WITHDRAWN FROM
STERLING HEIGHTS PUBLIC LIBRARY

WITHDRAWN FROM
STERLING HEIGHTS PUBLIC LIBRARY
STERLING HEIGHTS PUBLIC LIBRARY
40255 DODGE PARK ROAD
STERLING HEIGHTS, MI 48313

RAVISHING

RAVISHING

A Novel

ESHANI SURYA

ROXANE
GAY
BOOKS
New York

Copyright © 2025 by Eshani Surya

All rights reserved. No part of this book may be reproduced in any form or by any electronic or mechanical means, including information storage and retrieval systems, without permission in writing from the publisher, except by a reviewer, who may quote brief passages in a review. Scanning, uploading, and electronic distribution of this book or the facilitation of such without the permission of the publisher is prohibited. Please purchase only authorized electronic editions, and do not participate in or encourage electronic piracy of copyrighted materials. Your support of the author's rights is appreciated. Any member of educational institutions wishing to photocopy part or all of the work for classroom use, or anthology, should send inquiries to Grove Atlantic, 154 West 14th Street, New York, NY 10011 or permissions@groveatlantic.com.

Any use of this publication to train generative artificial intelligence ("AI") technologies is expressly prohibited. The author and publisher reserve all rights to license uses of this work for generative AI training and development of machine learning language models.

FIRST EDITION

Printed in the United States of America

Book design by Norman E. Tuttle of Alpha Design & Composition of Pittsfield, NH.

This book was set in 12.5-pt. Garamond Premier Pro by Alpha Design & Composition of Pittsfield, NH.

First Grove Atlantic hardcover edition: November 2025

Library of Congress Cataloging-in-Publication data is available for this title.

ISBN 978-0-8021-6468-1
eISBN 978-0-8021-6469-8

Roxane Gay Books
an imprint of Grove Atlantic
154 West 14th Street
New York, NY 10011

Distributed by Publishers Group West

groveatlantic.com

25 26 27 28   10 9 8 7 6 5 4 3 2 1

for all the sick girls

. . . the irony is that your body keeps the score because your mind wants to forget the tally.

—Fariha Róisín, *Who Is Wellness For?: An Examination of Wellness Culture and Who It Leaves Behind*

RAVISHING

Her mouth drops into a hesitant *o* when she first looks at herself in the mirror.

The girl on the screen films whenever she can. Her phone's camera, a hungry eye, beckons. But she doesn't mind being wanted. The more people keep watching her, keep calling her the best of the best, the more her mind loops with clever visuals instead of memories she'd prefer not to fall asleep to. So she records. So she posts—online. So, she presses her phone to her chest and waits for the comments to come in, all of them for her.

Today, the girl on the screen uses her thumbnail to slice open a box. Inside, a tube. Inside that, a product she layers over her face. Now she starts filming, and as the cream is absorbed there is a twist and a tug, like something caught needs release. It hurts, but in a good way, like floss parting the gums around a tooth, startling the mouth with blood. The girl's features rearrange and for a split second her whole face looks mangled. She doesn't flinch. In editing, she speeds up the process so no one notices when things go gruesome.

The girl's face sculpted, elongated, augmented exactly as she wanted it. She smiles, both at that and at how her view count ticks up as soon as she posts. Her followers send her blue hearts, green hearts, whatever color heart their fingers hit first. Some crimson ones, too. *Blood*, the girl thinks again, then makes herself forget.

Later, the girl on the screen deletes her video and reposts a better version of it. She edits out one clip—her mouth, in that hesitant little *o*.

PART ONE

CHAPTER ONE

The whole party moves like a single animal, lumbering back and forth between the foul juice-and-liquor concoction haphazardly set up on the weather-cracked patio furniture and the in-ground pool where four boys play a game of chicken. One of them shouts a long "fu-u-u-ck" as he goes tumbling into the water, but Kashmira doesn't look up. She stands between a seated boy's legs and angles her mouth against his. Though Tej bites her lip too hard, she doesn't stop kissing him. Tonight is about nothing but becoming someone new in the wake of her father's call a month ago. The call during which Vinod announced not that he was coming home after a year and a half of forgotten holidays and missed school ceremonies, but rather that divorce papers would soon arrive in the mail.

"You're better at this than I thought you would be," Tej slurs.

Kashmira says nothing. She never shows up to these parties, though the guest lists are made up of South Asian kids from her so-called family-friendly suburb, Marlton, and the rest of South Jersey, too. Today's party, on the second Saturday in June, is just a fifteen-minute drive from her house, but sometimes the hosts live much farther away. Because there aren't as many brown teens here as in Edison or Jersey City, people travel for these things.

But regardless of distance it always works like this: One of the richer kids' parents go out of town, usually to some big wedding, and everyone starts texting about what alcohol to bring and what lies to tell the "aunties and uncles." While Kashmira sometimes ends up on the text chains, no one really ever expects her to come. People have been calling her a loner since her father left, and even in the years before that, she rarely hung out with the other brown kids anyway. Tonight, though, she intends to change all this, to become someone new amid the blaring Bollywood music that some self-appointed DJ cuts with rap.

So far, none of the thirty or so attendees have acted surprised at Kashmira's presence, possibly because they're already too far gone on punch and hormones to care. The only one who notices her is the boy she is draped over now: Tej, a stranger, who she can only guess is interested because he is tired of sleeping with his usual girls. After an hour at the party even Kashmira has heard the gossip that he has been looking for someone new, someone fresh. It doesn't matter. What does matter is that he circled her little wrist with his meaty hand and pulled her close and that she can pretend she is like the other girls here: flitting around the party in their light, lithe bodies.

"Have I even seen you around before?" Tej says. He blinks up at her, waiting.

"You would remember meeting me," she tells him. It sounds awkward, but Tej laughs. She feels the rumble of it under the hands she settled on his chest.

"You need more punch," he says. "Come on, it's inside."

Holding on to one of her belt loops, Tej leads her around the perimeter of the yard, where the grass is due for a mow. His thumb creeps under her waistband while he pulls her along. It feels for her hip bone, and she lets it. Inside, they pass the kitchen, where juice litters the island. Neither of them stops to ask about if they should be refrigerated. Instead Tej opens the door to a bedroom, and there, he sits Kashmira on the bed and sprawls next to her. The mattress is firm beneath her spine as she lays back. Tej's stubble comes in at the underside of his jaw. She touches it. Then, they kiss.

It's Kashmira's first kiss, all messy tongue and alcohol stink, but she decides to enjoy it. She lets Tej pull her on top of him, and doesn't stiffen when he grabs her ass so eagerly it puts her off balance. When she collapses, it just gets them closer, and he nuzzles her cleavage. Then he goes back to her shorts and undoes the sole button with an easy tweak of his fingers.

"You should, you know," Tej says, unzipping his pants and gesturing.

She knows what he means, even though she hasn't done it before. When Tej stands, Kashmira slides off the bed and onto the carpet. Instead of looking at Tej's erection, she glances in the mirror, hoping she'll see a clear-eyed girl, in control, pressing her hand against the muscular thigh of one of the most coveted boys at this party.

But no.

In the mirror, she sees the specter of her father, Vinod, animated in her face. Reflected at her, in her, are his heavy-lidded eyes, his crooked nose, his squarish jawline. That face that contorted in fury whenever she did the smallest thing wrong. That face that went scarily blank after he yelled himself hoarse. That face that never loved her enough and doesn't love her now. Pain runs through her abdomen, and she gasps, but her breath won't come in or out, and this leaves her panicked, digging her nails into Tej's thigh without meaning to.

"Shit, let go," he says.

"I—I—"

"Hey," Tej says, nudging her shoulder.

Kashmira just shakes her head. Yes, people have always told her she looks like her father. Vinod used to say it himself. But now, for the first time, she sees how impossible it is—how impossible it will always be—to escape the man who so easily fractured the girl he demanded she be.

She can't look any longer.

Kashmira lurches out of the bedroom even as Tej calls out to her. She is crying, she realizes, as she flees the house and crosses the lawn back to the luminescent pool. Her tears are glimmering, too, and heavy. Her father would've said something like, *I told you hanging out with these people would make you cry.* Likely he wouldn't have understood the whole of her sadness, nor would he have tried. Shoes off, she sits at the edge of the shallow end and tilts her head back as her chest finally expands enough for a big breath.

Two feet dip into the water next to Kashmira's. A girl sits close, swigs from her plastic cup, and then scrapes at the rim with her bottom teeth. Kashmira narrows her eyes. It's Roshni Gupta, who she used to be so close with. These days, they barely encounter each other—only at school, when it's in session—and with distance has come change. Roshni looks different than she once did—not just older, not just more beautiful, but impossibly perfect, as she'd always wanted. A thing Kashmira has wanted to ask about, but can't. It bothers her every time she sees the her former friend.

"Someone's going to start wondering what's wrong with you," Roshni says.

Kashmira steals the cup from Roshni's hand. The gin burns her nose and throat the same way it did when she was eight years old and accidentally sipped from her father's glass, thinking it was water. At the time, she swore off alcohol so vehemently Vinod snorted and told her she'd see one day. And maybe he was right. Kashmira drinks until it's gone.

"Oh my God," Roshni says. She snaps Kashmira's spaghetti strap. "I'm already regretting coming over here."

"No one asked you to check on me."

"*Loving* this attitude of yours."

The two of them have known each other since the first day of kindergarten, when their teacher confused them in the attendance lineup. Roshni thought it was fun having a twin and made Kashmira stand next to her for the rest of the year. Kashmira didn't mind; Roshni's rowdy giggles made her laugh, too. But the next year, when Roshni begged Kashmira to come over for pretend game after pretend game, Kashmira avoided asking her parents' permission for a playdate. She knew her mother, Ami, would defer to Vinod, and he had never allowed her to make real friends with another Indian girl.

It was noticeable, the way Vinod kept Kashmira and her five-years-older brother, Nikhil, away from the other brown kids. Often Roshni asked why Kashmira didn't go to Hindi lessons at temple or to any of the South Asian beauty pageants that Roshni attended annually as part of the little-little-miss division. But Kashmira answered none of these questions, because at the time she didn't understand why with her paternal grandparents—who they visited only twice a year despite their being her and Nikhil's only living set—Vinod tolerated his kids participating in puja, while elsewhere he harbored a deep-seated hatred of what he called "traditional shit." In their own house, Kashmira and Nikhil were careful not to edge too close to anything Vinod disapproved of, like ordering a fully vegetarian meal at a restaurant or asking if they'd ever get to visit India or trying on one of the saris their mother kept hidden in the back of the closet, because if they did their father became a stranger, his rage somehow turning him taller, broader, stronger, louder.

"I'm protecting you the best I can," Vinod hollered once, pushing past both of them. The bulk of his body forced them to huddle against the wall. "And you won't fucking cooperate."

Whenever these types of outbursts happened, Vinod would stalk through the apartment, collecting his keys, his wallet, his dog—his coat if he needed it. He'd leave without telling them where he was going and for how long. And though the children were left with their mother, Ami's presence never comforted Kashmira. Instead of hugging Kashmira or reassuring Nikhil, Ami repeatedly called Vinod's cell phone, begging him to forgive them and not to leave them, while the children hung back and gnawed at their fingernails. It went on like this until Vinod decided to come back, sometimes smelling of drink or cigarettes or perfume. At his return, the two siblings would cry, and the dog would lick their faces even wetter—though over the years, Nikhil stopped with the tears. But Kashmira couldn't; she was always so afraid when her father was gone, both because she felt safer in his absence and because she wasn't sure who to be and how without him. Perhaps it made sense. This oscillation between needing and not needing is sometimes the only way daughters like her understand how to keep fathers like him close. Whenever Kashmira wept, Vinod pulled her into a long embrace, breathed deep against her neck, and said things like "I know. I never wanted this life either."

Vinod would have hated her at this party, Kashmira knows. He would've hated her standing next to Roshni. And while Kashmira reminds Roshni of none of this history, the other girl leans closer anyway to say, "So what gives? You never show up to these things."

"Well, I'm here now," Kashmira says.

Roshni rolls her eyes. "God, you can be so unbearable, you know that?"

Kashmira crumples the plastic cup so it collapses into a twisted shape. It isn't unlike Roshni to be snappish like this, though they did end up calling each other friends once. For years, actually, because despite Kashmira's fears about asking Vinod to let them play, it had all worked out, thanks to Nikhil. When Kashmira told him that their father said it wasn't good to be around girls like Roshni, eleven-year-old Nikhil inflated his cheeks with breath, then blew out the air hard. He said, "I'll handle this." When she protested, he blew another breath right into her face to get her to listen. "I said I'd talk to him."

Somehow, incredibly, Nikhil had persuaded Vinod to change his mind, at least part of the way. Vinod agreed to let the girls hang out, as long as Kashmira never called Roshni's mother, Lalita, Aunty; or watched Bollywood movies; or stayed over for Saturday night chaat with them. It felt like a loss to not enjoy these experiences with her new friend, but just being around Roshni soothed Kashmira anyway. The other girl had her own familial issues, like Lalita, arbitrarily and aggressively venting over how her daughter was such a disappointment—in school, in social courtesies, in her looks. What had she done for the gods to punish her with this failure of an only child? Roshni's father never defended his daughter, and that, coupled with how spiteful all this reproach was, forced Roshni to tears, not unlike Kashmira's. But at least the girls learned to lean on each other. They always found a way to distract each other when things were really hard, and that made the friendship special to them both.

Years passed; Kashmira and Roshni turned fourteen. They hung out every week, often on the days Roshni went to her kathak lessons. She had been learning the dance for what seemed like forever, and it had become part of their routine for Lalita to drop Kashmira off at home before the classes. Kashmira would linger on the stoop, still waving, until their car lights had long turned out of the parking lot. She wished she could go too, in the same way she craved long summer visits to her grandparents' house. She knew others who did this type of sojourn with their families and returned changed, seemingly more whole and assured of who they came from and what that meant. Kashmira wanted to experience that surety in her life. Still, she never asked her father for a visit like that—or for the lessons.

And then a balmy April day. Roshni was running late, and Lalita didn't have time to swing by Kashmira's house. Instead, she took both girls to the studio and sent a dashed-off message to Vinod and Ami about it. That was bad. Worse was that the teacher wouldn't let Kashmira sit through the lesson without participating. She stationed Kashmira in one of the middle rows, and while Kashmira promised herself she would slip away after warm-ups, it didn't happen. As the girls began their footwork, she found she could hit the same marks, at least at the slower speeds—and then, just like that, she was one of them, a brown girl in the same rhythm. After class, the teacher put an arm around Kashmira and said she had clearly enjoyed dance and she ought to come back soon.

But of course, she wouldn't return. At dinner, Vinod cut coldly into his chicken and interrogated Kashmira about the afternoon.

"I didn't mean for it to happen," she said, holding her own fork and knife tight in her two fists. Nikhil was out of the house at college by then and unable to intervene. But maybe, if she groveled enough. "I promise. I—"

"How was it?" Vinod asked, before taking a slow bite.

Kashmira paused, unsure if her father wanted a real answer. She thought for too long. As his brows furrowed, she understood that he had expected one response only, and she hadn't given it.

That time, he left for two full days. When he returned, there was no more Roshni. Hangouts stopped, and because Kashmira was afraid of doing anything else to anger her father, so did partnering up on class projects and sitting together at lunch. The rift between the girls was abrupt and wide, though ever since then, Roshni has always found her own imperfect way to bridge it. Whenever she can, she goes out of her way to needle her former friend, just as she is now. It's retaliation, Kashmira understands, for abandoning Roshni in the prime of their girlhood—but it's also mingled with concern. Under the insults, a question: *Do you know I still care?* Most of the time, Kashmira can tolerate these complicated exchanges, but today she wants more. She wants someone to help her. Roshni had been that person once.

And so, as the party goes on around them, Kashmira mutters, in response to Roshni's jibe about her being oh so unbearable, "Maybe I'd be a more normal person if I could just forget about all my shit. But that's impossible when I look just like my fucking dad."

Roshni flips her hair over her shoulder and combs it out with her fingers. Under the flickering outdoor string lights, her expression is unsure in a way Kashmira has rarely seen. Or maybe it isn't only the expression. Roshni's face shudders strangely, and as the minutes pass, it seems to shift: Shadows play differently on her face as her nose grows rotund, as her cheekbones whittle down, as her brow drops, heavier than before. Kashmira blinks, wondering if the alcohol has gotten to her—but it can't be that because Roshni gasps and presses her palms into her cheeks, as if trying to hide.

"What the hell?" Kashmira says.

She peels Roshni's hands away. And then, there it is. She'd been right. Roshni had done something to her face, because now the dusky skin, the clumsy features that Kashmira used to know stare back at her. Kashmira blinks, and while she does, Roshni, who—thanks to her mother—has always been self-conscious about her looks, dips her chin to her chest and rummages in her bag for a tube of some product. She rubs its contents onto her face quickly and says nothing, not even when Kashmira whispers her name. And then, it happens again. After a few long minutes go by, Roshni's face shudders a second time as her features begin switching back to the delicate charm of before. It doesn't seem possible, and yet.

"Your face," Kashmira says. "You changed it."

Roshni tucks her hair back behind her ears and sets her jaw in the way of girls who refuse to question any of their choices. "Maybe I did. Maybe sometimes I want to be someone else too. Just like you, right?"

As they stare at each other, a brief, knowing smile crosses Roshni's mouth. It's true, she wasn't there when Vinod disappeared eighteen months ago—this time for good. She wasn't there to see the door, locked so carefully; or the knife resting on the edge of the sink, coated in peanut butter as if Vinod had just made a sandwich to go; or the missing dog, taken from his spot by the fireplace, along with his half-chewed rawhide bone; or the note that said Vinod saw what he had done to them but he couldn't stop, so he was going to leave—to save them and himself. She wasn't there either when Kashmira isolated herself for eighteen months, worrying that Vinod would return one day only to leave again if she didn't behave. And Roshni wasn't there this week, when Kashmira realized that Vinod would actually never come back and that now Kashmira needed to pretend he didn't exist, the same he pretended she didn't either. Roshni hadn't been there for any of this, and still, in her own way, she understands.

Kashmira's onetime friend reaches for her shoes, black heels that she holds at shoulder level. Then she nudges Kashmira, urging her to stand. Soon, they're up, swaying slightly and blinking at each other in the night.

"Come on," Roshni says. "Let's see how it looks on you."

They move through the party, dodging drunk make-outs, boys wet from the pool, and Roshni's friends who somehow all want to talk to her at this very moment. Once inside the opulent, high-ceilinged house, they see a line for the first-floor bathroom, but Roshni says she knows where to go so they won't have to wait. Upstairs, apparently. They slip into another half bath, and Kashmira perches on the edge of the closed toilet while Roshni hands her a tissue to wipe her face. When Kashmira takes too long to clean up, Roshni uses another one to wipe under Kashmira's eyes for her.

"I was doing it," Kashmira says.

"And I'm helping you."

Roshni plucks Kashmira's tissue out of her hand and replaces it with a sleek glass tube exuding an expensive sheen. Scrawled on the side, sophisticated cursive teal letters: *Evolvoir*. Underneath, in block text, the name of the product: NuLook. Kashmira traces the lettering with her finger. Less overwhelmed than she was out by the pool, she realizes she knows this brand from ads and some viral posts on the short-reels app VidMo. More importantly, last month her brother was finishing up interviews for a job with Evolvoir to work on this product, but—she pauses her hand—she doesn't know what happened with that since she and Nikhil haven't spoken since

Vinod's divorce announcement. Yet another thing their father has ruined. She weighs Roshni's tube in her hand and finds it heavy.

"Obviously you don't usually wear makeup," Roshni says. She points to the thick eyeliner Kashmira smeared around her eyes for tonight. "So I'll do it."

She strokes white cream onto Kashmira's face, and then they both wait as the product takes time to disappear into her pores. At first, Kashmira thinks nothing will happen, but then suddenly something twists so hard that she bites the inside of her cheek and reaches her hands up to wipe the product off, to stop this. It's too late, though, the cream is doing it, changing her. Roshni points to the mirror, and then, yes, a new face takes the place of her old one. There it is, both awkward with its lopsided cheekbones and misshapen nose—the product seems to work better on Roshni than on her—and also lovely, because Vinod is nowhere to be found in it.

"Holy shit," Kashmira says.

It's easier to look at herself now, with her father's features changed, though a traitorous part of her wonders if this isn't just another way of losing him. Not unlike every time she relives the memories of his leaving—the door locked so carefully, the knife resting on the edge of the sink, the note. Strangely, those images are there now, edging into her consciousness until she sees them more clearly than this new face. And then nausea, like a sense of impending doom, clutches at her. But maybe it doesn't have to be like this. Kashmira closes her eyes. Vinod is already gone, and she is still here. In the darkness, she imagines herself passing through the world with this new face, dancing at a party, kneeling on a bed, forgetting about ever feeling like she never had a place by anyone's side. Wouldn't that be something? All she'd have to give up is a person who has already given up on her. She can do that. She can pretend he never existed. She can pretend that version of herself—the version tied to him—never existed too. As Kashmira opens her eyes again, she swallows hard. For some reason, the images are gone, but the nausea remains. But maybe it's just a side effect of Tej's ungodly punch. Yes, she decides, that must be it—because when she looks in the mirror again, this second face looks bright with possibility.

Kashmira says, "This is, I don't know, incredible?"

"Well, your cheekbones look creepy." Roshni rests a hand against the side of her own face. "It's because that formula is mine. You need your own product, but for that you'd have to get on and then off the wait list."

"There's a wait list?"

Roshni slips the Evolvoir tube back into her bag. "Ye-*ah*. You really need to get out more. Everyone wants this stuff, and they can't make enough. I got off the list because one of my dad's friends is an investor or whatever. No big deal, but I heard it's been like months of waiting for other people." She pauses. "I guess I could ask Anil Uncle—that's my dad's friend—to help you too. Then you could order it whenever you want. You know what? I will do that. As long as you . . ."

"As long as I what?"

"As long as you help me. I need someone who won't gossip with other people. Or, you know, someone who no one will believe if she does blab. And we used to tell each other everything, didn't we?"

"We tried to."

"Then we can try again, because"—Roshni shuts her eyes, suddenly serious as she confesses—"something's wrong." She points, unnecessarily, to herself, then lists off what's been bothering her: cramps in her lower belly, fatigue, and insistent diarrhea. All too often she feels this close to throwing up. "The internet says it could be an STD. Gross, I know."

There's an implication—sex—in Roshni's admission that bothers Kashmira more than the words themselves. How much of her old friend's life she has missed. They'd once promised to talk with each other about their first times right after they happened. Kashmira says, "Seriously? How many guys have you been sleeping with?"

"Don't *judge*. Are you seriously worrying about that after everything I just said?"

Kashmira is, because honestly the symptoms Roshni listed sound almost benign. The kind of things a person gets after drinking too much, as Kashmira has done tonight and—according to the rumors she has heard—as Roshni probably does most Thursday, Friday, and Saturday nights. Besides, Roshni is glowing under the bathroom lights, belying her claims of illness. Can anything be that wrong? It isn't as if teenagers like them get seriously sick, outside of heartache. And that, too, is possible to get over, Kashmira has to believe.

"I need you to take me to get tested at the clinic," Roshni says. "You know the one?"

Yes, Kashmira has heard other girls talk about a reproductive health clinic in Camden where they go for their birth control pills. But despite having knowledge of this, Kashmira asks, "Are you sure it's not just hangovers? They can be rough, right?"

"Yeah, but they don't last for weeks. It has to be something else."

"Okay, then why don't you just go to your ob-gyn or whatever if you're worried?"

"Because I don't have one. My mom doesn't think I need one of those until I'm married. She doesn't think girls my age have sex. And if I go see my regular doctor, she'll go in with me. I don't want her to know about all this." Roshni sighs and fiddles with her bangs. "What's the issue? I don't want to ask someone else or take a rideshare, because I don't want to go alone. And you have your license, right? I mean, you turned seventeen like six months ago. So it's perfect."

Though Roshni says all this casually, Kashmira feels a seriousness in it. Like someone drawing close to whisper a secret. She says, "You still know my birthday?"

"Please. How long were we friends?" Roshni extends her hand and raises her last and littlest finger. It's one of their old gestures: the pinky promises they made all the time for small and big things alike. "Kashmira, look, we can take care of each other, like before. I promise."

Roshni sounds sure, so sure, but Kashmira peers into the mirror one last time. Before she answers, she wants to see what she is agreeing to. What will come to pass. And then, there it is, her crooked face, for the first time tonight, smiling. Once Kashmira sees it, she can't stop looking.

Roshni's hand lingers in the space between them, waiting.

SERIES OF SHOTS – WOMEN APPLYING MAKEUP

A) TEENAGER with smooth, unlined face applies mascara in gray-hued school bathroom. Drops wand in sink in frustration.
B) WOMAN IN THIRTIES holding BABY, tries to refresh lipstick in car side mirror. Fumbles. Draws vicious red line across her cheek.
C) OLDER WOMAN swipes blush across her cheeks in bedroom. Opens door and smiles at HUSBAND. He frowns and turns away. She sighs.

FADE TO:
TEENAGER, WOMAN IN THIRTIES, OLDER WOMAN applying Evolvoir cream. Faces twist, then settle. Features sharpen slightly, like they've been surgically enhanced.

CHYRON TEXT: YOU ARE YOUR BEAUTY. EVOLVE YOURSELF, EMBRACE YOURSELF. LIVE FREE.

TEENAGER, WOMAN IN THIRTIES, OLDER WOMAN touch their cheeks in awe.

CHAPTER TWO

Evolvoir HQ, situated right in bustling, trendy SoHo, exhibits all the trappings of a reputable start-up. Modern white furniture. White walls, blank, except for the teal accent wall sporting the motto *Evolve Yourself, Embrace Yourself* in cursive. Coolly attired New York employees who straighten with purpose as soon as their computers ping. Everyone seems part of a strategic groupthink—one mind, one body—and when someone sends a TaskSquad message bringing some issue to the entire staff's attention, there's always a quick reply: already taken care of.

It's the second Monday in June and the beginning of Nikhil's fourth week here. As he adjusts his bulky over-the-ear headphones, his TaskSquad pings. The app operates like an immense chat room. It also sends him constant AI bot reminders to add "something fun" to his status. Nikhil comes up with an uninspired but acceptable answer each time. Today, he types, drinking coffee, listening to my favorite playlist (no top 40! 😊). Once a few 👍 come in, he minimizes his screen and pulls his headphones off. Job done, though he feels little enthusiasm for it. He works at Evolvoir because it was the first offer he got in this stagnant market. Nikhil graduated from college last December, and by mid-May, when the yes came in after a few weeks of interviews, he had applied for over a hundred positions. Though the Evolvoir opportunity was barely of interest to him, he had taken it in the midst of trying to parse out the chaos in his family: his father asking for a divorce; his mother falling apart; his sister, Kashmira, somehow ending up estranged from him.

"No Top 40, huh? Seems a little exclusionary." This, from Nikhil's deskmate, Michael, who has been slouching in his chair, adjusting his braided silver nose hoop, and pretending not to notice that everyone who walks by stares at him through the cubicle's glass panes. Perhaps he is used to the attention, handsome as he is, his lips always set in a disarming smile. So much the opposite of Nikhil, whose roughly shaven chin is only one of the weak points of his countenance.

"I'm careful about who and what I spend my time with," Nikhil says.

"This place, of course, must be an exception to that rule."

Michael laughs at his own joke and leans closer. His scent, mint underneath the cigarettes he smokes during breaks. It makes Nikhil wheel forward half an inch, then back. In truth, Michael's close presence thrills him. It has thrilled him since they met at the New Talent Orientation Breakfast, where Michael held Nikhil's gaze while they passed each other the tongs for the Danishes, and, later, their hands brushed at the fruit salad. After, he sat next to Nikhil in the circle of white chairs set up for their getting-to-know-you session and whispered dirty comments about which higher-ups must be screwing each other. Now the two of them often trade jokes and sly looks during the day.

"I don't know," Nikhil says. "I have sent out a few more resumes since starting here."

"So you can leave the Product Growth Team? Betrayal." Michael's arm rests against Nikhil's. It could be an accident, but Michael doesn't pull away immediately, and the touch lingers longer than a coworker's should. "I'm sure our fellow team members would agree."

They would. Evolvoir's staff is tight-knit and proud of the start-up, which has raised $20 million in Series A funding, amassed a quarter of a million followers on its social media accounts, and hired twenty happy new employees during the last six months' rapid acceleration. The company's core product, NuLook, comes as a cream comprised of revolutionary nanoparticles that can each be programmed to recognize and make specific changes in specific cells on an accelerated timeline. As the nanoparticles are absorbed into the face, they travel cell by cell—even into the eyes—until they encounter the correct area where they can affect bone and tissue growth, melanin levels, and more. Because each tube of NuLook must be specially created, Evolvoir maintains a robust wait list for the product—and this has only made the cream more popular, more coveted. Still, Nikhil would prefer to work elsewhere, at a place that does more than superficial beauty. He wants to help people, to save them from their worst circumstances.

If he were to think about it, Nikhil would say that this desire has to do with his family, which has very much made him who he is today. After all, his father, Vinod, always tried to guide his children, often by saying his catchphrase, "Fit in, and no one will bother you." Once, at the age of fifteen, Nikhil had decided to investigate the origins of this belief system. By probing his father, getting the right hints, and doing enough research online, he came to the conclusion that Vinod had been deeply affected by growing up around the targeted violence in Jersey City. He'd had to walk past disquieting HINDUS GO HOME graffiti on his street, and hear of the horrific beatings of young brown men all too regularly. Vinod had become even more fearful after the immense New York City terrorist attack during his twenties, which had somehow turned the country's citizens viciously against each other instead of prompting empathy and grace.

The pain of all this was, of course, authentic. But it was dangerous too. For it was the reason that Vinod wanted to be American, white American, impossible as that was. It was the reason he would do anything to achieve that dream, including tormenting his own family. Nikhil—who was born in the age of the internet, social media, and think pieces—saw in his father an internalized racism, and he wanted nothing to do with it. Nor did he want his sister and mother to continue to endure Vinod's damaged outlook. Vinod was the patriarch, but he didn't have to be. For years, Nikhil tried to convince them to give up on Vinod and his rules, tried to show them they could depend on Nikhil instead, but it never seemed to fully work.

And then, eighteen months ago, Vinod had left.

It was a boon, Nikhil thought, and doubled down on his efforts to support Ami and Kashmira. Though both of them carried on the same patterns as they had when Vinod was around—sure, perhaps, that he would return as he had before—Nikhil considered it just part of the process. In the meantime, to show them they could function without Vinod, he took on whatever load he could: Calling Ami every week and reminding her to make an effort with Kashmira. Helping her with taxes and with the dishwasher after it broke and flooded the apartment. Giving her lists of mental health services that took her insurance, and when she couldn't sign up, coming up with a hundred other ideas to help her self-sustain. He guided Kashmira, too: Checking his sister's mostly good report cards and choosing tutors for her when she needed one. Telling her what classes to take and what clubs to join to help get her into Bryn Mawr, her dream school. Finding her a used car to suit her driving needs. Likewise, he managed his own life: Working as much as he could to save the money he would one day use to buy a two-story house for his mother. Reaching out to NYU's wellness department for therapy and seeing an overworked clinician who decided because he was highly functional, maybe more so than some of his other peers, he could be done after three sessions. Dating very little so he could limit obligations outside of his family and career. Graduating first in the college's newest program, Social Justice Studies, so he could investigate the impacts of colonialism, internalized racism, and oppression and impart those lessons not only to himself, not only to his remaining family, but to the world at large. He felt that this work was good, purposeful, and even if Kashmira and Ami didn't seem to see what he was doing, he was sure things would get better from here.

But they didn't. Ami and Kashmira remained as concerned with Vinod as before. They followed all his old rules, despite the new patterns Nikhil tried to instill. And on top of that, Nikhil's job hunt was going poorly. His degree seemed to confuse job screening technologies, and he rarely got interviews; or if he did, he was never invited back for a second one because there had been "so many qualified candidates." Only Evolvoir, whose application he had thrown together randomly in desperation, was showing him much interest. One night in April, he collapsed into bed and slept for thirteen hours. He was exhausted, and needed something to change.

And then, like another boon, Vinod had texted—not called, as he would Kashmira, but texted—Nikhil to let him know the news about the impending divorce.

Nikhil had written back: good it'll be nice to never see you again. And then he thought immediately of his sister and mother. This would be it, he thought. The catalyst for them to truly estrange themselves from Vinod, because now they would see that Vinod was never returning and would never be worthy of them. Fully expecting this reaction, Nikhil video called Kashmira the night of Vinod's announcement—but his sister was skittish, with her pupils darting left and right. She told him how their mother had wept for hours. Then Ami had gone into the closets to look for old pictures to reminisce over.

"And then she found this box," Kashmira said. "She thinks it's Dad's. You know, since she's never seen it before. It was buried under some of the dog's old stuff. Anyway, she thinks Dad left something important in it, like a message, but she keeps talking herself out of opening it. I know she's overwhelmed, but, god, she's been a lot today." She paused. "It was kind of weird finding it, though. We weren't expecting it."

Nikhil had wanted Ami to clean out all of Vinod's old things months ago, but she had refused to toss the random shirts left in the closet, their old dog's blanket and toys, the legal pads left in drawers. Because of this, they found Vinod's stuff here and there all the time. But a box was strange. They hadn't found one before, and it did seem like it had been left behind—though likely accidentally, and not on purpose as Ami believed. Still, it could be an opportunity. Nikhil imagined journals, the wayward handwriting giving way to pages of awful confessions, or photo albums, each shot captioned in a way no one ever expected it to be with a terrible secret. Anything that might make his mother and sister back away, emotionally, from this man.

Nikhil said, "We should open it up, sort through it. I can come down next weekend."

"No, don't," Kashmira replied. "Honestly, I don't want to deal with it. We can just leave it in the closet for the rest of our lives, okay? It'll be fine there."

Nikhil stiffened. While he understood Kashmira might need some time, the way she said this made him wonder if she didn't want to confront the things in the box. If she didn't want to take the opportunity to divest from Vinod, even after all these years of Nikhil prompting her to. Perhaps it was because he was tired, so tired, but an insistent fear rose up Nikhil's back and into his neck, overtaking any logical thought. In his mind, even if there was nothing in that box, the act of keeping it in the house, like a shrine, would be like keeping Vinod close forever. And then what? Even with him divorced and gone, Kashmira and Ami would always be trapped in memories of that man? No, his mother and sister had to take this final moment in front them, had to use it to push Vinod out for good. Because if they didn't, everything Nikhil had done for them in his twenty-two years would be for nothing. He gripped the phone hard. The fear was morphing, as it often did, into anger.

"Do what I say," Nikhil said sharply. "Don't argue. It's for everyone's good."

His sister flinched, though at first he thought the expression was a delay in the connection. And then, voice flat and coming from behind her teeth, she said, "Seriously, Nikhil? If you're trying to be like Dad, you can stop. Don't try to take his place."

The anger took hold completely. He heard Kashmira's words like a proclamation, telling him she would always hold Vinod in her heart, no matter what Nikhil did—and it hurt. And so, without considering that this could be a misunderstanding, Nikhil laid into her, telling her he had been trying to help her for years and she just didn't appreciate that, telling her that she was obsessed with their father for no good reason. As he paced his studio apartment, his legs matching the pace of his furious diatribe, he vented frustrations that had been born of almost two decades of watching over her and their mother. Really, he hadn't meant to go so far, but he only realized what he was saying when Kashmira shouted back, "I can't believe you. Do you even care what it's like for me? I mean, I'm the one who looks like Dad, who thinks about him no matter where I go. But I guess you don't give a shit about any of that."

There was a deadness in her expression as she hung up on him that night. Maybe it was there when she blocked his number, too. Nikhil didn't know, but he could imagine. He did imagine, as he called her again and again, the connection never going through. Finally, past midnight, he threw his phone to the other side of the room, and slept fitfully—though Kashmira's words echoed through his dreams. *I'm the one who looks like Dad, who thinks about him no matter where I go*, she had said. Nikhil saw images of his sister looking in the mirror—seeing Vinod, talking to him, missing him—and they made him twist in the sheets he'd already sweated through.

But when the sun rose the next morning, Nikhil did what he'd done his whole life. He controlled his breathing, and moved forward. As he stripped the damp sheets from his frameless bed, he reassured himself by thinking that though he knew he had acted like his father, it was different. Unlike Vinod's, his anger was in service of the ones he loved, and thus the impacts of it would be fixable. He would just have to keep going, and then it would all work out in the end. It was in this frame of mind that he saw the official offer from Evolvoir that afternoon, accepted it, and requested a start date of just five days later, on May 20. At least this way, he reasoned, he would be able to pay his rent, while figuring out what to do about his career ambitions and, more importantly, the fight with his sister—which he would later find out was not just a fight but an estrangement.

Now, it's three and a half weeks later, and Nikhil is here, chatting up his deskmate. But before he can say anything more to Michael, TaskSquad pings. Keon, Nikhil and Michael's Young Talent Coach, also known as their YTC, also known as their boss if they were working anywhere else, writes in the #grow-big-grow-strong channel and tags the entire Product Growth Team:

—@prodgrowth we've got another yukiko video 😬 [URL]

When Nikhil clicks the accompanying URL, the link takes him to a Brooklyn-based Japanese American beauty-and-wellness influencer's VidMo page. Her latest short reel features a tube of NuLook. When it plays Nikhil's headphones, still around his neck, fill with distorted music as the already glossy-lipped girl on the screen resculpts herself by applying the product. As Nikhil scrambles to readjust his headphones over his ears, the girl on the screen fast-forwards her transformation. Her first face appears to dissolve into a second one with wider eyebrows, slightly lightened skin, a rounded chin, and cheekbones set higher than before. All of this sets off her new irises, which have become a swirl of green, brown, and gold, the color Nikhil imagines a wary tiger's would be. Behind this new Yukiko, a montage plays, featuring pictures of her and the girl whose face she has borrowed. They don't look the same—Yukiko actually looks even more striking, and has a small mole over her upper right eyebrow, which her bangs hide—but their resemblance is now unmistakable. Over the video, Yukiko speaks of the other girl, of the half sister she lost to an act of violence she doesn't name. *I've always been afraid*, she says, *that I'd forget what her gaze looked like in real life. But now, I can check any mirror and see it there.* Yukiko blinks so many times it isn't clear if perhaps she is holding back tears. And then, because Nikhil doesn't hit pause, the video restarts.

"What do you think?" Michael says. He watches over Nikhil's shoulder the whole time but balks at the third play. "It's a little morbid, using her feelings for clicks, huh?"

Nikhil doesn't answer, because he is reading the comments section, in which hundreds of people have reacted. Many of the responses are standard praise or jealous criticism, but some are deeper. These are replies in which the viewers talk about their own family difficulties, which have been exacerbated by the currently polarized political and social climate. Thanks to the recent presidential election, these commentators say, they've started thinking more deeply about their relationships—but, in many cases, therapy hasn't really helped. They can't get in with a decent provider on their insurance, or they can't afford the weekly sessions out of pocket, or it has taken too long to see progress. But now, Yukiko has offered them an alternative. She has inspired them to get on the Evolvoir wait list, because they want to transform their faces too: to look less like their abusive grandfather, to look more like their adopted mother, to look less like their white parent, to look more like something, anything. After all, if they can redefine themselves, maybe they can redefine their relationships to others, or even their lives.

"I don't think it's morbid at all," Nikhil says to Michael. He has never thought of using the product this way, but as he scrolls down the page, he thinks of Kashmira, pronouncing that she looks like their father and thus will forever be connected to him, haunted by him. It doesn't have to be that way, though. Nikhil says, "I mean, this application of the product goes beyond just beauty. It sounds like it could be healing for people."

"Doesn't look like Keon agrees with you," Michael says, as another TaskSquad message flashes across Nikhil's screen.

—@prodgrowth this kind of organic advertising is probably why we're getting an increase of requests for major face shifting. but as you may know, those asks are creating problems for us.

Keon sends a second message, a link to an article about the controversy around Evolvoir's nanoparticle technology. Set in a stark, black sans serif font is a transcript of a reporter's interviews with both public figures and private citizens who fear the potential of false impersonation due to the product's ability to so fully change faces. Two of the concerned parties have leveled lawsuits against the company in an attempt to demand more regulation, despite the fact that Evolvoir has established guidelines aimed at discouraging attempts to change one's race or to transform absolutely into any person, living or dead. This latter policy is likely why Yukiko's second face has a mole that her sister didn't. The Client Care Team member who worked with her probably used Evolvoir's facial recognition AI software in order to check her new look against a database of billions of images mined from the internet. The mole is a small but important way to differentiate Yukiko from her dead sister—and though Yukiko can cover it up, it's possible that if there was a legal challenge, the courts would then hold her, not Evolvoir, liable for false impersonation. It's hard to know for sure, though; no one has made a ruling on a case like this before.

—we're really thinking about how to manage these new complaints/worries, Keon says in another message. and to be proactive, we're considering limiting the facial alterations allowed during a consultation. just for new clients right now, though! we'll soft launch it now and see how many of them will be happy with small enhancements instead. (hopefully a lot of them . . . after all, 90% of our clients are generally only doing small changes.) we'll circle back in the future re: if this is going to be a permanent policy. 😊

Nikhil rereads the message, but he is only more turned off by it the second time around. He understands the concerns around lawsuits, of course; but it makes very little sense to him to restrict the product's capabilities. Not when a segment of clients do seem invested in using NuLook to change their faces more fully. And yet, half the team members are sending 👍 emojis to Keon. The other half send positive notes, like, you got it and we're on this.

"But this is totally diminishing what NuLook could do for people," Nikhil says.

"Is it?" Michael asks.

In response, Nikhil positions himself squarely in front of the screen and types with purpose—so much so that he hits Enter a little too loudly.

—@keon i'm trying to understand what you're saying, but it feels like yukiko is hitting on something really valuable with nulook that we should be paying attention to. i mean, we're in an intense political moment during which people are seeking mental health help, especially around family. it sounds like nulook could be a part of that.

Keon's reply is instantaneous.

—sure @nikhil it's definitely special 🤩. but it'd be better if they could do this emotional processing stuff without the major face shifting. keep this 🥸 but some of our board members aren't happy about the negative press and they want us to really double down on anything that could be misconstrued as impersonation.

—@keon but major face shifting is the point??

For the first time since he started at Evolvoir, Nikhil is sitting up. He can feel his pulse, excited, in his wrists, as a thought occurs to him. He has been bored in this job for three and a half weeks now. His sister hasn't spoken to him for just about the same amount of time. But with Yukiko's video, he sees a solution. He has just remembered that his contract states that after 180 days at the company, he will be offered a slot off the wait list to get himself or a family member the product. So his next steps are obvious. He will stay at Evolvoir and advocate for the importance of these major face shifts. Meanwhile, he will work on convincing Kashmira to speak to him again—so that, eventually, he can offer her that slot, so she can remake herself, can become another daughter, can carry another legacy.

On the screen, Keon is typing. Then not. Several people are typing. Then none at all. It seems no one is going to answer, let alone agree with him.

"Come on," Nikhil says, "Come on."

"You okay?" Michael asks. Turning, Nikhil sees that his deskmate is back on his own side of the cubicle. His legs are kicked up on another chair. His laptop, unplugged from the dual monitor, rests on his stomach while he types. He says, "Make sure to breathe."

Nikhil isn't thinking about breathing, but rather changing tactics. He works at a tech company. These are the type of people who want to beat their competition. That is what he needs to tell them. He types out a new message:

—@prodgrowth and one more thing. if we don't go all in on the major face shifts, someone else will. we know other people are working on this tech. what's going to happen when they figure it out? they go for the big changes? the public will see them as the risk-takers—the bold and exciting companies that want to make a difference. but they won't do it like we could. like we already are. i mean, look at the impact nulook is already making. let's keep the momentum.

This is right. This is the way to go. Nikhil knows it as he hits Enter, but it becomes clear as a column of new profile pictures, each accompanied by its own ping, claims the space on the left side of the screen.

—actually @nikhil has a point.

—we can't let opportunities pass by @keon.

—should we at least discuss this? we do want to stay on top, right?

"I'm impressed," Michael says. He grins at Nikhil, his tongue slipping out from between two even rows of teeth. Nikhil blinks. That tongue—Nikhil may have just gotten exactly what he needed professionally, but suddenly Nikhil is mesmerized instead by the shade of Michael's pink, provocative appendage. Michael, clearly not oblivious to this, wiggles his tongue and says, "I mean it."

Does he? Or is he just tempting Nikhil? Because, clearly, sitting there with his heavy boots casually showing off the city's wear and tear, Michael knows exactly how to get Nikhil's attention. He has been doing it since they met. Nikhil looks down at his computer keys and traces the letters *w o w* with his index finger.

Meanwhile, TaskSquad keeps pinging. The team reacts to each other's words with emojis: 😵 and 🫠 and ‼️ . Someone links to their favorite one of Yukiko's videos, and it begins a chain: another favorite, then another, until each one is someone's favorite. Keon has no choice but to reply. He cuts through the rowdiness with one sentence, brief but promising:

—fine. i'll escalate your thoughts to leadership.

―― ∽ ――

That evening, Nikhil and Michael leave work separately, but run into each other on the same Brooklyn-bound B train platform, a few blocks from HQ. When they board, Michael waves and sits in the seat closest to Nikhil. He spreads his legs wide, and Nikhil, who stands and presses his whole side into the metal pole, has to sink his teeth into his lower lip after accidentally staring too long at the inviting space there. Normally, he isn't so forward with men, women, anyone, but Michael seems to coax it out of him.

"You know," Michael says at the Grand Street stop. "We should have gone out for celebratory beers after your win with Keon."

"On a Monday? This late?" Nikhil says. It is just past seven. The work culture at Evolvoir is to stay at the office—or online if one is working remotely that day—until right around dinnertime, if not later. Though most of the employees don't get in until half past nine, the late evenings still drag. Nikhil says, "I don't know if I'd make it."

Michael fills his pockets with his hands, and his gaze roves across Nikhil's mouth. "And here I was thinking we were getting along."

The subway travels fast on its track, now above ground. The lights from the Manhattan Bridge stand out in front of the ombre sunset. As the interior of the train car lights up gold, everything feels lucky—Michael feels lucky—and Nikhil says, "We were."

They find out they both live in Flatbush, just a few blocks from each other, and Michael suggests a biergarten on Nostrand. It's about a thirty-minute walk from both Nikhil's studio apartment and Michael's three-bedroom, which he shares with roommates. They could transfer over to a bus from the Church Ave station, but Michael says the warm weather is worth strolling in, especially after being subjected to the cold office air-conditioning all day.

"A longer walk means less time for beer," Nikhil warns, but they take the slow route anyway, using the trek to talk about their favorite restaurants in the neighborhoods.

At the biergarten itself, the beers are dusky, and the picnic table is rickety. A mediocre band plays acoustic covers of '80s synth-pop songs, and no one seems to be listening except Michael, who taps his foot in time. Nikhil, for his part, sips his beer faster than he should. He is nervous, he realizes, because of Michael. Because of liking Michael. Suddenly shy, he drinks some more and lets Michael start the conversation.

"So, based on that thing about Yukiko, I get that you care a lot about other people." Michael snags a full bowl of peanuts from the three women sharing their table. One of them, wearing a light blazer that suggests she has just gotten off work too, makes a face, but Michael just shrugs and winks. Then he pushes the snacks at Nikhil. "You'll be able to drink more if you eat these."

Nikhil takes a peanut. "You think that's a bad thing? Caring about people?"

"Please. That's exactly what I was raised to do, too."

Michael tells Nikhil that his parents are down South. His mother attends the Black Baptist church in town, and after service she is always milling about, passing around petitions to send to the pastor about things like what brand of coffee should be served in the side lounge. His father, meanwhile, leads the choir and offers free services to the whole congregation at the local car wash he owns. When Michael visits, he helps out with the cars, too, and then takes an hour or so to talk to each patron, laughing at anecdotes about how their families have been in the months since he last visited.

"I take my nose ring out for that," Michael says. "But it's my favorite part of going home. I think you would like it too." He pauses, then says, "These days, it's hard to find genuine people, Nikhil. But you've always had an air about you."

Michael lists instances when he'd appreciated Nikhil's thoughtfulness. The time Nikhil grabbed him a cup of coffee from the kitchen after Michael said he hadn't had any that morning. The time Nikhil worked through lunch to help one of the interns with the first draft of a marketing brief. As he talks, Michael stretches his arms out and then rests them behind his neck. The whole time he keeps his eyes on Nikhil, who grinds the peanuts into paste between his teeth. He has never met someone who has paid this much careful attention to him before. This, he realizes, is what attracted him to Michael from day one. And now, as Michael's eyes flash in the night, Nikhil swallows hard. Those luxurious eyelashes, those spirals of hair escaping from under his shirt's neckline, those sensually round knuckles. It all makes Nikhil go warm, and he only goes warmer still when Michael says, "You're easy to notice. But that doesn't mean I actually know that much about you."

He asks about Nikhil's past, and Nikhil drinks more. The truth is, Nikhil never talks about his family, not with anyone. In college, his roommates only knew that he visited home a lot but not why. The few people Nikhil went on first dates with asked about his parents, but he dodged the questions. With Michael, though, he feels an urge to give himself up completely. Their knees brush under the table once. Nikhil waits. Once could be an accident. Michael smirks as they touch again. Twice is on purpose. And so, maybe because of the beer, maybe because of the touch, maybe because

Michael's interest seems honest and true, Nikhil does it: He shares a story from his past, one he hasn't ever talked about with anyone.

The moment was over a decade ago, but Nikhil remembers it like a sunspot on his memory. His sister, Kashmira, wanted to make a new friend. She was an Indian girl, this Roshni Gupta, and Vinod wouldn't have approved. But, Nikhil refused to let his sister be cut off so completely from one of the few other girls who looked so much like her at school and, with an eleven-year-old's bluster, he plotted to confront his father during one of their rare visits to their grandparents' house.

Lunch—roti sabji with daal, which Vinod ate, though with a spoon—was over. It was always strange to see Vinod in his childhood home, hunched under the long gazes of the gods who hung on the walls in paintings directly from Rajasthan. He always seemed caught between frustration and some nebulous guilt, especially when he ended up letting the family stay a few hours longer than he said he would on the car ride over. Vinod always did uncharacteristic things around his parents, Nikhil had observed. And thus, he believed that unsettling his father when he was already unsettled would be the best move. Arms on his hips, cheeks already red with pent-up feeling, Nikhil turned to his grandparents, both also in the kitchen, and said, "Did you know Dad won't let Kashmira be friends with one of the only other Indian girls in her grade?"

Both his grandparents looked up. Gaurav, from his Hindi newspaper, the one that claimed to tell all the news from east to west of the country, and Jaya, from cleaning a pan in the sink while Ami dried some of the other dishes. Vinod groaned low and met his parents' disappointed expressions only briefly. Then he glared at Nikhil, as if to remind his son—who just smiled innocently—that there'd be consequences for this later.

"One of the only other Indian girls? This is why I told you not to move away from Jersey City," Jaya said. "What were you thinking, Vinod? Raising kids in a lonely place like that?"

"He wasn't thinking," Gaurav said before following up with a rant about how they had raised Vinod to be a good boy with Indian culture, Indian values, Indian dreams—because even in this country, he was going to be the best he could be. Nikhil's grandfather added, "That was why you never ate meat or missed Sunday temple. And that was definitely why we never let you hang out with those skinny white boys down the street. What were their names? Brian, Shian, something? They were always smoking some thing or another."

"And now, look at what you're teaching your kids," Jaya said.

"I'm teaching them how to be in today's world," Vinod retorted, seemingly unable to take their barbs anymore. "I'm teaching them to do more than survive. To thrive."

"We've been thriving in Jersey City for thirty years," Gaurav said.

"Thirty-five," Jaya corrected. "We moved to the US thirty-five years ago, Gaurav."

Gaurav nodded, and then told Vinod that doing well in those thirty-five years had always come down to community. People getting together for carrom board nights. People making each other gulab jamuns for special occasions. People bringing back packets of paan whenever they could afford a flight back to India. Because they upheld these traditions, they had each other; and because of this, when the country abandoned them in that major New York City terrorist attack, they were still not alone. Gaurav's voice shook when he said this, and everyone in the room noticed. Ami dropped the dish towel. Jaya dabbed at her own eyes with the tail of her sari. Vinod, most importantly, stopped arguing. He took in the rest of his father's lecture with eyes closed tight, like his stomach hurt and he was wishing away not only the pain but the damned organ itself.

At the end of it, Vinod said, "No one ever should have turned against you in the first place, Dad. And maybe they wouldn't have if they didn't see us as different, separate from them—"

"It's very important to have your people, Vinod," Gaurav interrupted. "You understand?" There was a long pause; Nikhil's grandfather waited for Vinod to nod. Then, reaching out his hand to grab his son's, Gaurav said, "Then, you'll let her make her friends? Promise me."

Vinod hesitated, and Nikhil ran his teeth over his lip, hoping his gambit had worked.

"Fine," Vinod said. "If it really matters that much to you."

That was that. As Nikhil finishes this story, he takes a long swig of beer. He lets the malty flavor settle in his mouth—a distraction as he waits for Michael to respond. He has never shared this with another person before.

As Michael for his part clicks his tongue and says, "Your dad was struggling, wasn't he?"

Nikhil frowns. He had expected Michael to be indignant for Kashmira, or proud of Nikhil. Then, realizing that perhaps he hasn't clarified the impact of Vinod's behavior on the rest of the family, Nikhil illustrates Vinod's temper and cruelty by sharing a few more memories. Then he goes through the timeline of Vinod's initial disappearance eighteen months ago, Gaurav's death a few years before that, and Jaya's more recent passing too. Vinod had packed up soon after his mother's funeral, leaving little but half of his inheritance. It was enough for Ami to pay off the mortgage on the three-bed, two-bath apartment. At least there had been that—though when Ami offered Nikhil some of the money, he categorically refused to take it. By the time Nikhil is finished, he has given his deskmate more than he expected to. He looks down at his palms, which are sweating, and wonders: Is this only because Michael is the first person who has seemed like he really cares to know? He adds, to be clear, "You know, my dad fucked up a lot."

"Well, I didn't say what he did was good or right," Michael corrects gently. "I said he was struggling."

Nikhil considers this. Over the years he has revisited this memory, and he has come to understand that Vinod struggled with his relationship with his parents. He loved them and didn't want to cause them pain, but he also believed their culture was something he needed to protect his children from. That was why he compromised. That was why he brought the children to visit them, but only twice a year, to eat the food and do the prayers he avoided otherwise. That was why he kept his promise to let Kashmira and Roshni's friendship flourish for years to come, but only with the caveat that Kashmira must never participate in all the very Indian things that Roshni did. All of that makes sense; all of that, Nikhil sees. But at the same time, he finds he doesn't really care about this explanation for Vinod's behavior. What matters to him is the distress that the man brought on everyone else around him.

"Maybe he was struggling," Nikhil says. "But now so is my sister."

And then, somehow, he is explaining yet again. This time, he tells Michael about Kashmira and the box, the fight, the estrangement, the fact that Nikhil hasn't gone home to confront his sister directly because he is afraid it will just make things worse. He keeps going. He talks about how Kashmira would benefit from untangling herself from their father, though it has been hard to help her find a way to do it. He talks about how Ami hasn't been able to find a therapist for her and Kashmira, who takes the right insurance, has slots open after three in the afternoon, and doesn't come off as invalidating in sessions. And then he talks about his own issues with therapy: how he'd signed up during his junior year, intent on working through the trauma he guessed he had. The therapist, a graduate student also at NYU, had given him three sessions. The first, an intake, The second, a check-in. The third, a forty-five-minute good-bye, in which she told him that since he was getting good grades, graduating on time, and generally focused on having a future, he was better off than most of the kids she saw.

"I get it, these therapists are overworked, overtired, but their clients are suffering," Nikhil says. "It's not just my family. I mean, look at those comments on Yukiko's VidMo."

"I saw them," Michael says.

"Then you know how so many people could benefit from NuLook—our NuLook—as long as we allow major face shifts. This could really matter for people."

Michael leans back. Though the biergarten is thrumming with other, sometimes distracting conversation, Nikhil can tell from the thoughtful expression on the other man's face that he's been listening to every point Nikhil has made. Now, though, Michael says, "But how do you know people aren't just using the product for a quick fix? How do you know it's actually helping them?"

"And how do you know that it isn't?" Nikhil replies, voice hard. "Look, I've always been one to take a risk. Because trying to fix something is better than letting it stay broken. This isn't any different."

As the words leave him, Nikhil's phone vibrates against his thigh. In a blaze of optimism—the kind that people who truly believe they're doing the right thing have—he wonders if this might be Kashmira, serendipitously playing into his new plans to help her. Perhaps she has unblocked him and is reaching out; perhaps he can even tell her about the product tonight. But it isn't Kashmira's name on the screen, nor is it is a text. Instead, the message is from Keon, in the #grow-big-grow-strong channel on TaskSquad. He looks up and sees that Michael has seen the ping too, but is putting his phone away.

"We're off," Michael says. "Save it for tomorrow."

But Nikhil is too curious. He swipes through the notification to open the app, and reads Keon's latest:

—@prodgrowth leadership wants to continue limiting face shifting for new clients. if we see a major drop in sales or lots of complaints (or if one of our competitors actually gets their tech to work and starts going with big changes), we'll revisit, but for now, this'll be our policy. we're not anticipating too many problems, and we can bulk up some marketing to make up for the 10% we might lose. and re: yukiko, we'll be discussing more in the upcoming week, but we may need to contact vidmo and see about getting those videos taken down (without her knowing it was us, of course), just so she isn't advertising something we can't promise. more soon!

He must have had a late meeting with management. A nonsensical one, it seems. The decision is idiotic. Nikhil says this out loud as he passes Michael his device. His deskmate rolls his eyes, but scans the message.

"Like I said, idiotic," Nikhil says.

"Sure, maybe it is. But you can't do anything tonight."

Perhaps that's true. Nikhil isn't sure. He is still processing his emotions. The acute surprise at such quick, stupid news. The frustration and the irritation. The resignation that of course this won't be easy. The pressure now to figure out the next-best thing to do. Nikhil breathes long. At least there's no fear—no sense that everything he has done is in vain and has culminated in nothing—and thus none of the uncontrollable anger he shot at Kashmira last month. No, Nikhil is in a different place now. He has new ideas, new plans.

He says to Michael, "I'm not letting this one go."

"Fine." Michael raises his beer at Nikhil. Half of it remains. "But leave it for tomorrow, okay? Let Evolvoir stay at Evolvoir tonight."

Before Nikhil can respond, there is sudden pandemonium.

A bottle hits the table and its neck cracks. Beer spills across the wood and the air suddenly reeks of hops. The women—the ones Nikhil forgot he and Michael were sharing a table with—yelp and grab their handbags and wallets. One runs for napkins and returns with far too few. Meanwhile, Nikhil struggles to get his lanky legs over the bench while Michael swears as the beer sloshes into his lap.

"Sorry," one of the women says. But she doesn't mean about the beer, which she ignores as her friends scramble to clean it up. "But do you two *work* at Evolvoir?"

Aside from the sudden beer spillage, Nikhil isn't surprised by this intrusion. Someone interrupting a conversation isn't as uncommon as he would have expected when he first moved here. Sometimes it's a tourist. Other times, it's a fresh Midwestern transplant, missing the small talk of home. Every so often, it's even someone who wants him to ask them out. But Nikhil can't decide what category this woman, chewing on a strand of her long blond hair and peering at Nikhil and Michael over her heavy glasses, is in.

"We can't get you off the wait list or anything, if that's what you're after," Nikhil says.

"It isn't." The woman hands him a card, which identifies her as Erin Frankel from TechVIP, a digital tech publication that Nikhil knows because Keon sends the @prodgrowth channel articles from it at least three times a week. Erin says, "I'll be quick. The rundown is, I've been assisting on a story about Evolvoir, and I need a quote. But no one there has DMed, emailed, or called me back, and if I don't have something soon for my editor, she's going to be pissed."

Michael sops up the beer closest to him with an already-soaked napkin and tosses it toward a nearby trash can. "What kind of quote?"

"Just a quick comment on Evolvoir's summer strategy. Shouldn't take long and doesn't have to be anything that violates an NDA, okay?" Erin takes out her phone and swipes to a recording app. She pushes the device into the space between Nikhil and Michael. "I'm happy to buy your next drink. Or do literally whatever you want. You know, within reason."

"I don't know," Michael says. "I don't think I'm interested."

He cocks his head at Nikhil, perhaps inviting him to say the same. But Nikhil's mind is working. He's thinking about all the things he could say to Erin. Most of them boring, like *I haven't worked there that long, so I don't know.* But he does have one slice of information she would probably like. That same information that Keon just messaged all ten employees in the #grow-big-grow-strong channel. He looks at Erin, who looks back, curious at his silence. The recorder waits, curious too. Nikhil contemplates what to do.

But then, he already knows.

The truth is, he has only worked at Evolvoir for three weeks; he doesn't have the power to change Keon's and the other higher-ups' minds—especially when they've already made their decision. Other things, though, could. Things like external forces. Things like the media. If TechVIP reports on the changing policies and if there is an uproar, or general criticism in the industry, or disdain from investors, then there might be a chance to make the company on their resolution. Nikhil clears his throat. Revealing what he knows to Erin, he will be violating his NDA. But that doesn't scare him. After all, he is still the boy who, at eleven, ambushed his father and forced him to break his own rules in front of them all. To him, risk is an inevitable part of fixing things.

"Have you heard of Yukiko?" Nikhil says. "The VidMo influencer?"

"Nikhil," Michael says. "We were having a nice night."

But Erin is leaning forward, nodding, and now Nikhil knows he has her. He knows that even though people are tiredly finishing their last beers and vacating the biergarten, she will stay for this story. This story, which he knows he will tell well.

The girl on the screen conceptualizes each video as short, under sixty seconds—laconic not out of laziness but for impact—and still, she reshoots for hours. Her name is Yukiko. Her logo always appears onscreen, a calligraphed *Y* dovetailing into a tiny *xo* at the end of her initial.

This girl, the one on the screen, wants to feel something more than the brief dopamine hit elicited by the heart counters on her videos. She wants to feel better for good; her commenters assume she already does. When she first posted her face transformation, she feared people would call her melodramatic, attention seeking. Some did. Some still do. But others write that they sense in her the dawning peace they too long for. In this second face, she will be able to find closure, and these commentators wish to do the same. They will follow her, change their faces too, they say in the replies.

These are the words she rereads. These are the ones that reassure her that even if she isn't sure of what she is doing, it must be right. These are why one video has to become two has to become three has to become.

CHAPTER THREE

Three days after the party, Sachin, one of the boys who also lives in Kashmira's apartment complex, loiters by her car. She can see him from her front door, as the lot she uses is directly next to her row of residences. Sachin parks here too, as his apartment is in the parallel row, on the other side of the asphalt—but it's her car he is lingering by, not his own. Kashmira takes him in, as she often finds herself doing. Under one armpit, he holds the bound black notebook he is never without. The last time Kashmira peered over his shoulder to see what he'd been doodling, it was a two-column inventory of colleges. On the left side were schools in the tristate area. On the right, ones where he could easily double major in film and business. He hadn't written them alphabetically, but he connected all the repeats with dark, straight pencil lines. Under the other armpit, Sachin holds his signature video camera.

"Looking for me or something?" Kashmira says, walking toward him, car keys in hand.

He looks up, smiles with dimples. "Or something."

She and Sachin have waited at the same bus stop for five years. He moved in after she did, but sometimes she forgets this. He has been a constant in her life; so many times they encountered each other in the brisk early hours, even in the winters, before the sun had risen high enough to illumine the snow into crystal. They always chatted while waiting, and Kashmira's father didn't argue with this habit. He said small talk was allowed, though he did periodically remind her not to get too pulled in—that engaging too much, too deeply would only hurt her in the end. What Vinod didn't understand was that even in those fifteen minutes waiting for the bus, she and Sachin would get into it so genuinely, that time was often the most interesting part of Kashmira's day. How could it not be? Sachin talked and talked until he found a topic to lean into. Often, it was some movie he'd watched, but sometimes it was the latest political matchup or pop culture scandal. He never seemed to mind that she listened more than she talked, and sometimes that encouraged her to share an opinion or two of her own. They were never as informed as his—no one could read as much as Sachin did—but he seemed attentive to her perspective anyway. Sometimes he even opened his notebook and wrote down what she said. Once, when she asked why, he told her he liked to revisit lists of things curious people said before he went to sleep every night. She was curious, he said, because she had a gravitas few people their age did. He liked this about her. She smiled shyly when he said this but then Sachin veered the conversation into other things, as if he didn't want her to ask more about his feelings.

Nowadays, they both take their cars instead of riding the bus, but they chat when they see each other around, either at the mailboxes a quarter mile away or in the lot. Sometimes Sachin even comes by, asks her to hang out, and they sit on one of their stoops to catch up. Normally, Kashmira likes their moments, but today the timing is bad and she can't dawdle with him—not when she is leaving to pick Roshni up for the clinic appointment they'd discussed at the party. Though she still thinks Roshni is suffering mostly from drinking too much, Kashmira has to uphold her half of the deal they shook on that night in the bathroom. That deal is the only thing she's thought about since making it.

"I was on my way out," Kashmira says.

"Okay," Sachin tells her, pushing his long bangs to the side of his forehead. "But before you go, well, I was just thinking about that party a few days ago. I was there, you know."

"You were?" She should have realized. Sachin is always invited to everything. People consider him sort of weird but also sort of cool because he's so talented. Before he got his car, his parents drove him into the city all the time to attend cinema workshops, and his films have even been screened at a couple of local festivals. Wearing all black, he hangs out at the fringes of most social groups and never stays around long enough for anyone to get their fill of him. It has something to do with him wanting to maintain an outsider's observational viewpoint of things, as this allows him to take in the world in such a conscious way it feels more real to him than it did before. Or so he has said to her before. She wonders, briefly, what he paid attention to at the party. If he saw her go into the house with Tej. She isn't sure catching a glimpse of that would matter to Sachin, but what if it did? "You didn't say hi."

"I know. I meant to, it's just that I was filming. I needed some big party shots. I've been working on that movie for my college applications. Still trying to figure out what I'm trying to say about it all." Kashmira nods, but says nothing. Of course, he was thinking with his camera and nothing else. He's been talking about this project—depicting modern-day South Asian kids and their lives in the suburbs—for a year. He taps his notebook with his lean fingers when her silence continues. "You're keeping your thoughts to yourself today?"

Kashmira shrugs one shoulder. "You're the director."

"And now you're one of my muses." His eyes widen. "You were there, I mean."

"Right," she says, letting his first comment go, because she doesn't know if he wants her to address it. "I was there. But I don't know if there's any big point, other than us trying to feel like there's someplace for us to hang out on a Saturday night."

"Simple, but honest. Think the admissions committee would approve?"

Instead of waiting for an answer, Sachin laughs, a high, bird-sound chortle, and opens his notebook to write down what she just said. *Someplace to go.* She watches his hand with fascination, confused by how his lanky scrawl can make her casual words look meaningful. Sometimes she imagines him flipping through these pages, thinking about her at night. No—not her—what she has to say. But what if it were her? Yes, listening and talking and thinking matter, but so would sitting together and just holding hands, until their two bodies felt like one. Until it became clear that by mutually creating that moment together, they had truly arrived at knowing each other fully. Oh, but this is where she lets the fantasy end. She can admit she has some sort of crush on Sachin, but she can't give in to it. Not when he might not feel the same way back.

In the parking lot, Sachin finishes his sentence and snaps his notebook shut on the black graphite sketching pencil he uses. "You know, I even got some footage of you and Roshni the other night. I never thought I'd see you two hanging out again."

Kashmira tucks her hair behind her ears. At first, the filming flatters her, the way it always does when Sachin pays her attention. For the boy who is always looking at everything to focus on her? But her throat tightens when she realizes that—depending on when he shot them—if Sachin uses that reel, what he broadcasts into the world might be the version of her that wears her father's face.

"You shouldn't have filmed us," she says, pushing past Sachin to get to her car.

Inside, it's so hot she can barely touch the steering wheel. Because the air-conditioning doesn't work, she opens the window, swearing as she does so. Meanwhile, Sachin, who has dropped his black notebook after her sudden movement, stoops to pick it up. He rises in tandem with the moving window, and now she can see him clearly through the open square between them, his expression strained and concerned, as he says, "I'm sorry."

"Don't look at me like that," she says, softening. This close, she notices the faint shadow of his facial hair growing back. How he smells like toast and fresh-washed cotton. "Not when I was about to drive away."

He laughs, but not for long. Then he says, "But I really am sorry. For filming, but anything else I did, too. It's just, I didn't know the footage would upset you. Really, I caught you two by accident. I was just going for some faceless, nameless atmosphere shots, and I didn't realize what happened until later. I'm sorry."

"It's fine." His apology is so freely given, she knows it's genuine. Still, she adds, "Just don't use that footage. At all, okay?"

Sachin frowns. "I wasn't planning to. But you should at least look at it."

He hands her his camera. The footage, already queued up, begins with the moment when Roshni approaches Kashmira at the pool, and when Kashmira sees herself, she tries to give the camera back. But Sachin doesn't reach out to take it, which leaves her watching herself and Roshni talk with their miniature hands waving in frustrated circles, then get up and go. Sachin reaches into the car and hits fast-forward. Once he hits play, she sees it's her and Roshni later on in the night, from a distant angle. Here, Kashmira's face looks slightly off, so it must be after she and Roshni convened in the bathroom. Though, really, she can't remember this moment at all. Probably because after using the product, she had poured herself more punch, which had led to her being drunker, which had led to her having more nausea. This at least is visible in the footage. The filmed version of her leans her head against Roshni's shoulder, breathing in, one-two, and out, one-two-three-four, to steady herself. She even clutches her stomach at one point and lies in the grass. In other clips, Roshni, who'd also had more drinks that night, does the same. Everyone around them parties on, probably assuming they couldn't hold their liquor. Or that they'd taken something.

"You didn't seem like yourself," Sachin says. "Did you do something to your face?"

Even as she considers telling him, she shakes her head. Sachin would probably be intrigued by the product, but he'd have a hundred questions about it too. Maybe judgments too. She doesn't want to have that conversation with him, or anyone else right now.

"Well, the face thing is probably just the weird lighting from the pool. Also," she tilts her head, "we were all pretty drunk. So no one was acting like themselves."

"You disappeared for a while after talking to Roshni. I didn't know if there was something else going on."

"There was a long line for the bathroom. That's all."

He presses his lips together. "There's something else going on."

"Sachin," she says. "There isn't. And besides, why do you care so much? For the film?"

She assumes he'll say, *Yes, for the film, exactly*, but instead, he crosses his arms and stays silents. Kashmira studies him. Watches the gentle way his eyelashes brush the skin under his eyes. Watches his suddenly closed-off expression. She doesn't have too much experience with boys, and she doesn't know if he means anything by these questions. How complicated he is, how unlike boys like Tej, who make their intentions clear. How close he often feels to her, and then not at all, not while he has that camera and that notebook, helping him intellectualize everything.

She gives him a moment, and when he doesn't reply, she says, "I have to go. I'm late." Expecting him to move away from the car, Kashmira releases the emergency brake. But as she starts to reverse, she realizes Sachin hasn't yet given her any berth. She looks up, confused by his slow reaction, even as her car is backing up. But then he jumps—farther than he has to go—and the car makes it out of the space safely, and it never grazes him, and he never touches it either.

～∞～

The clinic is full when she and Roshni arrive. As Roshni checks in, Kashmira finds two chairs beneath a large television that cycles through colorful slides about consent and healthy relationships both with others and oneself. Some patients flip through magazines or scroll through their phones. These are the ones who let their names get called twice before they gather up their things and saunter into the back. Most of the others are nervous, though, like Roshni, who twists her hair elastic around her finger until it swells purple. Kashmira watches her cut off her circulation and wonders if maybe there really is something wrong with Roshni. Wonders what to do if there is.

When the nurse finally calls Roshni's name, both girls jerk their heads toward her. Roshni slings her purse over one shoulder and stands up. As soon as she does, the purse strap slips—off her shoulder, then past her elbow, her wrist, and to the floor. The entire waiting room watches as she holds her tight skirt against her thighs and bends down to grab it. Immediately, Kashmira is ashamed she didn't lean down to help.

Roshni straightens her outfit. "Aren't you coming?"

"Inside? Shouldn't that be private?"

"Don't *abandon* me now," Roshni says. Kashmira sucks on the side of her mouth. Someone else might not notice, but the way Roshni often emphasizes her words says a lot about what she feels. "Abandon" has more meaning than "don't" or "me" or "now." When they were younger, Roshni would often use that word in reference to what both sets of their parents had done to them. For good reason, maybe. Neither of their mothers came here today, and maybe that's for the best.

The nurse calls Roshni's name again and glares at both of them.

"Fine," Kashmira says, standing and taking Roshni's purse. "Let's go."

The hallway back isn't long, but it's very white. At a scale the nurse tells Roshni to step up so they can record her height and weight. Though Roshni agrees, she gets up backward and doesn't check when the numbers flash with finality. The nurse doesn't comment on Roshni's refusal to look, but she does say the digits out loud when she writes them down. Worse is that the nurse takes Roshni's vital signs—temperature, blood pressure, and pulse—and doesn't discuss any of the numbers, even though per what the girls learned in health class they seem high, and Roshni asks if she should be worried. When the nurse finishes, she directs them to a room down the hall while pulling another patient's chart from a desk. Neither Roshni nor Kashmira can figure out which door they were supposed to go through and they both cross their fingers, hoping they've chosen right.

On the exam table, Roshni shifts on the white paper and winces when it crinkles. Kashmira hooks her feet around the legs of her chair. Time ticks by. The doctor, a slight woman who immediately introduces herself by shaking both their hands, arrives late. Instead of apologizing, she straightens her coat, presses her fingers into the dark bags under her eyes twice, sits on a small wheeled stool, and asks why Roshni is here, what her symptoms are, when they all started, what her alcohol and drug use are, how many sexual partners she's had, what genders she sleeps with, and if she has ever been tested for pregnancy or sexually transmitted diseases before. The doctor is efficient, but the more she inquires, the more Roshni stammers.

"Does it sound like, you know, chlamydia or something?" Roshni says. She has the hair elastic back on her arm, but is snapping it against her wrist. "Or, god, AIDS?"

"If you're having unprotected sex, there are more common STIs and STDs to worry about than HIV." The doctor leans over to grab a pamphlet. She looks at it instead of the girls. "Genital herpes, for one. It's far more common than you'd think, and many carriers don't even know they have it."

"Is that what it is, then?" Kashmira says.

"I looked that up," Roshni says. "It didn't sound right."

"In general," the doctor replies, "your symptoms aren't clearly indicative of an STI or an STD. But we can do some testing here, along with a pelvic exam and pregnancy test to be safe. If nothing comes up, I'd recommend you reach out to primary care, who might also refer you to a gastroenterologist. Or somewhere else, since these are common symptoms of anxiety, too. It's not uncommon for girls your age to be experiencing that." She shrugs, as if to remind them that she was a teenager once and turned out all right, then grabs for a robe that doesn't seem thin until she hands it to Roshni, who unfolds it and holds it up. "That's for the physical exam."

"I've never had that done before," Roshni says.

"No one ever talked about this with you?"

Going even faster, as if all this invasiveness she is describing means nothing at all, the doctor tells them both how Roshni will fit her heels in the stirrups and open herself up to the cold. She shows them the speculum, and as Kashmira understands it, the instrument will wedge inside Roshni while the doctor does her exam. The doctor minimizes that, though, says there may be some discomfort, but she's sure Roshni can handle it. Then she describes the pap smear which might cause Roshni to bleed and stain her underwear. As Kashmira imagines a disgusting pattern, abstract and insidious against the fabric, the doctor indicates a stack of pads Roshni can use afterward.

"And you might not find anything?" Roshni rolls her eyes up to the ceiling, like she used to do as a kid when something scared her and she was trying to stop her mother from seeing. Remembering this, Kashmira can't help feeling a swell of sympathy, and she moves to Roshni's side so she can put a hand on her shoulder. After five long seconds pass, Roshni puts her hand on Kashmira's wrist. Her thumb presses on the inner part, where the pulse beats. She says, "You know, maybe I was just exaggerating my symptoms before."

The doctor pauses. "Can you tell me more about that?"

"I don't know."

The doctor's eyes flick to the clock hanging on the wall, then to Kashmira, who doesn't know what to do either. Somehow, by coming in here with Roshni, she has taken responsibility for all this. So, assessing Roshni's hunched shoulders, she tries to come up with something to say. "You asked me to bring you here. You must have had a reason, right?"

"Maybe it was *just* anxiety." Roshni says. "The truth is, I've only had sex once and we used a condom. And I do get sick to my stomach when I'm nervous, and things have been stressful lately, and maybe I just needed someone to listen." Her tone changes, more relieved now, as if coming to this conclusion has helped. "And you did listen. You did more than that."

She's right. Kashmira did do more. Because even if Kashmira brought Roshni here only because of the deal they made, their bargain hadn't included coming into the exam room or standing by Roshni or taking ownership of the conversation when Roshni faltered. Yet, Kashmira had still done these things, because how could she not? She knows what it is to be alone. And now the two of them, Kashmira realizes, are leaning into each other.

"I'd suggest the exam since we're here," the doctor says. "And the urine and blood tests as well. But it's up to you."

"Sure," Roshni says. "I'll do the second part."

The rest of the appointment goes like this: The nurse from before comes in and hands Roshni a cup to pee in. After that, she ties a tourniquet around Roshni's arm to coax a vein out, swabs the inside of her elbow with an alcohol pad, and then inserts a long needle with a tube at the end to collect the blood sample. Roshni looks away until the nurse withdraws the needle, shakes and labels the tube, then asks her to put pressure on the small wound with a small gauze square.

"You okay?" Kashmira whispers, as the nurse searches for surgical tape to stick the gauze in place. "I mean, was it worse than doing the blood drive at school or anything?"

"It was better than having to get undressed and stared at down there," Roshni tells her at a normal volume. But her voice wavers. Perhaps she, like Kashmira, was imagining cold fingers parting her, probing her. The doctor probably would have been kind, but she is still a stranger, performing her job while her patient pretends to stay calm at the intrusion. And what does calm look like anyway? Pretending the body doesn't exist under someone else's clinical hands. Roshni clears her throat, regains her usual strong tone. "I mean, ew."

"Yeah," Kashmira says. "Ew."

With the blood draw now done, they can go. Suddenly lively, Roshni hops off the table and collects her purse from Kashmira. The doctor, who still has a full waiting room just yards away, meets them at the door and hands them pamphlets on safe sex and relationships and stress and anxiety, all of which Roshni holds awkwardly until she can throw them away in the lobby with an irreverent shrug. No one stops her from doing this, or anything else. No one tells either of them that this might be a bad idea or that other things they can't even imagine will one day hurt them more than what hurts them now.

Even if they did, neither Roshni nor Kashmira would believe them, not yet.

The next time Kashmira and Roshni are together again, they watch from the kitchen doorway as Kashmira's mother holds a serrated knife to a collection of flower stems. Just ruffled carnations from the grocery store, common enough, but Ami levels the blade with a careful eye. The only sound in the afternoon quiet is the sawing of the knife as Ami cuts at a slant and then holds the carnations high, inspecting their lengths from all sides.

"What is she doing?" Roshni says.

"Nothing," Kashmira replies. "We should go upstairs for my Concierge appointment."

It's two days after the clinic visit, and Roshni has already gotten Kashmira an Evolvoir account. Or, more accurately, she has gotten Kashmira a secondary account linked to hers. The reason for this linking is complicated, but basically has to do with Roshni's father's friend not being able to get Kashmira her own off-the-wait-list account. It turned out that because of the relatively small amount of money Anil Uncle had invested, he'd only gotten ten accounts to give out, and he'd already shared them all. But, because he is an investor, and Evolvoir thus wants to keep him happy, they offered him this secret way to get an eleventh account. Kashmira was fine with it—after all, it didn't matter, as long as she could log in and attend the Evolvoir Concierge appointments where she would talk to a Client Care representative and order her products.

"Wait, I haven't seen your mom in forever," Roshni says. "Should I say hi?"

"No," Kashmira says. "I don't want to be late. Remember, you have to log me in for the first time, and we don't know how that works."

While this is true, it isn't really the reason for Kashmira's hesitation. Since her father's call, since going at it with Nikhil, since the party where she and Roshni linked pinky fingers, all Kashmira has wanted to do is separate herself from her dysfunctional specter of a family. She avoids her mother—and her brother, who calls Ami's phone regularly and asks her to put Kashmira on—by staying out as often as possible. Her car, the library, the coffee shop where she works as a barista, all of these places are preferable to home. In them, she can practice becoming someone else, the Kashmira with her second face.

"Oh, come on," Roshni says.

She takes Kashmira's hand and pulls her into the kitchen. Now they are both standing there in front of Ami, who looks up, smiles slightly, and says nothing. Roshni looks between Kashmira and Ami, confused, and this makes Kashmira feel like she has to say something to her mother.

"You got home early?" she offers.

"The grocery store was quick." Ami's blade slices on. "And Nikhil is supposed to call when he gets a chance. Kashmira, are you still not speaking to him after that fight—"

"Mom, no. I don't want to talk about him. Or to him."

Ami quiets, and Kashmira tries not to watch as she arranges the flowers in a small vase. Her mother replaces these every week. A habit that preceded Vinod's departure; back then, Ami did it because Vinod always appreciated fresh blooms.

"It's beautiful," he would say, pulling his wife against his chest, as though he really was trying to make something work between them. And perhaps he was. Vinod was capable of this kind of thing, capable of oscillating between two versions of himself: the one who held them close and the one who resented them for all they did wrong.

During these moments, Ami always burrowed her face into the V between Vinod's pectoral muscles. If she could, she would have made a place there for good, Kashmira thought. Her brother agreed, and theorized that it had to do with how, as an ungifted youngest child of four, Ami had spent more time working underaged at her parents' hotel front desk than enjoying their attention. Maybe she was used to begging.

But if Ami had been unobtrusive, even deferential, back then, it has only gotten worse since Vinod disappeared eighteen months ago. Since then, people—Kashmira's guidance counselor, the mailman, the cashier at the store—often ask Kashmira if her mother is okay. Kashmira always says yes, because Ami is functional. Every morning, she does don her badge before she heads to her hospital admin job. But then again, every afternoon, she comes home quiet and exhausted and dissociates into her old habits, like the flowers. After Vinod called to inform them about the divorce papers, she cried for two days straight and then filled the house until it smelled so sweet Kashmira gagged and escaped into her room. There, she wished she could go live with someone else—but the thought made her feel worse, because it led her to thinking, once again, about those summers she had wanted to spend in her paternal grandparents' house learning about her culture and history. How she longed for them. But they were both gone, and their house was sold, and Kashmira never got the chance to be close to them or the knowledge of her heritage that they had held.

It hadn't been easy and it still isn't. But now at least Kashmira has Roshni again, who interrupts the awkwardness between mother and daughter by waving, casually, loosely. She says, "Mrs. Mehta, it's nice to see you. I'm Roshni, remember?"

Ami looks up from the knife and, extraordinarily, seems interested.

"Of course I remember. You're Kashmira's friend," she replies, just like a normal mother would. Kashmira stares. She imagines Ami taking a nonobligatory interest in her. It could be the three of them—Roshni, Ami, and herself—at the table, giggling about something, interrupting each other with excitement. They could gossip, maybe about Tej—though Kashmira would need to sanitize the story of the other night. She could do it. She could talk about the party, too, and her bargain with Roshni. But would Ami be excited about Kashmira erasing Vinod's face from her own?

Before Kashmira can capitalize on this rare connection between them, Ami's face stiffens. Going back to the flowers, she says, "But you stopped spending time together. Your father told you to." She pauses. "Kashmira, I've been wanting to ask you. What do you think about your father's box? How about opening it?"

The box, the call with her brother, a month ago now. That argument, awful. The shouting made Kashmira want to hurl her phone and never be reached by anyone again. All she had wanted was to explain to her brother—her protective but loving brother, who didn't have to be quite so protective any longer—that she'd finally decided to let go of her father. But Nikhil took it all wrong and when he argued back, Kashmira thought that maybe he didn't see why she cared about this, that maybe he didn't know the impact Vinod had on her every day. She tried to say something about that, but nothing worked, and the yelling didn't stop, and panic charged through her whole body. She couldn't keep doing this, first with her father, then with her brother. So she hung up and blocked Nikhil from calling and texting, because how else was she to deal with it? The same night, Kashmira, wary of the box, its brown cardboard rough under her hands, began pretending it didn't exist. She put it back in the hall closet where Ami had found it without peeking past its flaps. She hasn't looked at it since.

"Actually, Roshni and I should go," Kashmira tells her mother. "We have things to do."

"What things?" Ami orders and reorders her arrangement, seemingly unsure of which flower should serve as the focal point of the whole picture. "Kashmira, I really think we should decide about the box. It must have been important for your father to leave it."

Kashmira presses both her hands to the top of her head and gapes at her mother. It's impossible to understand how Ami can be so fixated on Vinod and Vinod only when she has children to care for too. Yes, the man disappeared. Yes, he asked for a divorce. But Ami isn't the only one contending with such things. The silence between them draws on, interminable—until, finally, Roshni takes over.

"She doesn't have time to deal with the box right now because, um . . ." Roshni falters, obviously understanding that they can't tell Ami about the impending appointment, about Kashmira erasing Vinod out of her. "Because we're supposed to be doing dance lessons. Because I don't know if you knew, but I'm teaching Kashmira some beginner kathak. If I don't, my teacher will put her in with the five-year-olds, and that's just embarrassing. So I'm working out the easy stuff with her so she can be in the intermediate class at least."

It's a pointed thing to say, a reminder of what came between Roshni and Kashmira years ago. But it's also a poignant reminder of what doesn't have to come between them any longer. Kashmira recalls the sound of bare feet on wood, the sight of the teacher's clapping hands counting out beats, the scent of just-broken sweat in the room. She hadn't thought to join again, especially in a studio of mirrors, where her father's face would stare back at her the whole time. She wouldn't have been able to get through the whole hour lesson. But now, with her changed features, her new identity, she could go along with Roshni. She could dance.

"Kathak?" Ami says. "Your father would have—"

Kashmira cuts in. "Dad isn't here. So let's just forget what he would have done."

Because, yes, Vinod tried sometimes. Sometimes he was good to them. But it was never enough. He wouldn't have approved of lessons. He would have gotten up and left at the suggestion of them. He would have hurt them, as he already has, irrevocably. But Ami, who reaches for another flower, doesn't seem to want to accept this. She makes another cut into the fresh stem and then adds the carnation to the vase.

"Oh," Ami whispers. "Dammit."

This flower she cut too short. It barely peeks over the glass and throws off the entire arrangement. Ami presses her hands to her cheeks, and Kashmira feels her shoulders tense, as if preparing her for something. The flowers, wrong. Ami, wrong, too. What now? Kashmira hates seeing her mother like this. What an uncomfortable inversion of hierarchy, to have someone older collapse in front of her like this. How often has she seen it, in her time in this home? She longs for Nikhil, who is normally better in situations like this. But Kashmira can't call him. He, too, would ask her about the box. He, too, would tell her what she should and shouldn't do. Kashmira wavers. If she can't reach out to Nikhil, maybe she can sidle close and help her mother with her blooms. That, though, would give Ami permission to be this person, forever shaped by her former husband's presence or absence. No, what they need now is to forget that Vinod ever existed. They need to become the people they would have been without him.

Roshni scratches the back of her calf with one foot. "It's almost time, Kashmira."

—⁂—

Kashmira sits cross-legged on her bed, trying not to notice her face reflected in her laptop's dark screen. Roshni leans over, logs her on to the Evolvoir website. A teal loading icon appears, and then connection: the video first, then the audio. Kashmira feels her hands sweating against her laptop's hard shell and tries to force herself to relax. But how can she? How, when she needs this call to go well? A reminder pops up, alerting Kashmira that she needs to click I Agree to the session being recorded. She almost laughs. She thinks she might agree to anything right now.

"Text me as soon as you're done," Roshni says. "Are you sure you don't want me to stay? I mean, you stayed with me at my appointment."

"I've got this." Kashmira doesn't look away from her screen. Nervous as she is, she doesn't want to approach this as Roshni approached the uncomfortable, invasive clinic visit. These appointments are not the same. "Besides, you've got dance tonight, remember? Your mom will be pissed if you don't show up."

The reminder about the I AGREE button shakes, emphasizing to Kashmira that she hasn't made a selection yet. She checks the clock, sees that her session is supposed to be starting now, and gestures at Roshni to go, go, go. But Roshni stands firm, demanding Kashmira send her at least one message about how the whole thing went as soon as her half hour with the Concierge is done. It takes Kashmira promising twice before Roshni backs out of the room, making sure to close the door behind her. Only then does Kashmira click the I AGREE button; only then does a pale woman with evenly spaced freckles log on, looking artlessly delighted, as if there were nowhere else she would rather be. JORDIE, it says under her picture, and she waves until Kashmira waves back.

"Hi, Kashmira, am I saying your name right?" Jordie asks. She adjusts her headphones as Kashmira pronounces her name for her. "Okay, great. Really great. I'm so glad to meet you. Because there's nothing like getting to know someone in real time. The preassess just doesn't let me do that the same way that our first meeting does."

Actually, the preassess Kashmira submitted was more invasive than any introduction Kashmira had ever given: first a cheek swab meant to collect pertinent genetic material, then the in-depth evaluation Kashmira submitted through Roshni's account. The early questions, mostly collecting demographic information, were easy, but the long-form answers required more. *What is something beautiful about you that you'd like to emphasize?* the Evolvoir Client Care Team asked. And, *Tell us the parts of yourself you prefer to hide?* They'd asked for photos, too. Kashmira responded by sending images of her own face and one of her father's, with a thick X over it.

"Is there that much more to know about me?" Kashmira says.

"It's fine if you're nervous," Jordie replies. "Just take a deep breath for me. This whole process can be overwhelming, but it's really very fun once you get going."

At this point, Jordie shares her screen without warning. A 3D diagram spinning in a slow circle takes over, shifting Jordie's and Kashmira's images to a corner. Despite the digitization, Kashmira recognizes the rendering of her face immediately. She likes it best when it turns away from her; the side, where mostly only the cheek is visible, looks the least like her father.

"Cool, right?" Jordie says. "We used the photos you submitted earlier and created a replica of your face."

Now sounding like she is reading from a scripted explanation, Jordie continues defining the Comprehensive Face Mapping™, or CFM™, process in full. These steps are how the Client Care Team collaborates with each NuLook buyer to decide which facial changes to pursue, and so Jordie shows Kashmira how the 3D diagram can be nipped and tucked in various ways, narrating as she goes. Kashmira can fill out the lips while keeping the cupid's bow. She can whittle the nose while keeping the slope. She can bronze the skin—a half-step tone difference with a lot of sheen—but keep the clear pores. She turns the controls over to Kashmira, who fiddles with the diagram herself as Jordie explains that once Kashmira's facial plan is finished, it will be sent to the Product Personalization Team, who will then produce the specialized product and ready the package for delivery.

"That genetic material you sent over will be the basis for your product, by the way," Jordie says. "It's uniquely suited to your face. That's why you can't ever use someone else's product and get the same results."

Post the product delivery—and Kashmira's application of the NuLook—Jordie will schedule a series of follow-up appointments that make up "the iterative process." If needed, she and Kashmira will refine the CFM™ during these meetings, so the Product Personalization Team can update the formula accordingly. But even after perfecting the formula, there will be more appointments, during which Jordie will track Kashmira's progress to see how emotionally fulfilled—how lovely, how evolved—she feels in her second face. If she trends backward at any point, they can always begin again.

"You pay a lot of attention," Kashmira says. "Nothing gets by you."

"Trust is very important to this process," Jordie says. "It's important you open up to me."

"Okay," Kashmira says, without knowing if she'll be able to follow this directive.

"Great. So, let's start with why you sent me that photo of a man with a big X over him."

As Jordie minimizes the 3D face, her and Kashmira's tiny video squares expand again. Jordie's eyes are pixelated, blinking and waiting. Kashmira's eyes—no, Vinod's eyes—are like two black holes staring back at her. Those endlessly dissatisfied, endlessly exhausted pupils. She realizes she has to say something.

"He's my dad," Kashmira mutters. "Couldn't you tell? We look the same. But that's what I want you to change. I want you to get rid of everything in me that's him."

"Why?"

"Are you allowed to ask that question?"

"If it's part of your emotional wellness, I am."

The silence goes on until Kashmira relents. "Fine. All I see when I look at myself is him. All I see is how much I would be disappointing him. But you know what? That doesn't have to be me anymore."

Like before, Kashmira takes over the diagram's controls. As she toggles various settings, she enumerates which features she wants to change. Her forehead, the whole breadth of it. Her nose, with its too-large nostrils. Her upper lip, which goes absent when she smiles. Her eyes, perpetually downturned. She has more to say, more to do, but Jordie stops her, saying, "Kashmira, these are way too many changes."

Kashmira blinks. The diagram only tangentially resembles Kashmira's current looks. Not her father, not her mother—who she never resembled much anyway—not her brother, not her grandparents, not any combination of them. It is an amalgamation of pretty features and nothing more. Kashmira wants to like it. She believes she does.

"Just let me do one more fix," Kashmira tells Jordie. "Please?"

But then, as Kashmira goes to adjust her chin, the program freezes and an alert pops up. A large teal triangle—the same shade as the loading symbol earlier—with an exclamation point in it, flashing. When Kashmira tries to click out of it, nothing happens.

"What's going on?" she says.

Jordie hesitates. Her expression dips, morose, though somehow in a picturesque way. Then she says, "It is a nice face. But, Kashmira, Evolvoir policies state that we can't make this level of change to new clients' faces. There have been a lot of updates to our procedures, and this is one of them." A breath, not long enough for Kashmira to interrupt. "I know that must be disappointing to hear, but I don't want you to think we can't help you. We can do smaller tweaks for sure. Maybe we can step this back a little, restart."

"But you did whatever my friend Roshni wanted. I'm on her account."

"Unfortunately," Jordie says, "I can't comment on other clients or their situations. We can try something else, though. I'm happy to put you in for another appointment, so we can come up with an alternative face if you need time to think about it. And I can even offer you a discount for your first three months, if that helps."

What now? Kashmira doesn't know the right thing to say to sound firm, convincing. Instead, she wishes she could reach through their laptops to touch Jordie's shoulder. To feel its tough bones with hesitant, searching fingers. To show her that they're both real, that this moment isn't just a theoretical exercise but an opportunity to change a life. But they're far apart and at an impasse. Kashmira can only make contact with her screen, and that won't do anything.

She says, then, in a final try, "But this is the face I want. The only one I want."

"Kashmira, we want to help you." Jordie minimizes the 3D model, as if she doesn't want it to imprint on Kashmira any further. Her tone is fraught. Maybe like Kashmira, she feels this is her final try. "So, I'm happy to work with you again when you're ready. Or I can reach out if anything changes on our end. Just like you should feel free to reach out to me, too, if anything changes on yours. I'm here."

Here, but not. Kashmira disconnects the call before Jordie can. Mostly because she can't bear to be left wanting yet again. At least this time she can go first. Her screen goes dark. There is nothing left to look at—except there is. In the glossy black of her blank laptop, Kashmira can just make out her reflection, still and forever unchanged. And her expression, etched with agony.

Evolvoir Doubles Down on Major Face Shifting, Leading to Questions about Its Future

Erin Frankel | @frankesterin

As of this summer, Evolvoir, the beauty and wellness brand behind the buzzworthy NuLook, may be limiting the amount of face shifting they plan to allow customers. According to TaskSquad screenshots obtained by an anonymous Evolvoir employee, new Evolvoir customers will not be allowed the same extensive feature changes that current customers are. The policy seems to have already gone into effect in the past week, as a small handful of new Evolvoir clients have used social media to report discrepancies in what facial shifts are allowed for them versus older clients. Overall, changes have become more limited to enhancing features that already exist rather than remaking them.

[Video interview of new Evolvoir client sharing her experience]

This new approach appears to be a response to the controversy that has surrounded Evolvoir's innovative technology. The company is currently facing multiple lawsuits, with allegations of false impersonation at the forefront. In one instance, a woman in Massachusetts filed a lawsuit, claiming that her ex-husband used NuLook to look more like her so he could try to gain access to her workplace. While the attempt was not successful, the case has been brought to court as part of a conversation about tech regulation.

The controversy has also caught the attention of lawmakers. Last month Congressman Daniel Weber, R-Mass., whose office has been keeping close tabs on the aforementioned case, stated in a press release that "there is significant potential for misuse of this product. The possibility that people could impersonate politicians or other public figures is alarming and warrants scrutiny." But while Evolvoir's new policies may address these concerns, they may also create new questions, particularly in the regulatory space. While some individuals believe that face shifting could lead to false impersonation and privacy issues, others see it as the natural next step for self-exploration in this country.

"Technology is changing the ways we articulate who we are, and there is always pushback," said Sandeep Agarwal, of the Institute for Inventive Tech. "But some users are using this product as a means to re-evaluate their relationships to their family-slash-ancestry, their identity, and their individual futures. They believe it is helping their general well-being, and to take that away from them could create some big waves."

[Photo of Sandeep Agarwal]

Influencers are also concerned about the change in Evolvoir's policies. Yukiko, the creator behind the popular VidMo account @yukiko (616k followers), who uses NuLook to almost fully transform into her late half sister, shared that the product is vital to her mental health and well-being.

"Losing my sister was so hard," she said. "And it stays hard. Obviously on special days like birthdays and holidays I miss her. But even on normal days, I sometimes wish she was here instead of me. And with NuLook she can be. It tricks my brain in this really helpful way, and the sad feelings turn into better ones. I've found so many benefits."

Yukiko's content has been seen by many as both radical public self-reflection and commentary on grief in our society. Her videos receive high engagement, with many praising the product as a form of self-care and healing. As evidenced by the numerous VidMo responses to her work—many of which discuss their creators' plans for using NuLook to majorly face shift—her work has also become the inspiration for many others who want options other than traditional therapeutic services.

"I haven't heard anything about me not being able to use NuLook this way anymore," Yukiko said. "But if a policy like this is happening, that would really be a mess for some of us."

The potential change in Evolvoir's policies isn't only disappointing to these influencers; with Series B funding on the horizon, many eyes are on Evolvoir. Earlier this year, Evolvoir CEO Larissa Gertz Ross stated that she is "exceptionally proud of NuLook and its capacity to change the world," leading to excitement in the venture capitalist community. However, some major investors shared that their interest in Evolvoir is likely to wane if the company doesn't follow through on its claims of revolutionary face shifting and instead limits its capacity to dramatically shift facial features.

"We're not sure about a company that seems to be contracting its offerings," Jianhong Jiang, a representative from Surgere Partners said. "Especially if there's market interest in one of those offerings. Generally, we like to see start-ups embrace their market, not reject it. It's something we always look for when we're considering funding."

Similarly, Mike Powell, a representative of Forward Firm, said, "We are surprised—and disappointed—to hear that Evolvoir is pulling back on its promises and yielding to these external pressures. We're seeking strong leadership that doesn't back down when facing big questions that need big answers."

In the past, Evolvoir has expressed hopes to use its Series B funding to open retail stores and increase its global reach. Evolvoir diehards have also predicted that the company's highly anticipated second product offering—which Evolvoir has hinted will one day come but hasn't provided more information about—could arrive after this influx of investor support. Without a successful round, the company's capacity to grow will inevitably be limited.

In response to these concerns, Evolvoir representative and marketing and publicity manager Keon Phelps stated, "As part of our commitment to ethical tech, we're looking closely at the conversation about face shifting. However, we have no plans to cap Evolvoir's growth, especially in this critical moment in the company's lifespan."

CHAPTER FOUR

The glass conference room door, so heavy it barely slides open on its tracks. The day the article runs—four days after the biergarten—Nikhil takes his seat on one side of a long teal table. Across from him, Larissa Gertz Ross, the CEO and founder of Evolvoir, drinks water from a champagne flute and fishes one of the lemons off the side so she can suck on it before throwing it back in. Larissa is a relative newcomer to the beauty tech space and, unlike so many in the industry, doesn't come from family money. But while there are rumors she adopted a fake middle name to sound chic, at this point, it doesn't matter. She has made enough connections with powerful figures to make up for her humble beginnings.

"Your TechVIP article was a coup," Larissa says. After slurping on the acidic fruit her lips have a sheen, and when she talks, all the light attracts that way. She demands attention, Nikhil understands, and this kind of thing is the reason that Larissa was able to start Evolvoir and continue to hold on to it as it grows. "We've been getting calls from investors all morning."

"A coup?" It isn't clear to Nikhil if she means the word in the sense of an unexpected but welcome success or an unlawful uprising. As he sits back, the leather of his conference chair whines embarrassingly. He keeps his smile taut. It isn't as though he is surprised to be here. It follows that, because of Nikhil's clear public position on major face shifting, Larissa would be suspicious that he was the one to leak the TaskSquad conversations between Keon and the Product Growth Team to the reporter. Then again, the #grow-big-grow-strong channel is unlocked, so anyone at the company could have read the exchange and shared it with Erin. This is the argument that Nikhil was planning to make, though depending on Larissa's definition of coup, perhaps it won't even be necessary. For some reason, she doesn't seem as incensed about the article as he'd expected—and that makes him feel nervous, yes, but also curious. Nikhil says, "Should we talk about why I'm here? I assume it has to do with this anonymous employee referenced in the article?"

He'd gotten the promise of anonymity before he offered to show Erin the TaskSquad conversations. Michael had watched this interaction with equal parts humor and concern. It was a combination Nikhil was beginning to feel might be typical of his deskmate, who reached over to tap Nikhil's wrist when he said, "You barely know her, Nikhil. What if she's an intern?"

"You saw my business card," Erin said. "Unless you think I faked that like you think I faked my credentials?"

Michael held his hands up. In the end, though, showing Erin the TaskSquad conversation was important; it was what got Erin's editor on board with Nikhil as a source. Even then, the editor wanted a conference call with Nikhil, after which she determined they could use the information, as long as Erin could corroborate that the new policy was happening through other sources. That was how she ended up interviewing a new Evolvoir client who wasn't happy about the new facial changes rules. She'd made a social media post that hadn't generated much attention—she only had five followers—but Erin had found it. Through the article, Erin had amplified the post and the story, making the whole thing much more impactful than any of the higher-ups would have anticipated it being, especially in that first week.

For all this, Erin worked fast and did well. Nikhil hadn't even expected the article to come out so quickly; he only learned about its release this morning, when one of the midlevel employees posted the TechVIP article on the #all-press-is-good-press channel, and asked Keon and the other Young Talent Coaches if they'd seen it—or the ensuing public dialogue. When none of the YTCs replied, the other workers filled the chat with links to social media posts dissecting the article. Even if ninety percent of NuLook users weren't necessarily interested in major face shifting, much of the public was interested in talking about how this related to a larger conversation about wellness.

"Looks like you got what you wanted," Michael said quietly from his side of the desk. His tone dropped even lower, became even more dulcet as he added, "But you've taken a risk here, Nikhil. I wish you hadn't done this to yourself."

It felt as though Michael had touched Nikhil—though when Nikhil looked down at his arm, he saw that his deskmate had not. He met Michael's eyes, and then Michael scooted his chair a little closer, as if he knew what Nikhil had expected.

"It may end up being worth it," Nikhil said.

Four hours later, he received the message, not from @mark from the People Team or even @keon, but from @larissa, telling him to come by for an impromptu meeting—immediately. Now, he sits in this glass rectangle with her. A clock on the wall ticks loudly to mark the hour. This can't be Larissa's last meeting of the day—she should have people to please and other decisions to make—but her phone rests face down, and her gaze fixes on Nikhil even as she takes another sip of her water.

Larissa says, "If you want the truth, the article was a favor to me."

He's sure he has misheard her. But before Nikhil can say so, she slides him a bright-screened tablet. On it is a signed contract with both Larissa's and Yukiko's names. He reads the proposal in full to understand: Apparently, Yukiko will be joining the company as part of a new initiative, the Operation Wellness Team. The name is dualistic. Her role will require her to focus on clients who want to make big facial changes for their wellness. It will also ask her to consider the company's—the operation's—health as part of her decision-making. Her start date is in five days. Satisfaction rises through Nikhil so intensely, he presses his feet into the floor to steady himself. But then he remembers that just days ago the company had promised to do away with major face shifting, at least for new customers.

"What about the board?" he says. "What about the lawsuits?"

"What about you? You're in your CEO's office for breaking your NDA." She proclaims this with some bite, and Nikhil straightens. He hadn't realized that Larissa was still interested in indicting him for the article. But then she says, "It's obvious not much scares you. Not much scares me either. But the Evolvoir board is different than us. It hasn't been easy for me to get them to see my vision for this place."

Pouring herself another glass of water, she explains that when she and her team of researchers first began looking into the technology for NuLook, she had been sure that she was about to revolutionize beauty, to disrupt the industry. After all, this was different than using visual tricks like contouring to make facial shapes change. This was actually reworking features. This was giving people the power to actually change themselves, and thus take control over who they wanted to be. Knowing that the product was vital, and that it needed to get to the public as soon as possible, she began Evolvoir.

"But running a business is different from coming up with an idea," she says.

Larissa had played the game, and mostly convinced the board of her suitability as CEO. But over time her reputation soared. People began to describe her as inventive but overly ambitious, personable but overly stubborn. Because of this, her board refuses to trust her fully—and in fact, they've even held meetings to discuss bringing someone else in. Those conversations have only accelerated since the false impersonation lawsuits began.

She says, "I keep telling them, every company has lawsuits to some extent. It's the way the world works these days. They'll drag on for years and nothing will come of them."

This assertion is likely true. Nikhil has seen news of many tech companies settling suits without any harm to their reputation. He nods, and then keeps nodding when Larissa goes on to say that even if the lawsuits do amount to something, it really doesn't even matter. She loves her product. She loves what it can do for people, as evidenced by the Yukiko videos. So really, what's most important is harnessing the full potential of these nanoparticles and not undermining them. But the board, worried only about the company's long-term viability, has told her to appease the false impersonation critics and pull back on major face shifting, or they'll more seriously consider pushing her out. They, in the end, were the reason for the new policies—not Larissa.

"Their argument is, there's no one else that has caught up to our technology yet. So why not just focus on keeping our company afloat with the ninety percent of clients that only want to do small enhancements. In every single meeting they say we can make up the lost market segment—the major face-shifters—in other ways. They're particularly obsessed with the idea of creating a second product, one that can change body size or something." Larissa pauses. "But I'm not interested in that. I'm interested in the original product doing great things. Obviously that argument never worked with the board. But the article did. Do you know why?"

Of course he does. Crossing his arms, Nikhil says, "Because it showed them that the ten percent might also hold the key to Evolvoir's Series B funding. And even though you told them that a million times before, their egos were too big to listen to you until now."

Larissa hums with pleasure at his answer. "You are good. And that's why we're going to continue working on this together."

She plans to reassign him, she explains, to the Operation Wellness Team. His new role will be to support that endeavor entirely, but especially with any marketing and branding needs. No title change or salary increase, but it's a lateral move in his favor, she assures him. It will allow him to focus on the ten percent of clients he actually cares about.

"We'll assess the team's progress at three months, six months, nine months, and a year. I expect things to go well, though," she says, and then raises her glass, as if meaning for them to toast, even though Nikhil doesn't have his own drink in front of him. "What do you think?"

He looks at her champagne flute, elevated over the table. The deal is better than he expected. Against all odds, he and the CEO of this place want the same thing. Suddenly, he feels that his way forward is clear.

"Can I have some water?" he says.

Larissa smiles, gestures at a pitcher at the end of the table. Next to it, another flute is waiting. *Come on*, her hand signals, and Nikhil reaches.

It's five days after Evolvoir officially announced its new hire in a press release and a series of social media posts; three days after Yukiko waved at her followers and told them she was going corporate; and one day after the media requests were all expertly handled. Now the work can begin.

As part of the media frenzy, Keon, who is still Nikhil's YTC, is making the public believe that the policy reversal around face shifting was just miscommunicated. Today, he shares on Evolvoir's social media that the company is still allowing major face shifting, but not under NuLook. Instead, the company will soon be announcing another product, with a slightly tweaked formula, that will be given to those who want to configure their face in more extensive ways.

—@opwellness actually, we're just doing a slight rebrand of what we have, all the nanoparticles and stuff are staying the same, but we're changing the color of the cream from white to gold.

Keon is writing in the #be-well-sell-well, the new channel for the Operation Wellness Team. In the last week, he has pivoted his opinions from being anti–major face shifting to pro. Nikhil suspects that after Larissa got the board to change their thinking, it was easy enough for her to convince her subordinates—Keon and the other YTCs—to do the same. After all, they too would be worried about the Series B funding, knowing that a lack of money could lead to Evolvoir contracting and thus laying people off.

—we'll talk about it more at our first meeting tonight. which, don't forget, is going to be at an ☆ art gallery ☆!

It was Keon's idea to hold the first Operation Wellness Team meeting in a special location, and he's clearly proud of it. Maybe he isn't wrong to be. Nikhil can appreciate the thought behind discussing a rebrand at an art gallery that specializes in self-portraits. Besides, it feels like a nice way to welcome Yukiko, whose first official day in the office is today. Nikhil hasn't met her yet, as she has spent all her time in Larissa's office, so he can't wait for tonight, when he and Yukiko have their official introduction and, hopefully, discuss their shared vision for the product.

"I'll go if there's wine," Michael says from his side of the desk. "There's always wine at a gallery, right?"

Once again, he talks to Nikhil in a sporadic and unprompted way, like they're in the middle of a conversation that has just never ended. Like their being around each other is a constant part of their day. Just a few days ago, Michael randomly texted pictures of two dogs he saw in the park, a little one yapping and a bigger, aloof one. And then he sent an invitation to a weird Bushwick disco warehouse party that he heard about online. And then this morning, he told Nikhil about a bagel, a hemp seed one, from a new coffee shop he had discovered on a meandering walk to the West Village that he had taken during a prolonged, definitely-unsanctioned-by-Keon break. When Nikhil said it sounded okay, Michael produced the bagel and asked if he wanted a bite. After, Michael brushed the crumbs off Nikhil's collar without asking permission. As if he knew Nikhil would lean in to the touch. Nikhil did.

But as much as Nikhil likes Michael—sometimes falls asleep thinking of Michael's nose piercing, Michael's fingers warm from cigarettes, Michael's easy, unhurried gait through the company halls—he hasn't had time to give his deskmate the attention he can guess Michael would enjoy. Since his conversation with Larissa, Nikhil has thrown himself into his work, mostly analyzing the metrics Yukiko has emailed of her many, many social media posts. He's also started brainstorming content ideas for the rebrand when he has small pockets of time.

"There might be wine," Nikhil says. "And also, you have to go. You're on the Operation Wellness Team."

Privately, Nikhil speculates that Michael only volunteered for the team as part of a scheme to get him and Nikhil to spend more time together—because it isn't as if Michael seems particularly interested in the mission behind it. It isn't that he ever disagrees with Nikhil's points about how people need more mental wellness support or that he wasn't congratulatory when Nikhil told him about the meeting with Larissa, but rather that he always ends up pivoting the conversation to talk about something else, something more personal, often about Nikhil's past or his feelings. It's flattering in a way, even if Nikhil doesn't quite understand Michael's ambivalence.

"You're not wrong," Michael says. "But since we're both on said team, why don't we walk to the meeting together?"

Nikhil nods. "Sure. As long as we leave early. I want to catch Yukiko before everyone else swarms her."

The gallery is in the Lower East Side, on Orchard. Just outside, twenty-somethings lounge in the few, coveted outdoor eateries. To counteract the mid-June warmth, they sip seven-dollar margaritas and fan themselves with the paper specials menus. A few college students flash fake IDs from England, put on bad accents, and seem to get away with it. But inside the gallery, the scene is quieter, devoid of much but the security guard, the curator, the complimentary wine, and the canvases that hang on the walls.

Nikhil and Michael tour the edges of the place, discovering that everything in here is by the same artist. The show consists solely of triptychs that operate as self-portraits of the artist as he progresses through a series of emotions. Thoughtfulness to concern to understanding. Shock to hope to wistfulness. The one-word titles—among them, LOVE and HATRED—are like amorphous ideas. But the captions say more, like "Thinking of the first time I decided my freckles were a part of me" or "Thinking of the first time I knew the bullies were right." Nikhil stares at the door. These paintings aren't his taste. The problem isn't technical—the brushstrokes are practiced; the composition is easy to take in—but rather conceptual. The way the artist's face twists through so many sentiments and somehow never ends on a smile disconcerts him. All this irresolution, hung for viewing as if it should be celebrated rather than dealt with.

"It won't hurt you to look," Michael says.

But Nikhil is looking now—at Yukiko, who has just come through the door, arms wrapped around her torso. As always, she wears her sister's eyes, lit amber with curious swirls, but Nikhil notices other things now that aren't visible on screen: her fine ears, sporting delicate rings; her short torso and disproportionate legs; the je ne sais quoi in her expression that she's famous for. Standing at the edge of the room, she rummages in her bag anxiously, so anxiously that items slip out: an Evolvoir-branded teal tablet, a tube of product emblazoned with the same logo, a pocket-sized tampon, a phone with a haunting black-and-white optical illusion on its case, a dollar bill or maybe a five folded neatly into the shape of an airplane. This last thing Nikhil finds the most interesting, and wants to ask her about.

"So?" Michael says, watching Yukiko too. She has since dropped to her knees to pick up her things, but keeps getting distracted by her thick, undulating hair. Over and over, she tucks it behind her ears, like she can't get it right. "Is she all you were hoping for?"

An automatic yes would be a lie. Over the last few days, Nikhil has built up an expectation of Yukiko. That she would come in here with confidence, creativity, a clear conceptualization of what the product can be that matches his own. This Yukiko, though, seems mostly uncomfortable—that worries him. He says to Michael, "I just hope she can help us."

Michael slaps him on the shoulder, as if telling him not to be so modest. "God, fangirl a little. Tell her the truth, how you're obsessed with her videos." He lightly runs his teeth over his bottom lip. His right incisor shows. "Then I'll tell her how cute it is that you can't stop watching them."

"It's not cute. It's research. I've been trying to figure out an angle for the rebrand."

"Sure," Michael says. "Let's just go meet her."

They cross the room, and when they introduce themselves, Nikhil holds out a hand for Yukiko to shake. She takes it after a moment of hesitation. Her palm is sweaty and soft, tender and human. But then the grip goes firmer, so firm that it distracts him from the dampness against his skin. Like that, the girl on her knees is no more. *Good*, Nikhil thinks. He decides to assume that her strange demeanor earlier was nervousness around meeting her colleagues. He decides everything will be all right. But then she starts talking.

"I heard some gossip that getting me hired was your idea." Yukiko lets go of their handshake. "If that's true, I owe you. You know, the recruiter said the only way they could let me use the products the way I have been is if I joined you."

Nikhil thumbs his lip. Partially because Larissa hadn't mentioned this arrangement, but mostly because it bothers him that Yukiko addresses their collaboration first as an individual business negotiation instead of an opportunity to provide their users a tool to support their mental health journeys.

"I was part of the process," Nikhil says. "Personally, I'm most excited about Evolvoir taking your cue and pushing the product as something that can do more for people's wellness than just their looks." He pauses, assessing her reaction. Nothing. He wonders if maybe she doesn't understand. Maybe he's not explaining himself well. He searches for a way to convey why this matters so much, but something in him is stuttering, unsure what to say to someone he was sure would already understand. Is there something wrong here? All he manages to add is "I have a sister too."

"Oh," she says softly. "I see."

Before Nikhil can ask what exactly she sees and if it's the same thing he envisions too, Keon arrives with the rest of the Operation Wellness Team. The four other Young Talenters by his side immediately head for the alcohol, and then they take over the gallery, making overemphasized *ooh*s and *aah*s at each painting. They appear to be trying to impress Keon. Unlike Nikhil, who has been moved to the Operation Wellness Team permanently, all the other Young Talenters are still part of their original teams. All of them are volunteers and will likely end up with double the work because of this, but each of them is here in the hope that management will call them dependable or cooperative in their midyear evaluations.

"I should get over there," Yukiko says.

There's nothing for Nikhil and Michael to do now but follow Yukiko to the other members of the Operation Wellness Team, who've paused their conversation to stare at her. The closer Yukiko drifts to them, the more she exudes the girl on the screen. When she notices their interest, she laughs, though it is light and breathless, more the performance of a laugh than something genuine.

"We meet," she says. "Finally."

Keon begins the meeting officially, and they go around the circle, introducing themselves with their names, original positions and teams, and one fun fact about themselves. Perhaps Keon suggested this format on the way over, because they each have a tidbit on the tip of their tongue to share: Jordie, who went parasailing once and saw a great white shark; Greg, who drove through every mainland US state on his senior-year road trip; Alison, who traced her family line back to the *Mayflower*; and Morgan, who owned a menagerie of exotic snakes and had once been offered a sponsorship by a pet store. Michael, for his part, passes on the fact aspect of the exercise, while Nikhil offers up something about his favorite band and color.

"These guys have a lot of ideas for you," Keon tells Yukiko when they've all finished. At some point, he pulled out his phone and is now checking TaskSquad. "Someone start us up."

Nikhil isn't surprised when Jordie, originally from the Client Care Team, speaks up. He knows her as a brownnoser who only wants to be noticed. At every meeting they've attended together, she's asked the first question—which is usually a strategically crafted comment, meant to make her look smart, instead. Pointing to a canvas at the wall, she says, "This actually reminds me of a client I met with last week. She wanted big changes, so she might be a good starting point."

She describes the girl, seventeen or so, who, during the preassess, sent in a photo of her father with a vicious X over his face because she hated how much she resembled the man. She asked to change almost all her features. As he listens, Nikhil chews on a hangnail that isn't close to being ready to be bitten off. He feels something brush against his thigh and continues working at his finger as he looks down to see what it is. Michael, subtly trying to get his attention. He has noticed, it seems, that Nikhil is lost in thought, though he can't know that Nikhil is hoping this person, who wants to stop carrying her father around, is his sister. But that would be unlikely based on his last conversation with Kashmira. Nikhil tears a small triangle of skin away from his finger, knowing it will bleed. Jordie isn't describing his sister, but one day, if Nikhil does what he came here to do, she could be.

"Okay," Nikhil says. He moves closer to the painting that Jordie has identified as her entry point into this conversation. "That's good. So how do we use that for the rebrand? We want to convey to our clients that we're on board with total transformation, and we believe that it can bring them peace from family and identity struggles. We need them to see that our product can help solve things for them. Because it can. Right, Yukiko?"

In their earlier conversation, Yukiko had seemed disinterested in Nikhil's ambitions to expand the product's reach. But this she should easily agree with. After all, her videos are about the power of becoming her sister. So Yukiko should answer in a crisp, clear affirmative, and then they should move to the next point in their brainstorm. But she doesn't say *Of course* or *Absolutely, I have some thoughts on that* or *That's exactly the way we need to go.* Her eyes dart from his eager expression to the painting then back to him again. She doesn't seem able to give him what he needs. Everyone is staring at her, and she just barely gets out, "I don't know. Solve? Maybe, in a way."

"Wait," Jordie says. "Yukiko, do you not think the big changes are worth it?"

Quiet descends across the group, and the fear Nikhil had earlier tonight—when he wondered if something was wrong—intensifies. Nothing seems to be working and there seems to be no way forward. How sure he was about Yukiko, and the product, and helping people, and reuniting with his sister. But now, that's all at risk, and he has no other options, no other plans. The fear becomes anger, just like that, heated and pushy.

"Nikhil," Michael says in Nikhil's ear. "She needs help. Say something."

In the future, when Nikhil thinks back to this time, he will wonder what Michael really meant for him to do. Probably to reach over and touch Yukiko's arm and ask if she is okay. Probably to tell her to take a minute if she needs it. Probably to ask her to be honest about what she thinks and feels. They can take it, as long as it's the truth. But Nikhil does none of these things. Instead, he clears his throat and speaks for her, over her, and says, "Of course she thinks the big changes are worth it. Otherwise, why would she be making them every day?"

His tone is harsh. He can hear it as he says it. But his anger is still there, still roiling, still ready to be unleashed even further—until Yukiko seems to remember herself, who she is supposed to be in this moment.

"He's right," Yukiko says. She smiles in an almost manic way. "Of course he's right."

The group relaxes, pacified. Jordie murmurs that it must have just been a misunderstanding, and a few others nod. Michael, though, shifts nearer to Nikhil, and when they share a glance, he looks concerned. But the meeting is moving on. Keon is asking where they're going to take this conversation next, and Nikhil knows he has to be the one to answer, or who knows what'll happen next.

He leans forward to look at the painting that Jordie turned their attention to earlier. RENEWAL, it's called. He reads only the title rather than the full placard and doesn't waste time with the images themselves. He doesn't have to, because suddenly he knows what to do. Renewal—it sounds like coming alive again. That's what he has always wanted for his sister, for himself, for their family. Renewal.

When he proposes a name for the rebranded product, the team votes yes.

ReNuLook it is.

—⁂—

He and Michael, it turns out, aren't done with each other that night.

While the rest of the Operation Wellness Team finishes up the wine, Michael steps out for a cigarette. Nikhil lets him go without following, but then five minutes later, his phone rings in his pocket, and—because it's Ami, whose call he always picks up—he too exits the gallery, seeking a secluded spot of his own. The nearby alley, quiet and thus perfect for taking the call, isn't empty though. Leaning against the brick wall, Michael smokes his cigarette with the easy calm of someone planning to take as long as they want.

"You were looking for me?" Michael says.

"Actually, no," Nikhil tells him, covering the speaker on his phone. "I'm on the phone."

Today, his mother is keyed up, going on about the air-conditioning unit malfunctioning, the wasps in a nest around their back door, the gas prices that are cutting into the household budget. Nikhil advises his mother as best he can until she slows down. Then he says, "Mom, are you sure Kashmira doesn't want to talk? I have something to tell her about."

A pause on the other end of the line. Then Ami says, "I don't know where she is."

Nikhil pulls the phone away from his ear so his mother won't hear his intake of breath, so sharp, so utterly done. He doesn't know if his mother really has lost track of his sister's whereabouts or if Kashmira passed back the phone with a sour expression. Either way, he won't be talking to his sister tonight, won't be telling her about ReNuLook and how it'll be on the market soon enough.

"Your mom?" Michael says when he sees Nikhil pocket his phone. "She never even asked you how you were."

"She forgets a lot of the time." Nikhil squares his shoulders. Michael watches his posture. "It's the way she is."

"Then let me ask. How are you? It got a little intense in the gallery."

"I was doing the things I have to do."

"Taking care of people? Like you just were?" When Nikhil shrugs, Michael says, "You know, you should take care of yourself sometimes too. Or else you're going to burn out."

One man shouldn't have so many perfect smiles, and yet. Nikhil walks to the alley wall where Michael leans, not at all worried about his shirt sticking to some errant gum or stinking up because of pee. Nikhil draws even closer, and Michael doesn't create any distance between them.

"Take care of myself? How should I do that? By giving myself lung cancer?" Nikhil says, gesturing at the still-lit cigarette between Michael's fingers. As much as he hates smoking, he finds himself somehow jealous of that thin, burning cylinder, so comfortable under Michael's touch.

"Hah," Michael says. "You know, I could help you. Unwind, I mean." He puts his cigarette out against the wall. Immediately after, he pulls out his pack and assesses the number of cigarettes left inside. Then he says, "What would be so wrong with that?"

What would be? Michael holds out a cigarette, which Nikhil knows he won't take. Still, he makes the gesture to do so anyway. Leans in to grab it. And then their faces, suddenly so close. Even in this darkness, Nikhil thinks he can make out every pore on Michael's face. Not because that's possible but because he has looked attentively before under the glow of Evolvoir's cool overhead lights. They are so close, finally.

And then they are kissing—Michael making use of his tongue in ways Nikhil didn't expect so early in their intimacy. He fills Nikhil's mouth wholly, feeling out every space, even those behind Nikhil's molars. One hand drags long circles against Nikhil's hip, while the other pulls at Nikhil's hair, hard, in a way that makes Nikhil jerk his head up. That makes Michael laugh and kiss the underside of Nikhil's jaw. To Nikhil's embarrassment, he gets hard at that.

"This isn't," Nikhil says, between two kisses, "this isn't the right place for this. We're still"—there's another kiss—"technically at work."

But even as he suggests stopping, he reaches for Michael's belt. It's been so long since he has had sex, and Michael has been tempting him for a month now, and their hips are close, and now Michael grinds against him just slightly and the pressure is too much, too good.

That is, until he abruptly remembers a memory that isn't even his own.

Vinod, and his mother, and their first encounter. Ami often told the story of how Vinod noticed her in the grocery store, weighing a bag of shelled and veiny walnuts. He walked up to her and asked her what she planned to make with them, and she said they were on the list for her father, who liked them best.

"Even over pistachios?" Vinod said. "Or cashews? Are you sure he's Indian?"

Vinod had been a younger man in stories like this, still orbiting around his parents and the community they built in their two and a half decades in this country. This was before he decided their way of being was wrong, and, because he liked Ami's laugh, he asked her out. After that they kept seeing each other. Ami said no one had ever pursued her the way Vinod had. It only took a few months for her to meet his parents—who embraced her, loved her, suggested their engagement. Nikhil had once leaned in to whisper to Kashmira that he suspected up until this time their father thought he could make it work with Ami, that he could be the good husband everyone hoped he would be—though that didn't happen, as she well knew. Kashmira had whispered back not to interrupt the story, because back then, she still hoped her parents could make it work.

Nikhil pulls away, uncomfortable. He and Michael exhale in tandem.

"You're thinking something," Michael says. "You can tell me."

"Maybe," Nikhil says, even as Michael kisses him again, this time at the corner of his mouth. That gentlest touch makes Nikhil's eyes close. And still, he steps further back, away from the wall and into the open space of the alley.

He and Michael are an arm's reach apart now. But Nikhil needs the space. He doesn't know why his mind came up with that memory, but its appearance feels tricky and complicated. He shakes his head, trying to dispel the discomfort. That time with his father was a long time ago, and doesn't matter now. It doesn't.

He reaches out his hand. Michael takes it, and Nikhil holds on, as if to tell himself, *Really, what's there to worry about?*

Sharper angles, heightened colors. The girl on the screen refines her videos with the help of a team. The changes are noticeable, and the viewers comment, critical and unsure. Who is she now? She types out answer after answer, but nothing suffices, except another video.

As always, she wears her sister's face, though at first no one can tell. The shot is of the girl's back, until she turns. Then, a new take. Her head, leaning against a window. Then her sternum, moving up and down as she breathes. The clip replays.

In the caption, she writes, *you've all been asking about the latest videos and i can't lie. i can't. i am trying to make things better. i am trying to be better, do better. i want you to see that, please.*

What the girl on the screen—and the viewers—don't yet understand is the toll this takes. How much it requires to become this person, when another version of her could have existed and been held in so many embraces.

CHAPTER FIVE

Almost two weeks pass after Kashmira's painful first call with Jordie. It's still June, but sometimes Kashmira forgets the real date. She has returned to lazing about the house and avoiding people, mirrors, windows, and anything else that reflects her face. She leaves the house only for her low-wage summer barista job and gets away with this because Ami, per the usual, spends most of her limited time outside of work caught up in her own routines, except when she shares the occasional prepared meal with Kashmira: frozen mac and cheese in an oven that makes the house hot unless the air-conditioning kicks in; chicken alfredo, just add water, now microwaved into gloop. Both foods that Vinod added to the grocery list, especially after visits to his parents' house. Kashmira pushes the pasta around her plate, leaving thick smears of white sauce, and answers in brief when Ami awkwardly asks her how her day was and then somehow transitions into talking about Vinod. In truth, it shouldn't be so hard, continuing to live with her old, unchanged features. She has done it for seventeen years. But the ache of who she could have been in another face palpitates brutally in her chest.

At least she has Roshni. They see each other once a day during this time, and usually hole up in Kashmira's room. Some of the time they scroll on their phones and send each other VidMos. Some of the time they listen to pop music, upbeat tracks with bitter lyrics. Some of the time they study for their upcoming standardized tests. But most of the time, they talk. Kashmira has questions about what Roshni has been up to in the years since they stopped hanging out; Roshni has her own questions about Kashmira too. They detail their histories, from the clubs they've joined at school to crushes to family conflicts. Roshni tells Kashmira when her negative test results come back from the clinic. Kashmira tells Roshni about exactly what happened in the bedroom with Tej. After a while, Kashmira can't think of anything she hasn't told Roshni—and that's when she realizes they are friends again.

Of course, when she tells Roshni this, on the eleventh day after the call with Jordie, the other girl just smiles, looks at her hands, and says, "Well, yeah, obviously we're friends. But I bet we both still have some secrets. Like what's going on with you and Sachin? He is literally always texting you."

He isn't "always" texting Kashmira, though he is sending her periodic updates about his vacation with his parents. She responds to these, albeit more distractedly than she would have before this summer. After all, much of her writing-related energy is going into collaborating with Roshni to compose daily multi-paragraph complaints to Evolvoir's Client Care portal. Roshni, who is worried that Evolvoir's new product guidelines will affect her too, suggests Kashmira ask why Evolvoir isn't letting her "fully evolve herself to embrace herself." Isn't that their tagline?

On the twelfth day after the call with Jordie, before Kashmira can send a message, a response blinks onto the app.

Let's me and you schedule a meeting, Jordie writes, and they do, and now, just two days later, Kashmira crosses her legs and waits on the bed as the video and audio connect for their scheduled session.

Like Kashmira, Jordie sits in the same position as before—with the same headphones, the same practiced smile. She waves at Kashmira and says, "Is this still a good time?"

"I wouldn't have logged on if it wasn't," Kashmira says.

The rudeness feels earned. No matter how much Jordie cites Evolvoir policy as the reason Kashmira can't change her face the way she wants, it doesn't matter. Inside the company is a concept that Kashmira can't see the shape of; Jordie is a person, and thus easier to blame. But she is also a person who was been trained well, and rather than reacting to Kashmira's tone, she pulls up the Comprehensive Face Mapping™. It opens to the latest 3D diagram, the one with all the changes Kashmira input during their last session. How lovely that face is, Kashmira feels, not for all it is but for all it isn't.

"I have some good news for you," Jordie says, and then describes a cream called ReNuLook, which, in all honesty, sounds like the same product as NuLook, just with updated packaging. But when Kashmira says this, Jordie insists that ReNuLook is for those who need to change their faces to better their mental health and wellness—not just to look prettier. Then she adds, "The point is, if this is still the face you want, I can put in the order right away. I just need you to say yes."

It never occurs to Kashmira to ask more about this new product. All that matters is that Jordie offers next-day shipping, free of charge. All that matters is that the product comes in a neat rectangular teal package, as promised. All that matters is Kashmira sitting down to unbox it. She tosses the cardboard and welcome pamphlets to the side, digging instead for the tubes wrapped in tissue paper. In one, a reversal cream that can remove any facial changes in ten minutes. In the other, the product, viscous and glistening gold instead of the white Roshni's was. The instructions are specific and simple: Use every six hours. Start with a clean, dry face. Dispense the product. Then using your fingers, rub the product onto the face. She does so, in small, resolute circles, making sure that the product penetrates every pore, from her forehead to her collarbone. Only then will the new, second face be able to interrupt the old one's authority over her life. She waits. Then rubs again. Then leans over the sink, trying to get a proper angle to see in the mirror. The instructions include a small-print disclaimer: RESULTS MAY VARY. But Kashmira refuses to believe that this warning applies to her. Her second face will persevere. It must.

And then she feels it, the deep tearing sensation, under her skin, under her sinew, under her muscles and veins and blood. The second face twists into being. New eyelids, new cheeks, a new top lip, none of it Vinod.

Trembling, Kashmira touches her face, her reflection, her face again. Images she prefers not to think about come harshly. Her father's back, always so stiff, always leaving. Gone, gone, gone then—and gone, gone, gone now. With one hand, Kashmira covers her mouth as nausea takes over, swirling. She remembers that this happened before when she used the product, but this time she also recalls Roshni, seated on the edge of the clinic's exam table. Anxiety, Roshni had said. Anxiety had caused her symptoms, including feeling sick to her stomach. Well, that makes sense for Kashmira. Like Roshni, she too is anxious, if only because she now has a chance to ignore all the emotional horrors inside her, just by gifting herself a new face to live in. And that knowledge of this better—this best—self will change everything about how she traverses the world, wherever she chooses to go.

Terrifying. Yet also everything.

After she gives herself fifteen minutes to stare at her face—newly changed, for the first time—Kashmira texts Roshni an impeccable photo that she takes outside her apartment. The mid-morning light accentuates every detail, and because Kashmira loves the look of it, she takes another three photos and sends them too.

Immediately, her friend responds, now that's a face. now what do you wanna do with it?

Kashmira, who has been considering this question herself, thinks of the conversation she and Roshni had with Ami a few weeks ago in the kitchen. She thinks of the thing that she has always wanted to attend, but couldn't, just because of her father. The thing that tore her and Roshni apart. She replies, what if I go to kathak?

Roshni loves the idea. Without hesitation, she calls up her teacher, Hemaji, who doesn't like students joining up in the middle of a semester—even if it is the summer—but does like Roshni quite a bit and might make an exception for one of her friends. They talk, and once again, Roshni acts as quite the negotiator: She ends up suggesting that though Kashmira is a beginner, she ought to join the intermediate class instead, since there are teenage girls enrolled in it instead of just five- to nine-year-olds like in the lower level. In exchange for Hemaji letting Kashmira stand in the back of this class, Roshni agrees to attend too, but as an extra set of eyes, helping out whenever she can.

you don't have to do that, Kashmira says. you've done me enough favors.

i like hanging out at the studio, Roshni writes back. but know that i do expect you to drive me.

Drive her Kashmira does. Just two days later they head to the studio for the first lesson.

The room, built of wood and mirrors, is busy when they arrive. Students swap gossip from the past week. Students warm up. Students loop ghungroos around their ankles. Roshni sits on the floor to do hers, but Kashmira leaves her ankles bare. As a beginner, she isn't allowed to wear ghungroos yet, even if she is in an intermediate class. In the past, this discrepancy between her and everyone else would have reminded her of her otherness and made her falter. She might have conceded that her father was right, that she shouldn't be here. She might have left the studio altogether. But this Kashmira, now on her third day of wearing her second face, just smiles and waits. One day she'll wear the ghungroos too; the person she has become can do anything.

The hour mark draws near, and as class begins, all of the dancers line up. At first, too many of them stand in the front, but Hemaji, wearing her severe, gray-streaked bun, clicks her tongue and they concede their places to make up the middle and back rows too. Kashmira walks past them all to the last line, but, as with the ghungroos, she doesn't mind, not even when the girls whisper to each other, wondering if anyone knows who she is.

"We have a new student," Hemaji announces once Kashmira has found a spot. The others nod, almost in unison. They've all noticed her, Kashmira sees. Hemaji does too, and she says, "Good. Make sure to welcome her after class."

Then she claps her hands, and the girls all turn to face a wall-length mirror. In it, they watch their movements, comparing each gesture to Hemaji's or their neighbors' or their own from the week before. They also steal glances at Kashmira and then wink at her when she catches them looking. Once or twice, they even make little gestures at her, encouraging her to change her posture this-way-to-the-right or this-way-to-the-left, and she does, and they clap lightly. It moves her, the way they accept her—though Kashmira wishes for a brief moment that it had been this simple when her father was still around. But then Hemaji starts the tanpura machine, the students begin their taatkaar, and Kashmira forgets this thought. Because as everyone's feet pound the smooth floor in time, she too finds a rhythm. How satisfying it feels to beat her heels alongside the other dancers. Almost as if the soles of her feet have been waiting for the sharp sting of contact all this time.

"Remember to smile," Hemaji calls out.

Kashmira doesn't have to remember. Her cheeks hurt from beaming, and they keep hurting. They hurt through basic movements. They hurt through the longer pieces, though Kashmira hasn't learned these steps and can't follow along without Roshni guiding her. They hurt through the end of class, as all the students do their chakkars, spinning again and again as the air breezes past them lightly.

An hour goes by like this, until Hemaji has all the girls come to a stop so she can dismiss them with a reminder that their autumn recital is coming up in three months, and that they must keep practicing. The students, who've slouched so their spines have fallen out of dancers' proper alignments, shift back and forth on their feet.

Class is over, and they want to chat while they pack up their bags. But unlike them, Kashmira isn't ready to go, and though the other girls leave once dismissed, she lingers on the dance floor, unsure what comes next, but reluctant to lose the feelings this class has given her.

"You picked it up well," Hemaji says, joining her on the floor. She surveys Kashmira's body up and down. "Not too bad at all. Maybe you'll even be ready for a part—a small one—in the recital this year."

"Thank you," Kashmira says, tucking the hair that loosened from her braid behind her ears. "I'm just glad to be here. I've been wanting to come for a long time."

"Of course you have. These are your traditions, too."

At this, a sudden memory: Kashmira's grandparents, arguing with her father while she waited by the front door. They had wanted to take her to the temple that day, to play Holi. There would be clouds of color in the air, and she would wear white. Though her father said they'd stayed long enough and they'd already done a puja, her grandparents told him that she should know more of her culture, more of the things that had been carried across the miles that were taken up by the ocean from here to there. Kashmira was too young to understand all that, but she did know she wanted to be smeared with color, the way she had seen it done to other people in videos about the holiday. In those clips, everyone had been laughing, showing their teeth, which were plastered with orange, pink, yellow. She wanted to see it. She wanted to do it. And even though Vinod hadn't allowed her to go to the celebration, she still spent the evening fantasizing about how it might have been if she had. What if, what if, what if. It doesn't matter; her grandparents are gone and will never return. Her vision swims at the thought.

But then Hemaji, maybe seeing Kashmira caught in this remembrance, reaches for her. The movement is gruff, in the way of everything Hemaji does, but that isn't what matters. Not when she pats Kashmira's cheek—once, twice. The touch, brief but meaningful, like an anointing.

Tonight, another party.

This time, they are a county away, celebrating July Fourth with beer pong. The host sets up four tables, and there are lines to play. Girls sling their arms around boys' shoulders and tell them they should be on the same team. These same boys tease the girls back and make them promise not to fuck up all the shots. Roshni, caught up in all this, laughs so hard some guy has to grab her around the waist to keep her from tripping herself and him.

"Roshni," Kashmira says, edging closer to her. "I need to reapply."

Roshni pitches toward Kashmira. "Do you need me to come?"

Kashmira shakes her head. At first, she worried whether she could feasibly come to another one of these parties, especially after the incident with Tej in the bedroom. But he had apparently passed out after their encounter and didn't remember anything that happened between them. According to Roshni, there aren't any rumors of Kashmira's freak-out and no gossip about how she is one-on-one with boys.

"You could try again," Roshni had said earlier as the two of them drove to the party. "He'll be there. He always comes."

Kashmira had pretended to be busy adjusting the rearview mirror. She did want to try again, not exactly because of Tej but because of how his approval represented an entry into this other world of brown-kid shenanigans. Before, she hadn't been able to become the girl she wanted to be with him. But tonight maybe she could. Why, then, did she suddenly think of Sachin, at the bus stop or on her doorstep watching her? Why, then, she did think of how under his gaze she felt seen, but always at a distance? Why, then, did she wish he would press his thumb to her collarbone and then trace the line of it all the way? He was the boy from before, she reminded herself, and then accidentally cranked the mirror too far down.

"I can help you with Tej," Roshni offered. "That is, unless you have someone else you're interested in?"

They arrived at the party then. As they walked into the backyard, Roshni looped her arm around Kashmira's. Immediately, they were busy. One of the girls from kathak, Prithi, waved to them, and then, at one of the beer pong tables, someone handed over two clear shots. One, two, three, drink, and then again. After, they found a group of girls and stood with them. As they all caught up, the girls paid each other fawning but genuine compliments on their outfits, their hair, their makeup, whatever they could see. Everything, Kashmira realized, was fine. And then after more drinks, it became good, so good that now Kashmira feels like she can go find Tej, as long as she first reapplies her face.

"I'm going inside," Kashmira says to Roshni. "I'll be back. I just need a mirror."

"Hurry," Roshni tells her. "You know Tej always has a million girls all over him."

Kashmira walks fast, but then as she enters the house, she finds that the first-floor bathrooms have a line. Not wanting to wait, she considers what to do, and then remembers Roshni escorting her upstairs the last time they attended a party. Kashmira takes a flight of stairs and then follows the hallway to an open door. Inside the room, sports posters feature prominently on the wall and a small basketball hoop hangs from the back of the closet door. This is someone's bedroom, she realizes, and almost turns. But then a mirror inside catches some light, and when she sees her reflection, she forgets to care about her intrusion.

Drawing close to her reflection, Kashmira sees that her face hasn't changed yet. This makes sense; she is only at five and a half hours after her last application. Still, to be safe, she applies another coat of ReNuLook. Slick and easy, except for the wave of nausea. This issue has affected her since her first application, but she expects she'll eventually adjust. That's one of the many reasons she now wears the product at all hours—hoping to get used to it—and only uses the reversal oil when she thinks her mother might be paying attention.

Still, Kashmira presses her palm into her cheek. Though the sick feeling will come and go, she wrenches the window open to push her head through, hoping the early July breeze, listless as it is, can dispel it at least a little.

This is when she realizes she isn't alone.

Outside the window, she sees Sachin, of all people. He has crawled out onto the little outcropping of roof past the window, and sits with his legs dangling. He holds his camera in both hands. Kashmira takes a moment with his silhouette, which she knows well from all the years. She can imagine what his expression looks like right now: thoughtful, but in an obsessive way, as if he has to figure out everything that moment or else. She pauses. She could recognize him anywhere, but he can't say the same for her any longer, can he?

Sachin turns his head. "Is someone there?"

Kashmira told Roshni she'd be back soon to look for Tej. But it's been a month since she and Sachin have properly talked, and he hasn't seen her second face, and for some reason, she wants to know how his pupils, dark and observant, will track the changes in her. She wants to know where they'll linger. Kashmira slides half her body out the window. When Sachin sees her, he stares until she says hi very low, the way she used to do at the bus stop. Only then does he furrow his brow and reply with her name.

"It's me," she says. "It's makeup."

"That face-changing stuff," he replies. "Since when have you been into that?"

"Since, I don't know. A bit."

As she tries to get further out onto the roof, Kashmira struggles to maneuver on the unfamiliar surface. Sachin sets his camera down and reaches out, as if to steady her—but his fingers don't go far enough. Ultimately, she is the one who lowers herself down successfully. Then, there is silence. He doesn't mention anything about how good she looks, even as she settles closer and makes sure she isn't sitting in shadow.

Finally, she says, "Don't you want to be down at the party?"

"Nah. I never know how to act at these things." Sachin picks his video camera back up. "Don't get me wrong. I like these parties well enough for people-watching. Life always looks better in my camera. That's why I'm up here, filming." He runs his knuckle against the edge of his camera's lens. "You might have ended up in a shot or two. Sorry. But they're just—"

"Faceless, nameless party shots. I know."

She doesn't mind being filmed as much when she wears the product, but she doesn't tell him that. Mostly because he acts the same with her as he did prior to her changing her face, and she can't be sure what that means. Instead, she asks how his movie is going and if he has actually started doing any storyboarding yet. He drums his fingers on his knees.

"I'll tell you," Sachin says. "But you have to be nice about it."

"When am I not nice about your film stuff?"

He cocks his head. "True. It's just, I think I bit off more than I can chew. The whole writing, directing, and producing my own movie thing is hard." He tells her more about how far he has gotten in the story. Mostly, he has focused on the characters, who all sound like they are based on people they know. Roshni and Tej, for sure. She tells Sachin this, and he fiddles with one of the buttons on his camera. "I'm writing about South Asians in suburbia, and they're decent subjects. I think I'm getting to the heart of them, which is good."

She smiles. "And am I going to show up at all?"

"Well, it's hard to add you in when I haven't really figured you out at all," he says. Then he looks up and gestures at her face. "And tonight you've complicated things even more."

This isn't what she expected, though Sachin doesn't hesitate when he says this—which means either that he doesn't think it could possibly hurt her, or that saying it is more important to him than her feelings. Either way, it means he thinks they're close enough for him to be honest. Still, his aloof ruling about her choices makes pain cut through her chest. To distract herself from that, she digs her fingers into the shingles, and she doesn't stop even as it ruins her nail polish.

"You don't like my face? That's the problem?"

"I'm just not sure why you're doing this to yourself."

"Then why don't you come down there with me and find out?" Her voice has climbed in pitch, but she doesn't care. How cruel that Sachin of all people doesn't understand that sometimes people hate who they are and have to do something about it. He, a filmmaker, so sure he understands people enough to put them on a screen, should. So maybe it isn't that he doesn't get this concept but rather that he doesn't see her as everything she is. Almost as if this narrative doesn't fit the character he built for her. How upsetting the idea of him looking past her like this. "Or are you just going to analyze me from behind your camera where it's safe?"

"You could just tell me—"

"What? So you can put it in your notebook? And then later in your film?"

"I didn't know you didn't like the notebook," he says. His voice cracks with surprise. She blinks at the sudden emotion in him, but then he clears his throat. "I don't know. I thought it was a way to open up to each other."

Kashmira thinks of all the words he's collected from her. Words she meant over the years, words often born of her experiences with grief and otherness and the loneliness of knowing everything she ever did would be measured against what her father thought she should be. These words—important and smart but somehow not everything. Not when there is so much complexity hammering inside her that she isn't even sure she knows how to make sentences out of it all. If only Sachin would try to experience her life with her instead of just talking about it. She needs that from him. But he doesn't know how to be in the moment with her. After all, he won't even touch her when she stumbles. And she needs to be held, to belong somewhere properly.

Kashmira looks down at the scene below, where people look like happy figurines playing games with each other in the yard, dancing when the right music comes on, drinking when the bottle goes around. Slowly, she stands. This time, Sachin doesn't even act like he is steadying her. This time, she isn't sure she needs to be steadied. She leaves the roof first, and she doesn't see what Sachin does next. If he follows her, if he leaves the party altogether, if he secretly stays up there to watch her and all the rest of them as they cavort deep into the night.

―⁂―

Tej plays beer pong on the near side of the pool. He holds up the ball whenever he makes a shot, and the group, including Kashmira and Roshni, cheers for him. Tej's partner, a sophomore, sweaty in the humidity, never makes her shots and giggles when she misses. If she thinks Tej will find this endearing, she is mistaken. He keeps looking past her at the rest of the party to see what else is out there. When he sees Kashmira, he holds her gaze until she smiles. Then he shamelessly gestures with two thick fingers for her to make her way over to him.

"Go," Roshni says, pushing Kashmira forward. "You can do this."

Kashmira weaves her way through the tight throng of spectators. When she gets to the table, she picks up a stray ball and hands it to Tej. Even though most of the cups on the table are tipped over and the game is ending, this is only at its start. Their fingers brush, and Tej's attention is hers, even as the sophomore makes another shot.

"Thanks," Tej says to Kashmira. "You know, I wasn't sure who I was going to run into tonight, and―"

"Don't tell me you were looking for someone else," Kashmira says.

New lips form the right words. She doesn't even have to look at Roshni to know what to say. Not in this face—not when everything is better. Isn't it? Deciding not to think about Sachin up on the roof, Kashmira runs her fingers over Tej's forearm, where the hair grows thick and coarse. He grins so giddily that she knows he's already wasted on whatever liquor he stole from his parents and brought tonight.

"No way. No one else." He hands her the ball back, warm from his touch. "You play?"

She doesn't. Still, Kashmira hip checks Tej so she can take her place on their side of the table. Someone has reset the cups in a tight triangle, and they take turns, flirting as they go. A hand on her waist. A wink in the dark. When Tej stands close, Kashmira decides it's time. She holds the ball at eye level. There is one leftover cup, and she could aim true, or she could falter and let the ball arc to the right or left, a near miss. These two options epitomize the two types of girls at this party: those who explicitly tell their target what they desire and how, and those who can't find the skill to take what they want. But tonight, Kashmira has a sense she doesn't have to be either. The ball flies long, hits the edge of the attached deck, and rolls away.

"Oh," she says, coy, because she, like Tej, finds all this delicious. "Was that the only ball? We better go get it."

It wasn't the only ball, not at all. But Tej points to one of his buddies and tells him to tag in. Kashmira waits for him to take her hand, and he does. They go past the beer pong table, past the crowd, and past Roshni, who smirks at Kashmira. Neither Tej nor Kashmira glances at the ground for the ball. All of this is an excuse. What they want is privacy. That's why they keep staggering, wayward, until they arrive at the driveway next to the silver flanks of all the fancy cars that kids parked here tonight. In one of the cars farthest away from them, two dark shadows bob together, in and out. It's obvious what they are doing. Tej's hand, on the small of her back, already moving lower, suggests he notices it too.

"Which car is yours?" Kashmira says. "I want to see."

It's a sleek sport sedan that she imagines he likes to speed in. He unlocks the car and its lights flash red in the night, probably startling the couple in the faraway car. Tej and Kashmira don't wait to see. When Tej opens the driver's side, she nimbly slides past him, taking the seat he expected would be his.

"Hey," he says.

"Get in," she tells him, feeling surer of herself than ever, especially when he does.

Kashmira's knees are far from the wheel, but when Tej sits in the passenger seat, all the space in the car compresses. She notices everything about him: the deep razor burn under his chin that must have stung, the scar on his lower lip where perhaps he bit through during a bad lacrosse play, the crease between his eyebrows she is sure will bother him when he grows old. He looks as closely at her, but she doesn't worry what he sees in her second face.

And then, a door slams. The other couple leaving maybe. Tej reaches near her, ostensibly to turn on the radio. His arm brushes her right breast. He does this on purpose, she knows, just as she leaned forward at that exact moment, too, to give him access. She wants this, and everything is clear between them. As Tej draws back, his hand drops right to her thigh and stays there.

"You're beautiful," he says and then pulls back to see if his line works.

It does work. Not because he says it but because she does feel beautiful. Kashmira boldly cups his penis through his pants. Though he isn't hard enough yet, his thighs tense. Soon, she can wrap her hand around the length of him as he leans into her and buries his face in her cleavage. She listens to his breaths. They guide her until he pushes her hand away, grabs the back of her head, and kisses her hard. His teeth pull at her lower lip, separating it from the rest of her for one brief moment. He can do anything to this body, she realizes, and she will allow it. Why not? This new self is just waiting to become.

"I want you," he says. "I want more."

Somehow, they make their way to the back seat. Kashmira accidentally kicks Tej in the ribs not just once, but twice. Her heels are sharp, but because they are young, these and all of their violences only seem like passion. Or, if not passion, the ecstasy of naivety, where everything and anything is allowed and the future is just something to wait for. Kashmira rises above Tej and catches a glimpse of herself in the rearview mirror—now askew. She looks like a dream, hair mussed, face unrecognizable. She forgets everything, including the discomfort she endures to make this version of herself happen. Kashmira throws her head back, and Tej takes it as a sign.

He takes over, finally, and thrusts. It hurts, splits her even, but she moans anyway and soon finds pleasure in her own sounds. In the midst of this, Tej ends up on top, and when he comes, he yells out gibberish. More pleasure. The crushing weight of him makes her feel how real this moment is—how it's everything she wanted—and even as each final stroke rubs her raw, it still satisfies, really satisfies. Later, there will be blood, but she won't mind. Not this time, anyway. In the end, he lays on top of her for a long minute, and she can hear the thump in his chest. *That was so much better than I expected*, his heartbeat claims. *So much better*, his soft mouth insists when he kisses her new face one more time. *Good*, her hands, spread along his spine, tell him, *good*.

PART TWO

CHAPTER SIX

Weeks go by, bright flashes of a summer well spent; and then toward the end of July the season pivots on her.

It begins with Kashmira's mother, who knocks on her bedroom door one evening while Kashmira readies herself for her fourth kathak lesson. In Ami's arms, the box she believes Vinod left behind for a reason. The one that Kashmira had since hidden under the winter gear in the back of the hall closet.

"We could open this now," Ami says, without asking where Kashmira is going. Luckily, Kashmira hasn't yet put on her ReNuLook. She planned to apply it right before she slipped out of the apartment, to avoid her mother's seeing her. "What do you think?"

"You want to open it together?" Kashmira says.

She stares at the cardboard cube, its dented edge, its slightly yellowed look. These days she does think less about her father, except at the six-hour marks, when the product wears off and she has to reapply. Then, her father, shutting the door in her face, every time. Then, the acute sense of loss and separation. And after that, the waves of nausea. Her body doesn't seem to want to let go of that man, and it stupidly tells her so. But she says back to it, *Get over it.* Because it's time to. Because what is she holding on to, when she now has: chatting brightly with her coworkers at her barista job about the shapes their scars take after particularly bad steam injuries; and driving with

Tej to a shaded, quiet part of town, where almost no one can catch a glimpse of them climbing atop each other in the back seat; and walking into someone's party, picking up a drink like she is owed one; and laughing with Roshni, their teeth shining like crescent moons in the night? She is still sure that her queasiness must only be a response to the still-new, still-overwhelming rush of learning to put away the old to become who she really wants to be: a girl who has never been hurt before. And she will be that girl, no matter how anxious it makes her. This box, though, won't help anything.

"Come on," Ami says. "It'll only take a few minutes."

She weighs the box in her arms and cocks her head. The gesture, so childlike, has worked on Nikhil before. Kashmira's brother will do anything their mother wants—the bills, car repairs, hour-long conversations about how she won't be alone when she is old—just to make Ami feel safe, feel secure. If he were here, he would've taken responsibility by now, opened the box for her. But if for some reason he hadn't, he would have called their mother's decision to open it progress. He would have applauded her for finally confronting its contents. He would have sat with her, comforting her if she needed it.

Still, when Ami cocks her head to the other side, Kashmira says, because she is not her brother and has found solace in operating outside their mother's emotional needs, "I'm busy."

"Kashmira, your father wanted us to look at these things."

No, it's Ami who wants to look at the things. It's about her, as it all too often is. But if her mother will always put herself first, then so must Kashmira. This time, she doesn't waver when her mother asks for help. Instead, she replies simply, "I have to finish getting ready."

She slides past Ami, careful not to let the box touch any part of her. When her mother asks her to wait, Kashmira doesn't stop. Ami can do what she wants, whether that means taking the thing back to her bedroom to open it alone or calling Nikhil or leaving it. It doesn't matter at all—or so Kashmira tells herself as she closes the bathroom door, leans against the sink, and waits for her mother's footsteps to pass.

Soon, there is silence outside the door, and Kashmira applies her product. As always, the dissolution of features hurts. As always, images come—the door locked so carefully, the knife resting on the edge of the sink, the note that said her father was tired of pretending. Kashmira winces at the nausea and holds on to the edge of the sink. Her face is changed, the way it has been every time. *Beautiful*, she thinks. *And not enough*, she thinks after that, when she remembers that though she can erase so much, her mother will never see and her mother will never understand. A truth that feels hard to digest. A truth, she decides, she would rather ignore.

Suddenly, her stomach cramps—hard, in a way it never has before.

The urge to go is strong, and Kashmira collapses onto the toilet, still pushing her clothes down her thighs as her stomach tightens again. She empties her bowels in hard thrusts. One, then another, then one more. It goes on for longer than she expects, and though it's gross, she can't help looking between her legs, shocked by it. The smell—distinct, sulfuric, and different than usual—embarrasses her. Kashmira presses her lips together and wonders what this is. Nerves, yet again? About letting go not only of her father or of that box but of her mother too? It must be. But this is all just part of the process—of getting better. Kashmira breathes in and out, trying to calm herself, trying to settle her stomach. Then, once she thinks she can manage, she flushes fast. What her body has just evacuated spirals down the pipes, gone.

Then, a knock, like the one on Kashmira's bedroom door earlier. Ami's voice just outside.

"Kashmira," she says. "Kashmira, are you—"

It doesn't occur to Kashmira that her mother might have heard the sounds in the bathroom. Might be asking if she is okay. All she can think is that Ami is back to talk about that box, that damn box again. So, still huddled over the toilet, she yells back, "Can I just have some space? *Seriously*."

A pause, and then, "I'll leave you alone."

One day, Kashmira will look back at this moment and wish she'd allowed herself to recognize that pretending things are okay doesn't mean that they are. One day, she will wish she'd understood that not knowing how to be okay is part of being alive. For now, though, she deludes herself.

Kashmira parks in Roshni's driveway, looks up at the sprawling, expensive house, and honks her horn. Five minutes, then ten minutes pass, but Roshni doesn't come out, not even when Kashmira texts that her ride to dance is here. The lateness is unlike Roshni—who fears that if she misses the start of class, Hemaji will tell Lalita she's been slacking, not practicing enough, not being expressive enough, not following through on her potential enough—so Kashmira gets out of the car to ring the doorbell. Her side is still aching from earlier.

When no one answers the door, Kashmira jiggles the handle. To her surprise, it's unlocked, and she can walk right inside, past the entryway, into the house itself. She takes it in for a long moment—because although she lives only seven minutes away, it's the first time since making up with Roshni that she has gone past the Gupta's foyer. Wonderfully and strangely, it all looks how it once did: the same ferns stationed in gilded pots; the same photos of Roshni from first- through third-grade picture days on the walls; the same middle school accolades adorning the fridge, though they are now partially obscured by newer, shinier high school achievements. The farther Kashmira ventures inside, the younger she feels. So many memories in this house, so far away, they seem more like dreams. She almost expects Lalita to emerge, wrap a fleshy arm around her, and tell her to make sure Roshni is keeping up on her homework. She almost expects to see a child version of Roshni, that small girl with sticky fingers from the fruit she always wished was something junkier and sweeter in the fridge. She almost expects to see herself, giggling uncontrollably at some nonsensical, adolescent joke. She sighs. Maybe it isn't right, but she has always remembered this house fondly, even if she knows it isn't the utopia she imagines. Even if she knows that Roshni's parents are so demanding that all too often she has talked about getting out of here by whatever means possible, in a casual but not, in an *I'd never do it, but what if,* sort of way.

Kashmira walks on, in the direction of Roshni's room. It's also mostly unchanged, except for the push-up bras hanging on the bedposts. Kashmira surveys the space, then notes that the door to the attached private bathroom is ajar. She peers in. And then, there is Roshni, seated on the toilet and rubbing her arms as she moans through tears. She hunches over, and there is the sound of something hitting toilet water echoing across the white porcelain.

"Roshni? Are you—"

The other girl looks up. "Kashmira? What are you doing in here? Get *out*."

Of course Kashmira does—but she doesn't go far. How can she? She and Roshni have unspoken responsibilities to each other. They take care of each other however they can. Kashmira lets five minutes pass before she returns. Now Roshni has finished, though she is still crying. Even as she washes her hands, she periodically swipes at her nose. Snot coats the back of her hand, and then she has to pump the soap into her palm and begin again.

"I'm still here," Kashmira says. "I came to see if you were okay. You were late."

"Not by much." Roshni gestures toward the ghungroos on the bed. "I was coming."

Kashmira steps into the bathroom and then steps back, both because of the smell and because Roshni glares at her. But even from her vantage point from the edge of the room, she can see it, the red ring around the toilet bowl, just a bit lighter than the color of blood. Is it blood? Kashmira thumbs at a dry spot on her lip. It scares her, the idea of Roshni staining the bowl in this way. It doesn't seem like anxiety—which Kashmira had thought both she and Roshni were suffering from—could cause that.

"That's not blood, is it?" Kashmira says, trying to understand what this toilet bowl color means not only for Roshni but also for her, who was just straining over a toilet bowl herself fifteen minutes ago. "Do you need to go back to the clinic?"

"No, I don't. And yes, it is blood." Roshni closes the lid and stands with her arms crossed. Her attitude is so different than when they went to see the doctor. Then, Roshni had wanted to talk—had wanted someone at her side holding her hand. Now, Roshni keeps both her mouth and her hands rigid. But it makes sense in a way. Kashmira probably shouldn't have mentioned the clinic, which had been humiliating. Not only because of the doctor and nurses but also because Roshni had been so sure it was the right place to get help, and it hadn't been. Of course she wanted to avoid going back there. Of course she wanted to pretend all this badness had never happened to her at all. Kashmira can understand that. Roshni says, "I don't want to talk about it anymore. Unless, I don't know, it's happening to you too?"

Kashmira doesn't move her head. Not a nod, not a shake. "Why would you ask that?"

"Well, because of the product," Roshni says. Her mouth twitches, like she wants to start sobbing again but won't let herself. "I mean, that's what it has to be, right? I think I've always known that."

"I'm not sure. I'm still adjusting to mine."

"So nothing's happening to you?"

When Kashmira doesn't answer, Roshni sinks to the bathroom floor and rests her chin on her knees. Then, she starts saying things, things like how all she wanted at first was slightly lightened skin, but then she thought of more changes she could make: a smaller nose, prominent cheekbones. After all, Lalita had always wanted the perfect daughter, a title gained not just by book smarts and awards but also by the kinds of looks that would turn a man's head when the time came. No matter what accolades Roshni came home with, Lalita worried instead about how dull looking her daughter was, how unmarriageable she would be.

"She *always* wanted to fix me," Roshni says, her breath hiccupping after the word "fix." "She was so happy when she saw me with it on the first time. And Dad was just happy to see her happy."

Roshni wets her lips, but these aren't the lips Kashmira got used to this summer. It's obvious what has happened: Roshni is late on her next product application and that's why her mouth thickens, then widens; her cheekbones fall; her eyelids go heavy; and her skin darkens—deep and burnished. Roshni puts her hands to her cheeks, in the same movement she made the day she introduced Kashmira to NuLook. And still, she talks, stumbling through the words as her mouth changes shape.

"I thought I was just nervous at first," she says. "But I hate how it feels to use it. I hate how it makes me relive all the horrible things my mother has ever said to me. And I hate thinking about how I have to keep changing myself just to make her happy. It just, it makes me feel sick. Nauseous, and my stomach hurts, and now it's more than that, it's, well, you saw."

"But you're still using it," Kashmira says, dropping down beside her friend. "And you let me use it too. Why didn't you tell me?"

"Because if I told you, you wouldn't have wanted to use it. And then I wouldn't have had something you wanted. And then you wouldn't be my friend anymore." A laugh, maybe unbidden, comes out of Roshni. "And anyway, how could I keep it from you when it makes so many other things better?"

This Kashmira can understand. She thinks of her own toilet from today, bloodless, yes, but not clean. If Roshni is right, it will one day fill with red too. And then what? A place like the clinic, maybe a future of people in white coats ordering vials of blood for tests and endless questionnaires of family history with details no one can remember, invasive procedures, embarrassing in how bare and vulnerable they make her body. Maybe—or maybe not. Maybe a little blood means nothing and will pass, as long as they keep to their raucous nights, their happy laughs. Kashmira looks at Roshni, who has reached up near the sink to grab the familiar glass tube. She rubs the product into her face. Soon, both of them will glow in their transformed faces, and that is what matters. They are only teenage girls, after all. They are only trying to make it through this summer.

"Maybe you should lie down," Kashmira says.

"Maybe," Roshni says.

She walks past Kashmira, back into the bedroom, slipping her shirt off as she goes. Her body is thin, its spine reptilian with protruding vertebrae. Kashmira stares, but then Roshni finds a sweatshirt in her drawer and pulls it on. She moves with resignation as she wrestles her way into bed. As she pulls a heavy duvet over herself. As her face keeps shifting. After she sinks onto her pillows, she pats the covers, indicating that Kashmira should sit next to her.

"I can't go to the lesson today," Roshni says. "But you can. Or you can stay if you want."

Kashmira comes close until she's nestled next to Roshni in the place where she used to lounge on this bed so many years ago. Roshni emanates heat and her musk is pungent vanilla, like she has been trying to cover her real scent with too much deodorant. But her face is starting to look right again, immaculate, as it now always does. Kashmira presses her hand against Roshni's forehead, ostensibly to check her temperature. Really, she wants to feel that second face under her fingers, to remind herself it is just as real as the smells and sights from today.

"We don't know what's really wrong. Not for sure," Kashmira says, drawing her hand away from Roshni's warm brow. She means they don't understand the physical symptoms, but also the ones in their minds. The ones Roshni was talking about when she said she was tired of reliving bad memories. Kashmira has her own flashbacks, but it doesn't seem like the right time to say this. Not when Roshni is exhausted and they are both overwhelmed. Besides, she has a feeling her old friend can already guess she is experiencing something like that.

Roshni sighs and moves her head closer to Kashmira's shoulder. "Don't worry. If you don't tell anyone about me, I won't tell them about you."

The two of them stay like that for a long time, neither saying anything more.

It feels like the best they can do.

―⁂―

The next day, Tej drives twenty miles north from his house, picks Kashmira up from her place, and then drives to the spot they've used the last two times they've been in her area. Here, at a quiet trailhead for the thirteen-hundred-acre preserve Kashmira rarely frequents otherwise, Tej expects it to be as it always is: They turn the radio up, Tej puts his hand on Kashmira's thigh, and Kashmira unbuttons her blouse. She expects that, too, but she can hear her stomach—its small groans—the whole time and fears Tej can too. She clenches her lower abdomen and buttocks, afraid of what might happen if she doesn't. She went to the bathroom once before she left the house—liquid again. Still, she says nothing and, in the end, because she has been sleeping with Tej for almost three weeks now, and because his body responds well to her touch, she can make him throw his head back in pleasure at least.

Later, they dress again and sit in the car, idly listening to a disc jockey tell misogynistic jokes. This is another part of their routine—they usually stay this way for fifteen minutes or so, probably because Tej believes it more respectful than rushing her off—but today, Kashmira turns the sound down.

"What?" Tej says. He wipes at the side of his mouth, at the facial hair he just started growing out. Kashmira isn't a fan of it, though she hasn't told him this. "Do you want to leave already?"

"No," she says, hands on her abdomen. "Well, yes."

She hates that they have to leave early. Not because she likes Tej all that much, but because she is supposed to be able to do this. As they drive, Kashmira notices things like the way Tej cuts close to the curb when he makes turns and how he checks the rearview mirror so many times to make sure the cars behind him aren't following too closely. He seems unsure when he steers, which she appreciates. She, too, is unsure of things. Since she found Roshni crouched over the toilet yesterday, Kashmira hasn't stopped thinking about the two of them and their sicknesses. What might change, what more they might lose, what they should do. She rests her head against the window.

"What is it?" Tej says. "You're not sick, are you? I can't have you throw up in my car."

Kashmira shakes her head, hitting the glass with her forehead when she does so. "I'll be okay."

"Then what's going on?"

She thinks of Sachin then, as she sometimes does when she is with Tej and their conversation runs out. Sachin wouldn't be here in the car with her, holding on to her thigh with confidence. But he would be someone she could say something honest to. Except she and Sachin only wave at each other these days. Tej is who she has here.

"Well," Kashmira says, "do you ever feel like you thought you were doing exactly the right thing and then you really, really weren't sure you were?"

She expects Tej to think about the answer at least, but instead he starts laughing. The sound of it, brazen and overbearing. It makes her press up against the window harder, unsure what to make of it.

"Tej, stop," she says. "What's so funny?"

He keeps laughing. "It's just, are you saying you think you're bad in bed?"

"What? No. I never said that."

"Sure you did. Why else would you be so nervous?" Tej says. "But you don't need to be like that. You're great. You do everything right."

As they turn into Kashmira's neighborhood, Tej pats her knee. Jerking away from him only makes Tej laugh more and makes Kashmira feel worse. Maybe she should have wrapped her hair around her forefinger and stared up at him from under her eyelashes and pretended that sex was exactly what she was talking about. She could say something about how glad she is that he likes the way she touches him. She could even suggest that they drive back to their spot and do it one more time before he drops her off. But no, her stomach is gurgling, so that wouldn't be an option. Instead, Kashmira runs her fingers over Tej's. His hand is still on her skin, but his touch doesn't mean as much as she thought it would. Under his touch, she feels noticed but not seen. She wonders if this is all that being with someone is about. It isn't as if she knows, having only seen her parents' ever-increasing distance as an example. But how do people keep doing this forever? This misattunement, this misalignment, with two people slipping close but never taking the time to listen to the stories in the other person's breathing. She thinks maybe if she were with someone she actually knew and felt something for, she could try. Maybe if she were with someone who knew her and felt something for her, too, they might both try. The clarity of that realization makes her open the car door too soon, before Tej has even slowed down. Still sitting, she slams the heavy metal shut before Tej notices.

"So, we're good? See you soon?" he asks when he has finally parked.

"Thanks for the ride," Kashmira says.

∽

In the parking lot between their apartments, Sachin gets out of his car just as Kashmira gets out of Tej's. They're on the side of the pavement closest to Sachin's apartment—Tej doesn't know exactly which unit is Kashmira's and just stops in whatever parking spot is empty—and so she and Sachin are closer than they have been since the July Fourth party. The truth is, since that night on the roof, they haven't been talking as much. Maybe it has to do with her. She has changed, and so the relationship between them has too. But Kashmira misses him. Her stomach aches when she thinks this. As Tej drives away, she looks back at her apartment—thirty or so yards away—and then glances at Sachin again.

"Kashmira," Sachin says with an odd emphasis, like he expects her to shake her head and say she goes by something different now. The sun is setting behind them, and Kashmira wonders if Sachin's back feels as warm as hers does. "You're with Tej?"

"I thought you knew," she says, gesturing to the camera he carries with him always.

"I didn't catch it."

He sounds jealous, which perhaps she should have anticipated. After their time on the rooftop, when his voice cracked when he talked of opening up to each other, she has sensed that he might like her in some way. She has also sensed her own feelings for him for a long time now. But for anything between them to work, she would need him to reach out first from behind the lens and stand in the shot with her. Not that this matters—she has other boys, like Tej, now. Or does she? Her expression slackens as queasiness overtakes her again.

"What's wrong?" Sachin says, folding his arms.

"Oh, I haven't been feeling the best," she says. "But it's nothing."

"Just like that footage was nothing?" He kicks at the curb. "I wish you'd stop lying to me."

At the time he'd shown that video clip to her, she hadn't wanted to look. What she'd seen had been embarrassing, awkward—she and Roshni bent over into the grass, holding their stomachs. The way Roshni, especially, cast her face upward, clearly asking for something to stop. Pain, probably. At the time, Kashmira pretended not to see. Now, she isn't sure what to do.

"I said it was the light. And that Roshni was just drunk—"

"You said that about both of you." The wind blows through their hair. His mouth is so tight she thinks he might be angry at her. But no, actually, his expression is only a mirror of hers. He says, "I've always been there for you."

Kashmira knows this. Whenever she has told him things, he has always listened, at least in his own way. Maybe this time, he can do more. Maybe this time, he can take her hand and press it against his cheek and tell her that he doesn't blame her for who she has become and that everything will be okay. She sits on the very curb he kicked, her shadow long in the sun. He sits beside her, his thigh a perfect parallel to hers. Half an inch closer and they'd be touching. But they aren't, not yet. Kashmira stares at her hands while she tells him, haltingly, about her and Roshni feeling unwell. About them suspecting it might be the product. To her own ears, she sounds so vulnerable, and the whole time she waits for him to at least brush his hand against her shoulder or her knee, but he doesn't. When she looks up, she sees that he has opened up his notebook and is writing things down in big, looping letters. He is doing exactly what she suspected he would.

"Sachin, what the hell?" Frustration rises in her chest. "Can't you look at me instead of that thing?"

"I'm trying to understand, that's all," he says. His eyes are glassy—with what emotion she doesn't know. "And I'm just trying to figure out what to do next. I mean, you need a doctor, obviously. But maybe there's something else too, maybe we could use that footage I have as proof, and—"

"Don't," Kashmira says.

She can't listen to him talk about what's in the notebook or in his camera, not when what she needs is for him to just tell her body it has company in his. That's all. But Sachin just sits on the curb, circling his thumbs around each other, thinking. And now, her abdomen contracts with pain. She gasps, quiet, but urgent. She has to go—again.

"What?" Sachin says. "Don't, what?"

"Just leave it alone," she tells him, standing and then swaying on her feet as another spasm overtakes her. "Pretend I never said anything, okay?"

"You can't be serious." Sachin stands up too. He has height on her now, and he leans down and she thinks maybe—maybe he'll hold her close. But he doesn't. Instead, he walks two or three paces away. Before she can take her leave, he returns and says, "Why did you tell me all this then?"

"Because," she says. "Because I thought you would make me feel better."

"Well, don't you see that I'm—I don't know." I'm what? It should be easy for him to come up with a word. For someone who writes scripts all day and all night, he should know what he is trying to say. It could be whatever he wants: staying with you, about to hold you, going with you where you need to go. But he said it himself the night on the roof: He has always been an observer. His hands make indiscriminate, confused gestures, and he says, "Don't you see that I'm thinking? About how to?"

Kashmira—her whole body clenching now—says, "Don't you see that's not enough for me?"

SERIES OF SHOTS – WOMEN CRYING

A) TEENAGER in car, holding on to steering wheel in death grip. Skin slick with tears. Reverses car and starts driving.
B) WOMAN IN THIRTIES at funeral caressing framed picture of dead mother. HUSBAND puts hand on her shoulder. She turns away from him and presses picture to her chest.
C) ELDERLY WOMAN in darkened bedroom. Pulls bed covers over her head even as phone rings continuously.

FADE TO:
TEENAGER, WOMAN IN THIRTIES, ELDERLY WOMAN dab ReNuLook cream on their cheeks.
Faces twist, then settle. Features not just sharpened, but surgically recut. The women look different, completely different.

CHYRON TEXT: YOU ARE YOUR BEAUTY. EVOLVE YOURSELF, EMBRACE YOURSELF. LIVE FREE.

TEENAGER, WOMAN IN THIRTIES, ELDERLY WOMAN touch their cheeks in awe.

CHAPTER SEVEN

Late July, and Nikhil tweaks copy and designs ads. The ReNu-Look, or RNL, announcement got plenty of attention online, but Keon wants to make sure the initial excitement translates into a long and impatient wait list they can show to Larissa as evidence of a successful marketing campaign. For half the day, Nikhil jots down catchphrases that might entice more potential clients; for the other half, he edits videos to make them more aesthetically pleasing, once again for those same imagined buyers.

"Break soon?" Michael says from his side of the desk. He finishes his work—more data-oriented than Nikhil's, mostly related to tracking feedback from clients—faster than everyone else and wastes the rest of the day sending memes over TaskSquad to the few people he likes at the company, Nikhil included. "Or are you still flexing your art skills over there?"

"Is that sarcasm?"

"Just seems like you're putting a lot of work into this."

"I have a responsibility to RNL," Nikhil says, pointing to his screen. "And we have a meeting soon."

Ostensibly by accident, Michael bumps his chair against Nikhil's, but Nikhil pushes his heels into the ground and holds his seat steady. They aren't dating exactly. As in, they haven't labeled it, but they have held hands walking down the street and they do kiss and they do go out when they can. But Nikhil is more reluctant to spend time together. The more he and Michael get close, the more old remembrances come up for him—mostly of his father. And besides, Nikhil's to-do list has taken over much of his time. Keon demands excellence, and Nikhil is willing to work for it, as long as he remembers who this work is for. Soon enough, Kashmira will forgive him. Soon enough, he will get her the ReNuLook so she can rid herself of Vinod's face. In the meantime, Nikhil is proud to learn through VidMos and product reviews that more and more clients are sure they're on their way to feeling mentally better now that they're using ReNuLook.

His first ploy having not worked, Michael leans back in his chair and slides his nose ring back and forth in its hole. Nikhil watches his fingers with interest, then swallows hard. Michael knows what this little suggestive action does to Nikhil's libido. "Five minutes won't hurt you."

Nikhil considers saying that he needs the five minutes to perfect this edit, then send it on to Keon for approval, all while sending feedback to one of the interns on the guest list for the ReNuLook "Autumn is for Change" party they're planning for late September. But then a TaskSquad message pings in the #ads-shmads-etcetera channel. Keon, as always.

—@opwellness anyone look at who exactly has been getting off the wait list for RNL?

Answers filter in: unhelpful emojis ☹ and 😒. Nikhil, also unsure where Keon is going with this but not wanting to add his own questioning emoji to the list, opens up the Evolvoir Consumer Database to investigate further.

He doesn't use this tool much, since the Product Growth Team generally isn't interested in individual clients, but rather in the full self-reported demographic picture, so they can see who's engaging with what products. Client Care usually sends that information along every month, and it's due in a few days, so everyone can see how the first thirty days have gone for ReNuLook. But while Nikhil doesn't spend much time in the Consumer Database, he does know how to use it, because he sometimes checks out the two tabs—one for NuLook, one for ReNuLook—to see if Kashmira's name is anywhere on either. So far, he hasn't found it, though he does think he may have run across her old friend Roshni Gupta on there. But from what Nikhil knows, those two don't talk any longer.

The Consumer Database has various categories at the top reflecting the demographic questions Evolvoir asks clients when they sign up. Though most people assume the company needs the answers for product development purposes, this type of data shows up most often in aggregate for internal stakeholder meetings and marketing discussions. Nikhil sorts the ReNuLook list by wait list placement number to see who has gotten off and subsequently received the product already. He rubs his forehead. It's not good. The wait list order isn't actually determined by when users signed up, but by an algorithm that ranks them according to how likely they are to, one, continue paying for the product month after month, and two, bring in new customers. Apparently, the algorithm has mostly privileged consumers who have self-identified as white women between the ages of eighteen and thirty-five. There are so many Sarahs and Emilys. The homogeneity is concerning. When Nikhil mentions this in the chat, Keon types back quickly.

—exactly. did we seriously not keep an eye on this? because our clients have already noticed. they're saying we used @yukiko's name and face to sell our product, but we're not giving RNL out to a diverse clientele. there are comments online about how we're racist and how we don't want to sell to clients of color. some major vidmo accounts are even suggesting that people stop buying from us in protest. and that journalist for techvip has reached out. so we need a course of action ASAP on how to spin this. what've you got?

Nikhil re-sorts the list using the demographic filters and finds that there are more clients of diverse backgrounds on the wait list. But although many of these people signed up on the day RNL was announced—a fact Nikhil can check based on the listed timestamp—they won't receive the product for months due to their placement at the bottom of the list.

"Shit," Nikhil says, clicking aggressively as he exits out of the Consumer Database. This isn't at all what was supposed to happen. Nikhil had wanted to extend ReNuLook to everyone who needed it, not just one segment of the population—although if he had chosen just one segment, it would have been BIPOC clients, many of whom he is aware have less access to competent mental health services. All in all, though, Nikhil had wanted ReNuLook to create more equity for people seeking wellness options. To learn that a discriminatory algorithm of all things has upended that hope makes him burn. "Shit, shit, shit."

"Hey." Michael wheels over and places a placating hand on Nikhil's arm. "It'll be okay. They'll rework the algorithm."

"That'll take time. I'm guessing they don't even know what's causing it to behave this way. Or if they do, they'll still have to work on retraining it with new data."

"They'll do it, though."

"And in the meantime?"

Nikhil pulls away from his deskmate's touch. Michael wants to support him, but Nikhil worries that the other man is too cavalier about issues like this. Michael has never been as invested in the big facial changes as Nikhil, and that still seems true. Nikhil slides an inch or two away from Michael, and opens up Keon's message. But he doesn't know what to write. He doesn't want to think of a way to "spin this," but he does want to come up with an idea of how best to get RNL into the hands of a more diverse clientele while the programmers look at their internal systems.

Another message from Keon comes in while Nikhil flexes his fingers over his keyboard:

—no one has any ideas? what happened to my dedicated team? fine. we'll be discussing this tonight at our next @opwellness meeting.

This is the meeting he and Michael are meant to go to. The one that Michael suggested taking a five-minute break before. But

Nikhil needs that time to brainstorm. Even as Michael stands and mentions that they can slip out and grab some coffee or some CBD water or whatever Nikhil thinks will help get his mind moving, Nikhil shakes his head and tells him to go on without him. He'll see him at the meeting. The more Michael argues, the more Nikhil stares at his computer resolutely.

"If you want a break, you can take one without me," Nikhil says. "I have to think."

"I know," Michael says. "But this can't be your whole life."

"It's not." Nikhil tries to sound convincing, even as he opens up his notes app to make a bullet point list of items he could bring to the meeting. "It's just that this is important."

This time, the Operation Wellness Team meets at a small art gallery six blocks from the first one, but still in the Lower East Side.

—i've learned there are a ton of places showing self-portraits right now, @keon had said when he announced the location last week. it'll be nice to create a tradition. we did good work last time we were there.

This show, called *In the Archives, I Archived Myself*, is a series of self-portraits the photographer captured while exploring his family's history as refugees of a war fifty years ago. According to the artist's statement, his ancestors fled their homes, but he only learned of the extent of their history after his mother's recent death. He found a letter she had written to her sister—but never sent—tucked in the folds of a white salwar kameez the artist had never seen his mother wear. This discovery moved him to study the past further.

Michael and Nikhil walk through the photographs together. Michael had eventually given up on asking Nikhil to take a break, and they made their way over to the gallery together once Nikhil was ready. Now, the two of them stop in front of a print in which the artist cleans his glasses.

"I like this," Michael says. "Thoughts?"

Most of the scenes are personal, like this one with the glasses. They include the artist smiling wistfully as he flips through a book, hugging his brother among some library shelves, pressing two fingers against his lips while he waits in line to use the copier, crying one solitary tear as he flips through an old photo book.

"It's something," Nikhil says, swirling his third serving of wine in a plastic cup.

He's torn. As much as he would prefer to ignore the exhibition and focus on the real reason they're here—the meeting—the photographs do affect him. He thinks of his father at his own mother's funeral. Jaya had died after her husband, leaving Vinod parentless in this world. In the afternoon, after the service but before people came by to spend time with the family and share memories, Vinod poured himself a glass of gin and was drinking it in his parents' old kitchen. He and the rest of the family hadn't come here often in recent years, as Vinod had put more and more distance between himself and his parents' Indianness. When Jaya died, Vinod said he hadn't even realized how sick she was.

"She would have hated this," Vinod said to his son there in the kitchen, gesturing at the alcohol. Nikhil, who was only sitting by his father because Ami had asked him to, said nothing while Vinod held up the glass and stared at its translucence, as if it held an answer. "They both said it. Good Indian boys don't drink."

He went on about growing up, about being told so often who he ought to be. His parents had made it sound simple. As long as he did the right thing, he would prosper and honor them all. And what little boy didn't want that? Especially when his parents were already suffering from an ineffable sadness of losing so much of themselves by coming to this country. Vinod had done what they'd asked until he couldn't do it any longer. Until he felt he needed to find his own way, a better way, to deal with the overarching cruelty he witnessed at the hands of people who beat brown men with pipes just for daring to exist. People who murdered clerks in gas stations. People who yelled slurs and spit, because why not? So, he left his culture—and his parents—behind. But it wasn't like he didn't yearn it, for them.

"And still, look how it all ended up," Vinod said. "Look what kind of son I ended up being. What kind of father. You already resent me, don't you? And who knows what you think of yourselves."

It was the first time that Vinod had properly acknowledged what his actions had done to his children. Before then, Nikhil wasn't even sure his father understood that his robust denial of their brownness, along with his hostile abandonments of them, mattered. Apparently, he did. Vinod wiped his eyes with the heels of his palms, but Nikhil didn't know what to do. He was too old to forgive easily, and he had already developed his own worldview, his decision to reshape his family into what he thought was best. And yet, here he was, picking up his father's gin and looking at it too, curious if anything valuable really could be seen in it.

Nikhil looks away from the photographs. He doesn't tell Michael this memory. He doesn't want to dwell. They're here not for that, but for ReNuLook.

"It's something?" Michael says, repeating the phrasing Nikhil used earlier. He searches Nikhil's expression. "Something good?"

"Just something," Nikhil says, but articulates nothing more until Keon claps his hands and tells the Operation Wellness Team—Michael, Nikhil. Yukiko, Jordie, and the others—to circle up in the center of the room.

"So," Keon says when they've all taken their places. "The algorithm issue is obviously a big part of today's agenda."

A few people raise their hands, but their comments are mostly apologies for not noticing the problem earlier. No one has anything useful to say, and after almost twenty minutes pass, Nikhil cuts into one of Jordie's digressions to say, "Look, the algorithm is the programmers' problem, but I don't think we can wait for them to fix it. I'm thinking we move fast and manually get more BIPOC onto the wait list ASAP. Like, this week."

"Actually, I think we need to slow down," Yukiko says from the other side of the circle.

He stares at her, and his first thought is of the dark circles in the hollows beneath her eyes, visible even with her second face on. His next thought is that she's doing it to him once again—just like at that first gallery meeting, she's undermining his ideas, his mission to engineer this cream into a salve for those longing for it. And he has put so much into this. And there's nothing else that feels worth doing anymore. Nikhil won't have this taken away, he won't. The familiar pair of feelings—fear and then anger—sets in.

"Slow down? Isn't TechVIP already writing a story on this?" They are. After Keon said so in TaskSquad, Nikhil texted Erin, and she confirmed that she was the writer for the article. When she asked him if he wanted to comment, he told her that he would get back to her when they had a plan. What if they never have one? "Slowing down would just create more problems."

"We need to be careful," Yukiko says. "You're pushing too hard. I know you care about the product, and about the people using it—"

When the anger fully takes over, Nikhil doesn't yell, but his clipped tone and dismissive words tell her exactly what he thinks. In a stream that no one can interrupt—not even Michael, who tries to step closer to slow him down, or Keon, who says something like "hey, hey"—Nikhil goes off, telling Yukiko that many of their BIPOC clients probably already have less access to therapeutic help for their problems. How can she be okay with withholding the product from them too? She needs to focus on what's at stake. People's wellness. Or does she not care? Or is she too scared to stand up for what they're trying to do here?

"You have to listen to me," Nikhil says. "I know what's best here."

Only now does he realize how quiet the group has gone. They shift their eyes and feet in collective discomfort. Someone clears their throat, someone else straight up says "jeez." Nikhil feels his pulse pounding through him, so hard he swears he can hear it.

He knows he shouldn't have gotten so heated. But what if he can't help himself?

When Nikhil looks out across the circle, he sees Yukiko bite her lip. A somber acceptance crosses her face, but when she speaks, her cadence mirrors that which she uses with her online viewers. "Okay. In that case, fine. I'll leave it up to you." She winces suddenly. "You know what? I need a minute."

As she heads in the direction of the bathroom, Keon casts a disappointed look at Nikhil and says, "I think we all need a minute. We'll revisit this in the morning, after we've all had some time to think, okay?"

The group murmurs in agreement and disbands, disappearing into various corners of the gallery. Keon leaves too, but not without telling Nikhil he'll be sending an invite over for them to schedule a chat. Then, only Michael remains.

"Jesus, Nikhil." Michael brushes close, and Nikhil feels the familiar softening. Of course Michael has lingered. Of course he wants to do something for the man who isn't quite his boyfriend but could be—with the right push. Of course he wants to take care of Nikhil, as he always does. Michael says, gentle and knowing, with one hand on Nikhil's lower back, "You're so worked up. There's no way you can be alone like this."

⁓

Wine is heavy on their tongues.

After heading back down to Flatbush, they stopped at a discount liquor store and bought two bottles of cheap cabernet sauvignon. Screw-top, because Nikhil didn't think he could find his bottle opener, which made Michael laugh and ask how someone could manage to lose things in a studio apartment. Nikhil had shrugged and, after checking for cops, opened up his bottle to drink right there on the busy sidewalk.

Now, in Nikhil's studio apartment, they have nowhere to sit but the bed. They talk about things, some of which they will remember in the morning. They also do things they won't forget: Michael somehow drunkenly pressing his cheek to the top of Nikhil's head, Nikhil somehow angling his face in a way that makes him kiss Michael's neck, their mouths somehow against each other while their hands slide up each other's thighs. Nikhil wants to escape what enrages him; Michael obliges, sure he can give his partner something better.

That night, they fit two into a bed that usually only takes one. Their clothes, in the way, come off. Their skin, hot from the alcohol, makes the mattress warm. They sweat and then taste it on each other. Deep under the covers, Michael works his tongue against Nikhil's cock, giving so much attention to a large vein that runs through it. Nikhil leans back into his pillows and doesn't make too many sounds until Michael looks up and asks him to. When Nikhil is close, Michael pulls away and smiles at him, as if to say, *I don't want this to be over yet*. Nikhil tugs on his hair, urging him to be faster, more efficient.

Then, more kissing, up and down the long planes of each other's bodies. In the middle of it, Nikhil knows that tomorrow he will look at his bed and think of this moment, of them in the dark apartment, unable to distinguish what belongs to whom. And why should they? They hold each other the way they expect someone else to hold them too.

―∞―

In the morning, Nikhil wakes up thinking about his father, of all people. That memory, at the funeral, with the gin. It must have something to do with Michael; the more Nikhil spends time with him, the more open his mind seems to be to these recollections. He closes his eyes again, and only sees the gallery and all its photographs. When he opens them, he sees Michael, lounging on his stomach in Nikhil's bed, scrolling through his phone. Still curled on his side, Nikhil tries to discreetly wipe the drool from his cheek. He feels hungover; he is hungover—and unprepared to talk about what it means for Michael to take up space in his apartment in this casual way. His phone pings, and he reaches for it without thinking.

"You're up," Michael says, dropping his own device.

He kisses Nikhil good morning with possessive teeth. His breath is fresh, so he must have sneaked into the bathroom and used Nikhil's toothbrush earlier. Maybe it's good that he wants to come off clean, desirable, even after they've already spent a sensual night together. The kiss happens—until it doesn't, with Nikhil too late, too distracted by his phone to press back with honest fervor.

—@prodgrowth who's got something for me? says @keon.

"What time is it?" Nikhil says. Ten in the morning, his phone shows. Far later than Nikhil would ever be for work. He throws his covers back and tries to stand, though his head hurts. "We didn't set an alarm?"

"I turned it off. We need to sleep. But it'll be fine. Just message Keon and tell him you took a sick day."

Nikhil stares at Michael. "We were going to talk about the algorithm today. I'm not ready for that discussion at all. I'm barely up."

Ideas come in through TaskSquad. Around and around the rest of the team goes, discussing what they might do or say to Erin. Most of the plans center on throwing her—and any other journalist—off. More sidestepping the wait list problem than solving it. Nikhil comments 👎 to those replies, hands sweating as he thinks about what could happen if the team chooses to focus only on PR and not on the larger problem of inequity around the product. They'll only be doing what Yukiko said last night, then: slowing down.

"Aren't you hungry?" Michael, who hasn't checked his own phone again, says.

Because Nikhil lives in a studio apartment, the kitchen is barely a foot from his bed. Luckily, it comes with a freezer and fridge, though Nikhil rarely uses either. Michael sits on the edge of the mattress and rummages. Then he holds out a yellow box covered in mouse cartoons. Nikhil bought it because waffles are easy to throw into the toaster oven, though he skips breakfast most days and drinks coffee at Evolvoir instead. "Can I eat these? And please tell me you've got some of that good maple syrup. You know, the real shit?"

"Michael, I don't have time for this." Nikhil stands but doesn't move to get dressed or brush his teeth. He is typing another response to the group, telling them to focus on the real issues, and not just image. He looks up, expecting Michael to be nodding and slipping on his shoes, but instead Michael has turned the dial on the toaster and is now further assessing the contents of Nikhil's fridge. "Are you even seeing these messages?"

"There's barely anything in here. Am I going to have to teach you how to grocery shop?" Michael slathers his toaster waffle with the low-quality, mostly-corn-syrup maple syrup that Nikhil has. Then he licks around one of the little squares. "Kidding. I also spend way too much time in my bodega."

—i'm still not sure we need to act quickly, @yukiko says through Nikhil's phone. can't we give it some time, see how things play out?

—larissa is concerned about this, so we need to be too, @keon writes back.

"Okay," Nikhil says, pulling washed underwear and pants out of a drawer. He can feel the anger coming on, just like it had last night. "Michael, I've got stuff to do with work. Yukiko's putting up blocks again."

Michael grabs a paper towel. "Maybe you should try seeing her side of things, then. Maybe she's got a reason." He wipes his mouth. "But how are you going to accept that she might be a complex, confusing person when you can't see that about yourself?"

Still getting dressed, Nikhil pauses at the side of the bed. Shirtless as he is, he feels strangely exposed and uncomfortable. The feeling makes him more irritable. "What is that supposed to mean?"

"I mean, I saw you at the gallery. You wouldn't talk to me, but I'd bet you were thinking about your family." Michael takes another bite and smiles when Nikhil won't answer. "Of course you were. I mean, we talked about them that night at the biergarten. You don't come from easy people."

"I know that."

"But do you?" Michael gestures with his breakfast, and a few crumbs flake off to the side. "Do you really get that? Do you get that your dad left you more than money for your inheritance?"

Michael speaks, then, of the cycles of fear that turn into anger. When Nikhil feels hopeless he succumbs to rage, because it's easier than feeling scared. These are the same patterns that Michael has heard Nikhil describe when he speaks of Vinod.

"I know I can be like him." Nikhil throws his shirt on over his head. When his head pops out, he says, "We're all like our parents in some ways, right? But at least I'm trying to do something good for people."

"What if he was too?"

Nikhil falters—because he knows Michael is right about this much. Vinod had believed his rules protected him and by extension his family; and though those rules' existence and enforcement had made their lives hell, Nikhil has always known that Vinod's behavior wasn't meant to be cruel. What Nikhil hasn't realized, though, is that this logic is the same that he uses about his own anger. He has always believed that what he does is for some greater good, unlike his father's selfishness. But the greater good might just be in the eyes of the beholder. Nikhil picks at his lip. He isn't ready to think about this. He isn't ready to confront it. He is shaking, he realizes, first from fear and now from the very anger he and Michael are discussing.

"And what about you?" Nikhil says. "What is it you're trying to do? Because all I see is someone who fucks around for the hell of it. I mean, where's your passion for doing something in this world?"

"Definitely not at Evolvoir." Michael laughs and eats some more waffle. "I'm not about selling things or working in big corporations. I mean, I do it for a job. But my life, my community is elsewhere." He gestures between himself and Nikhil. "It's between me and other people. Real people."

Nikhil grits his teeth. There's something imperious about the way Michael makes these statements—as if Nikhil doesn't have people he loves and cares about in his life—and he wants to say something back. Something that will dig into Michael the same way Michael digs into him.

Nikhil says, his voice really too loud for this tiny apartment, "I mean, as another person of color you'd think this would be important to you, too. You know, getting products to people who look like us. Who might need them for mental health reasons. I mean, don't you care?"

A pause. And then.

"As another person of color? That's reductive." Michael looks calm as he says this. He licks at one of the soggier squares of waffle. His tongue flicks and laps up butter as he waits for Nikhil to answer. But the longer it takes, the more his tongue muscles its way into each corner, aggressively now. "What exactly do you think a person of color—a Black man—is supposed to be like?"

Nikhil hesitates. He had expected this argument, the kind he might have made in a class or on the internet, to work. To him, it only makes sense that people like them, people of color who, through their work, have some proximity to power, ought to take responsibility for those who've been struggling. But Michael has somehow spun this.

Michael devours the rest of the waffle, then continues with his mouth full, "No answer?"

"I didn't mean it like it sounded."

Michael swallows. Then he drags his fingernail through the crumbs left on his plate. It seems like he wants to say something, but he doesn't. Over time, the crumbs all stick to his skin, and there's nothing left for Michael to distract himself with. "Have you ever even considered the standards you hold people to? The boxes you're always putting them in?"

TaskSquad pings before Nikhil can answer.

"You're not going to look at that right now, are you?" Michael says.

But Nikhil is. Because this argument isn't going his way, and that just makes him angrier. He needs to divert his attention, change this trajectory. He takes out his phone and checks it again. All anyone has sent are bad ideas. But that's okay. Nikhil sits on the edge of the bed, ignoring Michael and thinking about what to say. What they need is some way to bring more of their marginalized clients into the fold—immediately. It shouldn't be this hard, and he refuses to be a hypocrite and he refuses to let this conversation in TaskSquad go on without his input. He thinks, then, of what he would want for his sister, if she refuses to ever call him back, if she can't get the products through him. Maybe another referral, from someone else who has used the products, loved the products. Maybe the type of referral that would put Kashmira right at the top of the list, no matter what. He quickly messages the group:

—@opwellness i've got it. first thing, we'll move our clients of color to the top of the wait list manually. but now, we've got to do some damage control too. really show everyone that we're committed to diversity.

—yes, @keon says, agreed. and?

—let's do what we did with @yukiko. let's bring on more people who share identities with the diverse customers we want to attract. we can do it with a VIP program 👍⭐

Nikhil looks up from his phone. His feverish anger is passing, but Michael is putting on his shoes, and Nikhil suddenly feels unsure of what has just happened between them. A crumb clings to Michael's impeccable lip.

"You're leaving," he says.

"You're more worried about your phone than us," Michael replies. "So, yeah. I'm going."

Nikhil's phone vibrates again. 👏 and 💅. Keon has already decided on a cutesy name for the initiative, the BIPOC Beauty Babes Program, or BBB. They coordinate the rest easily. They'll identify loyal clients of color from the NuLook base who might have an interest in RNL, then gift rolling product rewards to clients who bring in five successful referrals of verified people of color monthly to RNL's wait list. Client Care will immediately move these new names to the top of the register, so they'll get their product quickly and efficiently. Down the line, some of these additions may become VIPs, too. Nikhil skims the replies. All positive, but one person is missing. He scrolls back up, but no, Yukiko hasn't said anything since her earlier input about slowing down. In fact, her status is set to gray—away—now.

"I think you're going to wish you handled this differently," Michael says, quietly.

Nikhil looks up, only now noticing that Michael is still in his apartment, that he's lingering by the door. Haunting the space, as this conversation will later haunt Nikhil.

The conference room where Nikhil and Yukiko meet Erin boasts transparency—the sliding glass door, the glass table, the glasses that wait next to the pitcher of lemon water that Larissa poured from just a few weeks ago—but it is only a mockery of the truth. Two days after agreeing to the BBB program, Keon decided to announce it through a TechVIP article, and he nominated Nikhil and Yukiko to be the spokespeople for it. But neither actually knows what the other is thinking, what the other wants to say. Though Nikhil has ventured over to her desk—not sure if he'll ask her what's up between them, but maybe—Yukiko never seems to be there. He often sees her in the hallways wiping her hands on her legs before nodding at him, then turning a corner. Something, he thinks, is wrong.

"It's nice to meet you both," Erin says. She had called Nikhil and talked to him about how they should act around each other. Their ruse—that they've never met and that he wasn't her source—protects them both. Finger hovering over the Record button, Erin pushes her phone toward both Nikhil and Yukiko. "Should we get started?"

"Fine," Yukiko says. "Nikhil?"

Erin lobs questions that Nikhil was told how to answer. Both he and Yukiko received a PR dos and don'ts document from Keon over TaskSquad yesterday. The list of don'ts was longer than the dos, though the dos came first. Do use our company's statement of values as a basis for your responses (use your employee handbook or the official press kit on our website for this!). Do be forthcoming on the interesting details (we want to be a story!). Do give them personality (you are a real person!). Do appropriately communicate your hopes and dreams (we're growing and we want them to know that!). The don'ts were all noted without Keon's pithy comments. Don't answer more than what has been asked, share any business strategies and/or financial projections, call out or disparage any other company or entity, air any grievances with HR or leadership, and so on and so on until Nikhil lands on the last point: Don't discuss anything covered by your NDA, including, but not limited to, the origin of Evolvoir products, their formulas, their testing, or their safety.

Nikhil messaged ✔ back, though he took a long time to send it. He thought of Michael in his apartment, on his bed, a ring of sweet syrup around his lips. How the other man told Nikhil he didn't know how to take care of anyone, just the idea of them. How while Michael was saying this, Yukiko was asking them to slow down and Nikhil didn't know why. As he thought about all this, he considered asking Michael to talk again, though his deskmate was and still is avoiding him. He considered not agreeing to the interview. He considered, instead, forwarding the TaskSquad messages Yukiko had once sent, the ones in which she'd said let's give it some time, let's see how things play out. Perhaps he could add to those words, *I have no idea what this is about, but we should listen.* But he didn't. He couldn't bring himself to.

The interview goes on for a half hour, and the questions continue to be things that Nikhil feels prepped for. Yes, Erin asks them in a trickier way than other journalists might, but for the most part, Nikhil is able to explain Evolvoir's response to the allegations of racism, the new BBB program, and why having an initiative like it matters.

"Are we done?" Yukiko says when there is a lull. She has been folding and refolding a small paper airplane—not unlike the one made of a five-dollar bill which spilled out of her bag the day she and Nikhil met. Something about the careful way she does it makes him want to ask her where she learned, how she learned to do it. But now isn't the time. When Erin nods to say the interview is over, Yukiko stands with her hands pressed into her left side. But before she leaves, she adds, "Can I have your card?"

Erin hands her one. Instead of saying thank you, Yukiko backs away, one foot behind the other, as though she is waiting for them to say something else and saving herself the effort of turning back around. When she reaches the door, she pauses in that space between in and out. Then, when no one offers her anything else, she goes.

After they watch Yukiko step out, Erin regards Nikhil with a journalist's appraisal and says, "What's going on there?"

Nikhil folds his hands together and tells her that he doesn't know. When she presses, he shrugs again and says the same. Finally, Erin stands up, puts a hand on his shoulder, and reminds him that lately, what's been good for him has been good for her.

"So I'm here," she says. "You can talk to me."

He wishes he could, but Nikhil knows nothing about how to word this realization: For the first time, he isn't so sure what he ought to be doing or not doing. It should be easy enough to tell her this and wait for her response, but he hasn't had much practice in this kind of trust.

The girl on the screen, ugly under drugstore products instead of NuLook, ReNuLook, any look. She paints her lips in too many colors, her eyelids, too. The colors muddle, but she draws double wings, triple wings, quadruple wings until her eyes are as sleek as cats. Then, suddenly, she flips her head down and back up. Her hair tumbles in curls, until—

There she is—or there she is not.

Her new face, her sister's face, smiles out from the screen, placid and dewy, with an unnatural gleam that could be mistaken for perspiration but should not be. Of course not.

"Everything is okay," she says, "if you tell yourself it is."

She never responds to any of the comments.

CHAPTER EIGHT

The message says that they need to talk.

That morning, around eleven, Kashmira arrives at Roshni's house and she sees the other girl on the porch. It's been four days since she found her old friend crying in her bathroom. Something since then has shifted, because Roshni now wears her old face bare, devoid of the product. Kashmira frowns. They'd texted yesterday afternoon and everything seemed okay, but this Roshni doesn't say hello, doesn't acknowledge Kashmira at all. She just drinks lemonade, with her legs thrown languidly over the side of the chair. Not sure what else to do, Kashmira drops into the seat next to her and pours her own glass from the pitcher. But when she drinks, she tastes vodka, harsh and searing.

"It's kind of early," Kashmira says, pushing the glass away. "Why are you drinking?"

"Surprised you caught on. There's barely any alcohol in there. Cheers." Roshni waits for Kashmira to pick up her drink. They knock rims hard enough to chip the glass. Kashmira traces the edge of hers and thinks she might feel a notch, so she covers it with her finger. It makes her feel better, but then Roshni says, "Sachin has footage of me from a party. Did he tell you that? Or wait, you must have already known. You hang out, right?"

Roshni treats her drink like a shot. Kashmira watches her throat, long and elegant, as she swallows hard. Usually, Roshni treats alcohol like a social lubricant, a way to get funnier, giddier. She uses it in a crowd. Often, she drinks too much—but not like this. This reminds Kashmira of her father and his gin. The way he relied on it to relieve the pressure of his emotions. Those, though, are memories she tries to avoid.

Still, as she spins her mind away, pressure builds in her abdomen. The waves come frequently these days, and she hates it. Yet, she still believes she can have the life she wants—because she did for the month or so when she passed her days with a proper teenager's unbridled joy. Work, kathak, Tej, parties, it had all been there. Actually, it still is—she still gets called to go out, still dances, still lets her body split open under someone else's—if she just focuses on the good parts and not the newly bad ones. Kashmira holds on to her chair and hopes she won't have to get up and rush into the house for the toilet.

"Sachin and I see each other, sometimes." Kashmira pauses. "Less these days."

"He fucking showed up looking for my mom," Roshni says. "He fucking showed her some recording he had. Of me."

Confused and still catching up, Kashmira tries to imagine the scenario Roshni glosses over: Sachin, with his camera tucked under his arm, knocks on the Guptas' imposing front door. Lalita answers. Looks him up and down, trying to remember if she knows him from temple or perhaps somewhere else. In her eyes, he must be gawkish, with all that height that makes his clothes rise up over his wrists and ankles. Not the kind of boy she encourages her daughter to pursue. Sachin asks to be let in. And then what? Lalita backs away, into the foyer, as he steps inside to show her the footage? Would he do something like that? Would he reveal what Kashmira told him in their last conversation? She wants to say no, but Sachin has always battled with social conventions. He should never have gone to one of his peers' parents, but maybe he did anyway. *Fuck*, she thinks.

"I didn't know he was going to do that," Kashmira says. "I swear."

"Well, he did. And then I had to confess. And now my mom is sending me away because she thinks it's all in my head. She says it's to get help, but I'm talking away-away. Hundreds of miles away. It's fucking crazy."

Roshni slams back more lemonade; perhaps the drunker she is, the more she can convince herself this isn't her fate. The place she describes isn't a hospital or an institution but somewhere called The Center, located in Upstate New York. There, the so-called guides believe that a person brings sickness on themselves through bad habits and personal failures. There, in the rolling hills—soon to turn burnished orange in the autumn months when she will still be there—Roshni will learn to suppress her sadness through long periods of isolation during which she will meditate on her shortcomings and path toward betterment. After enough weeks there, she'll wake up one morning, cured of the bad thoughts that make her sick. At least, that's what happened with one of Mrs. Gupta's friend's daughters.

Roshni wets her lips, her tongue saturated with all the lemonade, all the vodka. "I already tried all that repression bullshit. That's basically what this makeup is."

"It's not bullshit. It helps us. We agreed on that."

"But now it's not working. My mom is pissed. She thinks I'm a fuckup and now I'm getting sent away. To a place where they're *also* just going to tell me how fucked up I am. You think I want that?"

Kashmira shakes her head. She knows Roshni's nightmare is unyielding criticism, the kind that cuts a person down to their core. In this moment, her old friend is facing an unexpected reversal: The product that once saved her from the horror of her mother's condemnation is now the reason she has to bear more of it. Perhaps now the cream doesn't seem worth using, not the way it had before.

"They could send you to a place like that, Kashmira. And you'd be all alone again. I *know* that's not what you want either." Roshni picks up her phone from the table next to her. She holds it up in one hand as she scrolls to the Evolvoir app with the other. The icon expands to a window on her screen, just as she whispers, perhaps only for herself to hear, "I don't have a choice. I'm giving it up, and you should too. Maybe then we can both stay. You know, together."

"Hang on." Fear, as intense as her now-throbbing stomach, beats through Kashmira as Roshni navigates to her settings, where her finger hovers over the Delete Account button. Kashmira knows her friend can be impulsive. "Our accounts are linked. If you get rid of yours, you'll be getting rid of mine too."

"I know," Roshni says, and Kashmira hates her for it. Because it isn't Roshni's decision to make. She doesn't know if Ami will send Kashmira away. She doesn't know, even, if Kashmira will get as sick as she did. So far whatever Kashmira has is manageable enough for her to continue on with her life. And even if it weren't, it would be Kashmira's decision and no one else's to stop using the product, to stop being this new person.

In the moment before Roshni presses Delete, Kashmira lunges. Her chair teeters then crashes backward, but she ignores that and reaches for the phone. Even as Roshni pulls back, Kashmira gets her hands on the device. They must look stupid, playing tug-of-war with something so fragile, but they do it anyway. They wrestle over the table, then next to it, as Kashmira pulls Roshni to one side. Soon enough, the two girls crash together, their sternums knocking into each other, and Kashmira thinks she'll get the phone away from her friend. But Roshni elbows her in the side, right in the left lower quadrant that already aches, and Kashmira doubles over. The two of them part, panting.

"I'm deleting it for both of us," Roshni says.

This time, Roshni doesn't pause. Her finger doesn't hover. Instead she presses End Membership. When another prompt appears onscreen, she presses Yes, I'm Sure once and then again as the app gives her an opportunity to reconsider. Her finger moves fast, a quick triple tap, and then it's done. The app refreshes to a welcome page that displays the familiar ad with people touching their faces in wonder. Kashmira stares at it, even as the image blurs in her gaze. Her eyes dampen with tears, the way they had been that first night by the pool.

"How could you?" she says, thick-voiced. All their history, knotted and confused, hangs between them. The promises they made. The times they were friends—and the times they weren't. Is this just another rupture between them? Or was Roshni always planning to do this to her, revenge for the abandonment years ago? "We were supposed to watch out for each other."

Kashmira's stomach spasm peaks, and she leans forward. Sometimes this helps the cramping sensation, but right now it does very little. Her face feels hot and sick. She has to go and she has to go now. But where? The house towers above her, imposing, as if daring her to ask if she can go in. She and Roshni meet eyes, and the look between them isn't of pity, but knowledge.

"You can use my bathroom," Roshni says.

And then, all that's left between them is the warming lemonade, the ice going to water, diluting the sweet and the sour until everything tastes wan.

—⚜—

Sachin, she needs to find to Sachin.

Immediately after leaving Roshni's house, Kashmira returns to the apartment complex. There, instead of going home, she strides up the walkway to Sachin's place and rings the doorbell over and over again until he opens up. When he finally does, he stands in the doorway, feet bare, and blinks at her. But she doesn't give him a moment to ask what she's doing there.

"How could you do it?" Kashmira says. "How could you give her mother that footage?"

She expects an immediate apology, but when Sachin opens his mouth to respond, she doesn't get one. Instead, he says, "It needed to be done. I tried to give your mom copy too, but she never opened the door when I knocked."

She stares at him, this boy who used to be delicate with her feelings. His forehead is shiny, maybe from the guilt, but maybe just from the anxiety of her coming at him. Kashmira isn't sure.

She can't read him and it seems like he's turning into someone else, as much as she is, and she doesn't why or how. All she knows is she feels betrayed. It's a feeling she has obviously felt before—but never because of him. Suddenly, her whole body aches, from her knees to her shoulders and especially her abdomen.

"Why?" she says. "Why the hell would you think it needed to be done?"

He pauses, as though he didn't expect the question. As though the answer ought to be obvious to her. Then he says, "Because you told me to stop thinking. So I stopped. I just went with my instincts and did what felt right."

"Right to you. Not right to me."

He asks her, then, if she wants to come in. Maybe they can talk. She peers past him, at the living room. She's never actually been inside his place before, and she refuses to let today be the first day. No, she won't let him have this conversation on his grounds. When she shakes her head, his shoulders slump.

"Fine," he says. "But let me just say, I don't think your version of right and wrong is making sense. I mean, you've clearly got something going on. It shouldn't be so hard to let someone help you, should it?"

"How would you know?" Meanness makes her stress every word. But her tone, she believes, is justified. It isn't fair, after all, for him to talk to her about all her ugliness, all her sickness, with such a sense of authority. Just because he has witnessed a small part of it—through his camera, and her quick words, at that—doesn't mean he knows what it's like to live with pain burrowed inside as she does. She presses a hand against her side. "Why did you even bother to get involved?"

"I had a responsibility. I'm the one who filmed it first, after all."

Kashmira has a terrible thought then, because she remembers the night of the party when she and Sachin sat on the roof. He said he observed all of them from that vantage point because they were his characters, doppelgangers of the people he wanted—no, needed—to write stories about. But if that's all any of them—Roshni, Tej,

Kashmira—are to him, is it possible Sachin might have forgotten to treat them like humans? Perhaps he has been so diligent at writing down all his observations, dissecting and examining these people from afar, he's forgotten the consequences of playing with their lives. When Kashmira says this aloud, she hopes Sachin will deny it. But instead, he narrows his eyes and squints past her, up at the sky. When he looks back at her, his pupils are small, and it makes him look overwhelmed.

"I didn't forget you were people." His eyes rove over her face, chin to forehead, forehead to chin. There's tenderness in his expression—and a shy sadness, too. The softness she has known him to have seems to have returned—and it makes her wonder if maybe he hasn't changed at all, but that maybe he's having a hard time and needs another way of being, just like she does. He says then, "I don't think I'm saying all this right. It's just, if you're asking about me and my movie, the truth is, I haven't just been making it for the admissions committee. I've been making it for me too. Hoping I could learn something about the world in the process."

"Learn what?" she says.

He swallows. "You know my mom is white, right?"

She does, and so she nods. But then he tells her something she never knew: how hard that has been for him. For years, Sachin has oscillated between identities, trying to decide how best to define himself. He understands things about being brown—the Bollywood references, the temple traditions, the stereotypes upheld both inside and outside of the community—but in the end, he isn't sure that's enough, not when half his life is spent immersed in a whole other culture that he also doesn't entirely fit into. All of this keeps him a distance away from everyone, even when no one is asking him to stay away. This is why he hangs out in between social groups, keeping a camera to his eye like a barrier between his mind and the real world. He and Kashmira have the opposite and same problem; Sachin has had access to the world of brownness Kashmira has not; yet, he won't integrate into it, while that's all she wants to do.

"I thought if I could fit everyone else into a neat pattern, I'd know how I fit in too," But that was before you and your face and you getting sick."

Kashmira wraps her arms around herself, frustrated by what feels like an accusation. Like she has messed something up for him by trying to navigate her own difficulties. She says, "I don't know where this is going, and it seems like we're getting away from the point, which is—"

"Which is that I should've turned the camera on myself. I should've figured out why you were acting weird and pushing me away made me feel like I couldn't stay on the edges anymore. Why I felt like I had to do something to help you." He bobs his head over and over again. *Yes, yes, yes, I'm figuring it out just as I'm telling it all to you*, the movement signifies. And then, in a sudden burst, like that of someone suddenly sure of something, Sachin says, "I like you, you know. I have for a long time."

To Kashmira's surprise, he reaches for her hand. The warmth of his skin, like bathwater inching up her neck while she sinks in. Comforting, in the way she had always imagined it would be. His words matter more because of this touch; she hears them better because they're finally standing inside the same moment together. His sentences mean something real because he says them by her side, not from the distance to which she has grown so accustomed. How right it feels to have him wrap his fingers around hers and squeeze, all while telling her that he wants to be there, that he cares.

"Sachin," she says.

"Maybe I did do the wrong thing, though," he replies. "Maybe all I wanted was to be here. Like this. For you."

He raises their two joined hands to show her, and she smiles softly, because she likes being shown. But despite this, she feels herself backing away. She feels herself letting her fingers slip from his grasp. As she goes, his brows furrow, but he straightens his shoulders. He presses his lips together.

"Okay," he says, putting a hand—the hand that was just in hers—on the back of his head. "It's okay if you don't feel the same."

But of course she feels the same. Sure, he isn't the boy she planned to want, but maybe he is the one she has hoped for across the years. Maybe this is why every time they find each other's gaze they stay in the moment, unable to leave, like the two wary dogs that live in their neighborhood, circling each other until they recognize that their scents are more similar than not—or were more similar than not. Kashmira touches her face, still changed. And then she realizes why she is backing away. It isn't because of his transgression, his betrayal of her privacy. That she understands as doing the best he could. That she can forgive. No, there is another problem here: that of the path he presents her, where she goes back to the girl she once was, the girl he fell for however long ago. Because as much as he would like that for her, it's impossible. Because as she imagines it, right now, right here, she can't even figure out how she would fit herself back into those features, that history, that lonely world. She doesn't know how to be that person any longer. So really, the only choice she has is to figure out what to do so she can keep this new face.

Sachin steps away from the doorway, closer to her. His feet are still bare, and as soon as they touch the ground, they must burn. Still, he walks toward her and says, "Hey, Kashmira, hey. Look, no matter what you feel about me, I still want to help you, okay?"

She can only think of one thing to say. She shakes her head and tells him, "You can't."

For once, Ami is waiting for her when she returns home later that night.

She calls from the stove that she has dinner waiting, although Kashmira would prefer not to eat, especially not the heavy lasagna her mother has prepared for whatever reason. While her mother tends the meal, Kashmira dodges her eyeline. She excuses herself to go to the bathroom to "take a shower." There, she runs the water and then uses her reversal cream on her face. Then she returns to sit with her mother and push the sauce and cheese and noodles around her plate. Ami presses her fingers against the bridge of her nose.

"Where were you all day?" she says.

"With Roshni," Kashmira says.

A lie. Roshni isn't answering any of her texts. Instead, Kashmira was out with Tej, who called and asked her out just an hour after her argument with Sachin. She'd said yes, less for the sex and more for the reminder that things could still be okay, normal, if she let them be. She and Tej fucked in the back seat, twice, because of how much she wanted to believe everything would work out. After, he drove her back but told her he'd be hanging out in the area and promised to pick her up later, too, if she wanted a third time.

"But Roshni's mother called me. She said that Roshni isn't well, and you knew about it. She told me I should check on you."

"She was fine when I saw her. Besides, why is her mom talking to you about it?"

"She said I should know. As a mother, I should know." Ami fits her fingers around her wrist over and over again—nervously. Her discomfort is obvious. "Is that what you think too?"

Kashmira fixes her gaze above her mother's shoulder. She remembers the kind of mother Lalita was: abrasive at times, good for a laugh, but often tough on her daughter in ways that weren't fair. Ami is the opposite: delicate, prone to fits of crying. Both seem unable to see their daughters for who they are and what they need.

"I don't know, Mom. It's not my job to know."

Ami drops her wrist, but it doesn't make her look any more confident. "It's mine."

At first, it sounds like Ami is acknowledging her role, but then she keeps going on and on. She says many things, about how with Vinod gone everything has been different, how this fight between Nikhil and Kashmira hasn't made things easier, how sometimes she just doesn't know if she can get up in the morning. And the box, she says, is still there, waiting for her. She doesn't know what to do with anything—the box or her daughter or herself. She says all this and waits for Kashmira to agree, to appease her. When she doesn't,

Ami says, "Kashmira, you know as well as I do that your father was the one who was deciding how to raise you.

Kashmira drops her fork. The sound of it, loud and clanging through the kitchen. But she doesn't care. Not when her mother dares to privilege her father like this. She scowls at her mother and says, in the darkest tone she can, "He didn't raise us. There was so much he never did for us."

"Being a parent isn't as simple as you might think," Ami says.

Kashmira pushes her plate away. The lasagna is wet and slimy and too red. She can't eat it. She says, more to the empty space in front of her than to her mother, "It's also not as hard as you're making it. Literally all you have to do is put me first sometimes."

An intake of breath, like Ami might want to say something more. Or maybe like she is having some realization. But Kashmira doesn't wait. She rises from the table and leaves with a short proclamation that she's done. Then, in the bathroom, she texts Tej and asks him to come again, yes, soon. As she waits for him, she reapplies the product, and she does so with practiced ease. Images she expects come: her father leaving, replayed in her mind, the door, the knife on the edge of the sink, the note he left behind. Then more, new ones: Roshni and her lemonade, Sachin watching her move backwards, her mother gaping at her. So much has been lost, even as she tries to hold on. Kashmira's stomach aches, and she squats over the toilet. Though she hasn't eaten much, she's able to go a bit alongside deep cramps and nausea. When she thinks she's finished, there is more, coming out of who knows what recess of her.

The whole time she does what she always does. She thinks not of the pain but of what, in her life, she still has and what she still wants. More things are gone, but other things are still on their way. Tej is coming. They'll mess around. Maybe they'll go hang out with some of his friends, or maybe they'll see each other at a party later this week. She has her dance, she has her work, she has her routines. And maybe everything else—fathers, mothers, old friends, almost loves—meant to be lost if they're no help in getting where she needs to go.

Like all the times before, Kashmira sits on her bed and presses her finger against the Evolvoir app. But now she isn't sure who'll be on the other side of the video call. Because—as of two days ago—she isn't on Roshni's account any longer, she has to purchase her products some other way. For this reason, she has joined the ReNuLook wait list and has spent much of the last forty-eight hours sending Client Care message after message, suggesting that because she has been a loyal customer all summer perhaps she can have priority for the next appointment. Apparently, this has worked, because now she is here, though she isn't sure with whom or how the call will go. Really, she isn't even sure she should be on it, but what else is there to do?

The video and audio click on.

"Kashmira, hey," Jordie says. Faultless as always, she smiles and waves. "I saw your name in the appointment scheduler and thought I'd take the call. What's up? Why are you going through the wait list instead of your membership account?" She clicks a few keys and nods before Kashmira replies. "Oh, I see. You had a linked account. We don't see many of those. But I guess it doesn't matter since you're not on that account any longer."

Overall, Kashmira and Jordie have maintained a decent rapport. Each time they have a call, Jordie assesses how Kashmira likes her new face, asking not only how she feels physically but also emotionally. They fill out a progress chart together, and Jordie asks questions like *How comfortable are you with the statement "I'm getting better"?* and *How easy would it be for you to stop using Evolvoir products at this time?* Kashmira answers on one-to-ten scales, and Jordie inputs the data. The output: Line graphs plot increasing happiness that doesn't quite match up with how she actually feels. But how good it looks, all those positive-trending, beautifully angled lines.

"I got taken off that account, but I want to keep up with the products. I can pay on my own," Kashmira tells Jordie. She isn't sure if this is true. She never saw the final bills Roshni was covering with her parents' credit card. Her barista's wages can only go so far. "I think?"

Jordie taps her lips with two fingers. "You do know our wait list is months long at least, don't you? And it's only getting longer."

Jordie opens up multiple windows—Kashmira's progress charts, her idealized 3D face, her original intake survey—on her screen share. The visuals overwhelm the screen while Jordie's voice cuts through the speakers.

"Not a lot of changes to your initial personalized formula, I see," she says. "And these progress chart numbers are steeper than a lot of our clients see. Do you feel good?"

What is good? Exhaustion wills her to bed too early with the kind of fatigue she can't sleep off; pain drills into her ankles and knees; acid creeps up her esophagus when she eats. But there is still hope when she puts on her new face. She is still better off than before. She is still almost the girl who other people look for at parties, who throws her head back when she laughs, who shows up every week to kathak lessons, who loses herself in long kisses with a brown boy for the hell of it, who can tolerate herself in a mirror.

"The product does what you said it would. And more," Kashmira says.

"And you'd recommend it to other people? On a scale of one to ten?"

"Ten being—"

"The highest." Jordie watches Kashmira, who watches herself on the screen. They must both see the longing in Kashmira's face. The way her jaw moves up and down as she chews the inside of her cheek. Kashmira almost doesn't even recognize herself, this girl who is so desperate. This girl who is so intrigued when Jordie says, "Look, I'll level with you. We've got this new program, the BBB. It's for people who can share the product with others, you know, do some word-of-mouth marketing. In exchange, you'd be taken off the wait list and given your products as soon as possible. But you'd only be qualified if you were completely sure about ReNuLook."

Completely sure, completely sure. Kashmira feels that phrase like needles on her skin. It pinches and pinches, prompting her on until she says: "Before I answer, is there any chance that some people might have a bad reaction to the product? That it might, you know, make them sick? Like with weird stomach symptoms?"

As soon as she asks this, she wishes she hadn't. Because she is sure about one thing, the most important thing: that she wants the product, no matter what the answer is. So when Jordie asks why Kashmira is even bringing up this question, Kashmira just flicks her hair out of her eyes and stays silent, hoping Jordie won't reconsider her as a candidate for this BBB program. But then Jordie smiles and shakes her head, almost patronizing, and says the products have been tested for both efficacy and safety and the majority of clients respond well to them. The word "majority" hangs between them.

"Then, ten," Kashmira says. She watches herself on the screen, face perfectly calm, even as her stomach groans in real life. "I'd definitely recommend the makeup to people, especially if that's what you need from me."

Jordie says, "Good. Because you'd be great in the BBB. And you'd get your products as soon as possible if you took on the role. I'm assuming you're interested?"

Of course she is. She always has been. Kashmira nods through Jordie's detailing of the program's terms and conditions. When Jordie says something about how Kashmira will be responsible for getting a few other clients of color to sample ReNuLook as soon as possible, Kashmira says that yes, she has plenty of people to ask. She thinks of the kathak students and the girls at the parties she goes to. Whoever, whatever, they'll work. She says yes again to a question she doesn't even hear. She is not Kashmira any longer. She is someone who would say yes to anything right now—as long it means the product will arrive soon. After she and Jordie rush through the answers on the enrollment form, Kashmira asks when exactly the package will arrive on her doorstep.

"I don't want to miss any days," she says. "Of wearing it, I mean."

Evolvoir Launches New Initiative to Expand Product Availability to BIPOC Customers

Erin Frankel | @frankesterin

Evolvoir, the innovative beauty and wellness brand known for NuLook and ReNuLook, is creating buzz this summer with a new initiative that prioritizes BIPOC customers. The program, called BIPOC Beauty Babes (BBB), aims to prioritize BIPOC clients on the ReNuLook wait list, ensuring timely access for those who "historically lacked access and quality care for mental wellness," according to Product Growth Analyst and BBB initiative team member Nikhil Mehta.

This new initiative comes on the heels of Evolvoir's newest offering, ReNuLook, a product that leverages the same advanced nanoparticles as NuLook but focuses on promoting full facial transformations that support clients who may be grappling with their family relationships and self-identities in a difficult political and social landscape. It can be used in conjunction with other therapeutic practices, but—according to data from Evolvoir's one-on-one client-concierge meetings—many people are using the product as their primary way to address their concerns. One such person is Yukiko, the creator behind the @yukiko account on VidMo (647k followers), who has worked with Evolvoir on ReNuLook and now the BBB. In Yukiko's VidMo videos, she reshapes herself to look more like her late sister and has found the practice to be "life-altering."

"That's why we started the BBB," Mehta said in response to Yukiko's claim. "Because this tech is so important, it's important to us to prioritize marginalized demographics getting access to our products."

The BBB initiative is gaining traction. The program fast-tracks eligible BIPOC clients—also known as BBB Team Members—to the front of the ReNuLook wait list in exchange for promoting the product within their communities. Any clients that the BBB Team Members bring to Evolvoir will also be able to skip the wait list. Five hundred BIPOC clients have already benefited from this program.

"This isn't just a marketing strategy," Mehta clarified. "Word of mouth is a powerful tool for spreading awareness, not just for the product itself but for the ideal of mental wellness."

While the allowance of "extreme facial shifting," as Congressman Daniel Weber, R-Mass., calls it, has come under fire, and Evolvoir faces legal challenges in several states, consumer demand remains high, with both NuLook and ReNuLook consistently selling out every month. Because of this, investors are showing interest—and despite doubts earlier this year, Evolvoir is now predicted to procure a high amount of Series B funding.

"Evolvoir is heading into new directions, and it's interesting, to say the least," Jianhong Jiang, a representative from Surgere Partners said. "Their brand is transforming the future of beauty and wellness."

Mike Powell, a representative from Forward Firm, said, "With initiatives like BBB, the company is expanding its reach and setting new standards for inclusivity and technological advancement in the industry, while also setting the stage for its own growth. That's the kind of vision we're always looking to support."

CHAPTER NINE

Another week, another Operation Wellness Team meeting. Today's art installation, on Prince Street, is more self-portraits. Nikhil has come to expect this. Unlike during last week's meeting though, he walks around on his own. Michael stands at the other end of the space and does not approach him. The pieces are collages of the artist's childhood photos, pasted together to make up the impression of her own face. Nikhil walks back and forth, gauging the art, pausing when he comes across a spread of a family picnicking on the beach and eating ice cream on some pier. Despite the distance between him and Michael, Nikhil's memories come easily now, like he has unlocked them for good. In his mind, he revisits the summers of his and Kashmira's childhood, when they would go to the shore and curl their tongues around soft serve on the Wildwoods Boardwalk. It was Vinod who loved this place the most, and he was the one who taught both his children how to lick their cones the most effectively. His father held up his own smooth ice cream and showed off each side, then demonstrated how to take long licks so nothing ever dripped. To practice, he bought Nikhil two ice creams a day for that week. It's hard to reconcile that man with the one who left them repeatedly, but there it is. But there is no one at the moment to share this memory with, and soon Nikhil drifts into the circle with Keon for the meeting.

Predictable conversation, mostly about how well BBB is going, consumes most of the first half hour. Nikhil knows all this, and he finds himself staring at Michael, who looks bored and ready to go. The muscle in his neck pulses, and Nikhil has to look away to avoid recalling their time together a week ago, and how that same muscle tensed when Michael held Nikhil close. Since then, Michael hasn't been talking to him much—and he has somehow switched most of his work-from-home days to line up with the days Nikhil is in the office

"Anything else we should discuss?" Keon says. "If not, we can end early."

"I have something," Jordie says. She hesitates, then adds, "I had this client asking if RNL can make people sick."

When Keon asks what kind of sick, Jordie explains that it'd been a quick conversation, and that all the client had mentioned was that the symptoms were "weird" and related to the stomach. The room hums with questions as she says this. Nikhil is part of this crowd, wondering things out loud. How can he not be? It's a strange and concerning allegation to say the product is related to some illness.

"I mean, I know we're FDA-approved and everything," Jordie says. "So, I just thought I'd check in, since I'm not really on the product development side of things."

"Neither am I," Nikhil replies. "But it just doesn't make sense to me that the product could be related to stomach issues. People aren't ingesting the product. Why would it have any impact on their digestive systems?"

Jordie shrugs. "Yeah. It's more likely this girl got the stomach flu or something."

To Jordie's right, Yukiko shifts on her feet. Her face is angular and somehow pained, even with the product on. Her head bows as she breathes in and out more deeply than everyone else. And her arms look thinner. So does the tight skin over her collarbones. Yukiko uses the product every day; they're all aware of this. Nerves tighten in Nikhil's body as he wonders if maybe, possibly, there is something here that Yukiko knows about.

Jordie, perhaps having had the same thought, says, "Do you know, Yukiko? I mean, you've been on the products for a while now."

"I—" Yukiko says.

"Hold on," Keon says. "You don't have to answer that. Your health and medical information isn't anyone's business but yours, and I'm sure our People Team would agree."

"Well, if it has to do with our product, though," Jordie says. "Yukiko, come on."

The circle breaks slightly as the other Operation Wellness Team members shift away from Yukiko so they can look at her. There's pressure in the room now. People wanting answers. Someone asks Yukiko if she's feeling okay. If she's been feeling okay. Someone mentions that she has been looking pale lately, and what's up with that?

Yukiko flicks her gaze from person to person. Her eyes go fast, never stopping—except on Nikhil. Something in her gaze seems to say to him, *You, maybe you.* But then she shakes her head, and a nervousness fills her expression. The same type of nervousness that Nikhil has been feeling in his body for the last few minutes. Suddenly, he's sure everything makes sense. He's sure this is why Yukiko has been pushing back against ReNuLook, against Nikhil. He's sure this is why she didn't want to talk to Erin. The product is doing something to her.

"Thanks for your concern," Yukiko says. "But I'm fine—"

"Yukiko, all of you, enough," Keon says. "This isn't something we can talk about. So seriously, drop it."

Nikhil watches as his YTC tugs at his ear. He's right that they shouldn't be questioning Yukiko about her medical history in the middle of a meeting. It's very possibly illegal. But is it also true that Keon knows what Yukiko might be reticent to share? Is this why he interrupted only after she said the word *fine*, which seems to have calmed some of the questions at least? The rest of the Operation Wellness Team looks at least a little less worried now, though Nikhil feels his anxiety grow and grow. Luckily, it hasn't shifted into that familiar, brutal anger—though he isn't sure why.

"Thank you, Jordie," Keon says, "for bringing this topic to our attention. Please let us know if there's anything else at any point."

Keon closes the meeting; Operation Wellness Team leaves the gallery. Michael and Yukiko both seem to exit by some back way, because they disappear. So Nikhil walks out alone, though around him his fellow employees chat about what just happened in there and whether Yukiko really is okay. Their conversation sounds like gossip, like they don't believe that their product is the culprit and that something else—drugs, maybe—is. But Nikhil isn't so sure. He can't let go of all that's happened with Yukiko since she joined the company. He can't let go of her face in this meeting, or Keon's. He can't let go of the memory of ice cream. How his sister had learned how to eat it after him, and how he had pressed napkins to her wrists when she let the chocolate, the vanilla, run long over her skin. Nikhil had wanted that little girl to use the product, and he'd thought he would do anything to make it happen. But he'd never imagined that this cream, the one he has dedicated the last two months to, could hurt her.

If he had, he swears he never would have done what he has done.

―∽―

In the morning, Jordie recants what she said about the Evolvoir client who thought the product was causing an illness:

—@opwellness i rewatched the recording with girl i told you about last night. i realized i misrepresented what she was saying. i mean, it was really just a general question about side effects, nothing to be concerned about.

The rest of the Team seems to believe her, based on the 👍 emojis they send. But Nikhil wants to talk to Yukiko. He wants to hear from her what's going on. The problem is, he doesn't think she'll talk to him with the way things are between them.

So Nikhil looks for the person he knows can help him. Michael isn't anywhere. Not at his desk, where most Evolvoir workers always are; not in the break room punting Ping-Pong balls; not chewing on jelly beans in the lobby, waiting to get chastised for mooching the free candy for clients and partners. Nikhil checks TaskSquad to see if Michael put up a 🌡 to indicate a sick day—but no. Not knowing where else to look, Nikhil ends up in the kitchen, where he rips open the foil around one of the nut-free, soy-free vegan protein bars the company stocks the drawers with. The bars leave a faint aftertaste of chickpea in his mouth for hours, but chewing makes him feel better, like his body is doing something productive.

Eventually, Michael does show up. Wordlessly, he passes Nikhil, while fumbling with his keycard and a white Styrofoam takeout container from the hot bar at a nearby Asian market the two of them had first tried together.

"Where were you?" Nikhil says.

"I worked from home this morning," Michel says. "I had a whole thing with my neighbor's dog. It's been going on for a few weeks."

"It has?"

"Yeah." Michael wrenches the fridge open with enough force that the glass salad dressing jars in the door shake. "I've told you about it. Guess you weren't listening."

"It's true," Nikhil says. "My attention's been elsewhere. I know you know that. But I do think what happened at the meeting yesterday with Jordie and Yukiko was important. I was thinking we could something, like—"

"Do what?" Michael says. He presses his weight against the already-closed fridge. "I'm not a responsible person, so why would you ask me? I mean, I should be because of the color of my skin, but you know."

"I apologized for that."

"Actually, you said it came out wrong."

Michael walks across the kitchen. When he sweeps by Nikhil, their shoulders brush, but he doesn't stop until he gets to the doorway.

The space between feels vast, though Nikhil can count the distance in ceramic tiles. Just five. Then Michael takes two steps forward and makes the count three.

"What did you want?" Michael says. "Why were you looking for me?"

"I was hoping you'd help me talk to Yukiko," Nikhil tells him. "I'm not sure how to get her to talk."

Michael's mouth parts. "Jesus, Nikhil. You still don't know?" He laughs, gestures around the kitchen, with its perfectly lined up prebiotic sodas; its state-of-the-art coffee machine that grinds fresh beans before drawing a drink; its cold tile floor that nothing ever seems to stain, no matter what anyone spills. "No wonder you fit in so well at this place in the end."

"Just tell me," Nikhil says. "Please."

There's a pause as Michael deliberates. And he says, "Just listen to her. Think of her like a person. Just like you should have with your sister. Just like you should have with me."

As he talks, Michael's nose ring glints under the lights, and Nikhil watches it, captivated. He has the absurd desire to pull it out of Michael's nose and put it on his own finger. To wear it forever, as a reminder of how intimate—and horrific—this moment feels.

―⁂―

Nikhil's to-do list taunts him from the side of his screen, but he can't concentrate. He left the kitchen thirty minutes ago and still, he can't open his files to work, can't pretend everything is fine. Michael's words have cut into him, and then nestled deep. Nikhil clicks on TaskSquad and skims the conversations in all the channels he belongs to. The chats are full of discussions about things like adding new allergen-free soap to the bathroom to support anti-inflammatory lifestyles and starting an all-gender baseball team where they would use real balls and making sure it isn't the same intern in charge of changing out the coffee machine's filter every Friday. As Nikhil reads, he looks for Yukiko's name.

When he doesn't see her or her profile picture, he navigates to his @yukiko direct message thread. They haven't talked here much, but he wants to fill the page with her conversation. But what to say? Michael said to listen. Michael said to try to understand. This time, Nikhil writes Yukiko a quiet message, one she could easily ignore, but also might want to respond to.

—hi. if you want to talk, i'm here.

He tries not to watch for the tiny tick marks that indicate the message has been seen. He does, though, end up minimizing the window and then maximizing it three times, just in case he received a ping but TaskSquad glitched and never sent the notification. Minutes pass this way, until a message actually does come through.

—since when? @yukiko says.

The keys clack under Nikhil's fingers. His first message sounds too irritated—*you don't have to say it like that*—and he deletes it. His second message is too rational, like he is trying to invalidate her feelings—*look, things have been complicated for us as colleagues, but we should approach this in a better way*—and he backspaces over that one, too. But the third—the third is right, he knows. Michael has told him to be honest about his own flaws, to be real. And this, this is that. He sends the message without even rereading it.

—since now. look, i'm sorry about all the times before. i was wrong. and i know you don't have a reason to trust me, but i'm worried about you. i'm here, if you're willing to talk.

This time, he allows himself to wait for those two tick marks. They come fast enough, and then he sees the message that @yukiko is typing. She writes for a long time, long enough that Nikhil assumes she, too, is using the delete key.

And then, the message appears on his screen:

—meet me tonight.

⁂

This art gallery is, again, on the Lower East Side, on Broome. Yukiko says she'd rather talk there than anywhere else, so he agrees to come to tonight's exhibition. In this series of self-portraits, the photographer imagines how her family members would pose her for pictures if they could do anything they wanted. The first photo is a neutral pose, where the artist is wearing a white T-shirt and black leggings and is set against a beige wall. No tint to her face, her hair mousy brown, hands down by her sides, completely straight, not touching anything, not even each other. The artist gazes straight ahead without a hint of what she's thinking, and viewers are invited to walk back and stand with this first image for as long as they need before they move on to the next family perspective in the series.

"One of the reviews says you can change your experience of the exhibit by visiting the portraits in a different order," Yukiko says. She and Nikhil stand together at the entrance. At first, he had only recognized her by her long hair, already tucked behind her ears, though her hands moved to redo it anyway. When she turned, Nikhil saw that Yukiko wasn't wearing her second face. This first face, this original face, he knew too, from the start of some of her videos, but it was far less familiar to him. He didn't know why she had chosen to forgo her product. Maybe she didn't want to be recognized by a fan, or maybe it was something more concerning, more complicated. She hasn't said. Instead, she suggests an order for them to walk through the gallery. "Mother, father, brother first? Then maybe brother, mother, father the next time? Then maybe aunt, brother, mother, cousin?"

"Shouldn't we talk?"

"Let's do this first," she says.

He doesn't press or make her do it his way, though an impulse tells him to. It's hard at first to just go along with her, but he finds that it does get easier. They walk among the frames—thick braids of gold. Mother sees the artist posed as a very tall, very big larger-than-life doll wearing a blue gingham dress. Aunt sees the artist posed in a fetal position with a mobile looped around her neck. Brother sees the artist posed with her hair shorn on one side, the rest of it rainbow tinted. Grandfather sees the artist posed in a library, scribbling a formula with too many variables: x, y, z, even w. Mother, brother, aunt, grandfather. Brother, grandfather, aunt, mother. Aunt, mother, grandfather, brother. Grandfather, aunt, brother, mother. Each time Nikhil and Yukiko change the order, but one thing stays the same: Each time, Nikhil assumes that the first portrait in the sequence is the true artist, not a theoretical version of her.

"How would you pose me?" Yukiko says.

"Flying a plane," Nikhil tells her. Without difficulty, his mind reminds him of the little fighter jet she always carries around, the one he meant to ask her about. He never did. "Trying not to crash it. Especially with me as your copilot."

He doesn't mean for this to sound like a joke. The truth he's starting to see is that his directions always lead him back to the start of things, where he's meant to recalibrate, rethink not only his route, but his way of flying. But he hasn't understood this, and somehow, his instruments never balance, and he always sets off again before being ready. Isn't that what happened when he pushed his sister away, all over how he thought she should handle their father? Isn't that what happened when Yukiko told him to slow down and he refused? It's not a joke at all to say that he has been this close to crashing for a long time now. And still, Yukiko laughs and says, "So self-aware. I think I would have liked getting to know this version of you, Nikhil."

Yukiko walks him back to the start. This time, instead of looking at the first photograph, Yukiko stands next to it, as if she too is joining the show. The longer she stays like that, the more she embodies the artist—quiet, mutable, waiting to be understood. It strikes Nikhil that people spend a lot of time living up to images of themselves, instead of their truth: that they're just humans, trying their best to contend with the pain of an aching back, the embarrassment of bad breath, the agony of arms that are desperate to hold on to something solid.

"I've been thinking a lot about my own sister since I met you," he says.

"You brought her up once."

He had, in that art gallery. But he'd said it without explanation. By that point, he'd been too focused on what Yukiko could and couldn't do for his vision. And she wasn't like Michael. She didn't push him. And so, much had remained unsaid. Nikhil thinks of what Michael would tell him to do now, in this moment. *Tell her*, he would say, *what you need to*. Nikhil explains, then, everything he knows about Kashmira. It's uncomfortable at first—gentler than when he said all this to Michael in a burst of fluid anger. But the way Yukiko listens, intently blinking every time he pauses, tells him what he has shared matters.

"I wish things hurt less. I wish my sister never died," Yukiko says when he is finished. At first it sounds like she is trying to one-up him, but if he listens, really listens, he can hear that she is actually thanking him for sharing. Her gratitude is expressed as openness as she tells him her own history. "She was so perfect, you know? Did everything right, everything anyone ever asked of her. And still. It was never enough." She tells him how her sister died—in a fatal car accident. Yukiko had been in the front seat, but walked away safe, alive. She was racked with survivor's guilt, racked with the strangeness of her now-fundamentally altered family hierarchy, racked with how much she missed her sister, racked with how much she wanted to fill the hole in her. She says, in a whisper, "It never worked, you know, putting her face on."

Then she moans—so quietly Nikhil is sure he wasn't meant to hear it—and sinks to the floor, her back against the gallery wall. Her expression, as if she is overcome by the art and just needs a moment. But the longer she sits here, the more likely someone will complain. Already, Nikhil can see the other patrons staring. A guard is watching them too.

He crouches down to touch her arm. "Are you okay?"

"What does it really mean to be okay, anyway?" She stretches her legs out so her body makes a long capital-L shape. Her teeth are clenched, her eyes shifting, her voice at a tempo faster than it normally would be. "Maybe I'm not."

"You want me to take you somewhere? A hospital?"

"Maybe," she says. "This isn't new. I've been throwing up between meetings. Running off the subway to get myself to a coffee shop so I can go to the bathroom. I've wasted so much money on lattes I don't drink. I just need the code so I can shit." She laughs, but it's so sharp it sounds almost like the *fucks* and *goddammits* he mutters under his breath when things make him too angry. She puts a hand over her mouth and talks behind her palm. "The truth is, sometimes, most of the time, I'm so hungry, so, so hungry. And nothing I eat fills me up. And then when I do eat, it all comes out of me, like it never got digested at all. Like my body doesn't know how to process food anymore. What do you think that could be about?"

"I think you're sick," Nikhil says, trying not to falter as she describes this double life she's been living—one he isn't sure anyone's been privy to. "I think you need help."

"I tried to get it," she says.

This is when she tells him what he thinks is everything. The product, on her face. The surge of grief that came with it, reminding her that she would never be her sister and that her sister would never—could never—return to hold her. The feeling of that loss, somehow magnified by her desire to deny it. And yet, she went on anyway, ignoring the physical pain that came with it: the nausea, the stomach aches, the diarrhea that came and never left. It was easy to pretend she didn't hurt when people were telling her over and over again that she was doing the right thing. This was why she had even gone so far as to join the company when the offer came—anything, to keep wearing her second face.

"But then the bleeding started," she says.

The bleeding, impossible to disregard, not when it was coloring all her toilet water red. She had gone to Larissa, worried about what she had done to herself—what others might do, too. Larissa told her they'd look into it, but then they focused on the wait list issue instead. No one listened to her—not the higher-ups, not her colleagues. Yukiko doesn't look at him when she says this, but Nikhil understands she is thinking of him telling her they couldn't slow down, not ever. In any case, she searched on her own for evidence of the connection between the product and what was happening to her body.

"And I did find some, at least," she says.

But she doesn't look pleased. Just exhausted. Nikhil rests his head on the wall. A version of him in the past might have asked what proof she had. But this version can do nothing but feel his breathing go ragged as he imagines all she has gone through.

"I was wrong about everything," he says. How much he hadn't known. How much he hadn't noticed. How much he had pushed a product that could hurt people, all because he thought it could disrupt systems of wellness in this country. He thinks of Keon, cutting Yukiko off earlier. He thinks of what, maybe, the man knows. And he realizes that maybe, just maybe, he has been trusting the wrong people the whole time. He says, "God—what should I, I mean, tell me, what do you need me to do?"

Something changes in her face. Not the features themselves but the expression, as though she recognizes someone who she hasn't seen for a long time, someone she has been waiting to see. She clutches Nikhil's hand now and pulls him close enough that he can see the long lengths of her eyelashes, wet with tears.

"Do you know the reason I told you to come out here tonight?" she says. "It's because I knew if I could get you to listen, then I'd finally have someone on my side. You're not the kind of person who gives up on people." She leans forward and rests her forehead on his shoulder. When she speaks, she sounds muffled. But he hears her when she says, "Please don't call the ambulance yet. I just want to sit with you for a little while."

The girl on the screen's last video is scheduled to post a day after her death. No one knew, but no one could've stopped it anyway, even if they had: Her account is password protected.

In the video, the girl twirls in an office chair, recognizable by its teal hue. As she spins, the girl laughs, like someone told her a secret she doesn't want to believe but has to. The video is only a second or two long, but viewers keep watching, thinking it's longer. It takes a while for them to realize they're just watching the same clip over and over again. But there's a tell, a gesture that flags the end of the clip as it goes back to the beginning. If they pause the video at the very end, the viewers will see the girl on the screen open her mouth, as though she was about to say something.

what would her last words to the world have been? did she know they were her last words? a popular commenter asks, garnering thousands of likes.

Another commenter, a nobody upstart, posts, too, with a post-mortem of anything that could be of interest: the girl's dress, the color of her eyeliner, her posture, the computer screen in the background still glowing bright with some file. it's a list of names, they write. what do you think that means?

Guesses populate in the comments. Some are so wrong. Some are closer to the truth, though they don't know that yet.

The popular commenter responds, says, who cares, she's dead, my god, you people.

It doesn't matter. The people can't stop—and neither does the video. It loops back to the start, to the awful, grim laugh, the look of disbelief, the look of resignation.

CHAPTER TEN

Out in the studio, the tanpura drones on; in the last stall of the studio's bathroom, Kashmira wipes blood from between herself furiously. She goes as fast as she can, cleaning every reachable centimeter, but the blood still floats in the toilet bowl, a red inkblot for her to understand—or not. This could be an anomaly, just one time she strained too hard. Except, it happened twice this morning, too. Except, it isn't just the blood but also the two months of nausea, the two weeks of urgency at inopportune moments, the last week of long and insidious strands of mucus that escape her unbidden. She knows now how bad this all is—and that she can't pretend she isn't as sick as Roshni. But for now all she can do is flush, check that her blouse isn't tucked into her tight shorts, and make sure toilet paper isn't stuck to her shoe.

By the sinks, Roshni—wearing her original face, which made Hemaji and the kathak girls falter until she spoke—is washing her hands. Kashmira frowns, trying to figure out when she came in. Then she realizes she was in that stall for at least ten minutes, and, in that time, the door probably opened and closed, its creak unnoticeable over the sound of Kashmira's gut emptying.

"I know you feel terrible," Roshni says, eyes fixed on the pink soap frothing and disappearing down the drain. The color of it, too close to red. Kashmira would like to just use water—but she needs to get clean. She pumps more soap into her palm. "No matter how much you try to hide it."

"I thought you weren't talking to me," Kashmira says to Roshni. Their fight was a week and a half ago, and since then Kashmira and Roshni haven't texted or spent any time together. They haven't made any plans, not even for today, which is Roshni's birthday. Kashmira has yet to even acknowledge this, though apparently Roshni still showed up at the intermediate class to keep up her end of the deal for Kashmira's kathak classes. Kashmira squares her shoulders. Probably Roshni only came because the other teenagers in the class planned a celebration for her—not because her presence as the teacher's assistant guarantees Kashmira lessons. "I thought your mom was signing you up for some commune or something."

"Orientation starts tomorrow," Roshni says. "Then I come back to pack. And then I leave for good in like three and a half weeks, just before the school year starts." She pauses. "You know you looked bad out there."

She had. Kashmira had stood in the middle of the room, hoping that if she was surrounded by the other girls, Hemaji wouldn't notice her lack of energy. But it was all obvious: Kashmira's shoulders sagging with exhaustion while she did her taatkar. Kashmira missing a pose because pain had settled into her joints and made it harder to raise her arms. Kashmira rushing out in the middle of the fall recital choreography, messing up the careful formation she wouldn't even have been part of if Hemaji hadn't made an exception for her to start in the middle of the season. Of course, what Hemaji didn't see was: Kashmira only leaving so she could squat on the toilet and moan as her body gave way underneath her. Kashmira standing before she felt totally finished so she could get back and stop being such a disruption. Kashmira pressing a wet paper towel to her forehead to calm her low-grade fever. None of that was as visible as Kashmira's poor performance, so it made sense that when Kashmira returned to the rest of the class finishing their cooldown stretches, Hemaji called her up to the front.

"You haven't been practicing," Hemaji said as the other girls moved to their next position, this time pressing their noses into their knees while flattening their backs.

Hemaji's assessment was untrue. Kashmira had practiced all week, as best she could in the small apartment, not nearly as suitable as Roshni's long basement space, finished with long strips of plywood to complete the improvised studio down there. Kashmira moved the table and chairs out of her apartment's dining area and did her best, but she hadn't been able to recognize herself dancing. It wasn't because of the space but rather because of her body, which wasn't what it once was, no matter how good it might look on the outside.

Now, in the studio bathroom, the girls move to dry their hands. Kashmira considers handing Roshni a paper towel, but then she hesitates too long and Roshni has already grabbed one for herself. The distance between them is uncomfortable, though they have a history of such separation. This isn't the only loss to contend with either. As Kashmira blots her hands, she realizes what the issue is: In trying to curate her features, she has lost anything that has ever made her Kashmira. Here in the bathroom, there on the dance floor, she is unrecognizable to herself. And yes, all this is connected to that. Pain, again. She presses her hip into the sink, trying to stem the ache in her lower abdomen. The movement is subtle, but Roshni registers it.

"You're hurting," she says.

"How do you know?"

"It's constant when you're at this point." Roshni turns the faucet off and dries her hands on her thighs, leaving wet glimmers on her skin. Of course she knows about pain.

"Did anything get better?" Kashmira asks. "When you stopped using it?"

"I don't think so. It's hard to know. At least things haven't gotten worse." Roshni takes one last look in the mirror. She fiddles with an eyelash that has curled the wrong way, then straightens her earrings—diamonds that don't have a right side up. "You know, I was pissed at Sachin before. But he was probably right about trying to get us some help." She pauses. "I mean, I can't believe you're still using this stuff."

"I have to, I don't know what my life is without it. I don't even know who I am anymore."

That's it; that's the truth. It isn't so much about clinging to the product because she loves her new self or her new existence any longer. It's more about being afraid of what will happen if she stops being this person. Will she have anything left? She chokes out a small sob that feels like it's been sitting in her throat for weeks. All her dreams, all her fantasies, they're gone. She is only trying to survive. She can't bear to lose that option too.

"I know," Roshni says. "I *know*. But you have to stop. Come on, Kashmira, you know you're not happy."

What is she to say? Kashmira hesitates, remembering the promises she made. She's been offered another go-round with her second face. After her Concierge call, she messaged every girl she knew and asked them if they wanted in. So many had said yes. Tonight, she plans to sign some of the kathak girls up through the special portal in her app. That way, they'll bypass the wait list and be scheduled for their own appointments. And she'll keep getting her products. But for what? So, she can slather on another version of herself, a person whose perfection has only intensified how empty she has become?

The door swings open, and Roshni and Kashmira end their conversation and busy themselves in the mirror. Side by side, they finish, their bodies moving at the same pace, with the same motions. Water on, soap pumped, hands washed. They don't speak further, but Roshni looks at Kashmira's reflection and her forehead creases with something that seems as poignant as grief.

After dance, the lot of them—the teens from Kashmira's class, those from Roshni's class, and even Hemaji this time because the girls cajoled her into celebrating Roshni's seventeenth—head out for dosas. Kashmira goes along, though she isn't sure she can eat. As hungry as she so often is, food never seems to make that feeling disappear. Perhaps because it runs through her. Perhaps because the pit inside is so large. She isn't sure when she last felt full. Kashmira stirs a straw around in her mango lassi—thick, fresh, a drink her grandmother once made for her a long time ago—and when the waiter pauses by her chair to ask her what she wants for dinner, she shakes her head.

"Not hungry?" Hemaji says from the other side of the table.

"I'm not in the mood for dosa today," Kashmira tells her. "This is fine."

Hemaji purses her lips, but is distracted by another student asking a question. This is when Prithi leans over, her eager whisper staccato against the shell of Kashmira's ear.

"Hey," she says, "when are you going to sign me up for the product? Tonight, right? You said you would."

Roshni, her expression piqued, watches them. She knows Kashmira has a choice to make. If she gives out the product, she'll keep receiving more for herself. If she doesn't, she won't. Either way, she'll be losing things. So will the girls. Such is life, a constant negotiation of who deserves to lose how much, determining who will survive it and who won't. Roshni presses her lips together while Kashmira gestures to the waiter and asks for another lassi. She isn't hungry, but the dairy might cool her stomach. Or it might give her more diarrhea. Who knows.

"Kashmira?" Another girl, Malini, on Kashmira's left side, leans over as the waiter takes away her empty glass. "You are going to sign us up, right?"

Still not answering, Kashmira surveys the table. A few other girls order another drink as well, though some laugh and twist their hair around their fingers self-consciously. These are the ones who've said before that too much sugar causes acne and, oh, all those calories.

While the waiter bustles around the table, Kashmira watches all these faces, the ones that look eagerly for their drinks to come and the ones of girls who stare into their laps. She imagines that each night, before these girls go to sleep, they finish their routines in the bathroom and either stare directly at themselves in the mirror or duck their heads so they won't see. Either way, they each have their own relationship with those features, the ones they see every day. Either way, they deserve to know themselves as they are—not as they naively wish they could be.

"You can't have it," Kashmira says harshly, firmly. She doesn't stumble over the sentence, because the decision to say this is easier to make than she expected. Almost as if she made it some time ago and only had to convince herself to say it. "It's not good for you."

"But it's good for you?" Because Hemaji sits close to them, no one can say anything too loudly, but Kashmira swears Prithi mutters something into her drink, something like the word *bitch*. Louder, she says, "You've got to be kidding me."

"I didn't say it was good for me." Kashmira rests her hands against her stomach. "The truth is—"

Both Prithi and Malini push away from the table. Prithi's chair falters against the carpet, but she makes enough room for herself to stand up anyway. Her hip, clothed in the shimmering fabric she always wears to class, meets Kashmira's eyeline. Then, it backs away, as Prithi tells Malini she needs to use the bathroom. They make their way between all the tables and patrons, until they both head into the single-stall room together. Likely, they're going in to complain about Kashmira and wish bad things on her. It'll make them feel better, but Kashmira could laugh at the idea that they want to find solace in the bathroom. Then suddenly her lips quirk the wrong way, and she finds herself on the verge of crying.

Nothing about this exchange is subtle; no one misses Prithi and Malini's departure, or Kashmira's expression. And so, the whole table looks to the only adult there, Hemaji, to mediate. She doesn't disappoint. Her bun bobs as she says, "Kashmira, what is this? If this is about the recital, you should know I don't run my class this way."

It isn't fair to be called out for this. It isn't fair to be blamed. But everyone at the table is staring at her. A few girls look over to the bathroom and then take hard sips from their straws, as if judging Kashmira. Even if they aren't sure what transpired here, they know something did. And perhaps, because they've known Prithi and Malini longer, they assume that it was Kashmira who was in the wrong. Girlhood is always about solidarity, after all.

"It wasn't about the recital," Kashmira says. "It doesn't matter. I have to go."

She twists out of her chair and slings her purse over her shoulder. In her peripheral vision, she sees Hemaji rising, perhaps to pull her to the side, either to berate her or check on her. Kashmira doesn't think she could take either right now, and so she edges away from the table with a slight, short wave that clearly indicates a request to be left alone.

But then, one girl doesn't heed that warning: Roshni rises.

"Wait, Kashmira," she says. "Don't forget, you're my ride home."

Is she? Kashmira swings around, confused. They never discussed this; but Roshni seems sure. Even as the other kathak girls complain that Roshni is leaving so early from her own dinner, she just smiles and tells them that Lalita doesn't trust her to drive alone yet and so she has to go with Kashmira. Soon enough, the two of them are weaving through the restaurant together, with Roshni so close, she keeps stepping on the back of Kashmira's ankles.

Once outside, though, Roshni doesn't look for Kashmira's car. Instead, they both notice a familiar van at the same time. It's Lalita's vehicle; she has been waiting here the whole time. And so, in a way, Roshni hasn't lied. Her mother doesn't trust her to get home on her own now. Probably Lalita assumes if she isn't around, she'll be disappointed by things turning out wrong again. As Kashmira and Roshni walk through the lot, Lalita's headlights catch both girls and their shadows. Kashmira tries to say hello by waving. Lalita looks away, and honks to hurry Roshni along.

"Your mother hates me now?" Kashmira says.

"You were in the video, and she wants to blame whoever she can for this."

Kashmira scrapes her foot against the gravel. "She should blame herself, too, then."

"I don't know, maybe she does." Roshni rubs her arms, though it isn't cold. Despite having stopped using the product, her body remains concave, and she hunches over the missing space of herself. "It doesn't matter. Hating someone or not won't change her taking me to The Center." She pauses. "You did the right thing in there. The thing I should've done for you."

"You did do it for me. In your own way."

"I think I was too late," Roshni says.

Night swaddles the two of them close. Even with Roshni's mother just a few yards away, it suddenly seems as if they are alone, each waiting for the other to say the right thing. How many times have they abandoned each other over the years? None of these times has been voluntary, and yet. The sting of it. Words can't make sense of what they've seen of each other, but they don't have to just yet. Roshni catapults forward, her arms tight and smothering around Kashmira's neck, but in a good way, like she never wants to let go. Kashmira rests her chin on Roshni's head, right in the part.

"Okay," Roshni says after a while, though it isn't clear if she means that they'll be okay or that everything is already okay or that even if nothing is ever okay, they have to accept that too. "Okay."

Now, she steps back, pointing to her mother's car, saying she does have to go. Kashmira nods. Without her old friend's arms around her, she feels weightless, like she might disappear into the atmosphere.

After Roshni is driven away, Kashmira stands in the parking lot for a long time and wonders what to do with herself.

Two days later, Kashmira stands alone at yet another party. She used to love how many of them there were, one or two every week. Pool parties, drinking games, bonfires. All of it culminating in bodies seeking bodies past midnight, the moon shining high in the sky. Others might have found the consistency boring, but Kashmira remembers each of those nights as discrete, special moments, pivotal events in a series that once heightened her sense of belonging to a group of people who looked so remarkably like her. That was before the blood.

Because spirits make her gut cramp, she sits by the small fire someone started instead of pouring herself punch. The heat from the flames makes patterns on her thighs and soothes her stomach. She needs this; things haven't improved for her, even after giving up the product for a few days. Each time she looks in the mirror, she doesn't recognize herself, despite wearing the features she was born with. Nausea chokes her not only when she sits down to eat, but before and after too. Headaches put her to bed early and a terrible need to go to the bathroom gets her up in the morning. There, on the toilet, she empties herself for twenty minutes at a time. Really, she shouldn't have come to this gathering, but she didn't know what else to do with herself. She doesn't know, right now, who to be. And no one else seems to have the answer. Everyone at this party leaves her sitting alone, and Roshni is in Upstate New York, and Tej is over on the other side of the party, toasting something with another girl, some substitute he chose when he couldn't find Kashmira. Actually, he had found her, had lapped the party and then stood right in front of her, but he recognized nothing about her and moved on as quickly as he had arrived.

She stands, and this is when Sachin comes out of the crowd from god knows where and approaches her. Kashmira doesn't know what he was doing—if he was filming or what—but his expression is tight when he sees her. And he does see her; he recognizes her right away. She wishes she could say the same for herself, and as she thinks this, she feels her vision blur at the edges and darken when her side flares with pain. She reaches out a hand to try and stop herself from falling, but there is nothing to grab. She senses the feeling of hands on her, two hands, touching her, handling her so she can sit again. The hands don't leave her once she is seated and safe. They stroke her back, but she can only feel their pressure, not the intimate contact of skin on skin.

"Kashmira," Sachin says. "Kashmira, can you hear me?"

"I need to make a call," she says. Suddenly, this is the only thing that makes sense to do, the only way to come back to herself. "I need your phone."

His phone, because the man she calls might not pick up if he sees her number. Sachin hesitates, asking her if he can take her home, asking her if she needs to go somewhere else, and if so, who he should call to meet them there. Kashmira shakes her head and asks for his phone so many times that he gives it to her. She enters her father's number deliberately. There, in the middle of the party, amid the cacophony, she waits for him to pick up. And despite the odds, he does.

"Hello?" Vinod says, his voice so low it makes the phone tremble in her hand.

Hello, hello, hello. This does bring her back to herself. But not in the way she had hoped. She sucks in air, trying to stop the worsening pains needling through her. These she can feel. These are the only things she can feel. *Oh god*, she thinks. Oh god. Maybe she even says it to her father, right there, right then. The thought of that makes everything worse, and she fumbles the phone as she hangs up. But that, too, leaves her with something awful: silence, nothingness.

She presses her face into her wrists and cries. Sachin, at her side, whispers that he is taking her home, he is taking her home right now. She lets him. As they stagger through the party to his car, the moon shines above them, so bright, so sharp and clean and sure of itself, it goads her, asking why she can't be the same. *I don't know, I don't know, I don't know, I don't know*, she says in her head.

PART THREE

CHAPTER ELEVEN

Pain overtakes her. It has gotten steadily worse in the five days since her last rager, and now it radiates from her left hip bone into the entirety of her body. She was supposed to have done something about this; after leaving the party, Sachin dropped her off at home and made her promise to tell her mother she wasn't doing well. Kashmira had agreed, though in her confusion she would have agreed to anything. She fell asleep that night without saying anything to Ami, and since then, she has stayed mostly in her room, waiting, just waiting, because she is too scared to do anything else. In her bed, Kashmira rolls her knees tight into her chest. *Stay still*, she wills herself, hoping that if she settles, her body will too. So far, this hasn't worked. Her body as she thought she knew it has disappeared. In its place, anguish. Kashmira turns her face to her pillow as bitter tears run into her nose and mouth. She can't hold still any longer. She can't go on like this. But she has to. She says to herself, *Stay still, stay still*, unsure how loud her voice is or isn't.

This is when she hears the door opening. Ami looks through its crack while Kashmira massages the heel of her hand into her temple, hoping more pressure will alleviate the pounding in her head. With the other hand, she rubs her chest, trying to get at her lungs, which don't seem able to fill as deeply as usual. Her vigorous motions leave her skin a dark, suspicious blush.

"What's the matter?" Ami says. She comes inside, though she stops at the foot of the bed when she scans Kashmira top to bottom with wide eyes. "Kashmira?"

Not wearing her other face has made no difference. For a week, Kashmira has gotten sicker. The bleeding has gotten worse but even as she has considered being honest with her mother, she can't. She is too haunted by the way the doctor at the clinic suggested opening Roshni up and revealing all her insides. Clinical hands judging ravaged organs. Different ones they'd likely look at in her body, but what does it matter? She doesn't want that appraising stare on any part of her; not when she'd rather someone touch her with the understanding that this has gotten so bad not because Kashmira is stupid or negligent, but because she's just trying to make it through best she can. Knowing this, she has texted back brief answers to Sachin, telling him, i'm fine i'm just busy. Knowing this, she has skipped work and stayed in her room, waiting until this moment, when she can't wait anymore. And still, when she speaks, she lies, because that feels safer to do.

"I don't know, probably nothing," Kashmira says. "I don't feel that great, but maybe I just need some juice or something?"

"Just juice? Maybe we should, I don't know, check your temperature?"

Ami twists one hand around the other. Is she asking her daughter, who is so sick, what to do? Suddenly, Kashmira regrets even talking to her mother. Intent on ending the conversation, Kashmira pushes up on her elbows and tries to use her hands to get herself into a fully seated position, but her limbs shake, tiny tremors she can't see but can feel vibrating from her shoulders to her fingertips. She keeps trying. One more launch, one more effort, but instead, collapse. She lays there, expecting to be left alone in this crumpled position, but then Ami puts a hand on Kashmira's forehead.

"Do you feel cold? Open your mouth and put this under your tongue for me," Ami says.

In her mother's hand, a ther-mom-meter, Kashmira realizes, trying to put a name to it. Sometime in the middle of Kashmira's struggle to sit up, Ami must have left the room to rummage in the closet for it. Her mother, who does nothing someone hasn't told her to, is checking for fever. Kashmira covers her face with her hands. It scares her that something must be this wrong.

"It's fine," she says. She doesn't want to be poked or prodded. "I overreacted."

"I have to do this. I have to. Please, Kashmira."

Her mother is using a voice Kashmira has never heard before. But none of this is necessary. Juice is all she asked for. Juice—and someone to take away the vicious sparks of pain in her joints. Ami tells her to open, and Kashmira can't resist her mother wrestling the thermometer into her mouth. Nor can she coax her mouth to spit the thing out. Instead, the thermometer hangs from between her lips. The numbers climb, though not too high. The thermometer beeps loud and long to announce it's finished.

"It's not so bad," Ami says. But then she looks closer at Kashmira's eyes, which have gone blueish in the whites. "But something isn't right. I know it isn't." She says something about the hospital. Kashmira can't make out the words, either because her mother is mumbling or because sounds are hard to concentrate on. What is this? Roshni never talked about her mind not working right, but Kashmira might be more ill than her old friend ever was. She tries harder to listen, and hears her mother say, "Can you get dressed?"

When Ami hands Kashmira a wrinkled shirt that never made it into the drawer, Kashmira finds that she can't hold on to it. It falls into her lap, covering her like another blanket, coaxing her to stay in the bed, to sink down as deep as possible. Kashmira does, and then, instead of following her mother's instructions, she wails something unintelligible even to herself into her pillow. Something like *I don't want to go, I don't want to go.*

She expects Ami to back away from her suffering as she always has. But her mother breathes in deeply, then sits on the edge of the bed to untangle first Kashmira's right arm, then her left from the blanket. Then each leg. There they go, the two of them finding their way. Ami's touch isn't sure, but it's there as she pulls the pillowcase from between Kashmira's teeth.

"You're sick," she says, once Kashmira is free of the covers. Now Ami pulls her daughter's pajama top off her, like she must have done when Kashmira was a toddler. "It's time to get better."

But that's what I've been trying to do, Kashmira tells her—or at least thinks she tells her, but it comes out so strange, so garbled, it's as though Kashmira never said it at all.

The emergency department's waiting room is full, just like the clinic was. They're twenty minutes from home, and Kashmira scans the place for anyone she might know, anyone who might recognize her. No one. Or maybe someone; it's hard to focus on anyone's real face with her confused mind. Anyway, there's somewhere else she is supposed to be. Where? Kashmira imagines all the places from this summer: the cool shallow end of a pool; between a boy's two muscular thighs; the car, as greenery whooshes by and music plays alongside laughter; the Gupta house that still looks as big to her as it did when she was a child; her bedroom, at the mirror, changing her face but not what it has witnessed; the bathroom, sure her insides are all about to escape her while she strains into the pain; another waiting room, just as inscrutable as this one.

Kashmira clutches at her mother's arm, surprised that there is some comfort in the way Ami holds on to her too. Somewhere, a vending machine dispenses a soda. Somewhere, a nurse calls another person's name—or maybe hers, she doesn't know, she never knows. Across the room, someone is vomiting, and Kashmira can't believe it isn't her. Next to her, Ami continually checks the time on her phone, but the numbers barely move.

"We should just go home," Kashmira whispers.

"I don't know what we'd do there," Ami whispers back.

Then, triage. They call her back and never send her out again. The nurse gives Kashmira a warm blanket and an IV that takes three tries to insert because Kashmira's veins are so small—butterfly veins, the nurse says—or maybe "butterfly" is the name of the needle. One of the doctors pats her foot, which somehow wears a yellow sock now instead of the one Ami pulled onto it in the rush to leave the house. The same doctor asks Kashmira to tell him all her symptoms, so she talks to him about the exhaustion, so heavy; and the pain that is, she swears, somewhere around a ten on the scale he asks her about; and the bleeding, quick like a flame sprung from a match, on the tissue paper when she wipes. The more she talks, the more her head lolls back. Her eyes turn into slits she doesn't try to see through.

The doctor nods. He leaves. He returns. He leaves again. Returns again.

This time he says, after many other words, "You need a blood transfusion."

Though Kashmira has already forgotten the doctor's name, she tries to cling to the word "transfusion." The conversation is already moving on, though, as the doctor talks to Ami about consent. They keep talking, and soon after, the nurse comes in holding two bags that are so red, they look fake. Kashmira flinches when the nurse tries to attach the IV in her arm to them, suddenly disgusted by what they're putting in her.

"It's just blood," the nurse says.

"Whose blood?"

"People who want you to get better." The nurse holds Kashmira's shoulder to keep her in place. "Just stay still for me."

The nurse's grip is strong and sure. Kashmira closes her eyes and waits for her veins to burn. They don't. The blood drips into her at a steady pace as the minutes tick by. The doctor is long gone, then the nurse is too. There is time now, it seems, to wait. Ami collapses onto the edge of the bed, keeping her eye on the erratic heart monitor above her daughter's head.

"At least we made it," Ami says.

She talks for a little while about what they'll do next, finally getting to how she needs to call Nikhil and Kashmira shouldn't complain about it because her brother needs to know. Kashmira doesn't respond. She can't, because she is in too much pain. She has been for a long time now. This realization makes her shake. No, not just the realization. Her teeth chatter because she's afraid and cold—so cold. It whirls in her bones, in a cavernous place where one blanket, two blankets can't make a difference.

"What's happening?" Ami says. "Kashmira, what are you doing?"

She isn't doing anything. She just can't stop trembling, even as she wills herself to stare at the ceiling and empty her mind. Then the itching starts, all over, from her thighs to her shoulders to the back of her neck. She claws at her skin. It feels like someone else's, ill-fitting and wrong as it hangs off her body. She scratches faster, until her mother shrieks for a nurse.

Three people come running in. One Kashmira recognizes, two she doesn't. They page a doctor while taking her vital signs. Someone says something about a reaction—maybe allergic, maybe not. They don't know. Someone else says something about getting her to the ICU, a place Kashmira never thought girls her age could end up. It isn't right; none of it is.

"I'm not allergic to anything," Kashmira tries to say, even as a nurse grabs her hands and pushes them to the bed so she'll stop scratching at her face, her neck, her chest. "You don't have to take me away."

Kashmira isn't sure if she is slurring her words or not. It doesn't seem to matter. Someone says they have to go to be safe, a nurse detaches the blood bag from her IV, and someone else toes the brakes under the bed. Down the hall they go, and Kashmira's head aches from the whooshing lights, bright as they are. Everything moves fast and slow at the same time. She isn't sure if her mother is there, but someone takes her into a new room, where new nurses shake her and demand she sit up so they can clean her whole body with a small sponge and hook her up to the monitors again. After, they make her jerk her hips up to pee and show them she can. The doctors arrive to check everything in rapid succession, from her heart rate to the slight swelling in her ankles. They give instructions Kashmira can't understand. Then they nod their heads, pat her arm, and tell the nurses they can darken the lights.

Only after this is there some quiet, though that frightens Kashmira as much as the chaos did. She doesn't know what to expect in this silence, and when a nurse leans over her to adjust her pillow, Kashmira raises one heavy hand and tries to touch this woman's shoulder. She misses, and her arm falls back to the bed. Still, she tries again and again, because though the nurse doesn't notice, Kashmira needs her attention, needs to ask—though it feels hard to get anything out from behind her clenched teeth: *Is this what it feels like to die?*

It isn't clear what is a dream and what isn't.

A nightmare, waking, dreaming, a nightmare, sleeping. Strange and new. Strange and horrible. Kashmira sees faces she recognizes and faces she doesn't. Some nurses start off as strangers then become familiar, both in their features and in their movements. They check her pulse, her oxygen, her temperature. They adjust blankets. They lift her arm to scan her wristband, then set it down. One seems angry when she calls for help, and he tells her to please calm down when she starts clenching her hands in the flimsy sheets, asking for someone to come. When they ask her who she wants, Kashmira doesn't know. Instead, she sobs. Later, there is her mother, who sits in the corner and watches. There is her brother, who watches over her, his brows contorted. There is Sachin, adjusting the lens of his video camera, and Roshni, whispering, *I told you so*. Doctors come by too, to check her legs and take notes. Sometimes she swears she sees her father, then her dead grandparents hovering at the edge of the room, waiting for someone to open a door so they can linger in the doorway—one foot far gone, the other not. Every so often, she even sees her own face—the new one transposed over the old one and then vice versa. Both of them contorted in pain.

    Maybe it's right not to know what's real. For so long, she has been living as two selves, trying so hard to delineate between them, as though she could ever succeed. One time, in the middle of the night when she is no longer crying but everything still feels surreal and weird, Kashmira considers pulling the IV out of her arm just to see what would happen. No one would appreciate it, because she would make a mess on the floor with the *plink-plink* of her blood. Trails of it, leading back to her. And then all those people would rush to her and stare right into her naked face. But that isn't where the ugliness is anymore, is it? Inside her, things are swelling painfully, taking up spaces that her bones, her veins, her organs need. Inside her is something she can't ignore any longer. That thought is hers, until it isn't. She holds on to very few things here, in the place they call the I-C-U.

SERIES OF SHOTS – EVOLVOIR EMPLOYEES

A) CLIENT CARE TEAM MEMBER dabs at her eyes with a tissue. She blows her nose, but delicately.
B) PRODUCT GROWTH TEAM MEMBER looks through old Yukiko VidMos. He hearts each one.
C) PEOPLE TEAM MEMBER walks through the Evolvoir halls looking lost. She looks out the window and smiles sadly.

FADE TO:
CLIENT CARE TEAM MEMBER, PRODUCT GROWTH TEAM MEMBER, PEOPLE TEAM MEMBER dab ReNuLook cream on their cheeks. Faces twist, then settle. Features, not just sharpened, but surgically recut. The women look like a girl who once graced screens: Yukiko.

CHYRON TEXT: WE ARE YOUR BEAUTY. WE EVOLVE OURSELVES TO EMBRACE YOU. LIVE FREE. WE LOVE YOU.

CLIENT CARE TEAM MEMBER, PRODUCT GROWTH TEAM MEMBER, PEOPLE TEAM MEMBER touch their cheeks in awe.

CHAPTER TWELVE

How, Nikhil wonders, is the time after a coworker's death meant to pass? Yukiko's desk, a gravesite, twelve days after her passing. Her now-obsolete username lingers on TaskSquad channels and her old calendar invites still chime, reminding everyone of meetings that now don't have agendas. No one declines, out of respect. Then again, no one responds at all, and the work goes on while computer keys clack and coffee spurts out of the machine and the air-conditioning runs so high that everyone is shivering, though no one complains. When Nikhil messages Keon to ask about an office memorial at the very least, he gets exactly the kind of reply he should have expected:

—the people team is worried about how triggering the whole thing is. we're holding off, especially with the big autumn into holidays buying season we're preparing for.

Triggering, yes. Like her sister, Yukiko died suddenly; though instead of a car accident, her cause of death is a pulmonary embolism. Online, fans speculate if it could have been anything—something darker. Those rumors have reached the office, too, and Nikhil hears whispers here and there about what was said at the last Operation Wellness Team meeting. But only Nikhil knows the full truth of what Yukiko speculated about her health—her mortality—at the art gallery just hours before her passing. The memory of that night weighs on Nikhil, and at home, alone, he can't sleep. He can't stop thinking about her, curved into him, hugging his shoulders, her sad, weepy breath colliding with his skin. He can't stop thinking about how he called emergency services and then rode in the ambulance with her and then sat in the waiting room until her parents got there. He can't stop thinking about what to do with the information she gave him. Nikhil considers calling Erin, but he has nothing to give her except the anecdote about the gallery. He considers looking for some kind of paper trail, some way to substantiate Yukiko's claims about the product, but he doesn't know where to start. Sitting at his desk in his and Michael's shared cubicle, he replays Yukiko's old videos and rests his head in his hand.

"You know, it's okay if you're grieving," Michael says from the other side of the desk. He pulls his headphones off and assesses Nikhil. "Yeah, we only knew her for a few weeks, but it's still death. It still hits hard."

Nikhil blinks. It's one of the few days he and Michael are in the office at the same time. Still, Michael was the one who texted him about seeing Yukiko's passing announced in TaskSquad. Her death had occurred just after Nikhil had left the hospital and was announced online two days later. Normally, Nikhil would have responded quickly, glad to hear from the other man. But he didn't know what to say to this news. Even now, he isn't sure how to reply. How can he explicate the twisting emotions inside him? The reality is that he didn't know Yukiko well, even if he was moved by her work. The reality is that their relative distance from each other allows him to go on without her, and yet their relative closeness, after that night in the gallery, means he knows more than before and he feels he must do something with that information. The reality is that, in the end, the only reason Yukiko told him any of that was because he stopped trying to take over and fix things, and he worries that if he starts chasing after questions—what happened to Yukiko, who was responsible, how many others are like her, what could he do to stop this—he'll just be falling into the same trap of seeking control and messing up again. In the gallery, Yukiko had said she knew Nikhil would be on her side, but what did she mean by that? What did she want from him?

"There was something going on with her," Nikhil says in a hard whisper. "She was sick, Michael, because of the products. And I don't know what to do. I don't."

Michael's mouth thins, and Nikhil imagines that his mind is routing him back to that moment with Jordie, when she brought up clients getting sick. That moment when she'd turned to Yukiko, but then Keon had stepped in. The rumors that ensued after, though they'd quieted. But then, without Yukiko's testimony all of this is so unbelievable. And that must be what Michael lands on, because he says, "Are you sure you're not just trying to find a problem to fix, Nikhil? As a way to not feel anything?"

Maybe it's fair that Michael assumes this. After getting over the shock of Yukiko's passing, Nikhil had wanted to tell Michael that he'd taken his advice and talked to Yukiko one-on-one. He'd wanted to tell Michael everything about the conversation. But he isn't sure if Yukiko would've wanted him to. They'd left things so nebulous, she and Nikhil. Even now, Nikhil wonders if revealing to Michael that she really was sick due to the products is some violation of Yukiko's last wishes. The problem, though, is that because of all this hesitation Michael doesn't know what happened in the gallery that night—and thus he imagines that Nikhil hasn't changed at all in the last twelve days.

"I'm not sure what I'm doing," Nikhil says. "But if there are things I know, don't I have to do something? Like, I don't know, investigate? Go after this place? Use the media?"

He means the question sincerely, but Michael seems to take it as an opening to another argument—one that he doesn't wish to participate in. He picks up the strap of his messenger bag and slings it over his shoulder. As he does, he shakes his head slightly and says, "You've always been about big, business-world solutions, Nikhil. Isn't that how this whole thing started?"

He is turning. And as Michael swivels out of the cubicle, Nikhil has a sudden realization. That he and Michael are more similar than either of them realized: They are stubborn, and so confident that the way they think things should be done is the only way. Michael may not put people in boxes, but he does box up what he thinks it means to deal with them. To him, people just need people. Moments of connection, intimacy. And of course, that's what so many do crave. But there are still systems of power, of privilege, of industry, of business, of politics, of history, of capital looming large over everyone, including Michael, including Nikhil. Maybe Nikhil had been wrong to try to push a product—a manufactured thing, made to be sold—to solve the dysfunctional mental health system in this country. But if it hadn't been him, there still would have been Larissa, trying to change the world with her entrepreneurial dreams. There still is Larissa and the company. What is it, then, that they must do?

"Good luck out there," Michael says as he steps into the hallway.

Nikhil nods, thinking he would like to say it back.

⁂

Later that day, outside Nikhil's apartment, Erin Frankel waits for him, clutching her bag to her chest while looking down both sides of the street like she fears she'll miss Nikhil if she isn't paying attention. On seeing Nikhil, she waves. The gesture is so big that at least three other people on the street falter, thinking she must be someone they know.

"You weren't answering your phone," she says.

"I was on the train," Nikhil says. He feels tired after the work day, most of which he has spent debating his next actions. "How did you find my place, Erin?"

"I'm good at looking for people." She follows him up his stoop. "How are you? I know about Yukiko."

The way Erin says it doesn't make sense. Everyone who knew about Yukiko also knows about her death. Erin herself reported on it just ten days ago, two days after it happened. Somehow, Erin had even gotten an interview with Yukiko's grieving parents, but Nikhil had clicked out of the article, unable to read about them asking why and how this had happened to her. He reaches past Erin to unlock the door to his building, then turns and asks, "Do you know something? Something you haven't printed yet?"

Erin nods. "I have something for you."

She follows him up to his fourth-floor walk-up, and both of them are panting by the time they get inside. In the studio, Erin doesn't pause to look around his apartment or comment on the sparseness of his furniture. Instead, she settles on the bed and opens her bag to pull out a laptop, a notebook, and a cell phone Nikhil has seen before—its case a disconcerting optical illusion, its black and white lines somehow curving even when they are straight.

"Why do you have this?" he says, eyeing Yukiko's phone.

Apparently, the reason Yukiko's parents ever spoke with Erin for an interview was because of the phone. They'd been in the emergency department with their daughter when she told them that she wasn't sure she would be around for much longer. She asked that they make sure to give her device to Erin, begged until both parents had said yes. But then, with all the immediate postmortem arrangements, they forgot to actually complete the handover. It was lucky that Erin contacted them for the interview, which gave them an opportunity to give her Yukiko's phone. Since then, Erin has gone through it at least ten times. She swipes through the screens, showing Nikhil that much of the phone has been wiped, except for the email client, a cloud storage app, and VidMo. According to her, the last app is where the most vital data lives.

"In the drafts folder," she says.

Nikhil watches over Erin's shoulder as she navigates to Yukiko's profile page. There, a red notification badge shows unread messages in her private inbox—Erin had read some last night, but more keep coming in—and new likes and comments. Even now, people are watching her, engaging with her. Perhaps more so, even, than they had before her death. Erin ignores all this and swipes left to open the drafts. There, the screen displays a grid of videos, ready to be posted. Except the clips aren't of Yukiko, but of others who Nikhil doesn't recognize.

"She left a note for me," Erin says. "Asking me to show you this too."

Erin plays each clip in succession. The people, mostly women, have been filmed documentary style, speaking to a faceless person behind the camera. They talk about Evolvoir. They talk about getting off the wait list. So many of them were ecstatic to be chosen. They talk of wearing new faces that, at first, felt fitting. Felt right. But slowly those new faces leeched something from them. They talk of bleeding and exhaustion. They talk of pressing their hands against mirrors and crying when they see what has become of their bodies. They ask why they can't stop using the product, even when it hurts. By the time Erin and Nikhil finish watching the videos, the dull apartment feels claustrophobic. It's past midnight, and Nikhil's mind is all lethargic drift, both because of the late hour and the devastation they've heard about over and over again.

"Do you realize what she was doing?" Erin asks. Undercutting her question are the clips, replaying, but she doesn't stop them. Someone says, *I wasn't sure if what was happening to me was real.* Other people say, *I didn't want to believe it, but there's something happening to me* and *I'm so glad you reached out* and *I just ignored it until I couldn't ignore it anymore* and *I just kept hurting and hurting until I was sure I was going to die.* "Do you see what all this is?"

"Evidence," Nikhil says, through a stiff jaw.

He hadn't realized the immense inescapable breadth of all this. He knew Yukiko's story. He knew Jordie had one sick client. But this? This is more than he ever expected. He wonders, then, if in the gallery she had been testing him, making sure he could handle her story before giving him access to the others. He had passed, it seems, but he doesn't know what to hear in the sharing of these videos, other than that this is a disaster, one that he helped perpetuate.

Nikhil blows his breath out and looks around the apartment. He wishes the apartment were bigger, expansive enough to imagine Yukiko still alive in it. She would be there herself, showing them these videos. But then, it's the size it's always been: barely big enough for one—let alone two, let alone three.

⁂

That night, Nikhil's phone vibrates hard and wakes him and Erin. kashmira is in the icu, his mother's first text says. The second reads, please come home.

His body understands the words first. Horror rides high in his chest, even as his mind grapples with what is on his screen. It takes three long minutes for him to write back, what do you mean she's in the icu? Then he calls Ami, hoping to get faster answers. She doesn't pick up, not even when he calls a second time.

"Who is it?" Erin says. She groans and presses her forearm against her forehead while Nikhil texts his mother again with his brightness all the way up. "Who're you talking to this late?"

Nikhil glances at Erin, who fell asleep at the foot of his bed, while he tucked up toward its head. They'd ended up here by accident after Erin demanded they rewatch all the clips on Yukiko's phone while simultaneously reviewing her first watch notes about them. That part of the night feels far away now, even though it was only a few hours ago. But then, he hadn't ever expected a message like this.

"It's my mom. My sister is in the hospital," he says, somehow.

Three dots appear on his screen, followed by a long text. At first, an explanation of what happened—how Ami found Kashmira sick in her bed—then some clinical jargon Nikhil is familiar with but only in oblique terms. She says things like blood transfusions, reactions, numbers, cells. Because she works in the hospital, she actually understands some of what the doctor is saying. But Nikhil can't understand why Ami didn't call him as soon as Kashmira was taken back for triage in the emergency department. He gets out of bed to throw things into a duffel bag.

"What's wrong with her?" Erin says.

Mentally, Nikhil lists what he'll need to pack instead of answering. Two pairs of pants and four shirts and enough underwear for a week, at least. He can wash clothes at his mother's house. How about deodorant, a toothbrush, floss? He'll leave his razor behind, and probably his shampoo, but he can't forget his phone charger and laptop. The duffel bag is half full already, but he drops to the edge of the mattress and puts his head in his hands, overwhelmed. She's his sister. His little sister, who he has spent his whole life trying to protect.

Behind him, Erin, ever nosy, ever a journalist, has grabbed his phone. She reads the text messages and swears. Nikhil only nods. He is imagining the worst thing: Kashmira's pale face under hospital sheets, her body shutting down, the doctors not sure what to do with her. He imagines all that and it guts him. He has already felt her absence this summer—over that damn box, over their damn father—but he can't bear the true loss of her. This sister, who he has always held so close in his heart, if not his arms. His head is suddenly light. His feet are suddenly tapping of their own accord. Erin kneels on the bed and tentatively nudges Nikhil's shoulder from behind.

"Nikhil? Take a breath," Erin says. "In and out."

He can't. To breathe would be to release the pressure sitting inside his chest. To breathe would be to know what to do next. Michael says to grieve. Erin says to look at the evidence in front of him. Instinct says to run toward his sister and never look back.

※

The early morning B to the E takes Nikhil to Penn Station; the Amtrak takes him into Philadelphia; the rideshare takes him to sleepy, suburban Marlton. Partway through the ride to his mother's, Erin texts him and promises she'll handle what she can with Yukiko's phone. She tells him to just be on top of things at home, and he texts back: easier said than done.

The car drops Nikhil off in the parking lot near his mother's apartment. A couple walks by with their wirehaired dog. The woman is pregnant. Across the street, another woman is trying to talk on the phone while yelling at her children. They've been bouncing a basketball too hard, and it hits one of them in the face. But then a car parks next to the apartment, and a man gets out. The kids shriek and let the ball go. They tumble over each other to reach him, clamoring for a hug, while Nikhil walks on, up to the apartment. It's impossible for him not to think about his own father, who walked these same streets for years, sometimes to meet his family, sometimes to turn away from them. Nikhil wonders if his back stoops the same way, if the neighbors are wondering whether Vinod has finally returned after a year and a half. He wouldn't blame them if they do.

The apartment is as he remembers it. His mother has kept up her ritual with the flowers, though her most recent bouquet has wilted. Nikhil drains the water from the vase and throws the flowers away. He knows he should go straight to the hospital to meet Ami, but he worries about what to do once he gets there. Should he talk to the ICU doctors? Should he sit quietly and just try to take it in? He's so unsure, and it feels good, instead, to do something more obviously helpful around the apartment. He looks for more tasks. He checks the cupboards to make sure the dishes are clean. He restocks the paper towels and the toilet paper. He opens all the doors to see what else can be done: a closet, his mother's bedroom, another closet, and, finally, his sister's room.

Kashmira has kept her space messy and chaotic since they were children. That part hasn't changed, but now there are new posters on the walls, new books on her bedside table, new clothes in the closet. Nikhil slides farther through the door. How much of her life has changed in the few months he hasn't talked to her. And now—his presence here in her space is invasive, he realizes. But as he turns to leave, he sees a familiar tube on the dresser. Glass, with Evolvoir scrawled on the side in teal. Underneath, in block letters, the word RENULOOK. *No*, he thinks, and then picks the tube up and tries to gauge how much of the product she's used. By weight, it seems most of it. *No*, he thinks again.

His hand works of its own accord. Nikhil drops the tube, and it hits the side of the dresser at an angle that'll probably leave a crack. He wants to leave it there. He wants to let the product seep out and disappear for good. But it might have something to do with why Kashmira was hospitalized. Nikhil picks the tube up, hating that he has to. As he leaves the room, he shuts the bedroom door hard. His hand is slick, and so is the doorknob.

Back in the kitchen, he paces, wondering when Kashmira got off the wait list. He hadn't seen her name in the Consumer Database before. What will he find now? Remembering that he can, he opens his work laptop and logs into the matrix, hoping that maybe he won't find Kashmira there at all. Hoping that this was a mistake, and that this was someone else's product, left in Kashmira room by accident. Nikhil opens the search function, the one where he can input a name. M-E-H-T-A, he writes. K-A-S-H-M-I-R-A. He hits Go so many times the spreadsheet lags as it reloads, but then the purchases from the last few months populate.

Then, there it is: His sister's name.

At first, her account was connected to that of Roshni Gupta, who Nikhil didn't know she was talking to. It's an anomaly, this linked account arrangement, and it's why Nikhil never noticed Kashmira on the client list before. But her name is starkly present now, because she became a primary account holder when—he falters, seeing a colored tag by Kashmira's name—she joined the BBB. That's how she got her last batch of products, through an initiative he helped start.

Nikhil digs his fingers into his temples, like claws. Everything is coming together, just as it is coming apart. Kashmira is sick, and he can't pretend that isn't true. He has to be by her side, he has to linger in these moments with her, as Michael would tell him to. But in those moments he can't forget that her sickness very well may be one other part of the investigation Erin is undertaking at this very moment. Kashmira is both sides of this equation, as maybe Nikhil also has to be. But there is a balance here that he needs to make—if he can.

He remembers suddenly that he is expected at the hospital. He has to go.

---

you can see her now, his mother texts a moment later, just as he starts searching for the keys to Kashmira's car.

According to the rest of the message, Kashmira has been downgraded from the ICU to the general ward, meaning she can have visitors. Nikhil won't just be going to the hospital to meet Ami; he'll get to sit with Kashmira too. Knowing this, he throws himself further into the search for the keys, and when he finds them, he half jogs to the car itself. He makes the drive anxiously, and ends up taking two wrong turns on the highway. But he makes it. Once inside the labyrinthine hospital building, he asks staff members in every corridor for directions until he finally finds the right elevator to Kashmira's wing—and there, her room. Its door is ajar, as if waiting for him, but he hesitates. Earlier, he'd been so focused on arriving, he hadn't thought about what it would be like to be here, amid the antiseptic air.

Ami sees him through the gap in the doorway. She waves him in, and then there he is, in the room. As he enters, his sister makes a guttural sound and turns away from him.

"You're here," Ami says. "Finally."

"I left as soon as I could," he says.

Though he talks to Ami, he stares at Kashmira, small in the hospital bed. She keeps her thin shoulders straight, and even though her collarbones seem to undulate under her skin, she breathes in long, forceful breaths that insist he notice their presence. He doesn't recognize this illness on her. But at least he recognizes her face. That might not have been true before this hospital visit, when she was still using the product that put her in this bed. In his chest, agony.

Right then, his mother comes in for a hug, though he is surprised when she pulls away after just a moment or so. No tears from Ami dampen his shirt; his mother's eyes are wet-looking, but she doesn't cry on him. Instead, she goes through what the doctors have said: Kashmira has high levels of inflammatory markers in her bloodstream, and this likely has something to do with why her gastrointestinal tract has been bleeding. They need to keep doing tests, though, before coming to any conclusion. In the meantime, they've put her on IV steroids.

"Is the bleeding why you were in the ICU?" he asks Kashmira.

Ami answers because his sister refuses to. In the emergency department, Kashmira's blood panel also showed low hemoglobin—due to the prolonged bleeding most likely—and the doctors thought a blood transfusion would be best. But Kashmira's body didn't take well to it. Her allergic reaction led her to shake and itch, to the point that everyone knew something had to be wrong. The doctor ordered her into the ICU, though it was ultimately mostly for monitoring. The experience, Ami says, was harrowing.

"I left your father a message," Ami says. "He texted me this."

She passes him her phone. Vinod has written: i would only make things worse if i came, please send her my thoughts. He doesn't even write "love," though in a way, Nikhil appreciates that. It's not that he doesn't think his father feels that type of affection, but more that Nikhil knows he isn't capable of accepting his children as wholly as he needs to if he wants to say that word. That generational curse, the one Nikhil hopes to break. But there are many things he wants to do with his sister, for his sister—and wanting is easier than doing.

"He isn't coming," Kashmira says. She turns on her side to hide in her pillow. Her voice is muffled. "Dad isn't. You didn't have to either. No one had to."

"Kashmira," their mother says. "We talked about this. He's your brother."

Nikhil says, "You know I wasn't going to stay away."

But maybe she doesn't know. Nikhil sits on the side of Kashmira's bed. Her leg, next to him, moves incrementally away. He falters, unsure if he should reach out and move a strand of hair from her face. Her head lolls slightly, like she isn't quite all here.

"We have a lot to talk about," he says.

It's the wrong thing to say. Her expression closes even further, until it looks vacant.

CHAPTER THIRTEEN

The phlebotomist comes in the morning to draw blood. The nurse comes at nine to dole out her medication. The cafeteria sends up breakfast. Today is Kashmira's first full day in the regular wing, and she isn't sure how she likes it. This white-walled reality holds her and her brother and her mother together, but tentatively—and sometimes it seems like more than holding, like being closed in.

"Rounds started," Ami says. She moves greasy hair from Kashmira's forehead. There's much to orient themselves to, and this version of their mother is one of them. Something about being away from their apartment seems to have triggered a maternal instinct in her. A necessary thing to have right now, since Vinod hasn't flown back to Jersey to see his daughter. Ami texts him updates, but usually tosses her phone to the side after these exchanges. Almost like these messages are a formality, something to get through before she can focus on more important things. Ami has never interacted with Vinod like this before, and it puts Kashmira on edge. Her mother says, "I saw a doctor go across the hall. He'll be here soon."

She's right. Dr. Wilkes, a tall, slim man in a white coat, comes into Kashmira's room a few minutes later. He introduced himself yesterday as a family doctor who specializes in bringing specialties together—but outside of this witticism, Dr. Wilkes operates primarily in facts. He has already gone through Kashmira's medical history and now checks her chart see what the gastroenterologist, who saw her earlier today, documented.

"We got some of the infectious disease tests back, and those are all negative, so that's a start," he says. He's gentler than the doctor Roshni saw at the clinic but also patriarchal and procedural. Kashmira tries not to think about how many tests he might make her do, and consequently what he will see in her, if he says they need to look inside somehow, some way. He says, "Your body seems to have stabilized after the blood transfusion. The IV steroids they started you on in the ICU are probably helping with that. But you're still anemic, so we'll watch that. We're also going to do some other tests to see what else we can uncover about your condition."

Nikhil, who has been gazing down at the parking lot, crosses the room. He stands next to Kashmira and watches her. Kashmira tenses. When Nikhil arrived yesterday, she was overwhelmed not only by his presence, but by all that had happened to her in the hospital thus far. Since then, she has stabilized, and can think about her brother's arrival here. She's glad that he came. For all that's happened between them, she can't imagine going through this without her brother. At the same time, she does know Nikhil as volatile, and she worries what he'll do—when he'll get mean with her. Now, standing beside her, he looks at her like he's waiting for her to say something—and she doesn't know what.

When Kashmira tucks her chin, and Nikhil seems to take this as a sign to interject. Slowly, awkwardly, as if he isn't sure he should, he says, "She probably doesn't want me to say this, but she already knows what caused it." Nikhil slides his fingers along the wires that keep track of Kashmira's heart rate. She swears the electrical activity jumps when he asks, "You've been using those Evolvoir products, haven't you?"

At first, Kashmira thinks he is guessing—though she doesn't understand why he'd come to this theory at all—but then he reaches for a bag she hadn't seen him bring in. He pulls out a tube of product, one that is familiar to her.

"What is that?" Ami says.

Nikhil hands the product to Dr. Wilkes. The doctor twists it open and pours too much into his palm. Gold cream, with a luminescent sheen. Clean, smooth, the best product in the world, some would say. Dr. Wilkes holds his hand up to the harsh hospital light, then shrugs and washes it in the nearby sink.

"It's a cream?" Dr. Wilkes says. "A beauty product?"

Nikhil tells the doctor of things Kashmira never expected him to know: how the product works, how people have used it to change their faces completely, how sick it makes them. He discusses the symptoms in depth, and when he does, his face pulls into itself, sourly, painfully, as if something squeezes inside him uncomfortably.

"How do you even know what it does?" Kashmira says. She pulls her blanket up past her chin and to her mouth. She bites at a floss-like thread that has come unwoven. "Or what it might do."

His response is flat. "I've worked at Evolvoir for three months. I've seen what it can do."

"Nikhil," Ami says. "I don't understand."

Kashmira slumps. Her hair clings to the hospital bed, leaving it sticking up with static. All this time, he was at Evolvoir. Because he had yelled at her, because she refused to talk to him, she never knew. But what if it hadn't been like that? What if each of them and their relationship hadn't become a casualty of their father's cruelty. Kashmira dares a look at her brother. In him, she mostly sees their mother—but he also has features that match her own. By changing her face, Kashmira had lost Nikhil, too, and though she hadn't recognized it at the time, the anguish of that sat in her as well. Her stomach lurches, and the pain that streaks through her feels like her body saying, *Exactly, exactly, exactly*.

When Nikhil speaks again, he closes his eyes and his mouth trembles a little, and she wonders if he already knows the answer to the question he is asking. He says, anyway, "Why didn't you come to me?"

"How could I?" Kashmira says. "What if you didn't understand?"

Maybe he hears what else she means by that. *What if you abandoned me again?* He must, because his breath comes out as staccato, as panicked, as hers. This panic, so visible in him, echoes in every part of her: in the blood that hammers so hard and then leaks out of her, in the bones that are supposed to help her stand strong but have been aching in their pulpy centers, in the coiled organ inside her that grows puffy with inflammation and spits up angry pus. All this terror, apparently so connected. Nikhil and Kashmira stare at each other, but neither of them opens their mouth again.

Dr. Wilkes clears his throat. Their tension isn't his. He has a job to do, other patients to see, and after telling them that unfortunately beauty products aren't often carefully vetted and that he'll make a note in her chart, he says he also wants to investigate some other pathways. He puts the product back near Kashmira's bag. Then he motions for Nikhil to move so he can get closer to her and press the cold metal disk of his stethoscope to her.

"Here we go," the doctor says, listening to her heart and lungs. Everyone is quiet, and Kashmira can almost sense the *thump-thump* coming from her. Good, perhaps? Or perhaps not. She isn't sure what the doctor hears, but he pulls back and says just one more thing: "Listen, this place is going to bring up a lot of emotions. All you need to know is that all of that's allowed."

There are tests, many tests, but the worst is the colonoscopy, before which she drinks bottles of laxative prep solution and collapses on the toilet for hours, emptying herself.

It begins on her second day out of the ICU. The nurses have her on a liquid diet, and then she moves to the first of the two bouts of liquid. Kashmira drinks the prep solution without tasting it. When she mentions this, the night nurse tells her it's lucky her taste buds are so numb; she herself vomits every time she has to have a colonoscopy. Later, when Kashmira sits alone on the toilet, letting yellow bile laced with blood gush out of her, she notices how the numbness extends even to the way her stomach cramps and releases now. Her body is no longer hers. Maybe she's just muscles and bone to be manipulated by phlebotomists or radiologists or anesthesiologists readying her as she falls asleep so doctors can take long looks inside her.

The next morning, early, she wakes up from a fitful sleep and drinks the second round of liquid. All to start the process again. This time, when her stomach settles some, she feels so exhausted and so filthy, she decides to wash up despite how unsteady she is on her feet. At least there is a shower in the corner of her small hospital bathroom. In it, a dial says how hot the water can go, up to one hundred degrees, but it doesn't warm much except a small semicircle around her body. If Kashmira steps out too far to try to grab the shampoo her mother brought from home, she gets goosebumps immediately. Ami knocks on the door, checking in to see if she is upright, if she is okay, if she needs help.

"I'm okay, I guess," Kashmira says, still unsure how to respond to this new parent of hers.

As she cleans, she touches many uglinesses. Her matted hair; her face, littered with scabs from picked-at acne; her armpit folds, developing a white and smelly film. But then she stretches her arms up as high as they can go—ignoring the way her shoulders click and groan, begging her to be careful—her body shudders, and she flings herself at the toilet once again. Naked and cold, she huddles over it, shivering. Once enough time has passed, she stands and turns the shower off. Her body can't tolerate even that much right now.

Kashmira dresses in a fresh gown and a new pair of socks, complete with small pads on the bottom to prevent slips. Inspecting her reflection in the mirror, she touches her cheek, then strokes a line across her face, down to her jaw, over her lips, to her temple, over her eyebrows. She sees her father in every inch of her countenance. Her awareness of herself is returning, and as much as she hates this, she is grateful too. Because with it comes the history of her identity. Her father and everything that came with him and before him—that is so much of who she really is. It feels sick to have it embedded in her, and yet, better than not having it there at all. Kashmira brushes her teeth with the tiny toothpaste and gargles with the mouthwash the hospital provides. Her mouth smells better, at least.

Back on her bed, Kashmira waits for transport. Next to her, her phone is full of texts from people who are worried about her. Roshni, who has just come back from orientation at The Center and now has access to her phone. Sachin, too. Kashmira weighs the device in her hand and thinks about what to say back. The girl she once was would have sent a photo of herself at an artful angle, smiling despite it all. In the hospital, there is no good light. To Roshni she writes, well, i ended up in my own shithole. To Sachin, she sends, you don't know what it meant to me, what you did the other night. Then she drops the phone to the bed instead of waiting for replies to this vulnerability. She is already embarrassed but can't take back the truth.

Perhaps seeing Kashmira's expression, Ami—her eyes still gummy though she awoke with Kashmira hours ago—sits on the bed and presses her cheek against the crown of Kashmira's head. She says, "Everything is going to be okay, Kashmira. Trust me."

"Trust you?" Kashmira stiffens. "I don't even know you right now. This isn't like you, Mom."

Ami pauses, then raises her head. Kashmira finds she both appreciates this distance—which is what she is used to—and misses the ampleness of her mother's cheek against her scalp.

Ami says, "It's different here, so I have to be different. I have to see things as they are, not what I wish they were. Your father isn't here, but I am." She pauses, as if to let herself take this in. "You know, being here, away from the house, it's easier to see things as they are. You needed me, and I was there. But your father won't even come for a visit. But that makes sense. He never was there when it counted, was he? Only when it was convenient for him."

It's surreal hearing her mother talk like this. For a moment, Kashmira isn't even sure of who the woman she is talking to is. But then her mother puts her cheek back down on Kashmira's head, and the weight of it feels familiar, and Kashmira wonders if maybe she remembers it from when she was a baby and her mother held her close like this and she was too young to ever think Ami would let go.

Ami says, "How do you feel?"

"I don't know," Kashmira tells her. "Ready, I guess?"

And then transport arrives, and they seem to agree: She is ready, or if she isn't, it's time for her to be. Chipper even at seven in the morning, they beam at her, and ask her if she comes here often. What's funny isn't the joke, but how they crack themselves up laughing—and Kashmira joins them, because what else is there to do? But though they jest, their movements are precise as they tuck warm blankets under her sides, as they kick up the locks and ready her to go.

Transport makes the turn out of the room. The hall looks bright, and suddenly Kashmira feels a great forward momentum as they push her down past room after room. The dark bathroom is behind her; she has shot off, far away. Ahead of her, the procedure room, where people navigate the space with purpose, even while talking about their vacation plans for next month. A man wearing a surgeon's cap waits to set up Kashmira's anesthesia. He greets her with a high-five, while someone else hooks her up to the monitor. A third person shifts her to her left side, so she'll be in position for the scope. As Kashmira balances on her hip, she feels a sudden fear, realizing it's now really happening: in just a moment, the doctor will insert a camera into her, in just a moment he'll be thinking about the biopsies he needs to take of the inflamed tissue.

"It'll be okay," a nurse says to her, picking up on her suddenly tense body. She nudges Kashmira. "I was nervous before my first one too. But you'll get some really good pictures after. I bet you've never seen the inside of a colon."

Kashmira relaxes slightly. There, on the gurney, they look at her without horror. The twistedness inside her doesn't scare them; it's their job to look at it straight on, as just a condition of her body that must be addressed. She breathes, shows she can handle this too, and that same nurse leans over and tells Kashmira the anesthesia is starting. She'll feel it, in just a second. Kashmira nods, and then she does feel it. It starts with the scent of gas in her mouth and ends with a slow descent into quiet.

In the afternoons, Kashmira gets a notification that her test results are ready. They are the numbers from her daily blood draw, and they populate her phone screen sometimes even before Dr. Wilkes sees them. She notes what is high and what is low and tries to imagine what Dr. Wilkes must think. He isn't afraid of these values, she understands. To him, they are what they are.

Today she opens the app just as Dr. Wilkes knocks. The three of them—Nikhil, Ami, and Kashmira—look up and beckon him inside without tidying themselves or any part of the room. They've gotten used to his presence, the clipped reports he gives. The visits give their days a sense of structure and their understanding of this crisis a sense of scope.

"I heard you did well with the colonoscopy earlier," he says. "Tolerated it fine?"

"I think so," Kashmira says. When she got out of the procedure, the gastroenterologist said something to her and Ami in recovery, but neither of them understood exactly what he meant. They'd been waiting for Dr. Wilkes since, to explain in his measured way. "Why? What were the results?"

Dr. Wilkes stands at the edge of her bed and angles his glasses down his nose. The gesture looks serious, and Kashmira pulls her legs to her chest, waiting. In careful language, using phrases like "we believe" and "things may" and "it appears," the doctor explains that gastroenterology has preliminarily diagnosed her with severe ulceration in her colon caused by chronic inflammation in her digestive tract. The colonoscopy revealed this inflammation vividly, and the illness, a subset of something called IBD, is characterized by exactly the symptoms she's been experiencing. Dr. Wilkes tells them that the biopsies will be back in a few days, and they'll have more information then. For now, they believe it's likely she'll be dealing with flare-ups of these symptoms for the rest of her life. Kashmira's muscles seize at hearing this information, and she presses her forehead harder into her knees. Even if he notices, the doctor doesn't pause. He goes on, presenting the truth she'll eventually have to hear. He doesn't know if it has anything to do with the product they showed him, but they can keep investigating that too. Either way, he thinks this is a good step forward.

"How sure are you of any of this? Maybe she'll be okay after this one time?" Nikhil says before Kashmira can respond. Then he shrinks back into his chair, almost as if he regrets speaking. Kashmira doesn't understand. She still doesn't know what to expect from him. Sometimes he seems panicked, like he was about the product in front of Dr. Wilkes. Sometimes he is too forward and then unsure, like now. Sometimes he is even sweet, like when he came to see her after the colonoscopy and offered her some small globular peppermints that he'd read would help with post-anesthesia nausea. He hadn't realized she was only going into a twilight sleep, and that she didn't feel any sicker because of it. Still, she took the wrapped candies from his hand.

Dr. Wilkes says, "Gastro will come in and give you more thoughts on this, but I can start us off. The truth is there's a lot of uncertainty. The biopsies could come back and tell us something different, though that's unlikely. More likely scenarios are that we get the diagnosis right, keep you on IV steroids and then add a maintenance drug, get this under control, and you're good for life. Or, your doctors may have to play around with the treatment regimen some over the years." He pauses. "I wish we could give you a better answer."

Kashmira lifts her head just as Ami says, "But what about a cure?"

They don't have one at the moment. With autoimmune diseases, it is often a frustrating cycle where the body keeps mistaking itself for the enemy. It's a complicated process they don't really understand—sometimes genetic, sometimes environmental, sometimes a combination of that and more.

"Sometimes it just happens," he says. "But you can't blame yourself or what you've done. No one goes out and tries to get these diseases."

It's beyond her control, he means, except she isn't sure that's the case. Kashmira kept using the product when she knew she shouldn't have. Did that matter? Was the pain she felt because of the product or something else in her genes, in her home, what? These are answers she wants but doesn't know if she can get. Ami moves to her daughter's side and tries to discern the expression on her face. Kashmira isn't sure what emotion she is showing, but it makes Ami hand her some water and smooth her hair.

"Why can't I just stay on the steroids?" Kashmira says. "They aren't a long-term option?"

The IV steroids will help for now, she learns, and eventually they'll transition her to pills, which she'll take at home. But the steroids have side effects. Short term, she may experience blood pressure and heart rate changes, along with electrolyte imbalances, difficulty sleeping, and even mood changes. Long term, she may have to deal with stretch marks, thinning skin, decreased bone density, and an increased risk of infection. The steroids won't be suitable forever, so the doctors would rather consider a class of medicines called biologics, which they may even start her on in the hospital. These come with their own dangers, but with proper monitoring are generally better for patients and hopefully will prevent surgery in the future.

"The gastroenterologist will come by to discuss this more in depth," Dr. Wilkes says.

"Can you put a message in and ask him to hurry?" Kashmira says.

"I'll make sure he stops by. In the meantime, you need to take some time to process this," Dr. Wilkes says as he comes around the bed to check Kashmira's breathing once more with the stethoscope. In and out, in and out. These instructions are harder to follow than usual, and he tells Kashmira to take normal breaths. She tries as the doctor adds, "You know, if you have any other questions, I'm around."

There will be more questions, yes. But when the doctor leaves, no one speaks. No one wants to be the first to say the wrong thing. No sentence has enough weight to feel meaningful or enough lightness to make the tension ease. The first person to speak has to be Kashmira, but she is silent. She wants to sit, instead, with the realization that everything she ever imagined for herself will change now. Every person who ever knew her will now know a stranger. Every possibility of moving on from this, of forgetting it ever happened, dissipates. She closes her eyes and tries desperately to convince herself: *This is real, this is real, this is real.* The only good thing is that no one interrupts her. No one expects her to get over it here in this hospital room.

In the Staff Notices MiniSquad, @larissa posts:
 —@all i know there have been some concerns in the office as well as some inquiries from the press re: a small percentage of clients who may have reported some side effects related to our products, particularly RNL. rest assured, our QA team is still looking into this, but we're currently leaning toward this being an issue of product misuse by our clients. as you all know, we have strict product usage guidelines included in every box. we'll be connecting with any clients who contact us directly to discuss their dissatisfaction. if you have any questions or if you receive any questions from media (or others) regarding these situations, please reach out to your YTC or to me for guidance. and above all, remember: what we're doing here is making a difference for a lot of people! never forget that! ♥

CHAPTER FOURTEEN

Erin brings him the news, along with beer from her back seat. Nikhil takes one, and they crack their bottles open against Ami's apartment complex stoop. The evening has taken a cooler turn, and a slight wind wisps past their cheeks. Across the street, the lights in the apartments flicker on as dark descends.

"Are you going to tell me what's going on?" Nikhil says.

Nikhil hasn't heard much from Erin before this evening, and he hasn't texted her either. The last three days have been busy because of Kashmira's procedures and tests. Each day he drives to the hospital around nine to see what the day will bring. Most of the time, Kashmira says she is well enough, whatever that means. Otherwise, she doesn't talk to him much unless he pushes. Ami, who is always curled up in the hospital room's chair, has had more success with Kashmira than he has. A part of Nikhil is glad to see Ami finally being the mother his sister deserves; another part wishes that he too could be welcomed into this slowly easing dynamic.

At the same time as all of this, Nikhil is supposed to be working. And he needs to work in order to get a paycheck to pay his rent—so he can't quit Evolvoir, as much as he wants to, what with everything that he knows about the place now. Besides, he had proposed leaving that night Erin came to his apartment, and she told him he should stay for now, just in case they needed access to files or something else internal. It was a fair point then, before he needed to come to Marlton. After coming back to Jersey, he had asked for a full week of leave, but that was due to the upcoming autumn marketing campaign for ReNuLook. Keon's solution had been that Nikhil could work remotely for the time being due to the family emergency.

—just don't let things slide, @keon said. this is an important time for us. this campaign is going to increase the amount of clients we're serving.

Things have slid, of course. Mostly because he wants to be with Kashmira in whatever way possible. But also because he doesn't give a shit about the company after all that has been revealed by Yukiko's death.

"How's your sister?" Erin says.

"She had a colonoscopy yesterday," he says. "A colonoscopy, at age seventeen."

When he reveals the truth of Kashmira's condition, how her symptoms match those they've heard described in the recordings, Erin puts a hand over her mouth and asks if he knows for sure that she has been using the product. Nikhil tells her about finding the glass tube on his sister's dresser. Then he grabs his laptop from inside and returns to the stoop, where he balances the device on his knees and shows Erin the Evolvoir Consumer Database. Even though Nikhil now knows what to expect, his breath still feels shallow when the Find command works and pulls up Kashmira's name.

"God. I'm assuming this isn't easy." Erin lifts her own laptop out of her backpack, opens it, and shows him a series of PDFs, arranged by date. "And this isn't going to make it better. I got these off Yukiko's email client. I don't know how she got them."

Nikhil squints at one of the emails when Erin opens it. Yukiko was clever. She'd screenshotted the threads without the names and then re-sent them to her personal email as attachments. It effectively removed the name of whoever messaged it to her first, if anyone had. Nikhil runs his thumb over his bottom lip, wondering who her informant was or if she had somehow hacked into someone's account. He suspects the latter, though he may never know for sure.

In any case, many of the exchanges are damning. Before Nikhil was hired, back when they were still testing the products extensively, they'd had some issues with illness in a small percentage of users in their initial trial. They hadn't been able to pinpoint why, though one of the early product developers uncovered research about their particular use of nanotechnology. Apparently, it has the capacity to manipulate matter so rigorously, it can put a strain on the human body.

Larissa and her researchers ignored this research, apparently believing—or hoping, Nikhil can't tell from that the tone of the emails—that the rate of illness they were seeing was too inconsequential to be correlated with the product.

"But both NuLook and ReNuLook are impacting people," Nikhil says, trying to process what Erin is presenting to him. "Or they seem to be."

"They're affecting people with painful and traumatic family situations," Erin says. "They're affecting people who are changing their faces as a response to those circumstances. As an alternative to therapy."

She has more answers around this, having met with a researcher, Dr. Latoya Lewis from Princeton, who specializes in these nanoparticles. Dr. Lewis read the emails Erin brought and watched the videos Yukiko made of others who were sick. Then she and Erin talked for hours, trying to understand the contours of the situation. They'd brought in a few colleagues, too, who'd also come up with some theories.

"These nanoparticles make aggressive changes in the body," Erin explains. "Some people's bodies can bounce back from that. Some can't."

Nikhil asks her which people tend to be more vulnerable to the technology, and she responds, after swigging her beer, that often it is the people already having a cellular reaction to toxic stress in their lives. The next part is technical, she explains, but essentially those changing their faces in response to trauma were likely having an emotional reaction to the alterations.

"Grief, anxiety, that kind of thing. That's what Yukiko said too, right?" she says.

Yes, Nikhil remembers her in the art gallery, talking about a formidable surge of grief. He nods, but his teeth remain locked together in the back and he can't speak as he imagines what his sister felt when she used the product. What she went through each time, what terrible swell of emotion she must have downplayed in order to convince herself to keep using it. She'd wanted to change herself that badly; well, of course she had, the impulse to do so was hidden in both him and her, honed by the generations before.

Erin goes on, telling Nikhil that the emotional reaction may have been a form of retraumatization for some and that the repetition of the face changing may have increased toxic stress in the cells. This would have an impact on the immune system because of the swell of pro-inflammatory cytokines. She stumbles on this last word but gets it out, along with the next part: that such an escalation can lead to chronic illness.

"In this case," she says, "issues in the digestive system."

This metaphor isn't lost on Nikhil. The idea of thoughts coming into the body, not passing through. The idea, then, of them being absorbed into the body, staying there, stuck, until the colon rebels and forces everything out. All those people Nikhil had tried to help, suffering more now. His sister, his poor sister. He wishes he could go to Kashmira then, but there is more to discuss here. He wills himself to stay seated and listen as Erin says that what the researcher believes the nanotechnology accelerates what already could exist. Many of these people might have gotten sick anyway—what changed them was whatever they had already gone through—but the addition of the product has made them suffer faster and more. Not that this matters to Evolvoir. If Yukiko did speak to someone about it, as she claimed, the company didn't do anything. Maybe they're trying to figure things out internally; but Erin guesses that the conclusion of that won't satisfy either of them.

"They'll figure out some way to say they have plausible deniability," Erin says. "Maybe by saying that correlation doesn't mean causation. I'm not sure. But they've got good lawyers, and from what you've said about Larissa, she probably believes in the product too much to buy into it being too harmful to be out in the world."

"How did no one else catch this?" Nikhil says. "The FDA?"

"That's a fun one. They used a loophole and got the FDA to classify it as a cosmetic instead of a drug, so NuLook, and consequently ReNuLook, didn't have to go through as many stringent checks." Erin rests her beer bottle, still mostly full, against her cheek. "You know, this is exactly the kind of thing a journalist my age would want to happen. I mean, people would die to break this kind of story. But people *are* dying, already." She straightens. "I need to keep digging. And I think I need your sister's testimony. So far, I haven't been able to get anyone else to talk, and I can't release those videos without explicit permission. Your sister is probably our best bet for an interview that I can use to really bolster this article."

"She's in the hospital," Nikhil says, immediately not liking the idea of Erin using Kashmira. "I think she probably just wants to be left alone."

He expects Erin to back off but then she makes an unexpected point. How does Nikhil know what Kashmira wants? Maybe she'd welcome an opportunity to retaliate. Nikhil traces his lips with the beer bottle. It isn't that he thinks Erin is right about what his sister might want, but rather that he ought to ask her before assuming. This is what he has learned, after Yukiko, to listen and then do not what he thinks must be done but what comes about naturally.

But he hasn't even heard his sister out properly.

Nikhil taps the beer bottle against his teeth. It makes a soft *ding* maybe only he can hear. He says, "Let's see what happens. But I'm not going to rush her."

In the morning, Nikhil brings the box, a start to his apology, his explanation, his appeal for her trust, to Kashmira.

"Why do you have that?" she says, her lips sweating, her eyes sparking with mania. The steroids have been affecting her. But at least her diarrhea is under greater control and the bleeding has lessened. Soon, the doctors hope to start her on the biologic. Then she'll likely go home.

Nikhil places the box on the table. Their mother is out of the room getting breakfast, so it's just brother and sister. He sits on the edge of the bed and tries to remember how he'd approached Yukiko in the gallery. How the space between them had glowed with warmth and understanding, with an irresistible eagerness for more of this tenderness. He says, "It's where we need to start with things."

He spirals in many directions, explaining everything. How much he had wanted to make sure she wasn't stuck in Vinod's ways all her life. How their call had frightened him and he'd lashed out to avoid feeling the discomfort of that emotion. How he'd started at Evolvoir. How he had been behind all the initiatives that got her that second face. How he had learned about what the products could do to a body. He doesn't talk so much about Yukiko's plans for the public reveal of this information—or Erin's. He just wants her to hear this first part and come to her own conclusions. When he finishes, Kashmira's bottom lip starts to quiver. Nikhil angles his body toward her, ready to hold her, if she wants. Ready to do whatever she wants.

"I thought it was anxiety," she says. "I guess it was stress, but in a different way." Then she starts shaking her head to the point that he worries she'll make herself dizzy and throw up. "No, I knew it was more than that. It's just, I couldn't stop using the products. I thought I could fix all the sadness inside me by getting rid of it. But somehow that just made it worse."

When she calls herself stupid, he reminds her that it isn't her fault. That he wanted the same for her. He positioned it otherwise, thinking of what she ought to do to herself as remaking rather than erasing, but nothing about that is so different. Neither is it different from what their father did to them, or what his parents did to him before that. In the end, all of them have thrown out parts of themselves that they think don't match. In the end, all of them have felt unsure where to go, what to be, and how not to hate themselves. This illness is in him, too, just as it is in her.

"It's up to us to decide what we want to do with that," he says.

Kashmira points to the box. "And I'm guessing you think that would be a place to start? How do you want to handle it?"

"I want us to decide, together," he tells her. "If we need to get rid of it, we will. If we really think it's best to just leave it in the closet, that's fine too."

Kashmira holds out her arms, gesturing for him to deposit the box in her lap. He does, and she presses her palm against the cardboard, the rough, imperfect grain. She runs a finger down its opening, sealed with bunched-up tape, and nods.

"I think we should just open it and not expect anything," his sister says. "Whatever it is, just let it be."

They sit on the bed together, her hands on the flaps, his hands holding the key he uses to slit it open. One clean slash, and they're in. She opens the box and tips it toward Nikhil so they can both look. Inside, they find an old button-down shirt, folded neatly. A blank notebook with a few pages ripped out. A name tag from a conference Vinod went to annually, along with a pin in the shape of the host association's logo. Airline tickets that could have been tossed. Manila folders with no markings on them. A few business cards with no telephone numbers on the back, so maybe they were spares Vinod had never used. All in all, these items are things the siblings have seen before. And while maybe the fact that Vinod kept these things is of mild interest, really it's more likely these are items that just got tossed in corner one day and were eventually boxed up and forgotten. If anything, maybe the contents of this box are just a reminder that their father was a normal man. Fallible, selfish, yes, but normal too. A person who was just trying to make it through.

"That doesn't mean I forgive him," Kashmira says.

"I don't think you have to," Nikhil says, because he really does believe it. He doesn't want his father to return. He doesn't want to fold him back into their lives. What Nikhil wants is to accept the truth of him, just as he is learning to accept the truth of himself.

Kashmira pushes the box away as she rises out of the bed. Almost tripping on the blanket, she heads for the bathroom, simultaneously pushing her robe aside. Nikhil stays by the bed, though he can hear her emptying. One round, then another, then one more. When she returns, he helps her back into bed, where she begins to bawl.

Her tears are tiny things, dripping down her nose and cheeks relentlessly. Her thin gown is wet from them and underneath it her chest heaves so hard he does worry. All Nikhil wants is to draw her close, but Kashmira points to the tissues on the other side of the room, and so he gets them. Then he sits next to her and presses the tissue against her cheeks. He can feel her shaking under his hand, but soon enough she pitches toward him and rests on his shoulder.

―⁂―

Still parked in the hospital lot, just twenty minutes after leaving his sister's room, Nikhil makes a call. It rings and rings and no one picks up, Nikhil loses his nerve and hangs up before he gets voicemail. Then he reminds himself that just as he did with Yukiko and Kashmira, he has to try. He calls again. This time, it rings through and then the voicemail greeting comes on and Michael says, like someone who actually wants to receive a message, to leave one. So, Nikhil does, despite knowing full well that his isn't the voice Michael is welcoming. Despite knowing full well that the other man might ignore his message, might even delete it, just because.

"Michael," he says into the receiver. "It's Nikhil. Maybe you saw that in your call log. Anyway, I know we've been at odds. But I had to try to tell you something, at least."

For a second, the phone hums, almost like someone is at the other end. Nikhil pauses, waiting to see if maybe Michael has picked up. But no, nothing. He goes on, telling Michael first where he is and why. He describes Kashmira's condition and everything that has happened in Jersey since he arrived.

Then he says, "And now I see, being here, that I was wrong about things. I mean, you were wrong, too. But this message isn't about that. Or maybe it is. I'm not sure. I guess what I wanted to tell you was—"

The answering machine cuts him off. Nikhil dials Michael's number again. It goes to voicemail another time. Maybe that's for the best, because now that Nikhil has started this monologue, he has to finish. He talks faster now, so he can get it all out. This time, he says that he fucked up. He never should have said what he said to Michael about his responsibilities being tied to his identity. He never should have even thought it. Because what does he know about that? What does he know, just by reading articles and watching documentaries and making assumptions based on them? He had put Michael in a box. He had done it in the name of good politics, of helping people, when in actuality he was afraid to admit things were not going as they were supposed to. Michael had challenged him though, and because of him, Nikhil had reached out to Yukiko, who had then taught him to reach out to his sister. Only now does Nikhil understand the real, unending potential that can exist in genuinely tending to each other, without expectation.

A click. The message is too long and it cuts off again. Once again, he has to call back, wait for the ringing to go nowhere, and begin again. But why not? Maybe this is the very moment he needs with Michael too.

"It's Nikhil. One last time, I promise," he says.

There's more he has learned, more he wants Michael to know. He describes the moment in the art gallery when he connected with Yukiko. Then he describes her leaving him and Erin the phone, leaving them the emails, leaving them with the recognition that Nikhil, like everyone, cannot escape his responsibility to help, to do, to use his skills for others. Listening is the start. But there's more he can do, that he will do, when the time is right. He can't give up that part of himself—the part that springs into doing—fully, no matter how much Michael thought he should. And perhaps he doesn't have to. He'll find out, if and when Kashmira is ready to act, what she needs from him. He wonders what Michael thinks of this.

"Maybe you'll let me know," Nikhil says. "You know, I was going to tell you to call me back. But instead, I'll just say that I would like to hear from you. If you wanted to talk."

And then, just as voicemail starts clicking him off, he hangs up, sure he has given Michael all he can.

CHAPTER FIFTEEN

By coincidence, Dr. Wilkes stops by at the same time as the gastroenterologist, and the two of them catch Kashmira as she comes out of the bathroom, pulling her tiresome gown out of her underwear. One of her softly curved ass cheeks is exposed to the doctors, but now, seven days into her hospital stay, she doesn't care about such things. Doctors, nurses, even the administrative staff, they've seen it all before, and they keep telling her that, too. Over time, they've all gotten used to each other, and Kashmira doesn't even mind Dr. Wilkes's cool demeanor or the way the nurses sometimes gossip over her while taking care of some small procedure or how the staff gets mad at her for stacking her tray the wrong way every time. How used to this new reality she has become.

"Are you sure you have to keep tracking my pee?" she says, talking about the hat in the toilet that catches her urine so the nurses can be sure she is drinking enough. If not, they'll add fluids—along with the steroids—to the IV again. A bolus, Kashmira has learned they call it sometimes. "I swear, I had like three cups of juice with breakfast. No dehydration here."

"I think we can cease the monitoring for now," the gastroenterologist says. She addresses Kashmira, along with Ami and Nikhil—here for a second visit after delivering the box earlier this morning—who are both sitting in their usual chairs by the window. "We've also got an update on the biopsy results. They came back as expected."

This means Kashmira's official diagnosis is inflammation in her colon. This is why it feels like her whole stomach is coming out of her when she uses the toilet. Because both doctors agree they've investigated her issues fully, they'll now focus on treatment to achieve remission.

"Remission?" Kashmira says. "That's what they say about cancer."

"We say that about quite a few illnesses. But you don't have cancer," Dr. Wilkes says. Then the gastroenterologist reiterates the formal name for her condition: ulcerative colitis, an inflammatory bowel condition. Though it's lifelong and does come with an increased chance for colon cancer—as well as other complications—that isn't something to worry about now. Dr. Wilkes says, "You'll get used to the terminology."

They turn to discussing her treatment plan. Kashmira is lucky, because Ami's insurance plan is one of the rare ones that allows for some first-line biologic therapies. This means the gastroenterologist can start her on one here in the hospital, without her needing to try out other, often less effective drugs first. They'll also be keeping her on the steroids for now, as a bridge therapy, but she'll start to taper off them soon.

"So the biologic is a pill?" Kashmira says.

"An injection," the gastroenterologist replies.

One she'll have to do by herself every eight weeks, apparently. The nurses will teach her, the doctors promise, and it'll be easy. But Kashmira has a hard time believing that. She has never liked needles, and she always looks away during blood draws. All too often, the phlebotomists have to tell her to relax and stop sucking in her breath and tensing up. It makes their job harder, they tell her, and it makes it more likely they'll hurt her. The best course of action is just to close her eyes. But that won't be an option when giving the injection to herself.

"Does it have to be a needle?" Ami says, "Does she have to be the one to do it?"

Ami suggests that they could come to the hospital every eight weeks to meet a nurse who could do the injection. But Dr. Wilkes—benevolent but firm—tells her that most patients get used to doing quick pokes with pre-filled syringes. She'll be fine, the gastroenterologist agrees. While they discuss this, Kashmira traces a circle on the part of her stomach that the doctor told her to target for the needle. Two inches from the belly button, on either the right or left side. The skin there seems too soft and malleable to handle a jab; then again, no part of her has seemed ready for anything in this hospital, and yet here she is.

The doctors leave. A few hours pass. A nurse comes in to let Kashmira know that the pharmacy has gotten the order for the biologic and will be preparing it. They'll bring it up to her soon. At one point during their wait, Nikhil asks Kashmira if she is scared. She lingers on the word, so close to *scarred*, and says, "How could I not be?"

Her brother swivels his head at this quiet honesty. Surprise turns his features soft, and he tells her, "Yeah. Stupid question."

The medicine arrives. A box in a plastic bag, wrapped in a cooler pack, held in a nurse's hand. Inside it, instructions and a prefilled syringe and a packaged alcohol swab. Ami stands close, with her hand on the small of Kashmira's back. That touch, it's needed, because all Kashmira can do is remember right now. She feels far away, back in an isolated bathroom, in the huge house which served as the setting for the raucous June party that Kashmira had wanted to feel properly a part of. Roshni had slid a tube out of her bag and showed Kashmira how to change her body for good. Is this any different? As the nurse hands her the syringe, Kasmira forgets to breathe. But then, the air enters her lungs anyway. Her body works on its own accord, no matter what she tells it. It always has. She looks up at the nurse and nods. At this moment, she has to decide: If she can stand to do this, maybe she really has come to terms with all of what she is now.

The needle, at a forty-five-degree angle. The nurse teaches her how to do this, as she has others before: practiced, sure. It takes one jab, just one, to stick the needle in. More uncomfortable is how it has to stay inside Kashmira as she pushes the stiff plunger. Her hand shakes even as the nurse coaxes her to go on. Then the medicine, cool, surges through her abdomen. Already, it's doing something to her, even if she can't see the change. When the syringe is empty, the nurse guides Kashmira's hand back away from herself. Because Kashmira doesn't let go of the plunger, the needle comes out protracted, glinting in the light.

"You did it," Nikhil says. He touches her shoulder, which she realizes hasn't yet relaxed. "Kashmira, you did it."

And she has. A small pinprick, barely visible, mars her skin. And through that tiny hole, Kashmira imagines, what's inside can look out now, no longer fully hidden away.

───❀───

Sachin's eyes are wild as he takes it all in, from the whiteboard that says the nurse's name to the haphazard bottles of juice and soda on the side table to Kashmira's elevated arm, the one with the IV that won't stop screaming about being occluded unless she keeps the tubing as straight as possible. It's the day after she injected her first biologic, and she can only imagine what Sachin would feel if he saw her doing that.

Nikhil, who drove Sachin here, says, "He cornered me in the parking lot, and I told him he could come with me. Do you, I don't know, want a minute?"

"Yes," she says. She and her brother are doing better, and they are more adept at understanding each other now. That Nikhil asks her what she wants, what she needs, is nice, if a little awkward for her. Having new, more generous versions of those she loves both fulfills her and confuses her. Still, she smiles at her brother, and reiterates, "Yes, please."

Nikhil backs out of the room, and because Ami is taking a shower at home, Kashmira and Sachin are left alone. To Kashmira's surprise, he sits not in a distant chair but on the edge of her hospital bed, near her leg—where her mother has sat, where her brother has sat too.

Then she remembers Sachin's hands, his soft touch on her the last time they saw each other, and she knows that things have changed.

"Hi," Kashmira says. "You went after my brother? In the parking lot?"

"I saw him coming in and out of your house. And your text scared me." Sachin looks collapsed onto himself, like his worry is pushing on him from all sides. "I knew it was bad."

"I'm sorry," she says, and she means for many things, including how she left things between them. Including not allowing him in when he showed her that he wanted to try. By then, she had forgotten who she was and what it was she really wanted. She recalls the boy at the bus stop, who had always cared so much about her thoughts, her feelings. He hadn't come close enough, but he had accepted what he had seen. And now, he sits by her on this bed, no matter how hard it might be for him.

"No, I'm sorry," he says. "I spent so much time trying to figure things out about you—for you—when I should have just, I don't know, given you a hug. I mean, it's not that hard, is it? To give someone a hug?" His mouth twists. "But if you're okay with it, I'd like to be here now."

How can she not allow them this? The thing they've both wanted, probably for a long time. So much got in the way—missed signals, damning teenage insecurity, misguided beliefs that figuring things out alone would be better than doing it together—but all of that is passed. When Kashmira nods, Sachin runs his fingers along her arm, and it feels so good, she doesn't even mind if he feels the weird texture of old surgical tape stuck on the hairs there. Rather, she only notices her pleased sigh, a *finally*. If only they had started getting this close earlier in their lives. But no matter. She will make up for that lost time. And so will he, it seems. As they talk, they never stop touching each other. Sachin reties a string on her gown. Kashmira rests her cheek against his fingers when he is done. He tucks the covers around her again, clumsily.

Then he says, "I tried to look up what you have, based on what your brother was saying. Ulcerative colitis? I don't know if I got that right."

"You can just call it Kashmira Syndrome if you want. Apparently it's pretty unique for each person," Kashmira says. She means to joke, but her breath catches in her chest and she wheezes. Even if she is starting to come to terms with being here in the hospital, she hasn't yet figured out how to talk about what's wrong with her without struggling. Sachin grabs her a cup of water without asking if she needs it and allows her the time to regain her breath. When she does, she says, "You can write that one down in your notebook."

"You'd still want me to?"

"Sachin, I like your notebook. I just want you to be okay with putting it away once in a while."

He nods, then whispers, "I think I can do that."

She smiles, stunned by his naked honesty. The moment feels quiet, lovely, and then, at the worst possible time, her blood pressure cuff tightens, cutting it short. Sachin startles, jumps. Then he laughs at himself. But as the cuff deflates, his eyes track upward to the systolic and diastolic numbers on the screen above her head.

"Are those okay?" he says. "Do I need to get a nurse? Whatever you need, I'll do it."

It hurts him, she realizes tenderly, to see her hurting. It's not about the blood pressure, but about her in this bed. He wants to spare her this experience—or if he can't do that, at least make it easier for her. But for all that he wants to be the director, there are some things he cannot cut. Some stories take time to understand. She grasps Sachin's fingers and pulls at his hand until she can brush her lips against his skin. They both need this, badly.

He watches her dry lips purse and part against him, then says, "You've been so sick."

People as young as they are shouldn't have to watch each other's faces with this much worry. But when is anyone ever old enough to watch the person they care for lie pale and crooked against thin hospital pillows? When they kiss, they taste salt. Each other's tears, each with its own size and shape. It should ruin the moment, but Kashmira finds that their touch is only heightened by the sadness it sits inside. They kiss, and they kiss, and they kiss, even as the monitors keep running on.

Roshni, pacing outside the door as she waits for permission to enter the hospital room.

When Kashmira waves at her, she edges her way in and stares rather than coming in for a hug. Like Sachin, who first visited yesterday and plans to come again this afternoon, Roshni seems wary of the wires. But then the nurse who bustles in mostly unhooks Kashmira and suggests she sit in one of the chairs instead of the hospital bed. This way, she can keep her muscles working a little more than they would be lying down. Once Kashmira settles, the nurse brings her and Roshni cups of sugar-free Jell-O with plastic spoons. Strawberry for Kashmira and orange for Roshni. They trade flavors twice before settling on this. They will probably have to take turns in the bathroom after this, but they know it, so what does it matter?

"Took you long enough to visit," Kashmira says. She is sour about it, despite the fact that Roshni has texted her almost every day. She can't help but remember standing at Roshni's side at clinic—there for her when no one else was. "Too busy with the outside world?"

"No. Although the outside world is interesting. I heard rumors Sachin might be dating someone. People have been saying he was all over some girl at the bonfire party. I can't imagine that was anyone but you, was it?"

"He wasn't all over me," Kashmira says. "I wasn't feeling well. But, you know, he did come to visit, and—"

"He came? To the hospital?"

Roshni leans forward, eager for the gossip. And Kashmira can't help but give it to her. Tells everything about how later, at the end of the visit, Sachin had told her he wanted to ask her out on a date properly, but for now, would she be his girlfriend? How that moment had felt so precious—and right, after so many years of waiting for it.

"Oh my God," Roshni says. "Well, I'm glad he came. My mom almost didn't let me. She's obsessed with me getting ready to leave for The Center every minute of every day. I only have a week and a half left in Jersey."

As the two girls lick their spoons, Roshni talks about orientation at The Center. She begins with the scenery—which Kashmira understands as not a good sign, because Roshni has never cared about nature before—and describes the rolling hills as calming to look at. Strange, because everything else at The Center seems infuriating. The people who take care of Roshni—guides, they call them—woke her up early in the morning for tea and meditation, during which she was supposed to concentrate on thinking about herself and her body differently. She was supposed to ignore her aching joints, her stool covered in blood, the way she can't stomach anything more than soft foods. Instead, she was told to think about how lucky she is to be alive among people who care about her well-being. Every day they told her she was getting better—except every day she felt worse.

"And you told your mother that?" Kashmira, who has since forgotten to be irritated at her friend, says.

"She doesn't want to hear it."

"So she wants you to lie to her?"

Roshni stabs her Jell-O definitively with the spoon. "When hasn't she?"

Kashmira shrugs. She wrestles with her own Jell-O, but somehow a glob falls off her spoon and bounces away, under the bed. This makes Raveena snort and then joke about what the cleaning staff will assume after Kashmira is discharged. Maybe they'll think it is part of her liver or spleen. Together, they laugh until Kashmira has to lean back and rest her head so her breathing calms down.

"Tired? Me too," Roshni says. She extends her arm to show Kashmira how her limb shakes. "You see this? At least I can still dance." She drops her arm. "And at least I'm not in the hospital. I can't believe you ended up here."

"I don't know. I guess the product really fucked me up." Or perhaps she herself was more fucked up than Roshni to begin with. Of course, that's impossible to judge. Kashmira finishes her Jell-O and then, wanting more, reaches for Roshni's half-finished cup. They shared a cup of alcohol like this at the first party of the summer, she remembers, as she makes a half-moon indentation with her spoon. Then another one, until she has carved a star. She hands it back to Roshni with a small shrug. "But it's not so bad here."

"Really? I thought it would be hell."

Had it been? Kashmira looks at the room. The bed, slept in. The sheets, recently stained with blood and now clean. Earlier today, her IV site—the third one she has had during this visit—started aching so badly, the nurses had to take it out and replace it with a PICC line. After, her arm had bled and stained the white covers. It made her cry, this wetness sliding down her arm, because why couldn't her body manage something like a simple catheter? Why was it always causing problems? But as always the hospital staff hadn't thought of it this way. They'd been kind. They'd held pressure to the side and changed out her bedsheets, just like that. Her mother and brother had watched the whole thing, gazes tender. Years from now, she will probably remember these details and wonder how she got through this time The hospital stay will remain with her, another source of grief, when she notices how other people her age don't yet know what it's like to confront their own fragility. She pauses. A source of grief, yes, but also a source of solace. This is the only place in the world where she can just be.

"The thing about being here," Kashmira says, "is that it's okay to be fucked up. And it's okay to be sad about it."

"Oh," Roshni says and then hands her Jell-O back to Kashmira. "It's not like that where I'm going."

A brief pause. Maybe one of them should apologize for making the moment awkward. Except it isn't really. Between the two of them, they might as well tell the truth. So Kashmira says simply, quietly, "Remember when we just thought whatever you had would get fixed with a pill or something?"

"God," Roshni says. She rolls her eyes. "How stupid were we?"

They lean into each other then, resting their foreheads against each other. The past is the past. They both know it. They both will remember it. But what matters now is that they are not alone. Sisters, somehow, they know each other too well to pretend otherwise.

Lunch lately is better, now that Kashmira is allowed to order anything, instead of sugar-free, gluten-free, low-sodium options only, and today she eats mashed potatoes in a mountain with fatty gravy running down its sides. While her mother and brother sit at their chairs by the window, she forks the penne with the same zeal, filling her mouth, molar to molar with Parmesan. She knows she might regret this later—even on the steroids and biologics, her colon doesn't always tolerate foods well, and she will probably bleed—but she wants to be heavy and grateful. She sops up her pasta sauce with a piece of sourdough bread and thinks of what a miracle water and flour and salt and a bubble of life become.

While she eats, the doctor knocks, then enters and stands at the edge of her bed, as he has every day for the last eight days—ever since she got out of the ICU.

"I'm glad to see you've got an appetite," Dr. Wilkes says.

"It's decent," she tells him. "For hospital food."

He flips through her chart. "Well, here's some good news. You won't be eating hospital food for much longer. Your team and I have discussed it, and we're ready to discharge you."

"What? Already?" Ami says, standing.

She crosses to the bed and puts a hand on her daughter's shoulder. Nikhil, for his part, stays seated and appraises the doctor. Kashmira adds another bite of food to her mouth, but finds she can't chew it. Dr. Wilkes mentioned discharge yesterday and maybe the day before, but Kashmira hadn't really expected it. She figured something else would come up before she'd be sent away. That's how she thinks of it now, being sent away, because the hospital seems like a version of home now. Home, as in a safe place. Earlier in the summer, she had wanted to stay away from places like this, for good reason. There's so much wrong with medical facilities—in the often detached way they treat people, in the often cavalier way they approach pain—and yet, somehow, she appreciates how this place goes on, and on, and on, no matter how many bad days it has. Here, people have taken care of her. Here, her brother came back into her life. Here, her mother did too. Here, a boy kissed her, his warmth exactly how she imagined it. Here, her best friend held her close. Here, she learned that she can never excise generations of loss from her body and that she can learn to be okay with that. Here, here, here.

"I don't think I can go yet," Kashmira says.

"Between the ED and ICU, this is your eighth day here," Dr. Wilkes says. "You're not ready to leave?"

Unable to answer this without tearing up, Kashmira drops her fork. When she leans off the side of the bed, she tries to collect herself, but fears she can't. As she draws back upright, though, she catches Nikhil's gaze. He hasn't asked anything yet, which is unlike him. She considers this and realizes: He is here, but waiting for her cue, if she ever gives one. Slowly, she nods. She needs him to say something right now—anything. He nods back, and says exactly what she wanted to, but couldn't put words to:

"What about the rest of her care?" Nikhil says. "She's still sick."

The doctor addresses this as if he expected them to ask this question. "Unfortunately, the hospital is for acute, not long-term care. Once we've stabilized a patient, we need to consider the risks of having them stay here." He turns back to Kashmira. "You're more likely to get some kind of complication, like an infection, here than at home, especially when you're on the steroids and the biologic."

He says they don't want to see her catch something that would just compound her care. Rather, they would like her to find an outpatient provider able to follow her case long-term, in the way Dr. Wilkes can't.

"But," Kashmira says, not meeting his eyes, but instead staring at the square of his shoulders, the stethoscope that hangs against his chest—familiar things she never realized she would miss. "Are you sure I'm ready? To be home without, you know, all of this help?"

In her mind, she counts off all the people who've been there, who she feels she still needs. The nurse who brings her new graham crackers to replace the ones Kashmira nibbles on all night when she can't sleep; and the phlebotomist who comes by around six every morning and coos over the bruises on Kashmira's arms and tries to be gentle on the next stab; and the gastroenterologist who suggested with macabre wit that she put the pictures of her inflamed colon up on the fridge to freak out any visitors; and Dr. Wilkes himself, who has always told her, in no uncertain terms, that her body does not frighten him.

"The minute you get home, you'll forget to miss us at all," the doctor says. He steps forward with his hand outstretched. When she takes it, she finds his palm dry, very dry compared to her damp one. He's so calm, and she wonders if he will ever even remember her, the girl in the hospital bed, who wanted to stay. He says, quietly, "Just remember that recovery isn't always a straight line."

And then the moment is over. When the doctor leaves, Ami gathers their things. She alternates between throwing things out and putting them into one of the many bags they've accumulated. There goes the half-empty water bottle Ami always chews at, the magazines that Kashmira flipped through when she could keep her eyes open, the dirty socks on the floor that Kashmira kicks off her feet in the middle of the night. Nikhil folds a shirt half-heartedly when Ami hands it to him and shrugs when Ami says, her voice small, the way it used to be, "Home will be better, won't it?"

Maybe it will, maybe it won't. Time goes by. Kashmira's gastroenterologist stops in and repeats what Dr. Wilkes said. So does the hematologist she once saw. By now, the room is clean. Bags packed, half-eaten lunch in the corner. Nikhil paces, while Ami looks out the window at the cars in the parking lot. Kashmira considers hitting the Call button and asking them, once again, if she really has to go. It'll be night soon anyway. But no, an hour passes, but then the nurse arrives with a packet of instructions, which she goes over page by page, like a parting gift. Now, the PICC line. It takes more waiting, but another nurse, an experienced one, comes to remove it. The worst part is the tape pulling at Kashmira's skin; otherwise, it comes out easy. The nurse tells her to dress. The wheelchair will arrive as soon as it can.

Kashmira says she can wait. Because she can. Because once she sits in her old, unwashed clothes and they lift the brakes and walk her down the hallway, she will be leaving behind too many things. The lunch she never finished—the bread, with its soft crust. The half-used lotion she rubbed into her cracked hands. The last channel she watched on the television. The shape of her body in the bed. In minutes, that'll all be gone, so someone else can rest here.

PART FOUR

CHAPTER SIXTEEN

Kashmira doesn't know it, but she takes in the house much as Nikhil did when he arrived here. Though not that much has changed, her time in the hospital makes her run her hands over every countertop, makes her pick up the minutiae—the glossy magazines that had shown up in the mail, the mug that Nikhil left by the sink that morning. She presses her hand against the doorway, steadying herself as she moves from the kitchen to the living room. She does the same as she walks the hallway from the living room to her bedroom. It overwhelms her to see all these colors, to hear simple sounds like the neighbor's incessant wind chime, instead of nurses outside her room.

"Is she okay? Does she need something?" Ami says to Nikhil, who emerges from Kashmira's bedroom after putting her bag away. Their mother watches Kashmira from a few feet away, as if to give her a respectful distance to adjust. But in actuality, something shifted again as soon as they walked in the door. Ami, again, in her old patterns, retreats from the attentive motherliness she established for herself in the hospital. Kashmira remembers what Ami said to her in the early morning hours before the colonoscopy. Things had been different, so she had to be different. Here, everything is the same as it once was.

"Stop talking about me like I'm not here," Kashmira says over her shoulder.

"Maybe she needs time to get back to normal," Ami says, still to Nikhil.

"Mom," he replies. "What's going on with you?"

Kashmira pretends not to hear. In the hospital, her mother had to recognize that Kashmira, along with the others on her ward, existed in a suspended reality, where even the worst parts of them got to remain in plain sight. Over time, Kashmira had gotten accustomed to that too; but now, back in the world of the healthy, her raw and still-wounded self doesn't match. In her bedroom, Kashmira collapses onto her bed, then remembers to pull back the covers and tuck herself in. Returned to this normalcy—to whatever extent that can be true—she can't be so messy. She tussles with the blankets just as her brother steps through the doorway.

"Mom sent you?" she says. "Can't handle me on her own now, huh?"

"I know that was bad," he says. He helps her with the covers and then swaddles her with them. Kashmira burrows as deep as she can. "It's not your fault. She's doing her best, I think. But it's not enough."

"And you're doing *what*?"

"Trying to be here for you. That's it."

Kashmira clutches at the edge of the blanket with one hand. Harder, then less so. She watches that hand instead of Nikhil. "I don't know what you want me to do. I don't know what anyone wants me to do. I don't know who anyone wants me to be. Now that I'm"—she pauses—"back."

Nikhil touches her fist gently, right on the knuckle, urging her to open her hand. When she does, they both stare at her open palm, and the long grooves that cross it. Kashmira can't tell what Nikhil is thinking, but something about her soft skin, shining with perspiration and still babyish after seventeen years, seems to make him emotional.

"You can be whoever you want," he tells her. "Why is it any different here than in the hospital?"

"Because out here all anyone wants to see is good stuff," she says. When he asks her what it would mean for her to feel understood, to belong, she wiggles her fingers, feeling some soreness in her joints. Inflammation, still present. "I don't know. I guess I'd want people to know the truth. Whatever that is."

"Then you could tell people what you know." This is when her brother tells her about Yukiko and the videos she made of others like Kashmira. He tells her they haven't released the videos yet, but they will one day, because that's what the subjects wanted. He tells her that if she wants, she can do the same. "It might be cathartic."

"You never told me there were videos," Kashmira says. "And you have that girl's phone? I mean, how close were you?"

"Not that close," he says. "Mostly, I was trying to help you by helping her."

He pauses, maybe waiting to see what she'll say to that. Kashmira smiles just slightly, but he notices the change in her expression, and maybe he knows it's an opening. Her relationship with her brother, like two blocked arteries stemming from the same heart, is still learning to flow. Without their father, they could have loved each other more easily. But maybe because of their father, they'll have the opportunity to love more deeply. She doesn't know yet, but there are lots of unclear things waiting for her.

"It's whatever you think is best," Nikhil says. "I have a journalist friend who wants to help us. She thinks your story is important for going after Evolvoir. But she isn't going to push you either."

Kashmira considers. She wants to say yes. She wants to say no. Mostly, she doesn't know if she can articulate her identity—the entire arc of it—in a narrative she'd want out in the world. She pushes the blanket away, stands, and walks to her dresser, where Nikhil has arranged her orange pill bottles in a line. Some tall, some short, all of them marked with the dosage and the right time to take them and the name of the doctor trying to soothe some symptom. Before she left the hospital, the nurses reminded her to follow through with all the instructions or risk nothing getting better. Where the pill bottles are now is where Kashmira used to keep her tube of product.

Kashmira rearranges the bottles in order of height. Then color of pill. Finally, earliest to latest in terms of time of taking. She unscrews the top of the first one; it's already half an hour past when she should have taken it. She rolls her tongue and keeps a pill there. Then, with the bicolored capsule still heavy in her mouth, she asks him in crooked, clumsy speech to give her some time.

It takes her a long time to decide whether or not she should show up to her scheduled Evolvoir Concierge appointment. It's a follow-up that she put on the calendar before her hospital visit, but now it's the day after her discharge and she isn't sure what to do. In the time leading up to the appointment, she asks Roshni what she thinks, and her friend, who is still readying herself to move to The Center at the end of the month, says to absolutely skip the appointment. She asks her brother, who tells her it's her choice. She asks Sachin, who muses that if she decides to go, it could be good evidence. If she ends up taking her brother up on the offer to tell her story, she can use this appointment as part of the narrative. Sachin shows her a sneaky screen-recording app she could use if she wants to save the video for proof and then sends her a 🤫.

This last option is the one she likes best. A minute before the appointment starts, Kashmira starts up the screen recorder and then opens the Evolvoir appointment link.

"Kashmira," Jordie says, her enthusiasm amplified by her emphatic wave. "It's good to see you. You look great, as always. Actually, better than always."

This doesn't seem true. Like during every appointment before this, Kashmira scrutinizes her face in the video chat screen. She lays on the bed with her laptop balanced on her lower stomach, and the angle creates unflattering shadows on her face, especially in the folds under her chin and under her sharp cheekbones. Tiny spots of acne dot Kashmira's temples. Probably from the stress of being in the hospital for eight days. Probably, too, from taking so many drugs. And then there are her eyes. So wide, like they can't miss even the most marginal things. This is her face—her father's face, her grandfather' face, her grandmother's face—as it was before. But now honest in its grief.

"How have you been?" Jordie says.

"Not great," Kashmira tells her. "Really not great."

"Oh." Jordie looks appropriately disappointed for her. "Well, hopefully we can make it a better day today. Right? Should we begin?"

Kashmira leans her head against one hand. Fatigue overwhelms all her muscles. She wants to lie down. Then she remembers she already is. Being on this call might not have been the best idea, but Jordie has already pulled up the CFM™, and there Kashmira is, digitized again. Except this time, it's her with her so-called improved features. She takes it in, that face, swiveling back and forth. How expressionless it is. How blank. There's no history there, other than the history of erasure. Pretty can't take the place of real, she realizes.

"You know how this goes," Jordie says. "How have you been liking your second face? One being 'not at all' and ten being 'I love it.'"

Her second face? Jordie means this one on the screen. To Kashmira, though, her original face feels like the new one. It's the most truthful, the most evolved. Maybe she should say this, make the clarification, but she isn't sure how. Instead, she says, "I don't know what to think of all this."

"Let's talk about that on a scale from one to ten," Jordie says, not lingering. "How about a number?"

It slices through Kashmira then that all she is to Jordie is an appointment to get through. That's all she has ever been. She finds herself saying, bitterly, "Do you ever wish you could talk to your clients like real people?"

"I don't understand."

"Your products fucked me up," Kashmira says. She hadn't meant to bring this up. Her plan had been just to go about things as normal, record the call, and see what she could do with it. But Jordie looks at her with such impassivity. "I'm telling you and you're not listening. Your products, they really fucked me up, and I'm not the only one. My brother told me. He works there, at Evolvoir. You might know him."

Jordie pauses, then scrolls up to the top of the screen, where Kashmira's name, first and last, are written in capital letters. When she starts typing, the keyboard click-clacks faster than Kashmira has heard in the past. She says, "I thought you and Nikhil sharing a last name was just a coincidence. We aren't supposed to have employee family members in promotional programs like the BBB. He didn't warn you?"

"He didn't know. Now he does."

"Okay," Jordie says. "This doesn't have to be a big deal. We can just take you out of the program, and you can go back on the wait list. Then you'll just get your products like everyone else, and it won't matter."

"That's what you're worried about? Not how sick I was? Not that I was in the hospital for eight days? How about you put that on my stupid progress chart?" Kashmira means it. She wants to update those idiotic line graphs, the ones that chart how happy she is with every part of her body. She wants to have how she feels written down—recorded—a tangible blemish on their pristine files. "Let's put down a fucking zero for this session, okay? For every answer to every one of your fucking questions."

"I'm sorry," Jordie says. She bobs her head, like she is, but Kashmira can see her eyes moving back and forth, like she's reading off her screen instead of paying attention to the conversation. "But I'm not authorized to do anything with your charts right now, since we're going to have to reclassify your account."

Between them, the CFM™ still spins. Jordie hasn't changed the screen, nor has she properly acknowledged Kashmira's other accusations. Perhaps she remembers some training that told her not to engage with angry, rattled clients. Or perhaps she just doesn't care.

Kashmira doesn't know. All she understands is that Jordie has somehow composed herself enough to smile blandly and say that there'll be a follow-up email coming, and that Kashmira will be placed back on the wait list for the products, and that hopefully there'll be more soon.

"Now, other than that," Jordie says, "is there anything else I can help you with?"

Kashmira opens her mouth to say yes, of course, there are a hundred other things, but Jordie says goodbye, in a measured tone. The call disconnects before she even finishes the word.

The phone, with lines of black and white that somehow make enigmatic picture after enigmatic picture, on its back.

That night, Kashmira finds it on top of Nikhil's laptop in the living room. Curious, because she doesn't recognize it as his personal cell or something from work, she picks it up while her brother sleeps. This phone, she finds, is larger than her own. It also has a better camera. It also doesn't require a passcode. When she opens the phone up to the home screen, she sees that the only downloaded app, other than an email client and a cloud, is VidMo. By this point, she understands.

In the VidMo app's drafts are all the videos Yukiko filmed of Evolvoir clients. Each interviewee shares a story that mimics Kashmira's. Yet each divulges particularities that distinguish it from the others. Some talk about their histories of loss. Some talk about what scares them: dying, being a burden, being abandoned by caretakers. Some talk about the way the doctor described their conditions: kindly, clinically, obtusely. Some talk about who believes them and who doesn't: mothers who think it's in their heads, spouses who want them to go back to normal, best friends who stick around no matter what. Some talk about what they feel about their bodies now: pity, hatred, sadness at the understanding that their immune systems are just trying to protect them but instead are making things worse.

Kashmira takes the phone into her room. There, she calls Sachin and asks him to come over. Of course he will. Not only are they official now, dating, but they're also serious. Both of them have admitted their relationship feels like it started five years ago. Those bus stop conversations, those hangouts, those texts. They've liked each other for so long. Kashmira doesn't turn on the lights in the apartment, but Sachin is able to follow her through the living room and hallway soundlessly enough, despite not having spent much time here yet. In her room, she shows him the videos. There, she asks him to help her film herself.

"I want to share my version of things," she says. "But I'm going to post mine. Not just leave it in drafts."

"Are you sure?" Sachin sits on her bed and whispers. Only her bedside table lamp is on, and she can see shadows flickering over his worried face. "Didn't your brother say that reporter could help you?"

Kashmira shakes her head. Nikhil did say that—but although she trusts that her brother wants the best for her, she has to be thoughtful right now, as she tries to figure out how best to be in this world after her diagnosis. She worries that Erin will misrepresent things, by accident or not, and publish only a half-truth. No, Kashmira doesn't want anyone else sharing her story first.

It's with this deliberation that they start their work; Sachin holds the light and provides camerawork tips while Kashmira films her body. It's nothing scandalous, but it's revealing enough. She shows off her legs, her knobby knees. She shows her hip with the scar from falling off a bicycle almost ten years ago. She gives them her collarbones, her neck, where hives have broken out in response to all the medicines she has been taking. After this, she records a voice-over in which she tells her account, all of it. Why she wanted to use the product, what happened when she did, what seems to be coming next. She exposes everything she can, and in the caption she writes: *do you remember the girl who came before me? do you remember that she died? do you remember that you loved her? don't you ever wonder what happened to her, what happened to me?*

After this, she lets the video sit in drafts, while Sachin looks up how best to edit the clips and intercut them with other footage. It's easy enough, and soon they upload Kashmira's Evolvoir Concierge call recording to the app.

"What about the other videos?" Sachin says. "The ones in the drafts folder?"

Kashmira looks at these a second time. They would support her narrative, yes. They would make people pay more attention, yes. But she wouldn't want to do to these people what she is afraid Erin could do to her. Without their explicit permission—which she doesn't know how to get—she won't post them.

But then she thinks of someone else, someone reachable, whose voice matters too.

"We'd be in it together," she cajoles on the phone to Roshni, who thankfully hasn't left yet for The Center. "What do you think?"

"I think my mother would kill me," Roshni says.

It hasn't occurred to Kashmira to wonder what her own mother will think. Mostly, because Ami has gone back to drifting through the house, to looking to Nikhil for advice. Kashmira hates it. She'd had a brief flash of a cogent, committed mother in the hospital, but back home, that woman seems lost now. So what does it matter? Kashmira hangs up the phone as Roshni says goodbye. Sachin touches her elbow and she tells him what she is thinking: that it isn't her mother's reaction she is worried about, but her brother's. Nikhil has stayed soft with her since they returned to the apartment. But posting this video, going against his suggestion about the reporter—this may tilt him back toward harshness. She will miss him, if that happens. Miss his hands opening hers up to the air. But there's nothing she can do about that other than not posting. And that she can't do, not when she has come this far.

In the end, it is just Kashmira's account in the video—but it still seems like enough, still seems like something worth saying. She and Sachin gather around the phone and watch the finalized cut. He kisses her cheek, then her lips, firmly, reassuringly, as if to remind her that no matter what happens here. He says, "It's done."

As Kashmira hits upload, she sees the follower count. Thousands upon thousands, even after Yukiko's death. That means that her video won't disappear into the ether. Instead, people will click. People will watch. And what will they think of her? She can only hope they'll see what she needs them to see. She can only hope this will help her find a way to belong.

She hits the Post button and turns the phone off. Tomorrow, when she turns it back on, she'll see.

Some of the viewers are more interested in the girl on the screen's body than her words. They say they know what it's like to have a body that betrays them. They know it can be anything: a bad pimple on picture day, period blood that leaks through slacks, a knee that breaks during a soccer game and never heals right, a uterus that rejects a baby every cycle, a heart that gives out for no reason, a cell that just couldn't be copied right and then multiplies too far, too fast.

Some of the viewers want to know who this is, this girl without the face they are used to, and why she is here? These are the ones who ask a lot of questions, including: is she really sick? she looks okay on the outside, they say, maybe a little thin, but some girls are just thin. To them, without something obvious, like a mean rash or sudden hair loss or startling jaundice, there will always be doubt.

Some of the viewers are cruel because they can be. you people are always looking for something to complain about, they say, when they see the long swaths of her brown skin. A few others say that doctors are for old people and sick freaks that leech off the medical system. This, though, is not enough for them. They send her direct messages, anonymous behind their usernames—hateful. They call her words she has never heard before and never wants to hear again. They say, you people always want to blame someone else for your own problems. Blame no one but yourself, they mean. You should have been better.

The girl on the screen answers each comment with a single sentence, one she learned in the hospital just two days ago: recovery is not a straight line.

CHAPTER SEVENTEEN

All of it, on the same day.
 Nikhil wakes to Kashmira sitting on his bed, with wide, forlorn eyes. He pries the phone out of her hand to see what's going on, while she buries her face in a pillow and tells him she regrets doing it, regrets posting the VidMo. Meanwhile, his phone goes off with texts from Erin saying she's already halfway back to Jersey to talk to him face-to-face. She doesn't want them to communicate in writing right now. And then, his phone dings with a notice from @keon telling him that because of his poor performance at work and continued absence from the office, he's on probation.

Ami is out, at her hospital admin job, but even if she wasn't, Nikhil would have handled things the way he does. He sits with Kashmira first, and promises her he isn't upset about the video. He means this. Watching the video, he sees how she has told her own story with resolute honesty. She tells her history with precise, devastating detail. A thing like this requires bravery.

"I want to delete it, though," she says. "Look at all these comments."

They spend the next hour scrolling through the replies, both the public ones and the private messages. Kashmira's impulse to delete makes sense: It's unnerving, though perhaps gratifying, how many people are immediately obsessed with her. The great outpouring of sympathy feels like hundreds of well-wishers have lined up at their door. But then, there are the other comments too. The crueler ones make him want to go after these people somehow, some way. But his sister isn't ask him to do that. She just wants him to sit with her, so all he does is wrap an arm around her.

"What do you think?" Kashmira says. "Should I just get rid of it? Make it go away?"

"I think you should do what you want. But even if you do delete it, I'm assuming someone has saved a copy by now."

"Right," she says, and then puts her phone down. Her eyelids are still puffy from crying, and even now, she rubs at her nose. "Have you heard anything from work? I kind of told Jordie I'm your sister. I kind of told her everything."

He hesitates, lips quirking up then down. This, too, is brave—in its rashness, in its devil-may-care truth telling—but it's also not at all what makes sense when it comes to strategically moving against Evolvoir. Nikhil doesn't blame his sister for yelling the truth out during her Concierge appointment, but he guesses Erin, who in all the time he has known her has always been calculating, might not feel the same. The doorbell rings to mark her arrival.

"Are you expecting someone?" Kashmira says.

She sounds upset by the intrusion on their moment, and Nikhil explains Erin's already being on her way. "But you don't have to say hi unless you want to."

His sister doesn't know what she wants, other than washing her face. But her slipping into the bathroom gives Nikhil a few minutes to suss out Erin's mood. He opens the front door. Outside, on the stoop, Erin waits, flushed, as though she jogged from her visitor's parking spot to here. When Nikhil moves to the side of their entry, she brushes past him and sets up without asking at the kitchen table. There it is, laptop, notebook, phone, all of it.

"I can't believe that video went up. It changed everything about our approach, Nikhil," she says. "And that strategy was important to get this story told right."

"I think she did a good job telling her side," Nikhil says. His sister had done her best, and Erin isn't the one with the overwhelmed body and the overworked mind. "Do you really think either of us would do better if we were in her situation?"

"But what about facts? And evidence? The video didn't get any of the background that we now know." Erin presses her hands to her hairline, holding back her bangs. "We just, we have to move faster now. Is she here?"

"Yes," Kashmira says, walking into the kitchen and dropping into a chair. Her fingers skim the top of the table as she scrutinizes Erin's setup. "So, you're the reporter friend."

"Hi," Erin says. "Yeah, I'm the reporter. You're the sister?" She pauses, then maybe realizes she is being rude to a frightened teenager who only just reentered the world after being hospitalized for eight days. "How are you feeling?"

"I don't know, scared? Everyone's freaking out online. And I think Nikhil's going to lose his job."

"We don't know that," Nikhil says. "But Erin, I am on probation."

He opens TaskSquad to read @keon's message but notices, first, that the #all-press-is-good-press channel is 🔒 . Nikhil clicks the icon, but nothing pops up. Then, navigating to the thread between him and @keon, he sees that what he thought was going to be a text is actually a formal PDF from the People Team. It states that Nikhil has been noticeably behind on his tasks not just since he came to Jersey, but since his hiring. After this paragraph, they have included a list of projects he hasn't sufficiently handled. Most are about marketing NuLook, though the flagship product had been taken off his docket when Nikhil moved to the Operation Wellness Team and launched ReNuLook. But when Nikhil tries to navigate to those private messages with Keon for proof of that discussion, he finds that they've been scrubbed from TaskSquad entirely. All that's left now is the probation notice, which demands he return to the office immediately to create a performance improvement plan, or else he'll be fired.

"They didn't mention me," Kashmira says. She sits with her knees against her chest.

"True," Nikhil says. He rereads the PDF, annoyed. Not so much about coming to a head with Evolvoir—he'd expected, and maybe even wanted this since Erin came to him with proof of the company's unscrupulous dealings—but about them forcing him to accelerate his timeline and return to New York. "But they did make a lot of shit up."

Erin types quickly, taking notes on everything he says. "Well, probation isn't anything legally binding, and New York is an at-will state anyway. They're just trying to make some kind of paper trail for when they inevitably do fire you." She pauses to shrug at him. "Things are bad for them right now. Your sister's video is doing numbers and, on top of that, one of those fake-identity lawsuits is unexpectedly moving forward to trial. They're probably investigating the link between you and Kashmira, but right now all they want is to scare you out of filing for wrongful termination."

Sounding more practiced at this than Nikhil thinks she is, Erin details how they ought to move forward. The article is the most important thing, even with the video already circulating. What Kashmira gave them was an opportunity for traction, but they need to provide a good investigative report that both provides answers and opens up more questions too.

"We can do an interview with Kashmira too," Erin says.

"Me?" Kashmira replies. "I already said my side. In the video."

"You didn't talk to a reporter, though."

"Well, after the comments I got on this video, I'm not sure I want to."

Erin shuts her laptop. Her disappointment, palpable. While she can take some pull quotes from the video Kashmira already posted, the whole article might read as thin without a more in-depth profile of the person who has suddenly catapulted this story to the public consciousness. Nikhil imagines Erin mentally rifling through what she learned in journalism school, all those tips and tricks to make a source comfortable enough to speak. But why should it be Kashmira's responsibility to reveal herself further when she clearly doesn't want to? Nikhil looks at Kashmira, who looks at him.

"Don't make me do this," she says. "Please. Can't you just, I don't know, do it for me?"

The call comes around noon, while Nikhil is in the kitchen, finishing up making lunch for his sister. At first, he doesn't hear the vibrating device over the sound of the boiling pasta water, but then he catches a glimpse of Michael's name flashing across the screen. He lunges.

"Hello?" he says, while turning the stove burner off.

It takes a moment for Michael's voice to come through. The sound of the city overtakes it at times, a cacophony of other people talking, cars honking, construction that never seems to end. Nikhil presses the phone to his ear.

"Are you okay? What's going on?" Michael says. "You haven't been in the office for like two weeks. Things are, like, anarchy here. Something happened with one of the lawsuits. And then there was this VidMo on Yukiko's account. Jordie is saying the girl who posted it is your sister."

Nikhil leans against the counter. "Did you get my message?"

Michael doesn't respond at first. Either because he's thinking or because he's pausing while a truck rolls by, loud and unyielding. Finally, he says, "Yeah, I got it. I listened to it twice."

"You didn't call me back."

"I was," Michael pauses. "Embarrassed."

He hadn't wanted to admit that Nikhil was right and that in the end, they'd both had flaws in their arguments about what it meant to care for others. That was a hard thing to accept for a man who had always understood himself as someone with an uncanny understanding of community.

Things have quieted in the background. Michael must have veered into a side street or an alcove with a stoop. Once he can talk again, he says, "You had a lot to say about what I do and don't get."

At first, Michael had thought taking a few days to collect himself would be fine. He'd call Nikhil soon. But then he'd seen Kashmira's video. Not that he'd known it was Nikhil's sister at the time. All he'd grasped was that he found the footage horrifying. So had the entire office. Nikhil nods, though Michael can't see him. He can imagine the office: people huddled over their computers, meeting after meeting, discussions, secret conversations between employees trying to figure things out in the kitchen and the bathrooms and the stairwells. Many of them were probably worried about their jobs, but hopefully some of them had ethical concerns.

"I saw it then," Michael says. "I really saw how bad being sick is in the way your sister talked. And I realized I kept saying I didn't get involved in all this business shit. But that means I'm just letting them do this to people. If I care about real people, I do have to care about this."

After he says this, they are both quiet for a long time. They have an understanding, Nikhil realizes. That's what this silence is.

Then Michael says, "Look, I'm ready to be there how you need me to be. When are you coming back?"

Tonight. Earlier, in this very kitchen, he had he promised Kashmira she wouldn't have to be in the interview. They would find another way, other sources, other evidence. In that case, Erin had said, he had to go to the probation meeting tomorrow, so they could get as much information as possible before she publishes her first piece on Evolvoir. When Nikhil said he wasn't sure if he could leave home yet, Kashmira disagreed. She wanted him to stay, yes, but more than anything she wanted him to go after Evolvoir. That meant assisting Erin in any way possible. And that meant going to the meeting, but also getting a few things from Evolvoir, like examples of marketing copy, recent TaskSquad conversations, and ideally the minutes from the Operation Wellness Team meetings.

Tentatively, Nikhil says, "We could use your help with those last parts."

"Give the reporter my number," Michael replies. "I'll see what I can do."

Before he hangs up, Nikhil gets one more hit of the Manhattan's sounds. Michael must be on the move again, back on the sidewalk. The bustle reaches the phone—and then, the line cuts. But that's all right; Nikhil trusts this isn't the end of their conversation.

He and Ami fold laundry on the bed. A third of the pile will go to Kashmira's room, a third to the linen closet, and a third will stay here, in Ami's room. These divisions that don't include him, now that he leaves tonight. And though he'll return, for now Nikhil wants to leave things as good as he can. So when Kashmira came to him, asking if he would do one more thing for her—talk to their mother—he said yes. He wishes this were as easy as piling shirts in neat squares.

"What are you going to do when I'm gone?" Nikhil says. "You haven't said anything about that yet."

"Things are going to go back to the way they were," Ami says. She turns to the towels. When she tosses one to the side, not in any of the piles, it throws everything off. "Won't they?"

Nikhil digs into the remaining clothes. A metal zipper, still hot, brands him. "You know, Kashmira will still be sick. She'll need you."

Ami folds and refolds a shirt that didn't need to be folded in the first place. "I know. I was able to do it in the hospital. I was able to be a mother. I don't know why I can't here."

He does. In this very bedroom, Ami sleeps on the bed she once shared with her husband. It's concave in the middle, and it always has been. Nikhil used to imagine that his parents slept around the dip in the center, keeping a slice of air between them. The image, sad and yet comforting, because it's one from his youth. It isn't easy to let go of what was. Not for him, and not for Ami, who lives in this apartment exactly the way she did when Vinod was still here.

"This was his territory," Nikhil says, and when Ami nods, he opens his arms for her to rest inside. Her head presses against his chest and she keeps nodding as she tells him that she has considered what to do with this apartment, time and again. The mortgage is paid off, so it might be easiest to stay. Otherwise, it overwhelms her, the idea of packing everything up and getting out. It overwhelms her not just because of the logistics but also because these walls are all she has left of a life that may not have been perfect, but at least was hers. He lets her get this all out, and then Nikhil says, "And it's not just the apartment, is it?"

Ami steps back and sits on the edge of the bed. The mattress feels thin when he sits next to her. But he wants to be close when she says the next thing.

"He was the one who always decided how to raise you kids," Ami says. "We lived in this apartment and I did what he said. And that made him happy. And that made me happy."

"But he was—"

"Wrong about what he did and said, I know. Kashmira and I talked about that in the hospital." Ami traces the stiches on the bedspread with one finger. "But at least he had an idea about how to be a parent."

"You were a parent in the hospital," Nikhil says.

She laughs. A light, tinkering thing he doesn't usually get to hear. Then she tells him that she wasn't doing much in the hospital except staying by Kashmira, showing her that she wasn't alone. That isn't raising a child. Nikhil stares at her, until he understands that she's serious.

"But that's all she needs you to do, Mom," he says. "And you two can just figure it out together."

Because isn't that what Vinod had wanted anyway? For them to remake their lives? That was the reason he'd left, and he'd explicated that to them not only in his note but also in the actions he took afterward. Nikhil has been thinking a lot about how Vinod left them some of his mother's money. That inheritance. Once, Nikhil had said his father had done out of guilt. Perhaps he had, but perhaps he had also done it because he knew the power of a check on someone's future.

"One time," Ami says, after Nikhil suggests she use the inheritance to find a new place, a bigger, better place, "your sister told me I make being a mother too hard."

After this, she tells him that he should take some part of the money, too, because she doesn't know what will happen with his job. He nods. He has been considering this point himself.

"I'll think about it, if you think about yourself too," Nikhil says. "And Kashmira."

—⁂—

Years ago, when Nikhil first went off to college, Kashmira pretended to hide in one of the big cardboard boxes he packed all his T-shirts in. She came out only when called for dinner three times, and even then, her face had been tear-streaked. Nikhil tweaked her nose and promised her she could visit whenever she wanted, and he meant it. Today, there is no cardboard box. Just the duffel, half full, and Nikhil's laptop bag. Still, there is Kashmira, cross-legged next to his things, waiting to be packed up too. Yet again, it isn't possible. Yet again, he has to find a way to say goodbye for now.

"How about some ice cream?" Nikhil says, thinking of past summers with her. Cones, licked clean. Nothing was really simpler then, but it had felt that way. They can't get to the shore tonight, but Nikhil can still take her to a local place, one that he knows she likes. "I'll even buy you a sundae. The one with the face."

"That's for kids," she says, already slipping on her shoes. "I want soft serve."

So, she remembers those summers too. At the scoop shop, which smells of soft waffle cones being molded, Kashmira orders a sundae after all, maybe just to humor him. Fresh vanilla, with a smile made from a ripple of caramel. Three towering scoops. But even though all this dairy will pose a risk to her delicate digestion, Kashmira holds the giant cup in two hands and grins. Maybe because it feels right to end Nikhil's visit this way.

"I bet you don't have sundaes like this in New York, huh?" she says, as they find seats at a small table.

"We have better." He bumps her shoulder, but it's a little too rough. "Fuck, sorry."

"Don't say 'fuck' here," Kashmira says. People are starting to line up—it's a popular spot in town—and a toddler points and laughs at Kashmira and Nikhil's tussling. Then he pulls his sister's pigtail. "We'll get in trouble."

"Hey, you said it too. We're in this together now. Always have been."

Ice cream drips from Nikhil's cone and onto his leg. Kashmira hands him a napkin, then two. He wipes as she says, "Yeah. With or without Dad."

He watches her scrape the face off her sundae. The caramel falls to the bottom of the bowl. No longer smiling, no longer with any expression at all. They haven't talked much about Vinod since returning to the apartment. So much has happened, much of which is still because of him. Nikhil knows it, and his sister does, too.

"Are you doing okay?" he says. "With all of that?"

"I've just been wondering if he saw the video," she says.

It's hard to speculate. The video has made its rounds to so many places, but they don't know much about Vinod's habits any longer. Maybe his algorithm totally skipped over her face. Maybe it didn't. Either way, Vinod knows that Kashmira is sick. He still hasn't come back; he still believes his absence is for the best.

"Does it matter if he did see it?" Nikhil says.

"Maybe not," she says.

They go quiet, and Nikhil finishes the rest of his cone with quick licks. Kashmira, though, takes a long time to eat the rest of her dessert. She fills her spoon just halfway each time, and then even when the bowl is clearly empty she keep scraping at it. Nikhil takes it as a good sign, maybe that she wants to prolong their goodbye. But then, eventually, there are too many people in the shop for them to hold a table any longer. It's time to go.

Outside, the walk to the car is pleasant. Children laugh as dusk falls. Crickets chirp from a tree. Kashmira puts her hand on the door to the passenger seat and says, "I'll be okay, Nikhil. As long as you don't forget that we're in it together."

"Kashmira," he says, meaning to finish with *how could you think I'd forget?*

But before he can reply, she's in the car, playing with the radio. She fiddles with it, and then settles on Top 40—which she knows he hates. It's almost like she wants him to react, so when he sits in the car, he bats her hand away from the dial. In retaliation, she presses her hand to his cheek, leaving caramel residue on the stubble that has started to grow back into hair now that it's evening. They share a glance, and then she adds, "Okay. Say you won't forget."

So that's what this bit was about. She had needed a moment in the midst of this goodbye. And she'd gotten it. And now she can continue. Maybe they're getting better at handling partings.

"I won't forget," he says.

"Good. Because I'm scared, you know. The whole world's different now, and I don't know, maybe I'll need a sibling at some point."

"You'll probably need one more often than you think."

She rolls her eyes. "That's comforting."

Nikhil puts a hand on her wrist, keeping his grip as loose as the familiar hair tie that she won't take off until it snaps. He says, "I've got you. No matter what happens." He smiles. "Just promise me you'll call."

"Promise you'll pick up if I do," she says.

Kashmira leans against the window while Nikhil turns out of the parking lot. The road is clear. The sun is setting but warm around the lush oak trees. They could run any red light and still survive. Nikhil reaches over to pull her hair, like brothers do.

RE: DEFAMATION OF CHARACTER—
FOR LIBEL AND/OR SLANDER

This law firm is litigation counsel for Evolvoir LLC ("Evolvoir"). If you are represented by counsel for defamation-related matters, please direct this letter to your attorney immediately and have them notify us of that representation. We are investigating numerous false and/or baseless statements that you have made about Evolvoir in your social media post titled "the truth about renulook/nulook" ("the video"). These statements have been circulated by various media outlets as well.

Evolvoir is committed to providing their clients with safe beauty products. The products have undergone testing and have been used by thousands without incident. However, per the terms and conditions that each client is asked to accept, Evolvoir cannot guarantee that its products will have the same effect on each individual.

The video ignores this reality and instead spreads disparaging information intended to harm Evolvoir's reputation, slander its products, and destroy its consumer-company relationships. The video uses a personal medical experience as the basis of its claims and makes biased assumptions about the cause of the individual's illness that do not have scientific merit.

We demand that you remove the video from the VidMo app within twenty-four hours of receiving this notice.

CHAPTER EIGHTEEN

A doctor's office, her first after the hospital.
This primary care doctor holds some Saturday hours, and Kashmira is scheduled for the day after Nikhil leaves for New York. Unlike her GI visits, during which she will talk specifically about her colon and its health, this appointment is to discuss everything else—from any vitamin deficiencies to vaccinations she should get since she is now more susceptible to serious illness to the weird lingering hives along her neck to her lymph nodes, which are still swollen. While her mother sits in the corner, Kashmira settles on the white paper without changing into a gown. The nurse told her that this appointment was just to talk, that they'd have her change if needed. Somehow it's more uncomfortable for Kashmira to keep her clothes—gray sweatpants that make her inner thighs sweat, flannel shirt hiding her loose, casually bulbous breasts—on. She is more accustomed to stripping down and laying bare now than not.

"You're very articulate for your age," the doctor says after Kashmira goes through her medical history.

"No," Kashmira says. "I just went through some shit."

"Some shit" meaning the hospitalization, and also everything that came before and everything that came after. When she received the cease-and-desist letter, she'd been scared, but Nikhil promised to back her no matter what. So the video remains online, along with all the copies that people made and posted with their little edits and commentary. By now, more people have spent moments noticing her body than she ever expected. And so Kashmira has a sense that whenever she walks around, letting herself be seen—whether in the apartment complex or at the drugstore to order her medication or at the grocery store to pick up low-fiber foods that suit her digestion—others recognize her in a way they didn't before. In their expressions is a scrutiny like she has never experienced before, and apparently has no choice but to tolerate.

As the doctor continues the exam, Kashmira answers more of the clarifying questions with ease. Things like *When did this rash on your neck start?* and *Has it always been this color?* She knows how to talk to doctors now. They want clear, efficient answers with as much detailed observation as possible, and she is a good patient, because she can discuss her health the way they want. This doesn't surprise her after her time in the hospital. But what does make her swivel her head is Ami, coming in to add a few things here and there. She isn't as bold, as protective, as Kashmira has seen her before, but she's trying.

"Thanks, Mom," Kashmira says after Ami corrects her on the date her next biologic injection is due. Her mother squeezes her hand, and they leave it at that until later, in bed, when Kashmira replays the moment in her head and finds herself smiling.

In the end, the appointment goes well. All of Kashmira's symptoms are noted. A few more medicines—all topical—are prescribed. The one-month window between now and her follow-up is discussed. And therapy has been brought up. This last point is actually something that Nikhil and Kashmira have already talked about. They're both in agreement that they want to try getting back into treatment, though they know it may take some time to find the right practitioner, the right style, the right location, the right price, and the right time slot. Regardless, they want to try. Regardless, they are glad they have other support systems too. Kashmira's PCP is also pleased with this plan, and so the last thing she needs to do is get some blood drawn. Across the hall, though, the phlebotomist struggles to find a vein. The skin on both of Kashmira's arms is still bruised from the hospital, making it hard to see. A continued reaction to the trauma of the needle digging into her, apparently. The phlebotomist falters, saying she doesn't want to poke Kashmira more times than necessary.

"Try that vein," Kashmira says, running her finger over a spot she remembers the emergency room nurses used. It was the first IV site that had blown, but maybe it has since healed and can take another prick.

It works. One tube, two tubes, three tubes. They're done, except they aren't.

Outside, by the elevators, a harder examination. While Ami sorts Kashmira's next appointment out with the scheduler, Kashmira comes into the hallway. There, one of the kathak girls, Prithi, who wanted the products so badly she called Kashmira a bitch for not handing them over, is waiting, gauze on her otherwise bare arm. She scrutinizes blinks at Kashmira—having to get used to these old features of Vinod's instead of the manufactured face Kashmira used to wear—but eventually she gets who stands in front of her. Maybe she saw Kashmira's video, where she presented both her old face and her new one side by side, a before and after and now a before again.

"You see the doctor here too?" Prithi says. She checks to see where the elevators are. Kashmira does too. One seems stuck at the top of the building, the other at the ground floor. Prithi places a hand on her hip and says, "I saw your video. But somehow, you don't look as bad in real life."

Kashmira flinches at what sounds like a compliment. She said the same thing to Roshni that first night when they'd discussed the clinic. It's easy, even here at a doctor's, even after the video, for others to dismiss what has ravaged her body. Her thinness, her acne, even the moon face that has started up just this morning thanks to the steroids are all barely noticeable to anyone who hasn't spent much time with her or doesn't know her original face. She might look slightly off to them, if that.

"Look, I didn't mean it in a weird way," Prithi says, responding to Kashmira's silence. She thumbs at the gauze on her arm. "I mean, I know we've had our differences."

"I get what you were trying to say," Kashmira replies, because she does believe the other girl. In this world, it's a nice thing to congratulate others on looking well despite going through the hardest things. No one sees the erasure inherent in their words. So, she lets it go.

Still, as she turns away, Kashmira is left with one image: Prithi's arm, not yet bruised. She presses her fingers to her own mottled skin, wondering what will happen once it goes back to a simple brown.

―⁂―

Roshni is the one who coaxes Kashmira back to dance.

"It'll be the last lesson before I have to leave next weekend," she says. "Don't you want to come?"

It's the day after Kashmira's check-up at the doctor's, and Kashmira is tired. Every excursion out of the house requires more energy. But she does want to see Roshni. They haven't hung out since the hospital, because Lalita keeps Roshni busy with packing for The Center. When Kashmira tells Ami this, her mother offers to drive, and so Kashmira arrives on time, with her leggings on and her hair tied back in a sleek ponytail. As she gets out of the car, Ami puts a hand on her wrist.

"Would it be good if I stayed?" she asks.

"If you want," Kashmira tells her, because really, she isn't sure what the best thing for the two of them is. And yet, she finds herself appreciating that Ami is even considering hanging around the studio, despite this likely reminding her of Vinod.

"Okay, then," Ami says, and opens the car door.

They walk inside together and at first the other students don't recognize Kashmira. Not until, like Prithi, they remember her video, do a double take. Then, a few wave, though many of them square their shoulders and turn away, apparently unsure what to do with her. Hemaji, though, approaches and places a firm hand on Kashmira's shoulder.

She says, "I heard you were sick. You're better now?"

"I'm mostly here to watch, but maybe I can join in on the warm-ups," Kashmira replies. She looks over to where Ami has actually settled down by the wall where the girls leave their bags. "My mother will be staying, I guess."

Her voice comes out shy from the surprise of this, and Hemaji looks her up and down, as if assessing her endurance or strength. Whatever she sees, she seems to find it acceptable, because she agrees to let Kashmira out onto the floor. The only stipulation is that Kashmira stand by Roshni, who can help her take things down to half speed if needed.

"Hi," Roshni says, coming up from behind them. She leans an arm on Kashmira's shoulder, as if to check that Kashmira can hold up her weight. "Are you sure you're up for this?"

"You're the one who told me to come," Kashmira tells her and jiggles her arm to playfully throw Roshni off.

When dance starts, Kashmira stands in the center of the room, though somehow she gets pushed toward the back with each new warm-up exercise. It doesn't matter. She can hear the tanpura. When the taatkaar starts, she keeps up, thrusting her heels into the ground in time like the rest of them. It's fine, she assures herself, although her feet don't make the same strong sound as everyone else's now. And it's hard to lift her hands as high and keep them there. As Hemaji speeds up the count, Kashmira's breath comes in pants. Still, she tries to keep up, until the taatkaar gets faster and faster and everyone but her seems to be able to do it. A flaring pain makes her clutch her side.

"Don't forget to smile," Hemaji calls out.

The other girls grin, but Kashmira grits her teeth. She can't make herself smile. She can barely keep herself upright. Worse still, she swears everyone is staring at her now. The sick girl, who can't do the most basic of movements any longer. Blackness clouds Kashmira's vision and she sways in place, taatkaar forgotten. Then she blinks.

Roshni is talking to her. Roshni is drawing closer. Roshni has her hand on Kashmira's elbow.

"You need to sit down," Roshni says. "I'm sorry, I—yeah, I'm sorry."

She leads Kashmira to the edge of the classroom, where Ami presses a water bottle against the back of Kashmira's neck and asks her if she's okay.

"Yeah," Kashmira says, taking the drink from her mother's hand so she can gulp it down. "I think so."

She is okay. Kashmira's heart rate settles and her vision clears, too. But she knows she has to stay sitting, and it's humiliating to see the other girls dancing while she can't. Worse is when Hemaji starts them on their autumn recital piece, and Kashmira realizes they've gotten further along than she expected. At this rate, she'll never catch up. It's unlikely she'll be able to perform at all.

"You look upset," Ami says, leaning over.

Kashmira frowns, debating whether or not to confide in her mother. "It wasn't my best."

"But you looked good," Ami tells her. "You kept up in your own way."

Kashmira shrugs. When class finally ends, she stands, ready to get out of there. But then Hemaji strides toward her, Roshni in tow. The older woman stops in front of Kashmira, graying eyes sharp. Kashmira almost preemptively winces, imagining the scolding she'll get for trying to dance in that state. Instead, Hemaji turns to Ami.

"You should be proud of your daughter," she says. "After all she has been through, she looks good out there."

"Thank you," Ami says, smiling. "I thought so too."

"You really did," Roshni agrees.

There they are, the three of them, assuring her that what she did out there was good enough. Hemaji tells her, honesty coloring her somehow still-rough voice, that this dance is one of storytellers. Her dance is her own story, and even if it looks a little different, it's part of their tradition to share that history however she can.

"You still do need to practice," Hemaji says. "But I think it's a nice start."

That evening, after the dance lesson, Sachin comes over, and the two of them squish together on her soft living room couch to look through some of his new film. Lately, Sachin has been trying new techniques to include himself in the shots. Sometimes he sets the camera up in a corner and hopes it'll catch him while he walks through a room. Sometimes he wears it on his forehead and waves his hands in front of it. Sometimes he makes someone else film him, though this is his least favorite method because it feels inorganic. Kashmira watches whatever he tries and critiques each clip with whatever comes to mind. These days, when he takes out his notebook and writes down what she has to say, she feels glee, especially when he kisses her afterward.

Today, though, even as she rests her head on his shoulder and pulls their shared blanket up to her neck and watches the footage twice over, nothing comes to mind. She likes it, as she likes everything he does, but it registers only as that: good. When Kashmira tells him this, Sachin writes it in the notebook anyway, then touches her cheekbone with his pen-marked fingers.

"Did I show you the clip you're in?" he says.

It reminds her of that first conversation they had after her first party with the South Jersey brown kids. How he'd shown her some footage, and she hadn't wanted to look. That time, she was wearing Roshni's cream. This time, it's just her in her regular face, walking past the camera—and it looks fine, maybe a little puffy from the steroids, but overall, healthy enough. The image makes her breath hitch. How is it that inside her is still sick—will always be sick, even in that treasured state of remission—but the outside can heal so quickly?

"What's wrong?" Sachin says, leaning back to take in her expression. "I didn't realize you still minded me filming you. I thought, after the whole VidMo thing—"

"No, it's not the filming," she tells him quickly. "It's just the way I look now. Like at the doctor the other day, this girl from kathak told me I looked better than she expected. Even though she knows I was in the hospital."

"And that bothers you?"

"I guess." She tucks her hair behind her ear. "Even at dance, after I almost passed out, they still said I seemed pretty well."

Sachin draws her closer with one arm. "And in some ways you are."

At this, Kashmira pulls away, unable to understand how he could think that, when he himself visited her in the hospital and saw the tubing coming out of her. When he himself has seen her run to the bathroom in the middle of eating, because even now the steroids and biologics can't control everything. When he himself has heard the stories of her family and how their legacy lives inside her.

"You can't seriously believe that," she says.

Sachin purses his lips, and she worries that her high-pitched tone will send him careening back to his camera. That he'll put it between them again and look at her through the lens only. But no, he just reaches for her hand, smiling when she allows him to take it.

"I'm not saying you're not sick. Or that you're okay like how they want you to be. I'm just saying that you're healthy, alive, in your own way."

She tries to parse what he means, but then he is still going, hurtling through sentences. Soon, he starts to say lovely things, things she didn't expect. He says she's alive and well because when she is sad, she knows to cry. He says she's alive and well because she knows her body in ways few people ever will. He says she's alive and well because she is able to sit here with someone who loves her. He says that very word, *love*, and Kashmira blushes and stares down at her toes. She hadn't prepared for a moment like this, because she hadn't expected it to come so soon. But maybe what they've been through has opened up space for such deep feeling. After all, what can it be but love that has allowed them to keep coming back to each other in these most difficult of times? She exhales, seeing this. She exhales, and then says the truest thing. That yes, she loves him too. At this, he smiles so she has to grab onto his shoulders to steady herself.

When they part, he cups her face. He says, in the most serious of tones, "But I just want you to know that I know that even if you're well, you're still sick too. That's okay, though. If I know you, you'll figure out how to be both. One day, you will."

"Sachin," she says, because after those warm caresses she can't get anything out but his name. She swallows, gives herself a little longer to collect herself, and then adds, "If I had a black notebook, I'd put that in there."

"I'll get you one." Sachin laughs, that familiar sweet whistle of a laugh. How she loves to hear it. But then, he's already talking again, and she loves to hear that too. He says, with firmness, "Now come be in this shot with me. I think it'll be a good one."

After they take their video, they lean over the viewfinder together. Kashmira watches herself frame by frame. Each expression—laughing, smirking, pouting—is real and captured there for anyone to see. Now, she understands: Yes, her stomach still aches. Yes, her gut still controls her half the time. That is the truth of her. But so is this.

CHAPTER NINETEEN

Tuesday in New York. Nikhil's fifth day back in the city. He returned to the office Friday and met with Keon to have a conversation about probation and to create a performance improvement plan. All of it a farce, of course, but one Nikhil, knowing that Erin is still working on her article, played along with. He knows, though, that his firing is coming. As part of his probation, they've kept him locked out of TaskSquad channels and turned off most of his company cloud access, preventing him from viewing, downloading, or editing most Evolvoir files. That can't be standard for probation, Nikhil guesses. Most likely, Larissa and Keon are just conferring with their legal counsel on what to do with him; once that's decided, he'll face the full consequences of Kashmira's video.

He's just getting off the B train and heading to work when a notification pings on his phone. This isn't from @keon, but @larissa:

—@nikhil meet me in conference room two in fifteen. i assume you're already here?

Nikhil reads it twice, and then, instead of responding, continues walking down the clean SoHo street, his pace still leisurely—and even slower when he texts Michael a screenshot of Larissa's message. He doesn't rush; he knows Larissa just wants to intimidate him. It won't work. Not when he has already mentally resigned from the company. What's important to him now is helping Erin finish her article so the full truth of what they know can be read and understood by the public. What's important is making the world question Evolvoir.

In the lobby of the building Evolvoir is housed in, Nikhil takes the elevator upstairs. He stops by the kitchen for what he knows will be his last coffee here. It tastes, as always, slightly acrid, but he appreciates the warmth in his hand as he carries the cup down the hall. Now that he's here, walking around, he does feel nervous. The last time he was here he knew so much less and was so different because of that. He isn't quite sure how to hold himself inside these white walls any longer. He swallows another drink of coffee. He can't let that discomfort win; he must be sharp in this meeting with Larissa so as not to fall for whatever tricks she'll try. He sighs, breathes, keeps walking.

His phone pings again, but this time with a text notification.

shit, Michael says. i just got here. did you meet her already?

Nikhil pockets his phone. He's already at his and Michael's shared desk—and yes, Michael is there. As he draws close, the other man straightens and turns. Warm eyes, a welcome. Nikhil basks for a moment in their shared gaze. The two of them didn't see each other yesterday; Keon had spent the whole day with Nikhil going over the performance improvement plan. So Nikhil and Michael had only texted updates. At the end of the exchange, Michael had offered to skip his work-from-home day today and come in. Nikhil told him it was up to him, and carried no expectations about what Michael would decide. But he had hoped, and now that hope has turned into a bone-deep gratefulness.

"Well, this is it," Nikhil says, putting down his bag. "I think it'll be fine."

"It's unsettling when you're calm like this," Michael says.

"You'd like me to flip a table in there, wouldn't you?"

"It couldn't hurt."

They smile at each other, a little shy. It's different talking in person rather than over the phone. How nice it feels to be here, in each other's space. Nikhil already wants more. If only they could fall completely into each other like before, but no, not yet. Getting there will take time. Besides, Nikhil does have to go. But at least there was this moment to calm him. He needed it, to feel ready again. Now it's with this very confidence that Nikhil puts his coffee down next to his keyboard, like someone who intends to come back to finish whatever it was he started on that computer. Nikhil leaves this symbol in case Keon walks by. After all, he will reappear in Evolvoir's orbit. Not to work with them, but against them, certainly.

"I'll be here," Michael says. "When you're out."

"Thanks." Nikhil clasps the other man's shoulder. Squeezes hard, with meaning to. Michael cocks his head, perhaps surprised by the obvious show of emotion. But then he puts his own hand on top of Nikhil's, just as Nikhil says, "I hope you know I appreciate that."

After this, Nikhil makes his way to the conference room, where Larissa sits with her water. Lemons, again. He wonders what she would say if he called her predictable. Under her eyes, the skin looks thin and tired. He can tell she hasn't been sleeping. Instead of bobbing around, the lemons cluster at the bottom of her glass, seemingly stuck.

"Sit," she says.

Nikhil pulls out a chair and does so.

She goes on. "I was shocked, to say the least, to hear about everything you've done."

Her accusations come in succession: his initial breaching of trust when he talked to a reporter about hiring Yukiko; his ignoring his tasks while he was in New Jersey; his risking the autumn marketing campaign by shirking said tasks; his allowing his sister to get free products; his never informing the company of her illness and her suspicions that the product had caused any of it; his conspiring with his sister to spread slander online. Some of these are more accurate than others, but Nikhil doesn't debate. He knows there will be lawyers who will do that in the future. Larissa, for her part, sighs—a soft puff of air that serves as acknowledgment that while this was a lot to get out, it isn't all that's bothering her.

"I thought we were in agreement, Nikhil," she says. "You belonged here because you wanted the same things. You were on my side."

He thinks about this before he answers. There was a time when he and Larissa really had been allies, both of them motivated by the same desire to make a product that could disrupt the status quo. For her, the status quo of the beauty industry. For him, the status quo of the traumatized, devastated by difficult family histories and circumstances. Both he and Larissa had thought they could solve problems by using only their narrow perspectives, their narrow beliefs.

"I was on your side," he says. "Until I learned what that meant."

"I see," she says, though he can tell from her rapidly blinking eyes that she's overwhelmed by frustration, that she'd like to cry. Not that she will. The risk is too great that the gossip would travel to employees', board members', investors' ears. The conference room is made mostly of glass, and she's all too aware of people looking in to observe what she does. Instead, she says, "That's a disappointment."

Then, a knock on the door: a security guy, the one who works in the lobby downstairs. Larissa waves him in, and he stands next to Nikhil. The heat of his eagerness to escort someone out, palpable. He keeps his hand on his belt, though he doesn't keep a gun there.

"I'm assuming I'm fired," Nikhil says.

Larissa doesn't have to nod. The expression on her face says more, not because of some furious set of her mouth, but because each of her features sags. The look of a woman who has lost something. Pity brews inside him. He doesn't feel sorry because of her pain, but because she'll never know how wrong she is if she believes this is the nadir of how low a person can go.

He says, instead, "Then I've got nothing more to say. At this point."

"Security will monitor you as you pack up your desk," she tells him. "Leave your computer here. Your badge too. Anything personal you can take. Any other questions you have can be emailed to the People Team." Larissa slides away from the table. Light from a window illuminates her hair, her skin, her white teeth. She looks pearlescent. Closer to how she looked in the past when they met in another conference room. "You should know that my lawyers will be in touch."

He doesn't doubt it. But for now, his time with Evolvoir is over, so is the end of his obvious complicity. To others, it'll look as though he is no longer responsible for what happens here, but who's to say? He can only hope that his whistleblowing helps lessen the damage that his fight for big facial shifts may have created.

Security walks him down the hall. As he passes, programmers, product developers, marketers, interns glance up. He wonders what they, his now former colleagues who all have a hundred to-do list items to get to, are thinking. What rumors they've heard. Perhaps they're all hoping they never have to suffer this fate. But perhaps some of them might wonder about the claims in Kashmira's video, might wonder what they aren't being told, and whether they should look into things at Evolvoir more deeply. Maybe, just maybe, some of them will defect one day, too, but only after they understand that their work means nothing if they don't wonder who it touches and how. Nikhil tries to make eye contact with the employees, but slowly, they all drop their gazes and hunch back over their laptops. And so, Nikhil walks faster, ready to get out of this den of lackeys, who've bought into this place, just as he once had. But then, finally, Nikhil stops at the shared desk he used to sit at, and waits for Michael to notice him, and smiles when he does, smiles when he fondles his nose ring, smiles when he looks up at Nikhil and holds the stare.

"That's it?" Michael says.

"It doesn't have to be," Nikhil tells him—but then the guard tells them to stop talking, and Nikhil does, because he doesn't want to give the man anything to deliver back to Larissa.

Still, Nikhil takes his time with leaving. He packs a notebook he likes into his backpack, though the guard checks to make sure it doesn't have any pertinent company information in it. His business cards he throws away. The cup of coffee he pours down the sink in the kitchen. He takes the long way back to his desk. On the way, he stops in one more place: where Yukiko used to sit. The chair, teal leather and somehow cracking already. The quality, less than she deserved. He presses his hands against the back of it and wishes it were warm from someone sitting there. He remembers her, the girl on the screen, for a long moment, because she was the start of many things and the end of many other things for him. Without her, he wouldn't be where he is now.

Eventually, the guard tells him to get going, in a tone that suggests he should cooperate. Eventually, Nikhil backs away. And then, the chair goes back to being a vacant space, waiting to be filled.

Erin meets Nikhil, who is still being escorted out, right on the street outside the building, She holds up her phone, seemingly recording security directing Nikhil out onto the sidewalk. The way her fingers pinch at the screen, it looks as though she might be zooming in. Realizing this, the guard backs away, likely leaving Nikhil as the only clear figure in the shot.

"How did you know to meet me here?" he says to Erin.

"Michael texted. Right when you went into the meeting." She waves her phone at him. "It's too bad I don't get to cite you as currently working here. Readers love a good mole. But I'll just change it to 'former employee.'" Then, "Hey, which way are you going? To your apartment?"

He nods, and she starts leading the way to the B train. Her brain, he marvels, holds so much information. Everything about this investigation, including where he lives and how he gets there. Erin, though, doesn't seem unnerved by her own memory. She keeps talking as they walk, saying, "So, anything else you want to add to the article after talking to Larissa? My editor wants us to run at least part one soon."

"That's fast," he says about the article once he finishes giving Erin the account of his firing. "Kashmira will be glad."

"How is your sister?" Erin asks. "Not for the article. Just to know."

Nikhil tells her the latest. He has talked to Kashmira every night since leaving Marlton, and she sounds as good as can be expected. A few times she expressed that she's nervous about the article, and he tells her he understands. But he's happy that she says she also wants to focus on other things, like school starting up and her new boyfriend and her health. He's happy, too, that she's willing to tell him how she feels. The last time he said this, Kashmira said, "Get ready for more of that. Don't think I'm not going to hold you to your promise to always pick up my calls."

"I don't think I said always," he told her, and she laughed and laughed,

By the time he finishes telling Erin all this, they've walked all the way to the station. A swell of people comes up from entrance, signaling that a train has just come and gone. There they go, scattering in all directions, while Erin says she's glad to hear Kashmira is holding it together. Nikhil adjusts his backpack and then gestures toward the stairs. He says to Erin, "Are you this way?"

"No, I have to get back to the office. I only left to meet you." Erin shrugs. "I have a call with Professor Lewis again later this afternoon, and then one of the FDA regulators after that."

Nikhil shifts on his heels. He feels a sense of an ending, even though he knows he and Erin will talk again. They'll have to, depending on what happens with Evolvoir. But Erin's work is growing past Nikhil, and there are other experts and thinkers whose deliberations may start to matter more than his own. For this he's glad. What he and Erin have done over this summer is complicated. If not for them, perhaps the major face shifting would have stopped earlier. Perhaps ReNuLook never would have existed. But also, perhaps Yukiko would have still died from her illness. Perhaps in that other timeline, she never would have had her story told. Perhaps the company would never have been exposed, and Larissa would have eventually latched on to Yukiko's videos and found her way toward somehow allowing these huge transformations again. Perhaps everything would have been the same. So there's no use in Nikhil and Erin ruminating over what could have been better or worse. They just have to accept that what is, is—and that this is goodbye.

"You know, if I had to meet some journalist at the biergarten that night, I'm glad it was you," Nikhil says.

"Even though I spilled beer on you? Maybe I should try that trick more often then." Her smile is crooked. "If you ever end up at a shitty tech company again, let me know. We can take them down together."

"I wish I could. But I'm leaving this business."

When she asks where he thinks he'll go, Nikhil tells her, honestly, that he doesn't know. He explains about the inheritance, and how he has accepted it while he tries to land on his feet. What that means, he'll find out.

He says, "This whole thing, it's started something for me. I don't want to give up on what I've learned."

"You won't," she says, simply. Then she drapes an arm around Nikhil's shoulder. They must look awkward there—two people who clearly weren't expecting to touch, but are. But holding on to each other is a way of holding on to the moment. And then, as another rush of people exits the subway, they let go.

They are supposed to meet each other outside the row of apartment buildings on 147th and Third Avenue that Friday, though Nikhil doesn't know for sure if Michael will come. After all, it's eight in the evening, and Michael—who hasn't yet been terminated, but will be soon, once Erin's article comes out—has worked all day. Still, Nikhil, who got here a half hour ago, watches the bus stop from afar while a truck bumps to cumbia music and serves nopales tacos outside a nail salon. A few more minutes pass, and then Michael does too. He walks a few steps too far, notices Nikhil, sidesteps a little girl with a dollar store doll, then comes back.

"You made it," Nikhil says, elated. "Just on time."

"Are you sure it's okay I'm here?" Michael asks.

They're about to meet one of the other girls who used the product and got sick. María Elena is twenty-one, and going into her senior year of college, though she worries she may need to take medical leave this semester. She hasn't been hospitalized, but she has been struggling with her diseased colon for five weeks now and it has been hard to sit through her classes. Nikhil knows about her because she was because she was in Yukiko's videos. Nikhil has been thinking about visiting each of the interviewees, if they'll have him.

"I told her you were coming," Nikhil says. "Ready?"

They don't have to buzz in. One of the other residents holds the door open, and they walk up four flights of stairs—actually eight if they count the switchback between each floor—to get to the apartment. Nikhil is the one who knocks and thus greets the middle-aged Mexican woman who tells him, "Yes, please come inside."

The apartment is not air-conditioned, so the water glasses the woman brings immediately condensate on their sides. The girl, María Elena, meets them in the living room wearing her pajamas. Her hair is messy and tossed up in a bun. But she seems energetic enough to talk, and she settles on the loveseat with her legs making a butterfly, and asks them questions the whole time.

"We're the ones who came to hear how you've been," Nikhil says.

María Elena updates them on the progress of her illness. She has been seeing a gastroenterologist whom she doesn't like too much. He isn't very sympathetic and pushes her through the appointment too quickly. She wonders if there are others she can see. Nikhil nods and tells her he could look up her options if she wants. When she shyly asks if he knows any therapists she might be able to afford too, he says he'll look into that and have the information to her by this weekend. After this, he and Michael spend the rest of the afternoon listening to her talk about liquids best for hydration, nice nurses and less nice ones, and the different kinds of cures people have been hawking. In this latter part of the conversation, Michael excels, making María Elena laugh as he gasps at the next ridiculous wellness suggestion. He acts like gossiping with her is the only thing he would ever want to do. And although María Elena often has to stop the flow of conversation to get up and use the bathroom, Michael always easily returns to the subject at hand, never once forgetting where they were. *It's good he came,* Nikhil thinks. And of course it is. It's Michael, after all.

Eventually, when María Elena tires, her mother says she needs to rest. She gets fatigued easily nowadays and overdoing it could put her out for three days or more. They can't have that, not if she is trying to make it through the semester.

"Thank you," Nikhil says, taking María Elena's hand, "for your time."

"No one ever really comes around anymore," she replies. "People always want me to go out and I can't really go out that often, so this was nice."

He's glad to hear this. It's part of the point of what he's trying to do. Namely, giving people like his sister a place to turn. Namely, helping to make them feel seen. But he also wants to assist in tangible ways, ways that move them through the systems they'll have to navigate. That's why he offered to make a list of doctors for her. That's why he's also ready to help her go through her medical bills and request payment plans if she wants. It's also why he opens his wallet and offers her the hundred dollars of cash he brought.

"It's a late payment for your video," he says. "It's just the first installment."

It's a meager amount, but it's what he can afford right now. And it'll help some, for a few co-pays or out-of-pocket costs or pharmacy needs or groceries. Or whatever María Elena wants. It's her choice.

The only two things he hopes are that eventually, when he finds work again, he'll be able to give more, and that one day there'll be a settlement payout from Evolvoir, so María Elena and the rest of the company's victims never have to worry again.

When she thanks him, he says, "You'll call me, if you need anything else? Here's my number again."

"You can come visit again too," she says.

She leans in and Nikhil opens his arms to hug her while promising to return soon.

Outside at the bus stop, there's no one else waiting, so Michael and Nikhil sit together on the bench. After a moment, Michael turns to Nikhil amid the scent of tacos in the air. Nikhil's mouth dampens—both from the smell and from the way Michael looks at him. Curious, like he once used to.

"So this is what you plan to do now?" Nikhil's old deskmate says.

Nikhil points out that he hasn't yet figured everything out, having only been unemployed for a few days. But, he goes on, he has spent his mornings looking up ideas. He has even started toying with the idea of going back to school, perhaps for social work or psychology. Even if he does that, though, he won't give up on these visits.

"How many more are there?" Michael says. "I want to come to what I can."

He's glad, so glad that Michael appreciates what he is trying to do. He doesn't want to just pretend what happened at the company is over, even if he no longer works there. And he doesn't want to just work through whatever normal channels are out there—the law, the media, whatever. As Michael has taught him, there are other ways.

Quietly, Nikhil rests his head on Michael's shoulder. The other man stiffens, then relaxes. They breathe together, three, two, one, breathe, three, two, one, breathe. Then they part. It was just a moment. But maybe one day it'll be more. Around them, the street fills as the bus starts rolling down from an avenue away. People gather to talk.

People gather to smoke, to play music from a souped-up car, and to sing. They hold on to each other's arms. They make jokes that maybe they have made a million times before. No matter. They will make them again and complain if the others don't laugh. That's how it is, all of them, so happy to be here, together.

Evolvoir Products Linked to Mysterious Illness—What We Know So Far (Part One)

Erin Frankel | @frankesterin

Editor's Note: This is Part One in a multipart series about the Evolvoir scandal.

Evolvoir's popular face-shifting creams NuLook and ReNuLook are at the center of a growing controversy as troubling information suggests the company had knowledge about its products' destructive capabilities and retailed them regardless.

Last week, allegations emerged that Evolvoir's products may be causing a chronic inflammatory condition in some users. One anonymous client accessed the defunct VidMo account @yukiko (692k followers) and posted a video implying a connection between Evolvoir's products and the death of Yukiko, a former Evolvoir employee and avid product user who died of a pulmonary embolism as a side effect of her undiagnosed inflammatory bowel disease on July 12 of this year. The video quickly went viral, prompting other users to share their own adverse experiences, including symptoms like bleeding, diarrhea, cramping, and pain.

[Evolvoir Clients Remember Yukiko: A Gallery Slideshow]

Internal emails obtained by our team reveal that Evolvoir was aware of potential health issues. Initial tests showed a 0.005% illness rate among early users, attributed to the "aggressive" nanotechnology used in NuLook, and later ReNuLook. Despite this, Evolvoir assumed no link between its technology and the prevalence of the disease. Instead, the company moved forward with bringing NuLook to market as quickly as possible—even going so far as to leverage a Food and Drug Administration loophole to push the product through as a cosmetic rather than a drug, despite the use of complex nanoparticles that can alter the body extensively.

[Screenshots of internal emails with key phrases highlighted]

Additionally, a former Evolvoir employee, Nikhil Mehta, claims that Yukiko alerted the company to these same safety issues weeks before her death but that Evolvoir did nothing.

"She told me, privately, that she had talked to them," Mehta said. "And I witnessed a meeting in which she was bullied out of revealing information to the larger team."

Mehta's sister was behind the posting on @yukiko and has allegedly been adversely affected by the product. Mehta, who was terminated this week, believes Evolvoir severed their relationship because of his sister's coming forward. His claims have been verified by Michael Harris, a current employee at Evolvoir who was also familiar with Yukiko and the Operation Wellness Team that she was working on.

"She wasn't well," Harris said. "And she was clearly worried about what the product could do. That much was clear in that July meeting right before her death. Evolvoir leadership just didn't care."

[Photos of Mehta and Harris standing outside Evolvoir HQ together]

While these allegations will require more investigation, some are already theorizing about how the product could have made these clients sick. Professor Latoya Lewis, a Princeton University researcher specializing in this iteration of nanotechnology, is now looking into users' testimonies. She offered a reason for why some users are getting sick while others are not.

"Some Evolvoir clients might be retraumatizing themselves when they engage in major face shifting in order to erase reminders of past trauma, such as abuse or loss," she said. "This emotional stress, combined with the intrusive nanotechnology, could be triggering an increase in pro-inflammatory cytokines, leading to chronic illness. Investigating this link will take time, though."

[Embedded research paper about nanotechnology's impact on the immune system]

[Embedded research paper on relationship between toxic stress and chronic illness]

Evolvoir's legal representative, Oscar Perez, downplayed the concerns. "According to the FDA, there is no debate over the safety of our cosmetics, which is our primary concern," Perez stated.

When pressed about whether the FDA should reclassify NuLook and ReNuLook as drugs instead of cosmetics—which would lead to more extensive investigation of their safety—he added, "That is a nuanced conversation for the experts, not for unqualified critics."

However, these revelations have alarmed some Evolvoir users. A twenty-one-year-old student from Pasadena expressed her doubts, saying, "This stuff makes me wonder if they even see me as a person, or just a cash cow." On the other hand, a twenty-seven-year-old banker from New York defended the company, saying, "Everything can hurt you these days, from microwaves to cars . . . what are you going to do, not drive, not eat, not wear something that actually makes you feel good about yourself?"

[Gallery: Faces of Evolvoir Clients]

Lawmakers have already been engaged in legal battles with Evolvoir over identity theft concerns. Now, new lawsuits focusing on health and safety could be on the horizon, as well as questions about Evolvoir's future funding streams. When asked about these allegations, representatives from both Surgere Partners and Forward Firm refused to comment. But despite these challenges, Evolvoir continues to push forward with initiatives like the BIPOC Beauty Babes program and has not yet recalled any of its products.

"That's understandable," Sandeep Agarwal of the Institute for Innovative Tech said. "There isn't a clear link between their product and this illness. However, it's worrisome—to say the least—that Evolvoir bypassed scrutinizing the safety of their product in favor of getting it to the market. It speaks less to an interest in developing something to help people and more to ego and hubris."

As this story unfolds, we will continue to investigate and report on the implications for Evolvoir and its clients. Stay tuned for Part Two of our series, where we delve deeper into the experiences of those affected, and Part Three, in which we further investigate how NuLook came to market.

CHAPTER TWENTY

The last party of the summer reminds Kashmira of the first. It's the end of August, the Friday of Labor Day weekend, and school starts on Tuesday. Today is a last hurrah. Girls wear skimpy bikinis, while the boys splash their butts and thighs from the pool. A few people stumble, precariously close to the deep end. Cups float in the chlorinated water. Some litter the ground. It smells of vodka and cheap rum and fruit juices that should never have been mixed together.

"Are you sure you're feeling up to it?" Sachin said when Kashmira suggested going. "You've only been out of the hospital for a little over a week."

"I guess we'll find out," Kashmira told him, thinking of what he had said about learning to be sick and not. Earlier, she had found that balance at kathak, but only unintentionally. At the party, she would have the chance to try again, to really see what it means to be her whole self in the world. She said, "I'll take a nap beforehand."

In the end, she was determined to go, especially because the timing for the party was good. Ami had an event for hospital staff that night—some retirement party thing—and wouldn't be home. That meant Kashmira could stay out as late as she wanted without her mother checking up on her. The idea of this, she liked. After all, while she isn't regularly lying to her mother about her whereabouts any longer, she is still a teenager. Like other girls her age, she wants her mother to take care of her, but sometimes she needs her freedom too.

Ami, for her part, seemed to know something was going on though. As she finished screwing in her pearl earrings and was grabbing her purse, she said, "Be careful tonight, whatever you end up doing. I'll be home around eleven."

Then she hugged Kashmira so tightly one of her pearls left a small mark on Kashmira's forehead. It was nice, though, to be worried about like this, and Kashmira passed her fingers over it while saying to her mother that everything would be fine and that she would definitely text to check in.

After that, she and Sachin had driven together, and now they're at the drinks table, waving away handles of rum and tequila. They decided together that they wouldn't drink tonight—Kashmira because she can't handle it, Sachin because he wants to support her. They pour ginger ale into red cups and cheers. After, Sachin rests his arm around her shoulders while Kashmira takes in the scene. She realizes, as she sips her soda, that while she's back here with her old face, this time she's worrying less about fitting in and more about getting what she needs from this and letting go of what she doesn't.

"I see Roshni," Sachin says, pointing past the ice bucket.

Kashmira's old friend doesn't look well. She sits down, stands up, then sits again. Pale, she keeps her hands flush against her left side. Lalita probably thinks The Center—which Roshni is headed to tomorrow—will help, but Kashmira hates imagining her friend lonely in Upstate New York, hates imaging the staff there telling her everything is her fault and her fault only.

But at least Roshni has tonight.

She waves at Kashmira and Sachin, and then walks over, dodging kissing couples and groups of friends using their cell phone lights to fix their makeup on her way. When she makes it to Kashmira and Sachin, she stands close to them and fingers her collarbone. It juts out worse now. Kashmira wonders if Roshni can stomach food;

since the medicines, Kashmira has gotten better at eating. It feels good to be a little fuller.

"One last night out?" Kashmira asks Roshni.

"I guess. I shouldn't have come here," the other girl says, staring at her feet. "I just felt like, I don't know, it was what I had to do to keep up appearances before leaving."

"I think we're done with all that." Kashmira surveys the party, considering what she wants. She doesn't drink any longer and she isn't interested in flirting, but she doesn't want to go because it feels good to be around these people who, over time, have become familiar to her. If only they would make a place that fit who she is now; then again, really it is up to her to make that space for herself. She says, "Let's sit."

She, Roshni, and Sachin settle at the edge of the pool, where the girls had situated themselves once before in June. Then, Kashmira had dipped her feet in and thought of her father. How painful that had been, and still not as painful as what had come of her attempts to forget him. She thinks of Vinod now. How distant he is, doing what he has to do. She both misses him and doesn't wish he were here, but she allows that contradiction to exist. She wonders what he would do at a party like this, if it were him at seventeen. Leave, maybe, unnerved by the blatant brownness being celebrated around him. Stay, maybe, as his parents would have wanted, and try his best to follow the unspoken rules that would make him one of many. Neither option suits her; she is here to break the boundary of this or that.

"You both okay?" Sachin says to Kashmira and Roshni. "You're quiet. Need anything?"

As the water laps at her ankles, soothing, inviting, Kashmira pushes closer to the edge so she can submerge more of her legs. How would it feel to go all the way in? In the shallow end, boys play chicken yet again. Their splashes spray, keeping most people out of the pool. And besides, the party has its ways: Unless they are part of the group of popular boys, people don't swim. But Kashmira is no longer people, and she wants to get in. The summer is coming to a close, and she wants to immerse herself fully, as she is, at least one time and see how it goes. She stands, pulls her jean shorts down her thighs, and strips down to her one-piece suit. It isn't what the other girls are wearing, but it's what she found in her closet. It works.

"You're going in?" Roshni says.

"Someone other than Tej and his gang should," Kashmira replies.

She slips in somewhere around the five-foot mark and floats on her back immediately. The water, cool on her skin, rocks her. She likes how it rocks her. Its gentle pressure surrounding her soothes her stomach, and her muscles, too, which have ached since she got out of the hospital. She drifts along, arms spread wide, looking up into the night sky.

"How is it?" Sachin, who has started to strip to his boxers, asks.

"Come in," Kashmira calls back.

Sachin takes his shoes off while the water carries her back and forth. A few times she gets closer to the boys, including Tej. In the night, she can just barely see his familiar body glistening. It does little for her now, other than remind her of a time in her life that she has somehow already grown out of and still, like all her history, carries with her under her skin.

"Who are you? And what are you doing in here?" he yells. "Don't you see you're the only one swimming?"

She tips over and swims to the side, where she can hold on while staying mostly underneath the small waves. He doesn't recognize her. She finds she doesn't mind. She knows what happened between them, and what it did and didn't mean to her. That much is enough. She hollers back at Tej, "So?"

"So, it's just not how things work," he says. "The pool is ours."

"Sachin's coming in now," she tells him.

It's true; by the time she finishes the sentence, Sachin has slipped into the pool too, feet first. He freestyles a few yards and then shakes his head, so the water in his hair splashes her nose. She laughs and shoves at his shoulder, forgetting Tej for a moment. When she looks back, Tej has stiffened, maybe because being ignored by some girl, any girl, tampers with his sense of the rules of these parties.

"Fine," Tej says. "Do whatever."

They do. Maybe people stare at them. Maybe they gossip. But maybe they don't. No one kicks Kashmira and Sachin out of the party. The boys stick to their side of the pool, and Sachin and Kashmira stick to theirs, holding hands under the water. As the party goes on, Kashmira watches all the people, doing what they have done all summer. A few of them look toward the water at her, and, from this distance, it appears they are smiling. Kashmira smiles back, just in case. In a way, she is still part of all this. In another way, she is not. But the space she wanted, she has made.

After a while she emerges from the pool and squeezes water out of her long hair. Sachin, close behind her, hands her his shirt, which hangs low on her thighs, like a cover-up. Roshni stares at them, something unreadable in her gaze. At first, it looks like anger, but on second glance, it seems more like yearning.

"You should have come in," Kashmira says.

"I couldn't," Roshni says. "I don't know how you're okay being like this, in front of everyone. Like you don't care what anyone thinks."

Kashmira doesn't know what to tell her. In the end, it wasn't as hard as she thought it would be. She feels light, like the lithe girls she once wanted to be, but not because she looks or acts perfect. No, she feels light because in her imperfection, she has found an always swiftly tilting balance, a back-and-forth in her that allows for loss and joy, for sickness and health, for grief and hope. And even now, she is still learning about it. And even now, she wants more.

～

They leave the party early to preserve Kashmira's energy, and around ten Sachin drives Kashmira back to the apartments. Neither of them has had anything to drink, but they act without inhibitions anyway.

Kashmira lays her head on Sachin's shoulder. He presses his nose into her hair. Though he can't see her face from this angle, she has the strange sense that he's seeing her wholly, in a way no one has before. Her cheeks feel warm. She ducks her head.

Instead of parking near her place, Sachin settles the car into the spot directly in front of his apartment and asks her quietly if she wants to come in for a little while. His parents are out tonight, so she can be in his bedroom.

"Only if you want," he adds.

His hand on her knee, gentle. When she doesn't answer, he pulls back until his fingers are just touching her. He has misinterpreted her shyness, she realizes. He doesn't yet know what it means to her that the two of them aren't playing at what tonight should be. They're enjoying finding out what it could be. Kashmira slips her hand into his and nods.

Upstairs, she runs her fingers along everything in his room. The doorknob to his closet. The footboard on his bed. The edge of his dresser, cluttered with things he has collected over the years: photos of him and his parents, random notes from friends, greeting cards from the important people in his life, movie stubs that the local theater still gives out, old essays that have already been graded, all of it jumbled together, an amalgamation of what he is. She almost laughs, thinking how hard he works to figure himself out—through film, through the notebook—when the truth of who he is has always been here. He just never noticed. But she does. And she will. He strokes her back, along her spine, once.

"If your stomach hurts, just let me know," Sachin says. "The bathroom is down the hall."

It does hurt, but barely. An echo of hurt, really. She sits on his mattress; even as her left side pulses. It'll be there throughout all of this, but that doesn't mean she can't stay here with him, sprawled on his teenage-boy-mussed covers. Instead of pressing a hand on her abdomen, Kashmira pats the area near her, coaxing Sachin to sit. What she touches isn't the blanket, but the mattress, with its cool, smooth sheet that feels wildly sensual under her hand. When Sachin kneels on that spot, he leans forward, then waits. But she meets him, wanting his mouth on hers, her mouth on his.

"More," she says, when they part. "Please."

"Okay," he whispers.

He runs his fingers up and down the length of her body. When she responds by humming happily, he kisses the skin about her collarbone. His hand edges to her breast and his thumb circles exactly where her nipple hardens inside her bra. Her body shivers hot as she twists closer to him, and she has never been more thankful for her body, for letting her be here with him. She tips her head back. She wants to expose her skin. To feel it against his. Sachin unbuttons her clothes so sweetly, so tentatively, she has to push at his fingers to speed him forward. He kisses her wherever she asks. He groans when her hands skid over his throat, his hips. Naked, they curl into each other. Sachin, who seems to like her hair, uses it to draw her even closer. He touches her between her legs first, edging her open so she moans. Then she touches him, and the pitches of their soft, building gasps complement each other.

"Is this still okay?" he says when she lays back. "I'm not going to hurt you, am I?"

She doesn't really know. Kashmira hasn't done this since before the hospitalization. Inside her still feels cavernous and unknown, and the pressure might upset the delicate constitution of her bottom half. Or maybe it won't. She has no idea if she'll leak blood onto his sheets, or if she'll just whisper his name, low and needy, when he thrusts into her. But with him, she is willing to find out.

"I want to," she says.

Sachin holds her hand when he sinks into her. It feels right. Their hands fit together. He fills her up, not to complete her but to say, I'm here and so are you. Her breaths come fast and her hips speak back, yes, yes, yes, all of me and all of you, right here.

Even as it ends, Sachin keeps a tight grip on her hand. Then he rests it on his heart while they lay together, he reclining on his one pillow, she burrowing into his chest. He exhales long, satisfied breaths, and Kashmira looks up at him, taking in what she has never had the pleasure to notice before. The dip inside his collarbone, in particular, looks soft and vulnerable in ways that make her want to press her lips into it, gently, carefully.

On the other end of the room is a mirror, a large one. Sachin looks down at her, but she can see the two of them in her periphery. The image of them, impossible to escape, not that she wants to. This time, she sees Sachin tracing her features with his eyes, so sure, so grateful that she is the one there with him, no matter how complicated and strange she can sometimes be. This time, she sees them together, the two of them who wanted to be easy and legible to the world, who discovered they couldn't be, who fell into each other's arms anyway. This time, she sees her own face—with all its original features, even the ones that still sometimes make her heart ache—alive and open, witnessing its own deeply deserved existence with a wide smile.

The last encounter Kashmira has with Roshni Gupta is after the party, after Sachin's place, after Kashmira gets back to her own bedroom.

It's two in the morning, and Kashmira is sleeping, so she doesn't realize that Roshni has driven over to the apartment complex and is waiting for her in the parking lot. But then, Roshni sends text after text until the device vibrates enough times to wake Kashmira, who then dons a sweatshirt and stumbles out of the house. On her way, she trips on something—maybe her own sandals left haphazardly out on the stoop earlier, or maybe the crack in the steps, or maybe nothing. It doesn't matter. What matters is that the tiny twist of her foot sends pain up her calf and into her groin. She winces, and when she looks at Roshni's face through the windshield, she sees that her old friend does too.

Eventually, she makes it to the car. Inside, it smells like Lalita's lilac perfume, which reminds Kashmira of after-school pickups, during which Roshni's mother picked them up and then looked into the back seat and demanded to know if her daughter had picked at a pimple and made it bleed. It reminds her of the same Lalita, sometimes handing them each a polished apple and a square of dark chocolate as an afternoon snack after Roshni told her about them both getting A's on some quiz or test. So many memories, all of them complicated. Kashmira taps Roshni's bony wrist. The other girl's hand still rests on the steering wheel in the nine o'clock position. An ornament of Ganesh—remover of obstacles, Lalita once said—hangs from the rearview mirror, wishing them both luck.

"It's late," Kashmira says. "What are you doing here? Your mom let you take the car?"

"I needed to get out."

"You know the doctors are always saying rest is important. You shouldn't be out this late. You should be sleeping."

"I don't have doctors," Roshni says. "I have guides. And they're guiding me somewhere I refuse to go to. See?"

Roshni points to the back seat, at rolls of toilet paper, a few stray tampons, and a pile of clothes not even properly packed into a suitcase. Then she opens the glove compartment, stuffed with peanut butter crackers and bags of pretzels and the oat-and-honey granola bars that are always so hard to bite into.

Kashmira reaches for one of the snacks. "What are you doing? What is all this?"

"I'm leaving," Roshni says. "Because I can't take this anymore."

She, too, slides her hand into the glove compartment, but unlike Kashmira, she actually rips open one of the snacks. When Roshni sucks on a cracker, Kashmira feels her own tongue against the soggy, salty thing. Imagines, in that action, how much Roshni wants to control the crumbling. But she can't. All she can do is let it go mushy in her mouth and then swallow.

"Everyone wants me to get better," Roshni says. "I mean, everyone. My mother says she'll do anything to make me better. But I'll never be the person she wants me to be. So, I'm leaving." She pauses. "My cousin is going to school in the city. I'm going to stay with her."

So, Roshni means to run away. How blunt the confession is. Kashmira presses her back into the seat, bracing herself, remembering all the times she has endured people leaving, all the times she has left in her own way. The act of disappearing, so often a way to stop disappointing and stop being disappointed. Kashmira can't fault it, though she says, "Are you asking me to tell you you're doing the right thing?"

"Maybe," Roshni says, blinking. "You told me it's okay to be sad sometimes. But you don't seem so sad anymore. And I am. So I don't know what to do."

It's okay to be sad sometimes. Yes, Kashmira had declared a version of this, back in her hospital room. Mostly because by then she understood how grief could needle the muscles, the bones. It made sense to say it. But despite all she had learned, she hadn't known everything. She hadn't yet experienced looking at herself and seeing herself whole. Whole and joyful enough to laugh at least a little. Whole and joyful enough to enjoy the uncertainties. How Kashmira would love to explain this all to Roshni, if only her friend would believe her. But she won't, not until she finds it for herself.

"What I think is that it's okay to be happy sometimes too," Kashmira says. "You have the right to that. Wherever it is."

When Roshni doesn't respond, Kashmira opens her arms wide. She still hates good-byes, but at least she gets to have one here. And she will have it, because if Roshni does indeed leave, she doesn't want to wish she had hugged her one last time. The two of them lean forward, and though the embrace is awkward in the car, they make do. Kashmira closes her eyes. As she holds her old friend, she imagines that wherever Roshni does go—back to the Gupta house or somewhere else—it'll be lovely. Not because of where or what it is, but because she can imagine Roshni there catching a glimpse of herself in a window and realizing she is the girl in the reflection, the one worth looking at.

Later, from her bedroom window, Kashmira sees Roshni back the car up and pull out of the parking lot. Soon all that Kashmira can see are the brake lights. And then, they are gone too. Now there's nothing else to look at, and she herself should go back to bed. But before she does, Kashmira finds herself seeking the moon, that blemished, shining face studded into the sky so resolutely.

There it is. Dusky craters visible, but celestial, even in plain sight.

* * *

Acknowledgments

The making of anything, let alone a book, is far from an individual act. I owe many thanks to those who've ushered this project to life in so many incredible ways:

To the doctors, nurses, and other medical staff who have cared for me and comforted me through a decade of illness. To those researchers who work every day on chronic illness, trauma, and their intersection. Because of all of you, I continue to exist.

To Dana, Stephanie, Elizabeth, Khalid, Roxane, Irena, Noah, Amy, Joseph, Justina, Natalie, Rachael, and the rest of the Grove team for championing the book of my heart to print and beyond. To Maggie, and the Asian Women Writers mentorship program, who treated me with the greatest grace as I first embarked on the path to publication.

To the teachers who've let me experiment and fail or succeed or do something in the middle in their classes. There are so many of you, who put books in my hands, who told me I could do this. Most recently, thank you to the University of Arizona's MFA program, especially my dear thesis advisor, Aurelie, who is no longer with us, but who always treated my roughest work as precious.

To the literary community—the Claw, TSWT, Alys, Gabe, Jess, Josh, Katie, Kou, Maddie, Sam, Patrick, Wren—that has made me belong somewhere. To the journals and magazines who've taught me to edit and be edited. To the Mae Fellowship, which funded me so I could take the time to write.

To my friends and family, who see my passion for writing and never demand I do anything else. To Giri and Gita for encouraging me to do, not just say. To Solange, Julia, Anita, and Sanjay, for cheerleading. To Carrie and Dale, for always offering a safe place to work. To Rachna and Sunil, for teaching me, in their own distinct and invaluable ways, how to move in this complicated world. To Toomi, for keeping me company in the early hours. To Emily, Stephanie, and Quetzal, who've been there for this whole process, and longer.

And to Zach, who has never, not once, let me give up on my body or my book.